THE USBORNE
WORLD HISTORY
ENCYCLOPEDIA

THE USBORNE
WORLD HISTORY
ENCYCLOPEDIA

Jane Bingham, Fiona Chandler and Sam Taplin

Designed by Susie McCaffrey, Linda Penny,
Melissa Alaverdy and Steve Page

Consultants: Dr. Anne Millard, Gary Mills and Dr. David Norman

Contents

Medieval World

The Last 500 Years

Usborne Quicklinks

Quicklinks are links to specially selected websites where you'll find videos, quizzes, homework resources and activities.

Throughout this book, you will find recommendations for websites where you can discover more about the history of the world.

Downloadable pictures

All the maps and many of the pictures in this book can be downloaded for home or school use (but not for commercial purposes). Look for pictures marked with a ★ then go to **usborne.com/Quicklinks** and type in the keywords "**WHE**".

To visit over 800 websites selected for this book, go to **usborne.com/Quicklinks** and enter the keywords "**WHE**".

Online safety

Parents and guardians, children should be supervised online and follow our three basic rules:

★ Always ask an adult's permission before using the internet.

★ Never give out personal information, such as your name, address, school or telephone number.

★ If a website asks you to type in your name or email address, check with an adult first.

Site availability

The links at Usborne Quicklinks are regularly reviewed and updated but websites do occasionally close down, and when this happens we will replace them with new links at Usborne Quicklinks. Sometimes we add extra links too, if we think they are useful.

Discover Usborne Quickinks

Here are some of the things you can do at the sites we recommend:

★ Travel back in time to the age of the dinosaurs.

★ See ancient Egyptian mummies and explore the pyramids.

★ Investigate the ruins of Roman forts.

★ Visit Stonehenge in England and the Great Wall of China.

★ Discover facts about the Maya people and their amazing temples.

★ Find out what it took to become a knight and how to defend a castle.

★ See what life was like in the trenches during the First World War.

★ Explore the International Space Station.

Links to external websites

Quicklinks are links to external (non-Usborne) websites that have been selected by Usborne editors. Although they are regularly reviewed and updated, Usborne does not control these websites and is not responsible for their content or availability.

Prehistoric hand paintings on
a cave wall in South America

PREHISTORIC WORLD

Prehistoric World Quicklinks

Quicklinks are links to specially selected websites with videos, quizzes, homework resources and activities. Throughout this section, you will see recommendations for websites where you can find out more about the prehistoric world.

Here are some of the things you can do at the sites we recommend:

★ Examine fossils of some of the first animals on Earth.

★ Watch dinosaurs and other prehistoric creatures come to life in amazing reconstructions.

★ Discover more about mammoths and other giant ice-age animals.

★ See stone tools made by early humans.

★ Look inside caves filled with prehistoric paintings of horses, bulls and bears.

To visit the websites, go to **usborne.com/Quicklinks** and type **"WHE"** into the search box.

You can also download many pictures and maps in this book for home or school use. Look for pictures marked with a ★.

Prehistoric Time

Scientists believe that the Earth was formed about 4,550 million years ago. This is such a vast length of time that it is almost impossible for anyone to imagine.

People have been around for only a tiny fraction of the time that the Earth has existed. If you think of all of prehistoric time as just one year, then the Earth would have been formed on January 1, but humans would not have appeared until one minute to midnight on December 31!

Experts divide prehistoric time into several periods, each lasting many millions of years. The diagram on these two pages shows the main prehistoric periods. You can also see when different plants and animals appeared on the Earth.

SILURIAN PERIOD
(say "sy-loor-ee-un")

440 MILLION YEARS AGO

408 MILLION YEARS AGO

362 MILLION YEARS AGO

The first amphibians

DEVONIAN PERIOD
(say "div-ohn-ee-un")

The first land plants

ORDOVICIAN PERIOD
(say "or-doh-vishy-un")

The first fish

The first creatures on land

510 MILLION YEARS AGO

CAMBRIAN PERIOD
(say "cam-bree-un")

The first creatures with skeletons

550 MILLION YEARS AGO

The first soft-bodied creatures

PRECAMBRIAN PERIOD
(say "pree-cam-bree-un")

The first living cells appear.

The Earth's surface is covered with volcanoes.

4,550 MILLION YEARS AGO
The Earth is formed.

Hot, liquid rock pouring from a volcano

QUICKLINKS: For links to websites where you can discover fossils from key periods of Earth's past, go to **usborne.com/Quicklinks**

The first
flying insects

CARBONIFEROUS PERIOD
(say "carbon-iffer-us")

The first forests

290 MILLION YEARS AGO

The first
swimming
reptiles

PERMIAN PERIOD
(say "permy-un")

245 MILLION YEARS AGO

The first
dinosaurs

TRIASSIC PERIOD
(say "try-assick")

200 MILLION YEARS AGO

JURASSIC PERIOD
(say "jur-assick")

The first
reptiles

The first
mammals

The first birds

144 MILLION YEARS AGO

CRETACEOUS PERIOD
(say "cruh-tay-shuss")

The first
flowering plants

66 MILLION YEARS AGO

The first
humans

The first
horses

TERTIARY PERIOD
(say "ter-shuh-ree")

The first elephants

The first grasses

The first cats

1.8 MILLION YEARS AGO=

PRESENT DAY

QUATERNARY PERIOD
(say "kwot-en-uh-ree")

The end of the
dinosaurs

What Are Fossils?

Fossils are the remains of creatures and plants that lived millions of years ago. They provide a fascinating picture of life on Earth before any history was written down.

Fossils in the rock

Many fossils are made from animal bones or shells that have been preserved in rock.
It takes millions of years for a fossil to form, but the process begins when a creature is buried under layers of sand and mud, called sediment. This usually happens under water, at the bottom of lakes, rivers or seas.

Gradually, the layers of sediment covering the creature are pressed down hard until they turn into rock. This layered rock is called sedimentary rock. Water trickles through the rock and soaks into the creature's skeleton. The water has minerals dissolved in it, which slowly harden (or crystallize), turning the skeleton into a fossil.

Fossil of an ammonite, a sea creature with a pearly shell

The ichthyosaur's soft body rots away.

The skeleton is soon buried in sediment.

A sea reptile, called an ichthyosaur, being buried in the seabed

Layers of sedimentary rock

Fossilized skeleton

Fossil of an ichthyosaur inside layers of rock

Making shapes

Some skeletons that were buried in sediment have dissolved away, leaving their shapes in the rock. Some of the shapes have stayed empty, but others have been filled with hardened minerals, creating a fossil called a cast.

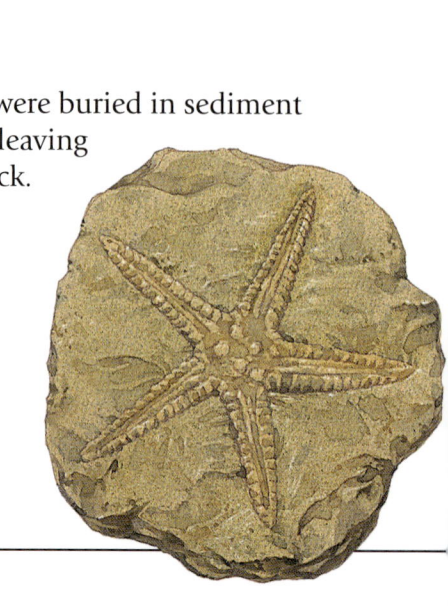

This shape was left by the skeleton of a starfish.

Coming to the surface

Fossils can now be found in sedimentary rocks on land, even though most fossils were originally formed under water. This is because, over millions of years, rocks that were once under water were gradually pushed up out of the water to become dry land (see page 23).

Buried bones

Experts have discovered many bones belonging to early humans and animals. Some of these bones were preserved in rock, but others were buried in very dry sand or in underground caves where no air could reach them.

The skull of an apelike ancestor of the first humans

Carbon fossils

Many plants and insects from prehistoric swamps were buried deep underground. Gradually, they heated up and turned into a sooty, black substance, called carbon. Most of the plants and creatures were squeezed together to make solid coal, but some formed delicate carbon fossils.

Soft-bodied survivors

It is very unusual to find fossils of creatures with soft bodies, but some have been discovered in the Burgess Shale, in Canada. These fossils were probably formed after a group of sea creatures was buried by a sudden mud slide. The mud then hardened into rock, creating very detailed fossils.

Fossil of a soft-bodied creature called Hallucigenia

Trapped in amber

The bodies of some insects have survived for millions of years. These insects were stuck in sticky sap that oozed from trees. When the sap hardened, it turned into a yellow stone called amber, and any creatures trapped inside were perfectly preserved.

A prehistoric insect trapped in amber

Leaving traces

Some prehistoric creatures have left clear evidence of their way of life. Footprints made by animals and humans and trails made by creatures like worms have been preserved in hardened mud. Some eggs and droppings left behind by animals have also turned into fossils. All these kinds of evidence are known as trace fossils.

A dinosaur leaving its footprints in soft mud

Clues from Fossils

Experts who study fossils are called palaeontologists. By piecing together information from fossils, they can build up a surprisingly detailed picture of life on Earth millions of years ago.

Beginning with bones

Most fossils found by palaeontologists show the bones, teeth or shells of prehistoric creatures. When they discover a set of bones, palaeontologists take notes, photographs and sketches before anything is moved. This helps them to understand how the skeleton fits together.

Flesh on the bones

Experts can get a good idea of what a creature looked like from the shape of its skeleton. Markings on bones show where muscles were attached, and the size of the bones suggests how heavy an animal was. Sometimes, other evidence can help to build up a picture. For example, fossil prints of dinosaurs' skin show that it was scaly.

Moving around

As well as studying skeletons to see how creatures moved, palaeontologists also examine fossil footprints and trails. Footprints show whether an animal walked with its legs close together or far apart, and whether it lived alone or in a group.

Chewing and eating

The shape of an animal's teeth shows what kind of food it could chew. Experts also examine fossilized droppings to see what creatures ate, and occasionally they find an animal's last meal perfectly preserved in its stomach!

This is a skeleton of *Stegosaurus*. Next to it is a picture of how this dinosaur may have looked when it was alive.

Large leg bones supported the dinosaur's heavy body.

Stegosaurus was almost as long as a bus.

QUICKLINKS: For links to websites where you can see life-size dinosaur skeletons, go to usborne.com/Quicklinks

Fighting off attackers

Bony plates and spikes on a skeleton suggest that a creature needed to protect itself from predators (hunters). Skeletons can also provide other clues to the way an animal defended itself. For example, *Stegosaurus* had a huge body and a tiny brain, so it must have relied on size and strength, rather than quickness and cleverness, to fight off attackers.

Bony plate covered with skin

Stegosaurus's tiny skull contained a brain the size of a lime.

Scaly skin

Stegosaurus had small, peg-shaped teeth for tearing up plants.

Fossil puzzles

It can be hard to know how fossil bones fit together. Experts used to think that the pointed plates on Stegosaurus's back lay flat like scales, but now they think that the plates stood upright. It's possible Stegosaurus may have used the plates to control their temperature, or to show off to other Stegosaurus.

Living fossils

Some animals alive today, such as crocodiles, look very much like creatures that lived millions of years ago. Studying these living fossils can help palaeontologists to understand what prehistoric creatures looked like and how they lived.

17

The Story of Life

Many of the plants and animals that lived in prehistoric times were very different from those that are around today. This is partly because lots of prehistoric forms of life have died out, and partly because all living things gradually change with time.

The first creatures on Earth were very simple animals. Over millions of years, these creatures changed, or evolved, into new kinds of animals. This process of change is called evolution.

How evolution works

The first person to explain how evolution works was a scientist named Charles Darwin, who lived from 1809 to 1882. His general explanation is still accepted by scientists today.

Charles Darwin

Darwin realized that no two animals are exactly the same. For example, one deer may have slightly longer legs than another. Long legs are useful for escaping from attackers, so this deer will be more likely to survive and have young. The young may also have longer legs, like their parent. Over time, a new kind of longer-legged deer could evolve.

These pictures show how, with a series of small changes, one kind of animal can gradually evolve into a completely new creature.

★ **4** Today's birds have hollow bones and no teeth, so their bodies are very light. Their strong wings are ideally suited for flying.

★ **3** Feathered arms grew into wings. This early bird had teeth, like a dinosaur, and a heavy body.

★ **2** Some two-legged dinosaurs grew feathers to keep themselves warm. Some also had beaks.

★ **1** This is a typical two-legged dinosaur with scaly skin.

Fossil clues

The oldest fossils that have been found all show extremely simple forms of life. Fossils of complex creatures, such as reptiles and birds, are only found in much newer rocks. This suggests that living things did not appear on the Earth all at once, so they must have evolved gradually.

Animal families

To understand how one kind of animal could have evolved from another, scientists need to find out which animals are closely related. They do this by dividing them into groups.

All the members of a group have something in common with each other. The more things two animals have in common, the more closely they are related.

The biggest groups are called kingdoms. For example, all animals belong to the animal kingdom. Inside this group, there are smaller groups, with even smaller ones inside them.

The smallest group of all is known as a species. Animals that belong to the same species look very similar and can breed together.

Lions and leopards belong to different species, but both of them are big cats and members of the cat family.

Here you can see how big cats fit into different groups within the animal kingdom. As you read down the page, notice how the creatures in each new group have more and more in common with each other.

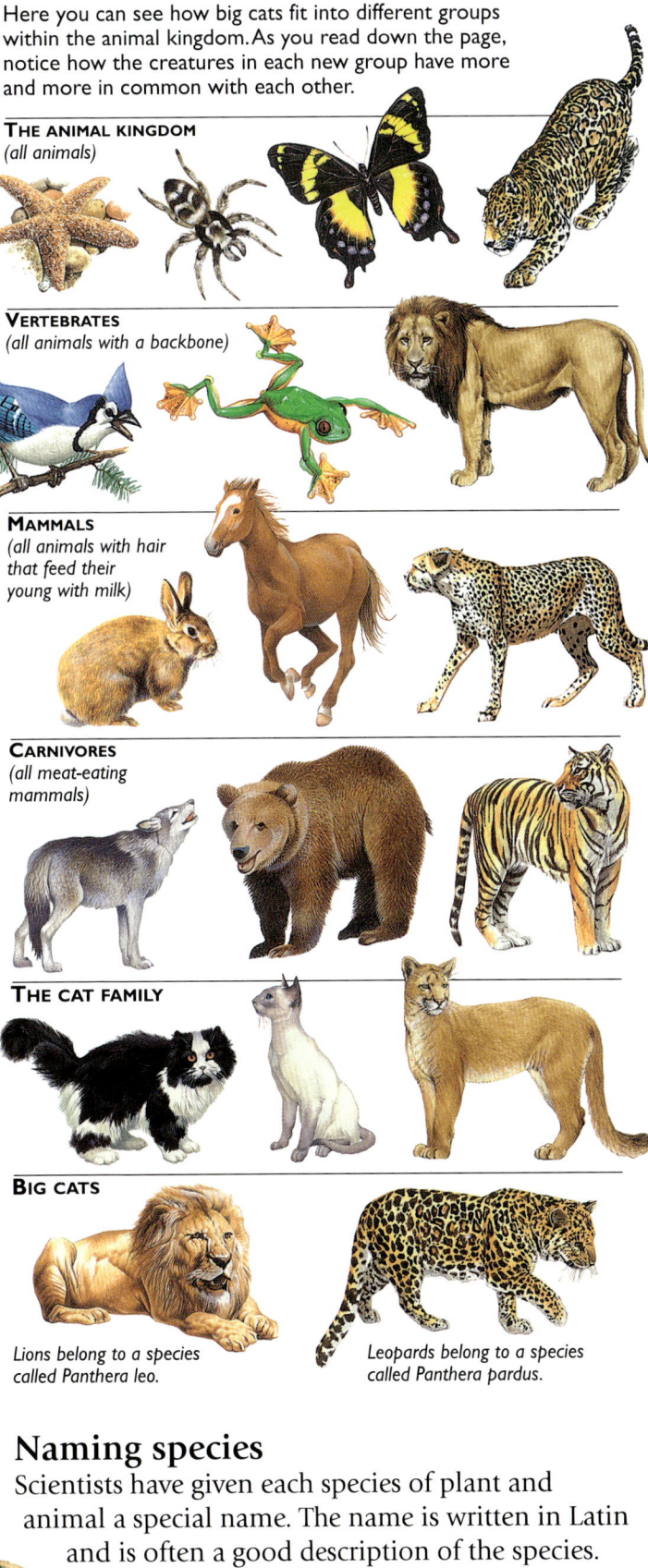

THE ANIMAL KINGDOM
(all animals)

VERTEBRATES
(all animals with a backbone)

MAMMALS
(all animals with hair that feed their young with milk)

CARNIVORES
(all meat-eating mammals)

THE CAT FAMILY

BIG CATS

Lions belong to a species called *Panthera leo*.

Leopards belong to a species called *Panthera pardus*.

Naming species

Scientists have given each species of plant and animal a special name. The name is written in Latin and is often a good description of the species. For example, the first humans that walked completely upright are known as *Homo erectus*, which means "upright man".

The Birth of the Earth

The Earth is a tiny planet in a vast universe. The universe is made up of billions of stars and planets and enormous clouds of gas, all separated by huge empty spaces. The stars are grouped in galaxies, each one containing millions of stars.

Our Sun is a small star in the Milky Way galaxy.

The Big Bang

Scientists think that the universe began over 15,000 million years ago with an unimaginably violent explosion, called the Big Bang. The Big Bang created a huge fireball, which cooled and formed tiny particles. Everything in the universe is made of these tiny particles, called matter.

These pictures show what may have happened after the Big Bang.

1 The fireball spread out and the universe began to expand. (It is still expanding today.) ★

2 As the fireball cooled, tiny particles collected into thick, swirling clouds of gas and dust. ★

3 The clouds pulled in more and more dust and gas. The gases became hotter until they began to burn, and stars formed. ★

4 Planets formed from some of the leftover dust and gases whirling around a star. ★

Planet Earth

The Earth was formed about 4,550 million years ago from a cloud of dust and gas spinning around the Sun. Gradually, the Earth grew hotter and hotter, until it turned into a ball of liquid rock and metal. Lighter materials floated to the surface, where they cooled into a hard, rocky crust. The rocks underneath stayed hot and liquid.

This cutaway picture shows inside the Earth, as it is today. ★

The Earth's crust is a thin layer of rock up to 65km (40 miles) deep.

The crust rests on a layer of hot, partly melted rock, called the mantle.

The outer core is made of hot, liquid metal.

The solid inner core is made mostly of iron. It is extremely hot.

A lifeless planet

For millions of years after the Earth was formed, nothing could live there. There was no water, no breathable air, and no protection from the harmful rays of the Sun. Volcanoes poured out red-hot liquid rock, and the Earth's surface was battered by giant rocks, called meteorites, that fell from space.

This scene shows how the Earth might have looked 4,000 million years ago.

There are no living creatures, because there is no oxygen for them to breathe.

Falling meteorites

The first oceans

Volcanoes on the Earth's surface sent out great clouds of steam and gas that collected in a thick layer around the Earth. As the clouds thickened and cooled, the steam turned into water, and it started to rain. It rained for thousands of years, flooding the Earth and creating the oceans.

Volcanoes pour out liquid rock from deep inside the Earth.

Liquid rock inside the Earth is called magma. When it reaches the surface, it is called lava.

The lava cools and hardens to form new rocks.

The surface of the Earth is dry and rocky. There are no plants.

Volcanoes belch out clouds of gas and steam.

This huge hole, called a crater, was made by a meteorite smashing into the ground.

Liquid rock bubbles up through cracks in the Earth's crust.

Boiling seas

Huge meteorites continued to batter the Earth until around 3,800 million years ago. As the meteorites hit the Earth's surface, they gave off heat. Scientists think that there may have been enough heat to make the oceans boil. This would have destroyed any very early forms of life.

THE EARTH

21

The Changing World

The Earth has not always looked the way it does today. Ever since our planet was formed, its surface has been changing. New rocks are being created all the time, and the land is constantly changing shape.

A giant jigsaw puzzle

The Earth's crust is divided into several huge pieces, called plates, which fit together like a gigantic jigsaw puzzle. Most plates are made up partly of dry land (known as continental crust) and partly of ocean floor (known as oceanic crust).

This picture shows some of the Earth's plates, with one of them lifted up.

Moving plates

The ground beneath your feet may seem solid, but it is actually moving. The plates that make up the crust are floating on hot, toffee-like rock just beneath the Earth's surface. This hot rock (or magma) moves around constantly, carrying the plates with it. Some plates are pushed together, while others are pulled apart.

This picture shows how the plates move around on the surface of the Earth.

North American plate

South America

Floor of the Atlantic Ocean

Boundary between two plates

This plate is made up completely of ocean floor.

South American plate

African plate

Ocean

The hot magma cools to form ridges of new rock.

Gap between two plates

As new rock is added, the ocean floor spreads sideways.

Oceanic crust (ocean floor)

Liquid rock from a volcano forms a new island in the ocean.

Hot magma (liquid rock) rises to the Earth's surface.

The magma spreads sideways, dragging the plates apart.

Making mountains

This is Mount Everest, which is part of a group of mountains called the Himalayas. The Himalayas were formed when the plate carrying India crashed into the continent of Asia.

When two plates are pushed together, the land crumples up at the edges to form great ranges of mountains. Mountains formed like this are called fold mountains. They include some of the highest mountains in the world.

Drifting continents

The Earth's plates move at about the same speed that your fingernails grow. Over millions of years, this movement can make the continents drift huge distances. About 250 million years ago, all the continents joined to form a giant supercontinent called Pangaea, which then slowly split apart.

These maps show how Pangaea split up to form the continents we know today.

200 million years ago

120 million years ago

60 million years ago

Deep-sea trench

Volcano

As the two plates collide, the land is pushed up to form mountains.

Continental crust (dry land)

Where two plates are pushed together, one is forced down under the other.

THE EARTH

23

The Beginning of Life

All living things are made up of tiny units, called cells. Cells are made mostly of chemicals called proteins, but where did these chemicals first come from?

Simple cells shown 33,000 times bigger than their real size

Chemical soup

About 3,800 million years ago, the Earth's surface was covered in volcanoes which poured out poisonous gases. The gases dissolved in the warm water of the oceans, producing a kind of chemical "soup". Scientists think that these chemicals reacted with each other to form more complex chemicals, like the ones that make up proteins.

From proteins to cells

Although scientists understand how the first proteins may have formed, they are not sure how these proteins came together to form something as complicated as a living cell.

The first cells may have formed in the seas. A film of proteins floating on the surface of the water may have broken up to form tiny spheres (balls) with chemicals trapped inside.

Cells could also have formed around hot water springs. The proteins may have melted together and then formed tiny, cell-like spheres as they cooled.

Another idea is that the clay at the bottom of shallow seas helped tiny blobs of protein to stick together and form some of the chemicals found in cells.

Blue bacteria

The first living things were made of just one cell each. They were rather like bacteria (germs). Millions of years later, some bacteria, known as blue-green algae, began to use sunlight and water to make their food. This process is called photosynthesis and it is how all plants live.

These blue-green algae have been magnified over 1,000 times.

Electricity from lightning like this may have helped the chemicals to react.

The first fossils

The earliest evidence of life on Earth comes from fossils known as stromatolites, which contain the remains of large groups of blue-green algae. Some of them are 3,500 million years old.

Some algae in the early seas became trapped in a kind of chemical paste. The paste hardened into a glassy substance, preserving the algae as microscopic fossils.

These fossilized algae were photographed under a powerful microscope.

A change of atmosphere

The Earth is surrounded by a thick layer of gases, called the atmosphere. For millions of years, the Earth's atmosphere contained no oxygen (the gas that animals need to breathe).

When plants make their food by photosynthesis, they produce oxygen. As the number of blue-green algae increased, oxygen began to build up in the atmosphere. This allowed many new forms of life to develop.

Strange, disc-shaped creatures drift through the water.

This creature, called Spriggina, is a mystery. It may have been a type of flat, crawling worm.

The first animals?

The earliest traces of animals are tracks left on the seabed by worms. The first animals had soft bodies, which do not fossilize easily, so it is very rare to find fossils of the animals themselves.

By 600 million years ago, a variety of weird and wonderful creatures had evolved. Some of them seem so strange that scientists are not sure if they are really animals at all.

The creatures in this scene lived in the sea from 600 to 550 million years ago.

The fossils of all these soft-bodied creatures were found in the Ediacara Hills of southern Australia.

These sea pens look like plants, but each one is actually a group of tiny animals.

Dickinsonia *(a flat, worm-like animal) crawls over the seabed.*

Creatures feed on the blue-green algae that covers the seabed.

Some scientists think Spriggina may have been attached to the sea floor by its "head".

Sea pens are attached to the seabed.

Tribrachidium, *a mysterious jellyfish-shaped creature, creeps along the sea floor.*

Shells and Skeletons

At first, life on Earth evolved very slowly. It took over 3,000 million years for simple cells to evolve into the first soft-bodied animals (see page 25). Then, around 550 million years ago, at the start of the Cambrian Period*, an amazing variety of new creatures began to appear in the seas.

Many of these new creatures had hard shells or outer skeletons to support and protect their soft bodies. Some of them also had legs with joints. Creatures with jointed legs and an outer skeleton are called arthropods.

Curious creatures

The fossils of some bizarre Cambrian creatures have been found in rocks known as the Burgess Shale, in Canada. These fossils are unusual because they show even soft-bodied creatures in fantastic detail. In some fossils, the animal's last meal can still be seen inside its body.

This scene shows some of the strange creatures of the Burgess Shale.

Sponges feed on tiny food particles which they suck in through holes in their bodies.

Marrella has long spines to protect itself from hunters.

A trilobite, a common Cambrian arthropod

The body is divided into segments.

Head

Each segment has a hard outer casing. This is the animal's skeleton.

Most sponges have spines to support and protect their soft bodies.

Wiwaxia's shimmering scales and sharp spines reflect the light and warn off hunters.

Marrella scuttles across the seabed, using its feelers to search for food.

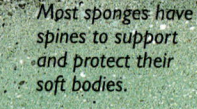

Worms burrow in the seabed to avoid being eaten.

Ottoia is a fierce worm with rows of hooks and spines around its mouth.

Aysheaia has spiky feet for climbing around on the sponges that it eats.

A worm called Burgessochaeta uses its tentacles to feel for food.

The first hunters

At the start of the Cambrian Period, some animals began to hunt and eat other animals. Soft-bodied creatures may have grown shells and skeletons around this time, as a way of defending themselves.

Find out about prehistoric time periods on pages 12 and 13.

Anomalocaris is the largest and fiercest of the Burgess Shale animals.

Jointed claws for grasping prey

This jelly-like creature is called Eldonia. The tube underneath may be the animal's gut.

This flower-like creature is called Dinomischus.

Mouth with sharp plates inside for biting

Pikaia swims by flicking its body from side to side.

Five eyes on short stalks

Opabinia has a long nozzle with claws at the tip.

Hallucigenia eats dead animals that it finds. This is called scavenging.

Dead trilobite

Hallucigenia has fleshy legs and spines on its back.

Stilts or spines?

Some of the Burgess Shale creatures are extremely puzzling. For many years, scientists thought that *Hallucigenia* walked on stilt-like legs and had tentacles on its back. Fossils found recently in China show that the "stilts" are actually spines on the creature's back. Scientists had been looking at the animal upside down!

Our earliest ancestors?

One of the most important creatures of the Burgess Shale is a small, eel-like animal called *Pikaia*. It belongs to a group of animals called chordates, which have a stiff rod running down their spine. Humans are also chordates, so *Pikaia* could be one of our earliest ancestors.

Scientists in China have recently discovered a chordate called *Cathaymyrus*, which is even older than *Pikaia*. Perhaps this is where the human story begins?

Cathaymyrus

EARLY LIFE

27

The Crowded Seas

Around 510 million years ago, many of the strange Cambrian creatures died out. They were replaced by an enormous variety of new creatures which thrived in the warm, shallow seas of the Ordovician and Silurian Periods. Some of these creatures, such as starfish, sea lilies and corals, are still around today.

Colonies of corals

Corals are tiny, bag-like creatures that live together in large groups, or colonies. They use their tentacles to sweep food into their mouths.

Corals

Tentacle

Corals have hard, chalky skeletons that support their soft bodies. Over time, the skeletons build up to form rocky mounds called reefs. The first coral reefs appeared 450 million years ago, during the Ordovician Period.

Starfish on stalks

Starfish belong to a group of animals called echinoderms, which means "spiny-skinned". Their cousins, the sea lilies, are rather like starfish on stalks. Sea lilies have lots of waving arms covered in sticky suckers, which trap tiny particles of food.

Arms

The stalk is attached to the seabed.

Fossil of a prehistoric sea lily
★

This scene shows an Ordovician coral reef.

Bryozoans, or sea mats, form a lacy network of tiny tubes.

This coral forms a chain-shaped colony.

This coral lives in a pie-shaped colony.

Trilobites hunt on the seabed.

Pieces of shell and skeleton from sea creatures help to build up a rocky reef.

Horn corals

Sea snails have teeth on their tongues for scraping food off the sea floor.

This is an early type of starfish.

Brachiopods, or lampshells, take in tiny food particles from the water.

QUICKLINKS: For links to websites about fossils of reef creatures from the Ordovician and Silurian Periods, go to **usborne.com/Quicklinks**

Sea lilies, or crinoids, wave their arms in the water to catch food.

Sponge

A nautiloid hunts for food.

The shell has hollow spaces inside which help the animal to float.

Tentacles covered in suckers for catching prey

Creatures in cups

Tiny creatures called graptolites also lived in colonies. A colony of graptolites was made up of lots of hard, horny cups all linked together. Each cup contained a single animal. Colonies may have lived on the seabed or floated in the water.

A colony of graptolites

Each animal puts out tentacles to catch food.

Horny cup

Powerful predators

Animals that hunt and eat other animals are called predators. During the Ordovician and Silurian Periods, predators became experts at chasing and catching their prey.

One group of predators were the nautiloids. They had excellent eyesight and long, grasping tentacles for catching food. Nautiloids were fast swimmers and moved around by shooting water in and out of their shells.

The most ferocious predators were the eurypterids, or sea scorpions. The largest of these was the giant *Pterygotus*, which grew up to 2m (6ft 6in) long. It had sharp pincers in front of its mouth, and used its tail as a paddle for moving quickly through the water.

Large eyes for spotting prey

Paddle-shaped leg for swimming through the water

This is a giant sea scorpion called Pterygotus.

The sea scorpion has caught a trilobite in one of its pincers.

EARLY LIFE

29

The First Fish

Fish first appeared around 510 million years ago, at the beginning of the Ordovician Period. They were the first creatures that had a backbone to support their bodies. Animals with a backbone are called vertebrates.

Jawless fish

The first fish had no jaws for opening and closing their mouths. They lived at the bottom of the sea, where they could suck up small particles of food from the seabed.

★ *Sacabambaspis*, an early jawless fish

— Hard, bony plating around the head and body

Fish with jaws

The first fish with jaws appeared during the Silurian Period. They are known as acanthodians, or "spiny sharks", although they were not actually sharks at all.

Fish that had jaws could use their mouths for grasping and biting, so they could eat a much greater variety of food. Many of them became hunters.

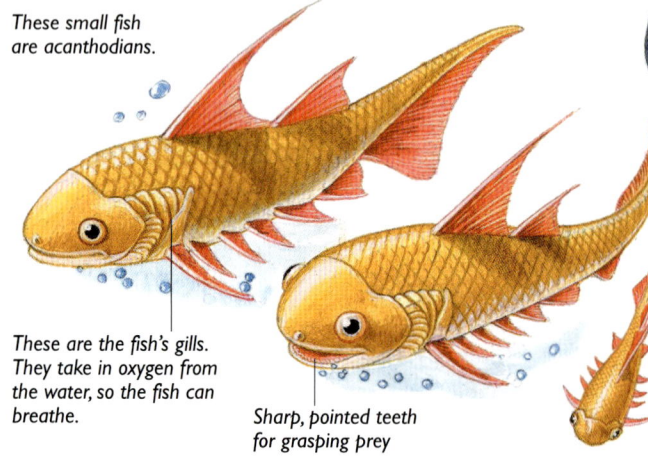

These small fish are acanthodians.

These are the fish's gills. They take in oxygen from the water, so the fish can breathe.

Sharp, pointed teeth for grasping prey

Fins help the fish to stay upright and move quickly through the water.

Ferocious fish

A group of fish called placoderms, or "plated skins", were particularly fierce hunters. Some placoderms were gigantic, and had powerful jaws lined with sharp, jagged plates of bone.

This picture shows some fish that lived during the Devonian Period from 408 to 362 million years ago.

This placoderm may have used its leg-like fins to steady itself on the seabed.

This is an early shark called Cladoselache.

The body is streamlined for gliding through the water.

As the shark's teeth wear out, a new set grows behind them.

Large, stiff fins support the shark in the water.

Spines on their fins make acanthodians difficult to eat.

The first sharks

Sharks first appeared during the Devonian Period. A shark's skeleton is not made of bone, but of cartilage (the same stuff that makes up the hard part of your nose). Cartilage is lighter than bone, and this helped the sharks to float.

This giant placoderm, called Dunkleosteus, is 10m (30ft) long.

The head is covered in curved, bony plates.

Jagged plates of bone for slicing prey

This is a bony fish called Cheirolepis.

An air-filled pouch inside its body helps the fish to float.

Flexible, fan-shaped fins help the fish to twist and turn in the water.

Jaws for snapping at prey

Bony fish

Most fish that are alive today have bony skeletons. Almost all bony fish belong to a group known as "ray fins". They have delicate, fan-shaped fins supported by fine, bony rods (or rays).

A few bony fish belong to a group known as "fleshy fins". Their thick fins are mainly bone and muscle, with a fringe of fine rays around the edges. It was from these fish that the first land-living vertebrates evolved (see pages 34 and 35).

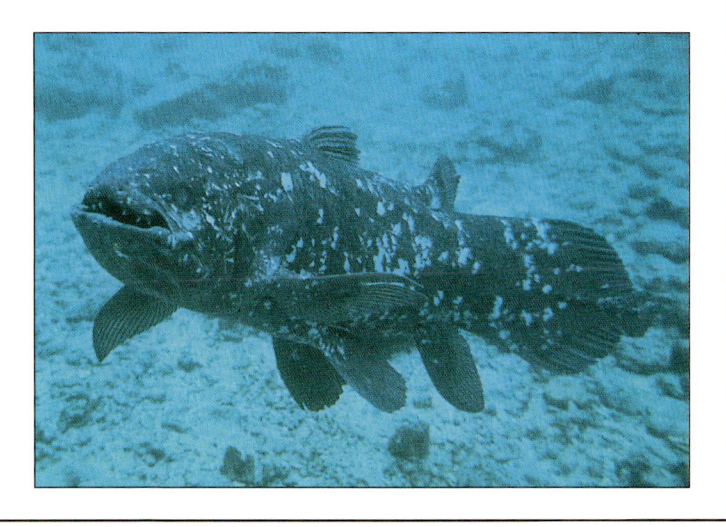

This is a coelacanth, a fleshy-finned fish which has hardly changed since Devonian times.

EARLY LIFE

Life on Land

Life on Earth began in the seas. For millions of years, the Earth's surface was scorched by harmful ultraviolet light from the sun, and there was almost no life on land. Simple plants, called algae, grew at the edges of the sea, but the rest of the land was rocky and completely bare.

Gradually, a layer of gas called ozone built up around the Earth. The ozone blocked out some of the sun's rays and made it possible for plants and animals to survive on land.

Plants on land

The first known land plants appeared about 440 million years ago, near the end of the Ordovician Period. They were probably relatives of modern mosses and liverworts, and they only grew in very damp places.

Modern liverwort

Problems for plants

To survive on dry land, plants need roots to take in water from the ground and a network of tubes to carry the water from the roots to the stem. The outside of the plant has to be waterproof, so it doesn't dry out, and the stem must be strong enough to keep the plant upright.

The first known plant to have all these features was *Cooksonia*, which appeared about 420 million years ago.

★ *Cooksonia*

Animals on land

Once there were plants on land, there was food for animals to eat. The first creatures to move from water onto land were arthropods, such as spiders, millipedes and insects.

This picture shows some of the plants and animals that lived on land around 400 million years ago.

This leafless plant is called Aglaophyton.

Inside here are tiny cells, called spores, which blow away in the wind and grow into new plants.

Rhyniella *is a tiny, wingless insect.*

Centipedes have poisonous fangs for catching their prey.

QUICKLINKS: *For links to websites where you can see fossils of the first land plants and animals, go to* **usborne.com/Quicklinks**

Spores and seeds

The earliest plants produced tiny cells, called spores, which grew into new plants. During the Devonian Period, some plants, such as seed-ferns, began to produce seeds instead of spores. Seeds are tougher than spores and can grow in drier soil. This helped plants to spread into areas where there was less water.

★
Fossil of a seed-fern

This is Asteroxylon. Its stems are covered in tiny, scaly leaves.

This plant is called Rhynia.

Capsule containing spores

Horneophyton grows in a bushy shape.

This scorpion has a poisonous tail for stinging its prey.

A mite sucking sap from a plant

Palaeocharinoides, a spider-like creature, hunts for insects, mites and grubs.

Cockroaches

A millipede feasts on rotting plants.

As dead plants rot, they mix with grains of rock to form soil.

EARLY LIFE

33

Fish out of Water

During the Devonian Period, the Earth's climate grew warmer, and there were long periods of dry weather. Lakes and rivers became shallower and contained less oxygen, so the fish that lived in them had to adapt in order to survive.

Lungs and legs

One group of fish, the "fleshy fins", had lungs as well as gills. This meant that they could breathe air if there wasn't enough oxygen in the water. They may have used their strong, muscular fins to push their heads above the water.

Why did fish grow legs?

Experts used to think that fish evolved legs so that they could walk to new ponds, if the pond where they were living dried up. Now, scientists believe that fish evolved legs and lungs to help them live in shallow water, rather than to help them get onto land.

A fleshy-finned fish called Eusthenopteron gulps air at the surface of the water.

Scientists believe that the muscular fins of these fish gradually evolved into four legs. The bones that supported their fins are very similar to the leg bones of land animals.

Fish with legs

One of the first four-legged animals was *Acanthostega*. It had gills for breathing under water and probably could not survive on land for long. With its short legs, it could move around in water even when the water was too shallow for swimming.

The fish uses its strong fins to prop itself up.

This fish, called Panderichthys, has four strong "arm" and "leg" fins, and no fins on its back.

— *Wide, fishy tail*

Acanthostega uses its flipper-like legs for swimming. ★

Gills for breathing under water

Slim, streamlined body for gliding through the water

Onto the land

About 365 million years ago, an animal called *Ichthyostega* appeared. It lived mainly in the water, but it could also breathe air and crawl onto land. It probably returned to the water to lay its eggs. Animals that live on land, but lay their eggs in the water, are called amphibians.

This scene shows some creatures that would have lived in a shallow Devonian lake.

The back legs are too weak to be any use on land.

Ichthyostega *drags itself around on its powerful front legs.*

A strong ribcage supports the animal's lungs.

Fishy tail

In shallow water, Acanthostega *pushes itself around on its short legs.*

Each foot has eight toes for gripping the bottom of the lake.

Wide, paddle-like back leg

Big bones

Ichthyostega had a strong skeleton to support its large body. Animals that live only in water do not need a strong skeleton, because their bodies are supported by the water. Without a strong skeleton, the body of a land animal would collapse in on itself, crushing the soft parts inside.

In the water, Ichthyostega *is a fast-moving hunter.*

Gills

Powerful jaws for catching fish

EARLY LIFE

35

Swamps and Forests

At the start of the Carboniferous Period, 362 million years ago, large areas of the world were covered in swamps. The weather was warm and wet, and these vast, steamy swamps were ideal places for plants and trees to grow. Thick forests of gigantic trees spread out across whole continents.

The trees in a Carboniferous forest were very different from those that are around today. The tallest trees were the giant clubmosses (moss-like plants with upright stems). They had green, scaly bark and reached heights of 50m (150ft).

This scene shows some of the plants and creatures that lived in a Carboniferous coal swamp about 350 million years ago.

Lepidodendron is the tallest of the giant clubmosses.

Meganeura, a giant dragonfly, has wings that measure 60cm (2ft) across.

A giant millipede feeds on rotting leaves.

A microsaur, a lizard-like amphibian, lounges on a fallen tree trunk.

Keraterpeton uses its long tail for swimming.

Diplocaulus has strange fins on its head to help it swim.

Gephyrostegus has spiky teeth for eating insects.

Creating coal

Dead plants and fallen trees piled up on the forest floor, and were gradually buried under layers of mud. Over millions of years, the plants and trees were squeezed until they hardened and turned into coal. This coal is still being mined in some parts of the world today.

EARLY LIFE

Big bugs

The Carboniferous swamps swarmed with huge insects, spiders and bugs. Giant dragonflies, the first creatures with wings, fluttered through the trees. Millipedes up to 2m (6ft 6in) long crept around in the dead leaves, and enormous spiders spun simple webs to catch their prey.

The age of amphibians

During the Carboniferous Period, a great variety of amphibians evolved. Some were small, lizard-like creatures that scampered around on the forest floor in search of insects to eat. Some hunted in the water like crocodiles. Others gradually lost their legs and could no longer live on land at all.

Like amphibians today, the early amphibians laid their soft, jelly-covered eggs in ponds or streams. This meant that they had to stay close to water. If animals were going to live successfully on land, they had to find a way around this problem.

This clubmoss, called Sigillaria, has no branches, just a clump of leaves.

Giant horsetail

Tree-fern

Short ferns and horsetails grow at ground level.

A spider waits for insects to fly into its web.

Pholidogaster, a large, crocodile-like creature, hunts fish and smaller amphibians.

This lizard-like animal, known as "Lizzie", may have spent all of its life on dry land.

Ophiderpeton is a legless, eel-like amphibian.

EARLY LIFE

37

What Are Reptiles?

Around 300 million years ago, a new group of creatures, called reptiles, evolved. These were the first vertebrates (animals with a backbone) that were able to live on land all the time, and they shared an ancestor with amphibians. Present-day reptiles, such as lizards, crocodiles and tortoises, show us how the early reptiles may have lived.

Keeping warm

Almost all reptiles are ectothermic, or cold-blooded. This means that they cannot produce their own heat. They rely on heat from the sun to warm their bodies.

A crocodile warming itself in the sun

At night, reptiles get cold and have to rest. In the morning, they lie in the sun until their bodies warm up. Then, they can start to move around in search of food.

Land legs

Animals that live on land need strong legs to lift their bodies off the ground, so they can move around easily. A typical reptile has legs that stick out on either side of its body. As the animal runs, its whole body twists from side to side, so its skeleton needs to be very strong and flexible.

Scaly skin

On land, animals lose water all the time through their skin. If they lose too much water, they dry up and die. Reptiles have scaly, waterproof skin to stop their bodies from drying out.

This picture shows *Hylonomus*, one of the earliest known reptiles.

Hylonomus is about 20cm (8in) long.

The long tail balances the weight of the animal's head.

Dry, scaly skin

The legs are attached to the sides of the body.

Eggs with shells

Reptiles lay their eggs on dry land, instead of in the water as amphibians do. Reptile eggs have a leathery, waterproof shell which protects the baby inside and stops it from drying out. The baby grows inside the egg and only hatches out when it is big enough to survive on its own.

Inside a reptile egg

The yolk provides food for the baby reptile.

Baby reptile

A bag of liquid protects the baby from knocks.

★ *Shell*

Recognizing reptiles

Scientists identify early reptiles by the shape of their skulls and jaws. The first reptiles had a more powerful bite than their ancestors. This made them better hunters and also allowed them to eat plants for the first time.

The first reptiles

The earliest known reptiles, such as Hylonomus, were small, lizard-like creatures. They were well suited to life on land and did not need to live close to water. This meant that they could spread out into drier areas. But at first, they lived in a world dominated by other scaly creatures.

Hylonomus *eats insects, such as these cockroaches.*

Sharp, pointed teeth for cracking open the bodies of insects

The reptile twists its body from side to side as it runs.

Long toes for gripping the ground

Hylonomus *has strong ribs and lungs to pump air in and out of its body.*

Synapsids and Therapsids

By 290 million years ago, at the start of the Permian Period, several new types of reptiles had appeared. But the biggest, most important land animals belonged to a group known as synapsids. They looked rather like reptiles, but they weren't very closely related. Some were meat-eaters (carnivores) while others (herbivores) ate plants.

Early reptiles

Pareiasaurus, an early plant-eating reptile

One group of small, plant-eating reptiles had chisel-shaped teeth which they may have used for digging up roots. Another plant-eater, called Pareiasaurus, was as big as a hippo. Pareiasaurus had strong, blunt teeth for grinding up plants. Its back and head was covered in hard, bony plates.

Synapsids

During the Permian Period, the largest and most successful animals were a group known as synapsids. Some early synapsids had a tall sail of skin on their backs, but scientists don't know exactly what purpose this served.

This picture shows some sail-backed synapsids.

The sail is made up of skin spread over bony spines.

Bony spine

It was thought synapsids used their sails to warm up, but experts now think they were for display.

Edaphosaurus is a plant-eater. Its jaws are lined with blunt, chisel-shaped teeth.

Dimetrodon is a meat-eater. It has two types of teeth for stabbing and slashing its prey.

When the synapsid walks, its long body twists from side to side.

QUICKLINKS: For links to websites about Dimetrodon and scientists' ideas about why it had a sail on its back, go to **usborne.com/Quicklinks**

Longer legs

About 270 million years ago, synapsids began to change. Instead of having short, sprawling legs, they developed longer legs that grew directly under their bodies. This allowed them to take bigger strides and move around faster. These later synapsids are known as therapsids.

This scene shows *Moschops*, a plant-eating therapsid, being attacked by a group of small, meat-eating therapsids, called Lycaenops.

Moschops may have used its thick, bony skull in head-butting contests to compete for a mate.

Moschops is 5m (16ft) long and has a huge, barrel-shaped body.

Back to the water

Although reptiles had evolved to cope with life on dry land, some of their relatives went back to living in the water. One of the earliest was Mesosaurus.

Mesosaurus

Mesosaurus had long, spiky teeth which it used to trap small, shrimp-like creatures in its mouth. It may have had a fin on its tail and webbed feet to help it swim.

Land and sea

During the Permian Period, all the Earth's continents joined together to form one giant supercontinent (see page 23). This meant that synapsids and reptiles could spread out to all parts of the world. At the same time, vast numbers of sea creatures died out, because the shallow seas around the continents disappeared.

The front legs stick out at the sides.

The back legs are directly under the body.

Lycaenops is a fast-moving hunter. It has huge fangs for stabbing its prey.

Long legs for extra speed

Changing Times

At the start of the Triassic Period, about 245 million years ago, the most common creatures on Earth were animals known as cynodonts (say "sigh-no-donts") and dicynodonts (say "die-sigh-no-donts"). These were both new types of therapsid (see page 41).

Tusks and beaks

Dicynodonts were plant-eaters. They had two tusks at the sides of their jaws for digging up roots, and a tough beak for slicing through plant stems. They ground up their food using sharp, horny plates on the roof of their mouths.

Early fur

Cynodonts had slim, dog-like bodies and long legs. They also had powerful jaws lined with different types of teeth for cutting, stabbing and chewing. Some cynodonts probably grew fur to help keep their bodies warm. They may even have been able to produce their own body heat.

Near the end of the Triassic Period, furry cynodonts evolved into a completely new group of animals, called mammals (see pages 60 and 61).

This scene shows some *cynodonts* and *dicynodonts*.

Lystrosaurus, a typical dicynodont, pulls up plants with its tusks.

Tough, horny beak

Lystrosaurus has a barrel-shaped body and short, stout legs.

Whiskers

Long, slim body

A cynodont called Thrinaxodon with its pups

Fur helps to keep heat inside the body.

QUICKLINKS: For links to websites about the first dinosaurs and how they were different from reptiles, go to **usborne.com/Quicklinks**

This dicynodont, called Kannemeyeria, is the size of an ox.

Kannemeyeria uses its sharp beak to cut through plant stems.

Cynognathus, a wolf-sized cynodont, is a ferocious hunter.

Some dicynodonts may have laid their eggs in underground burrows.

Rise of the reptiles

Meanwhile, reptiles were also evolving. In the Triassic Period, archosaurs, or "ruling reptiles" appeared. Early archosaurs had rows of bony plates along their backs. While they were resting, their legs sprawled out to the sides, but they could also tuck their legs under their bodies to help them run faster.

Lagosuchus, a two-legged archosaur, was a fast runner.

Eoraptor, one of the first dinosaurs, was a fast-moving hunter.

Later in the Triassic Period, some archosaurs began to walk on their back legs, rather than on all fours. They had a short body and a long tail to help them keep their balance.

Euparkeria, an early archosaur, ran on all fours.

The first dinosaurs

About 225 million years ago, the first dinosaurs evolved from small, two-legged archosaurs, such as *Lagosuchus*. Dinosaurs were different from other reptiles because they had longer, more upright legs that swung from front to back, instead of sticking out at the sides.

Once dinosaurs had evolved, many new types appeared. Their upright legs could carry a lot of weight and helped them to run fast. For the next 160 million years, they were the largest, strongest and fastest land animals in the world.

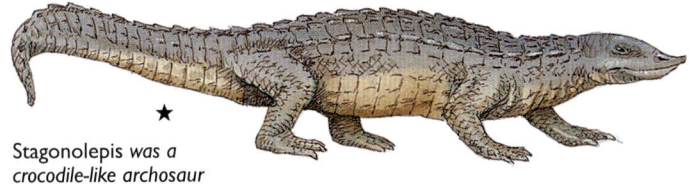

Stagonolepis was a crocodile-like archosaur with bony plates on its back.

Dinosaurs Rule

The first dinosaurs on Earth were meat-eaters. Meat-eating dinosaurs are known as theropods, which means "beast foot". All theropods walked on their two back legs and had viciously sharp claws on their feet.

The earliest theropods were fairly small, less than 1.5m (5ft) from nose to tail. They had long, powerful legs for running fast and used their clawed hands for grasping prey.

A wide variety of theropods evolved from these early dinosaurs. Many of them stayed small and agile, but others grew monstrously large.

Beaks and brains

One group of theropods, known as "ostrich dinosaurs", had beaks instead of teeth. They had larger brains than most reptiles and were probably fairly intelligent.

Gallimimus,
an ostrich-like
theropod
★

Ostrich dinosaurs were very fast runners, and may have reached speeds of over 55km (35 miles) an hour.

Small and speedy

One of the smallest dinosaurs was Compsognathus, which was no bigger than a pet dog. It hunted lizards and other tiny animals, and used its long tail to help it balance as it ran.

★ Compsognathus
chasing a lizard

Fast and fierce

Coelophysis was a ferocious and fast-moving hunter. It had a slim body with hollow bones, which made it very light and agile. It used its sharp, saw-like teeth to slice up its prey.

★ Coelophysis

Clawed hands for holding onto prey

Oviraptor ★

Crushing beak

Some theropods may have fed on fruit, nuts and seeds. *Oviraptor* had a strong, stumpy beak with sharp edges for cracking open nuts.

Killer claws

Deinonychus was only about 2m (6ft 6in) long, but it was a fierce hunter. It leaped on its prey and held on with its hands. At the same time, it kicked with the huge claws on its back feet. *Deinonychus* may have hunted in groups to tackle larger prey.

Tyrannosaurus is taller than a modern giraffe.

The dinosaur's huge head is 1.3m (4ft) long.

Deinonychus

Curved teeth with sharp, saw-like edges for ripping flesh

Tyrannosaurus *may have used its tiny arms to push itself up after resting.*

Huge hunters

The largest theropods belonged to a group known as carnosaurs. They had massive heads, strong necks, powerful legs and short arms. One of the biggest carnosaurs was Tyrannosaurus rex, which was 14m (46ft) long. As well as hunting for food, it may also have eaten dead animals that it found.

Tyrannosaurus is too heavy to run long distances. It lies in wait and then charges full-speed at its prey.

★ Tyrannosaurus rex charging at its prey

Gentle Giants

The biggest land animals that ever lived were a group of dinosaurs called sauropods. They were plant-eaters with large bodies, small heads, and extremely long necks and tails.

Early sauropods

The early sauropods were much smaller than their later relatives, measuring only 4-6m (13-20ft) from nose to tail. Unlike meat-eating dinosaurs, they walked mainly on all fours. However, some early sauropods could stand up on their back legs to eat leaves from trees.

An early sauropod

Huge and heavy

The really gigantic sauropods appeared about 160 million years ago, during the Jurassic Period. An animal named *Supersaurus* is thought to have been one of the biggest. It was probably 33-40m (108-131ft) long and may have weighed as much as 20 African elephants!

This scene shows some giant sauropods from the Jurassic Period.

Sauropods usually walk on all fours.

Diplodocus *has a strong, arched back to carry the weight of its massive stomach.*

The long neck is balanced by the weight of the tail.

Tiny head

Whip-like tail for lashing out at attackers

Strong, pillar-like legs

Diplodocus *is longer than two buses placed end to end.*

Like all sauropods, Seismosaurus *spends most of its time feeding.*

Weight lifting

Sauropods needed massive leg bones to support their great weight. Their backbones were also very strong, but they were sometimes cut away at the sides, instead of being solid. This made the animals lighter, so they had less weight to carry.

Hard to swallow

Sauropods had gappy, peg-like teeth which only grew at the front of their mouths. Teeth like this were ideal for stripping the leaves off trees, but were hopeless for chewing, so sauropods had to swallow their food whole.

Stomach stones

Plants and leaves are tough and very hard to digest, especially if they haven't been chewed properly. To help break down their food, sauropods swallowed large pebbles. These stones tumbled around in the animal's huge stomach, grinding the plants into a thick soup.

On its back legs, Apatosaurus can reach leaves high up in the trees.

Some sauropods have nostrils on top of their heads.

The dinosaur props itself up with its tail.

A group of sauropods can completely wreck a forest.

★

Brachiosaurus has long front legs, so it doesn't need to stand up on its back legs to reach the treetops.

Big bodyguards

Sauropods lived in large groups, or herds. When the herd was on the move, the larger adults walked on the outside of the group, with the baby dinosaurs in the middle. This made it harder for predators (hunters) to attack the babies.

REPTILES

47

Beaks and Crests

Some plant-eating dinosaurs, called ornithopods, were fast-moving and agile. They had bird-like feet and a horny beak for nipping off leaves and shoots to eat. All ornithopods could run on their two back legs to escape from predators (hunters).

Biting and chewing

One early ornithopod, called *Heterodontosaurus*, had large tusks behind its beak. It may have used these to defend itself against predators or rival males. *Heterodontosaurus* was one of the first dinosaurs to have cheeks. These stopped any food from falling out of the animal's mouth while it was chewing.

Heterodontosaurus ★

Small and swift

A small ornithopod called *Hypsilophodon* was a particularly fast runner, probably reaching speeds of 45km (30 miles) an hour. It had long legs and used its stiff tail to help it balance while running.

★ *Hypsilophodon*

Spikes and hoofs

Iguanodon was a large, heavy ornithopod, measuring up to 10m (33ft) long. It had a vicious spike on each thumb, which it used to fight off attackers. Its three middle fingers had hoofs, so it must have walked on all fours some of the time.

Iguanodon ★

Duck-billed dinosaurs

By about 80 million years ago, the most common plant-eating dinosaurs on Earth were a group of ornithopods known as hadrosaurs, or duck-billed dinosaurs. They had broad beaks, powerful jaws and thousands of small, sharp teeth for grinding up tough plants.

Broad, horny beak for slicing through plants

★ Adult hadrosaurs feed on pine needles and flowering plants, such as magnolia.

Incredible crests

Many hadrosaurs had strange spikes or crests on their heads. Some of these crests had hollow tubes inside. By blowing air through its crest, a hadrosaur may have been able to make booming noises to warn others of danger, or to attract a mate.

Corythosaurus ★

★ *Parasaurolophus*

Saurolophus ★

Mothers and babies

Hadrosaurs lived together in large herds. At the same time each year, the herd returned to the same place, so the females could lay their eggs. Unlike most reptiles, hadrosaurs guarded their eggs carefully, and looked after their babies until they could survive on their own.

This picture shows a group of hadrosaurs with their babies.

This hadrosaur is building a nest to lay her eggs in.

The nest is made of sand scraped into a mound.

The middle of the nest is hollowed out and filled with leaves.

This hadrosaur is guarding her eggs.

Each nest measures about 3m (10ft) across and contains up to 20 eggs.

This hadrosaur has brought back some berries for her babies to eat.

This baby is just hatching out. It is only 35cm (14in) long.

The babies stay in the nest while their mother goes to find food for them.

REPTILES

49

Horns, Clubs and Spikes

Some plant-eating dinosaurs were too big and heavy to escape from the fierce, meat-eating dinosaurs that hunted them. Instead, they developed a range of horns, clubs and spikes to protect themselves from predators.

Spikes and clubs

Ankylosaurs were covered from head to tail with bony plates. Vicious-looking spikes grew from these plates, and some ankylosaurs had a bony lump at the end of their tails, which they swung around like a club.

Bone heads

The pachycephalosaurs, or bone-headed dinosaurs, had a thick dome of solid bone on the top of their heads. They charged headfirst at their opponents, using their enormous skulls as battering rams.

Two bone-headed dinosaurs charging at each other
★

Head-banging contests

As well as fighting off hunters, bone-headed dinosaur males probably fought each other to prove which was the strongest. They may have banged their skulls together until the weakest gave up.

The dinosaurs' thick skulls are surrounded by a fringe of bony lumps.

Euoplocephalus, a very well-protected ankylosaur
★

Euoplocephalus can swing its tail with great force.

Plates, knobs and spikes protect this dinosaur.

Bony plates covered with skin

Pointed plates

Stegosaurs had two rows of upright plates running along their backs. The plates protected the stegosaurs from attack. Like the sails of some synapsids it's thought they may also have been for display, so Stegosaurus could show off to one another, or attract a mate.

★
Stegosaurus, the largest known stegosaur

QUICKLINKS: For links to websites where you can find out more about dinosaurs with horns, clubs and spikes, go to **usborne.com/Quicklinks**

Horns and frills

One of the last groups of dinosaurs to appear on Earth were the ceratopians. They had curved horns on their heads and a huge frill of bone around their necks and shoulders. Male ceratopians probably fought each other, as well as charging at attackers.

This picture shows two ceratopians. ★

Styracosaurus has a frill surrounded by horns.

Triceratops has three horns on its head.

Parrot-like beak for slicing through plant stems

Tough, scaly skin

Scary circle

Experts think that adult ceratopians defended their babies from attack by forming a circle around them. The adults probably shook their huge heads to scare predators away.

★

Ceratopians defending their young

Reptiles of the Seas

While the dinosaurs were living on the land, other reptiles were swimming in the seas. Reptiles probably entered the oceans about 290 million years ago (see page 41). Gradually, their bodies changed to help them live under water.

Early sea reptiles

By the start of the Triassic Period, about 245 million years ago, there were two kinds of reptiles living in the sea. Placodonts were turtle-shaped creatures. Some of them were good swimmers, but others spent most of their time on dry land.

★ A placodont called *Henodus*

★ A nothosaur called *Nothosaurus*

Nothosaurs had long, thin bodies that could glide smoothly through the water, and they may have had webbed feet as well. They used their big, sharp teeth for catching fish.

Swimming with flippers

At the start of the Jurassic Period, around 200 million years ago, a group of long-necked reptiles called plesiosaurs evolved. Instead of legs, plesiosaurs had big, paddle-shaped flippers which they flapped like wings as they moved through the water.

Sea monsters

Some plesiosaurs became ferocious hunters. One group, called the pliosaurs, had massive jaws full of sharp teeth for stabbing their prey. Pliosaurs hunted in the depths of the oceans, searching for sharks, big squids and other swimming reptiles. Some pliosaurs were enormous, reaching lengths of over 12m (40ft).

This picture shows some reptiles that lived in the Jurassic seas.

This squid-like creature is called a belemnite.

★ *Peloneustes is a fast-moving pliosaur.*

QUICKLINKS: For links to websites with exciting reconstructions of prehistoric sea reptiles, go to **usborne.com/Quicklinks**

All the sea reptiles have lungs, so they need to swim to the surface to breathe air.

Metriorhynchus is an early crocodile. It has flipper-like feet and a fishy tail.

A plesiosaur, called Muraenosaurus, moves its long neck around, searching for food.

Ichthyosaurs flick their tails from side to side as they swim.

Long, thin snout

Small flippers for steering

Liopleurodon is a fierce pliosaur with huge jaws.

This ichthyosaur, called Ophthalmosaurus, has very big eyes to help it see under water.

Underwater babies

Most sea reptiles had to return to dry land to lay their eggs. However, ichthyosaurs stopped laying eggs and began giving birth to babies under water. This meant that the ichthyosaurs never had to leave the sea.

Dying out

Around 66 million years ago, almost all the sea reptiles died out (see pages 58 and 59). Crocodiles and turtles survived, but today crocodiles live in fresh water, rather than in the sea. Turtles are the only present-day reptiles that spend their lives in the ocean.

Expert swimmers

The best swimmers were a group of reptiles called ichthyosaurs. They were shaped like dolphins, with streamlined bodies and large fins that helped them to glide swiftly through the ocean.

REPTILES

53

Flying Reptiles

Around 225 million years ago, during the Triassic Period, some reptiles evolved wings. These flying reptiles are known as pterosaurs. Pterosaurs may have evolved from tree-climbing reptiles which gradually grew wings to help them glide from branch to branch.

Sharovipteryx, an early gliding reptile, may have been an ancestor of the pterosaurs.

Flap of skin

Another idea is that pterosaurs were descended from reptiles called archosaurs (see page 43). Archosaurs ran along the ground on two legs, and some may have developed wings to help them catch flying insects.

Short-tailed insect-eaters

Near the end of the Jurassic Period, some new, short-tailed pterosaurs appeared. These pterosaurs could twist and turn in the air far more easily than their long-tailed ancestors. They probably caught fast-moving insects.

Pterodactylus slept hanging upside down.

Pterodactylus hunted insects.

Like all pterosaurs, *Pterodactylus had* excellent eyesight for spotting its prey.

Each wing was supported by a very long finger.

Leathery wing

Early flyers

By the start of the Jurassic Period, about 200 million years ago, several types of pterosaurs had appeared. They all had big, leathery wings, short necks and long, bony tails. Some of them flew over the ocean, catching fish in their pointed jaws.

Rhamphorhynchus was an early pterosaur that caught fish.

Bony tail

Pteranodon used the crest on its head to help it steer and balance in the air.

Pterodaustro trapped tiny sea creatures between its teeth.

Pouch

Bizarre hunters

Some pterosaurs developed very unusual jaws. *Pterodaustro* had an extremely long, curved beak, and its lower jaw was lined with thin, bristle-like teeth. It probably flew low over the sea, scooping up water and trapping tiny creatures between its teeth. *Pteranodon* had no teeth at all. It snatched fish from the water, then stored them in its pelican-like pouch before swallowing them whole.

Quetzalcoatlus had wings that measured more than 15m (50ft) across.

Keeping warm

Normally, reptiles rely on heat from the sun to keep their bodies warm, but pterosaurs could produce their own heat, like birds do. Pterosaurs were covered with fur, so they wouldn't lose too much heat through their skin.

Fur for keeping warm

Giants of the air

About 75 million years ago, during the Cretaceous Period, some gigantic pterosaurs evolved. The biggest of all, called *Quetzalcoatlus*, was the size of a small aircraft. Like all pterosaurs, these enormous creatures had very light skeletons with hollow bones, so they weren't too heavy to get off the ground.

On the ground, *Quetzalcoatlus* may have waddled on all fours.

REPTILES

55

The First Bird

For many years, experts were not sure how birds evolved. But now, experts think of modern birds (along with modern crocodiles and their relatives) as living members of the dinosaur family.

Dinosaurs and birds

Dinosaurs and birds are surprisingly similar. Dinosaurs laid eggs with hard shells, like birds do. Some even made nests, and cared for their young until they were old enough to survive on their own. Many dinosaurs had bird-like skeletons, and some had beaks.

Dinosaurs with feathers

In 1996, scientists discovered a fossil of a dinosaur called *Sinosauropteryx*. This fossil showed that *Sinosauropteryx* had a fluffy covering all over its body.

★ *Sinosauropteryx*

Other fossils have recently been found showing dinosaurs with short feathers on their bodies, tails and arms. Dinosaurs may have evolved feathers to keep themselves warm, or to attract a mate.

★ *Caudipteryx*, a feathered dinosaur

Flapping and leaping

Experts are not sure how feathered dinosaurs began to fly. They may have started flapping their arms while chasing insects, and accidentally learned to fly. Another explanation is that some dinosaurs learned to climb trees, and then began flying as they leaped between branches.

Early bird

One of the first true birds we know of appeared about 150 million years ago, during the Jurassic Period. It is called *Archaeopteryx*, which means "ancient feather". Although it had feathers and wings, like birds today, *Archaeopteryx* had teeth and a long, bony tail, like a dinosaur. It also had claws on its wings.

This picture shows *Archaeopteryx* in a forest.

A long tail helps to keep the bird steady in the air.

Into the air

Archaeopteryx was probably too heavy to take off from the ground. Instead, it scampered up trees, then launched itself into the air, hunting for insects. Once in the air, it could flap its wings quite powerfully. However, it may not have been able to change direction very quickly while it was flying.

This Archaeopteryx is taking off from a branch.

Strong legs and feet for running and jumping

Archaeopteryx hunts slow-moving insects, such as dragonflies.

Specially shaped feathers help the bird move smoothly through the air.

Scaly head

Archaeopteryx has pointed teeth for trapping insects.

Long claws for climbing trees

Pieces of a puzzle

Experts have known about *Archaeopteryx* since 1860, when the first fossil of this creature was found. The recent discovery that some dinosaurs had feathers has finally helped to prove the link between dinosaurs and birds.

★ Fossil of *Archaeopteryx*

REPTILES

The Death of the Dinosaurs

Around 66 million years ago, at the end of the Cretaceous Period, lots of creatures died out completely. All the dinosaurs became extinct, except for some feathered ones that had evolved into birds. Flying reptiles and most sea reptiles also died out. No one is certain why this happened, but scientists have given several different explanations.

Deadly rock?

Near the end of the Cretaceous Period, the Earth was struck by an enormous rock, or meteorite, measuring up to 10km (6 miles) across. As it hit the Earth, the meteorite would have smashed into tiny pieces, surrounding the planet in clouds of dust.

The dust clouds would have made the Earth cold and dark for months, killing off any creatures that needed warmth to survive. Without light, many plants must have died as well, leaving the animals with nothing to eat. The meteorite could also have caused massive earthquakes and giant tidal waves.

Huge clouds of dust spread out over the Earth.

The dust makes it hard for creatures to breathe.

This picture shows what may have happened as the meteorite struck the Earth.

Frightened animals try to run away.

Deep cracks appear in the shaking ground.

Lava shower?

Another explanation is that many volcanoes all over the world may have erupted at around the same time. The erupting volcanoes would have poured out vast amounts of hot lava (liquid rock) onto the Earth's surface, and sent clouds of dust and poisonous gases high into the air. These gases could also have caused harmful acid rain to fall.

Red-hot lava pouring from a volcano

Many creatures are killed or injured by pieces of flying rock.

Climate change?

By 66 million years ago, the weather all over the world had become cooler and more changeable. Dinosaurs relied on heat from the sun to keep themselves warm, and they may not have been able to cope with a changing climate.

Several causes

There is probably no single reason why so many animals died out. The meteorite must have killed off many creatures, but animals may also have been affected by a change in the weather.

The survivors

Mysteriously, some creatures did not die out. Some reptiles, such as lizards and snakes, survived, as well as most birds, insects and amphibians. Other survivors were a group of animals called mammals (see page 60).

Some creatures that survived

Dragonfly (insect)

Gull (bird)

Lizard (reptile)

Rat (mammal)

Frog (amphibian)

No one is sure why these animals survived, but mammals can produce their own heat, so they could have stayed warm in a cooler climate. Birds can also produce their own heat, and small reptiles, such as lizards, could have burrowed underground to keep warm.

REPTILES

59

The First Mammals

Around 200 million years ago, a new group of creatures, called mammals, began to appear on the Earth. The first mammals were tiny, insect-eating animals that looked like mice or shrews.

Megazostrodon, one of the first mammals ★

What is a mammal?

Mammals have hair or bristles on their skin, and feed their babies with milk. Their bodies are endothermic, or warm-blooded. This means that they can produce their own heat and stay warm, even when the weather gets cold. Mammals also have several different kinds of teeth, which they use for cutting and chewing a variety of foods.

Synapsid ancestors

Around 90 million years before the first mammals appeared, a group of animals evolved that had large heads, short legs and barrel-shaped bodies. They are known as synapsids (see pages 40 and 41).

By the start of the Triassic Period, some synapsids had become furry and had developed varied teeth. They were known as cynodonts. Some may have been able to stay warm all the time, like mammals. Experts believe that the first mammals evolved from small, furry cynodonts.

Thrinaxodon, a furry cynodont the size of a small dog ★

Living with the dinosaurs

The first mammals appeared around the same time as the first dinosaurs, but unlike the dinosaurs they did not change or develop fast. For more than 100 million years, until the dinosaurs died out, mammals stayed very small. They scurried around quietly, and usually only came out at night, when most other creatures were asleep.

This picture shows some early mammals in a forest at evening time.

The mammals try to keep out of the dinosaurs' way.

Some plant-eating mammals look like voles.

Mammals have large eyes so they can see at night.

Shrew-like mammal

Once the sun has gone down, the dinosaurs become cold and slow.

The mammals' strong sense of smell helps them to find food in the dark.

Mammals have good hearing, so they can tell when dinosaurs are coming.

Some rat-like mammals can climb trees.

Mammals can keep themselves warm, so they can stay active at night.

Egg-laying mammals

The first mammals probably all laid eggs, like their reptile ancestors did. However, unlike reptiles, the mammals fed their young with milk. Egg-laying mammals are called monotremes. Two types of monotremes still survive in Australia and Papua New Guinea. They are the spiny anteaters and the duck-billed platypus.

★ Duck-billed platypus

MAMMALS

61

Mammals with Pouches

The first mammals probably all laid eggs (see page 61), but around 100 million years ago some mammals started giving birth to very tiny babies. The babies crawled up into a pouch on their mother's stomach and continued to grow there.

Mammals with pouches are called marsupials. Today, marsupials are found mainly in Australia, but a few species live in North and South America.

Marsupial babies

Newborn marsupials are no bigger than a bee. The baby stays in its mother's pouch and drinks milk from her nipples until it is fully developed and ready to explore the outside world.

Diagram of a kangaroo, a present-day marsupial

★

Baby

Pouch

Placentals

A few million years after the first marsupials appeared, a different kind of mammal, called a placental, evolved. Placental mothers keep their babies inside their bodies until the babies are large enough to survive on their own. Most mammals alive today are placentals.

Placental babies

Before they are born, placental babies get their food from a part of their mother's body called the placenta. After the babies are born, the mother looks after them and feeds them with milk from her nipples.

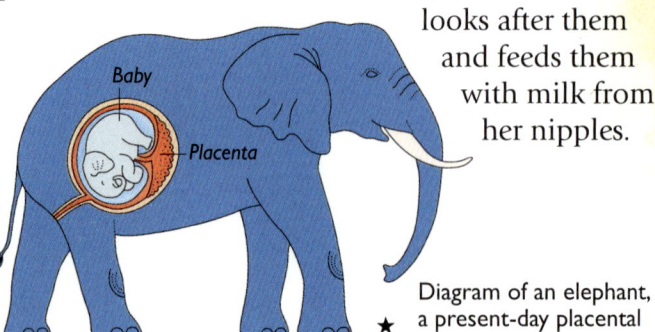

Baby

Placenta

Diagram of an elephant, ★ a present-day placental

Mammals spread out

At the time of the early mammals, the Earth's surface looked very different from the way it does today. All the continents were linked to each other, so marsupials and placentals could spread out across the world.

However, at the same time as the mammals were spreading out, the continents were very slowly drifting apart. This meant that some mammals became stranded in different parts of the world.

The marsupial Procoptodon is an ancestor of today's kangaroos.

Marsupials in Australia

Around 85,000 years ago, Australia became an island. By that time, no placentals had reached Australia, but a wide range of marsupials developed there.

This scene shows some of the marsupials that lived in Australia 10,000 years ago.

Diprotodon *digs up bushes with its paws.*

Thylacoleo *is a fierce hunter.*

Palorchestes *uses its short trunk to pull down leaves to eat.*

Procoptodon *is about 2.5m (8ft) tall.*

This young Procoptodon *is jumping into its mother's pouch for safety.*

Powerful legs for leaping

The rise of the placentals

In many parts of the world, the marsupials died out completely. This happened because placentals are generally better at surviving than marsupials. Tiny babies are safer inside their mother's body than they are in a pouch, and placentals are better at training their young to survive.

Marsupials survive

In a few parts of the world, marsupials have thrived. They have coped especially well in Australia because they are able to stop giving birth when the weather becomes too hot and dry for their young to survive. When the weather gets cooler, they start having babies again.

MAMMALS

The Rise of the Mammals

After the dinosaurs died out, around 66 million years ago, life became less dangerous for the mammals. They started to eat a wide range of foods and began to explore new places to live.

By 30 million years ago, a great variety of mammals had evolved. They spread out all over the world, and soon became the fastest, strongest and most intelligent group of creatures on Earth.

Plant-eaters

Many early mammals ate soft plants and leaves. Most of these plant-eaters were slow-moving and clumsy, and some of them grew to be much bigger than any land mammals today.

Rodents

Mammals with very strong teeth gnawed and nibbled at roots, bushes and tree trunks. These gnawing animals are known as rodents. Some of the early rodents looked like rats, rabbits and hares.

Palaeolagus, an early rabbit

Birbalomys, an ancestor of the guinea pig

Stylinodon, a badger-sized rodent

Uintatherium, a rhino-sized plant-eater ★

Didolodus, a pig-sized plant-eater

Tree-climbers

One group of mammals, called primates, learned to climb trees. Over millions of years, primates evolved into apes, and then into human beings. Most of the early primates looked like squirrels, monkeys and lemurs.

Smilodectes, a lemur-like primate

Branisella, an early monkey ★

Into the air

Some tree-climbing mammals grew flaps of skin between their legs so that they could glide from tree to tree. Around the same time, a group of insect-eaters gradually evolved into bats, with wings of thin skin supported by very long "fingers".

Icaronycteris, an early bat ★

Planetetherium, a gliding mammal ★

Meat-eaters

Some mammals ate meat, instead of plants or insects. Some of these early hunters looked like weasels and otters, and others looked like lions, wolves and bears.

Into the oceans

A few land mammals managed to move into the oceans. They developed smooth, streamlined bodies which were suited to life in the water. Slowly, the early sea mammals evolved into whales, dolphins and seals.

Pakicetus, the earliest known whale

Patriofelis, an early big cat ★

Cladosictis, an otter-like meat-eater

Basilosaurus, a ★ long-bodied whale

Hunters and Scavengers

Around 60 million years ago, some mammals began to hunt and eat other animals. At first, these meat-eating mammals were not very fast or clever, but gradually they evolved into expert hunters.

Early meat-eaters

The first meat-eating mammals were called oxyaenids. They had small brains, short legs and flat feet. This did not matter much, because the plant-eating mammals that they hunted were as unintelligent and slow-moving as they were.

Like most oxyaenids, Sarkastodon cannot run very fast.

Sarkastodon's teeth are not very good at tearing up meat.

This picture shows the oxyaenid *Sarkastodon* chasing a plant-eater called *Hyrachyus*.

Scavengers

Some of the early meat-eaters ate dead animals that they found, instead of going hunting. Animals that do this are called scavengers. Scavengers developed special teeth for crushing bones, so that they could eat the soft bone marrow inside.

Hyaenodon scavenging meat from a dead animal
★

Better hunters

Gradually, some plant-eating mammals became very good at running and started to live in herds (see pages 68 and 69). This meant that the animals that hunted them had to change too.

Cerdocyon, an ancestor of the fox

Hesperocyon, one of the first dogs

A new group of meat-eating mammals evolved that were fast-moving, powerful and cunning. These mammals, known as carnivores, had excellent hearing and eyesight, and a strong sense of smell. Today's dogs and cats are descended from these early carnivores.

Homotherium, an early cat

Dinofelis, a panther-like cat

MAMMALS

Hunting in teams

Around six million years ago, early dogs and wolves began to hunt in teams, or packs. This meant that they could hunt animals much larger than themselves. Some big cats, such as lions, also hunted in teams.

Today, wolves still hunt together in packs. These wolves are howling to other members of their pack to show that they are ready to start hunting.

Chasing and stalking

Dogs chased after their prey until the hunted animals were exhausted, but cats hunted in a different way. First, they stalked their prey (followed it very quietly), and then they pounced on it swiftly and suddenly.

Teeth and claws

Carnivores developed sharp claws for holding their prey, and long, pointed teeth for tearing up meat. Some big cats, known as sabre-toothed cats, had incredibly long, blade-like teeth, or fangs.

★

In this scene, a sabre-toothed cat, called *Smilodon*, is stalking its prey.

Powerful neck and shoulders

Smilodon uses its curved fangs for stabbing its prey and tearing up meat.

Another cat prowls through the long grass.

Smilodon pads very quietly on its soft paws.

Sharp claws for grasping prey

MAMMALS

Plant-eaters' Problems

The first plant-eating mammals (or herbivores) were slow-moving creatures with small brains. Most of them were the size of today's pigs or badgers, but a few were incredibly tall and heavy.

This is *Paraceratherium*, the largest mammal that ever lived on land.

Tough, leathery skin

Paraceratherium munches leaves from the tops of trees.

Paraceratherium is 8m (26ft) tall and weighs as much as four elephants.

Horns and tusks

The early herbivores wandered through forests nibbling leaves and plants. They were hunted by meat-eating mammals, and some of them developed strange-looking horns and tusks to defend themselves against predators (hunters).

Megacerops had two huge horns on its nose.

The growth of the grasslands

Around 40 million years ago, the weather all over the world began to get cooler. Gradually, most of the tropical forests were replaced by grassy plains. The herbivores were forced to eat grass, which is tough to chew and hard to digest, and many animals died out because they couldn't cope with their new food.

Roaming the plains

The grasslands provided plenty of food and the number of grazers increased rapidly. By 25 million years ago, the first deer, cattle, sheep and antelope had all appeared on the plains. They lived in large groups, or herds, that roamed over the grasslands.

Eating grass

Slowly, new kinds of herbivores evolved that were able to eat grass. Animals that eat grass are known as grazers. They have flat teeth with ridges that are very good at grinding. Grazers chew and swallow their food several times, bringing partly digested food back up into their mouths, so that they can chew it again. This repeated chewing of food is known as "chewing the cud".

This picture shows a herd of *Ilingoceros* (early antelope) being chased by wolves.

All the members of the herd try to stay together for safety.

A few animals cannot keep up with the herd.

This Ilingoceros has been surrounded.

The wolves run fast after the antelope.

It butts the wolves with its horns and kicks them with its hoofs.

Sharp, twisted horns

Eyes on the sides of its head give Ilingoceros a wide range of vision.

Springy hind legs

With their long legs and hard hoofs, the antelope can sprint for miles.

Herding together

Living in herds was safer for the grazers, because predators were less likely to attack a group than a single animal. However, herds were easier for the predators to spot.

Legs, horns and hoofs

Grazers developed long legs which helped them to run fast and escape from predators. Their legs also made them taller, so they could see farther across the plains. Many grazers grew pointed horns or antlers which they used to fight off attackers. They also used their hard hoofs to kick any animals that attacked them.

MAMMALS

The Horse's Tale

The first horses lived around 50 million years ago, when the Earth was covered with forests. They were much smaller than horses today (about the size of a small dog) and they wandered through the forests, nibbling soft leaves. Sometimes, the horses were attacked by vicious giant birds.

This picture shows a giant bird, called *Diatryma*, chasing *Hyracotherium*, the earliest known species of horse.

Disappearing forests

Gradually, the forests where the early horses lived were replaced by vast, grassy plains (see page 68). This meant that the horses had to change in order to survive.

Bigger and faster

By 35 million years ago, horses had grown longer legs for running on the plains, and had developed stronger teeth for chewing tough grass. They also lost a toe from each of their front feet and began to run on their strong middle toes. This new way of running made them lighter on their feet.

Diatryma is a powerful runner, but it can't fly.

Diatryma is 2m (6ft) tall.

Hyracotherium is only 40cm (15in) tall.

Short neck

Small, blunt teeth

Hyracotherium has four toes on its front feet and three toes on its hind feet.

The horse's toes spread out to stop it from sinking into soft ground.

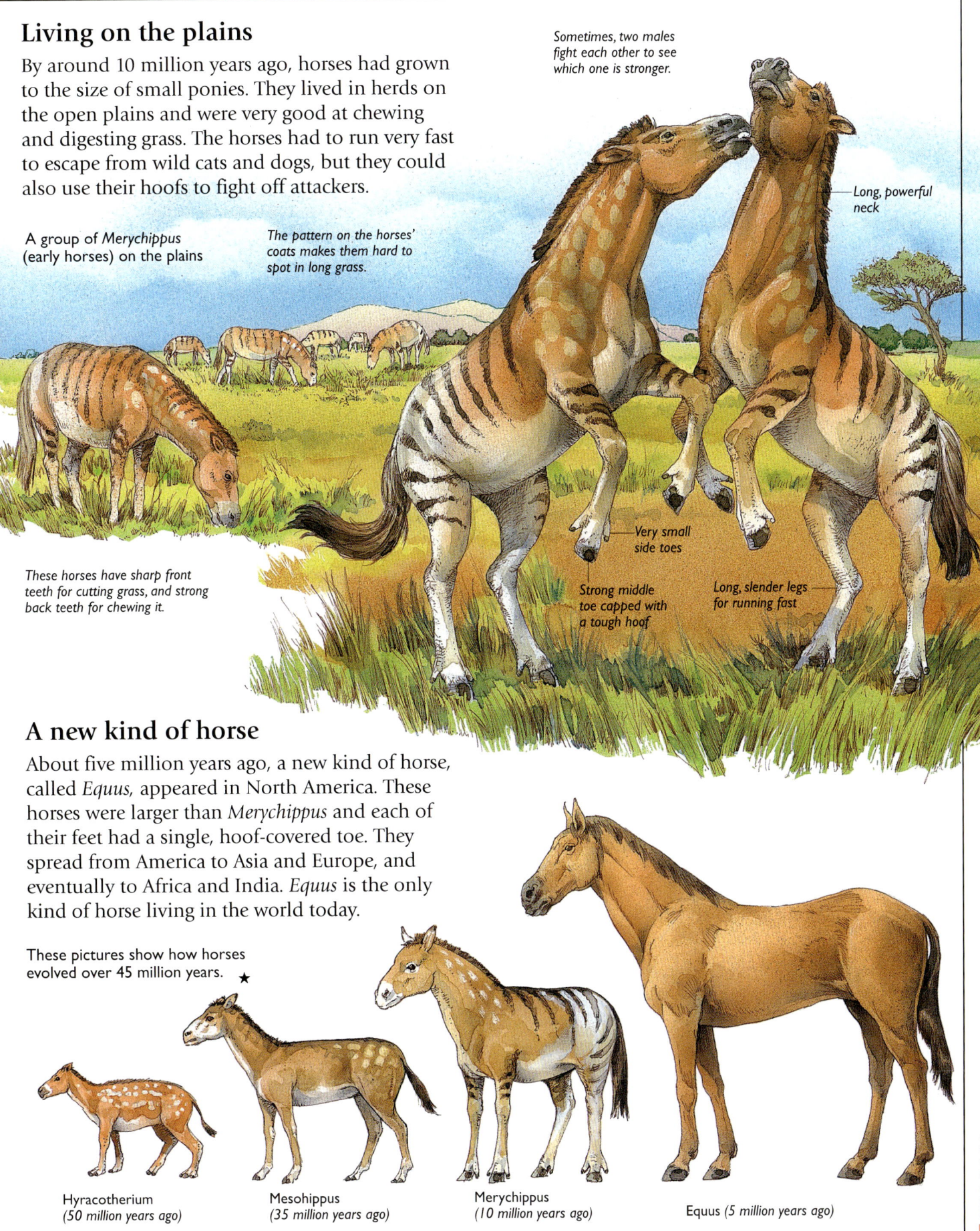

Living on the plains

By around 10 million years ago, horses had grown to the size of small ponies. They lived in herds on the open plains and were very good at chewing and digesting grass. The horses had to run very fast to escape from wild cats and dogs, but they could also use their hoofs to fight off attackers.

A group of *Merychippus* (early horses) on the plains

The pattern on the horses' coats makes them hard to spot in long grass.

Sometimes, two males fight each other to see which one is stronger.

Long, powerful neck

These horses have sharp front teeth for cutting grass, and strong back teeth for chewing it.

Very small side toes

Strong middle toe capped with a tough hoof

Long, slender legs for running fast

A new kind of horse

About five million years ago, a new kind of horse, called *Equus*, appeared in North America. These horses were larger than *Merychippus* and each of their feet had a single, hoof-covered toe. They spread from America to Asia and Europe, and eventually to Africa and India. *Equus* is the only kind of horse living in the world today.

These pictures show how horses evolved over 45 million years. ★

Hyracotherium
(50 million years ago)

Mesohippus
(35 million years ago)

Merychippus
(10 million years ago)

Equus (5 million years ago)

MAMMALS

71

Animals of South America

Around 50 million years after the first mammals appeared, the area of land that is now South America became cut off from North America.

Even though the mammals of South America developed completely separately from any other animals, many of them looked like mammals from other parts of the world. This is because creatures evolve to suit their surroundings, so animals living in the same kind of surroundings tend to evolve in a similar way.

Mammals with pouches

A wide range of marsupials (mammals with pouches) evolved in South America, although almost no marsupials live there today. Most of these creatures were hunters and many of them looked like meat-eating mammals from other parts of the world.

Thomashuxleya looked like a warthog.

Diadiaphorus looked like a horse.

Macrauchenia had a camel-like body and a short trunk.

Theosodon was an ancestor of the llama.

Toxodon looked like a hippo.

Argyrolagus was a marsupial that looked like a kangaroo rat.

Thylacosmilus was a marsupial that looked like a big cat.

Plant-eaters and gnawers

As well as the marsupials, many kinds of placental mammals (see page 62) developed in South America. These animals ate soft plants and grasses or gnawed at roots and branches. Most of them looked like plant-eaters or rodents (gnawers) from other parts of the world, but a few, like Macrauchenia, were very unusual.

Protypotherium looked like a rabbit.

Strange creatures

Two kinds of South American mammals were completely different from any other animals in the world. These were the sloths and the glyptodonts. Sloths had long, thick hair and moved extremely slowly, and glyptodonts had a bony dome on their backs to protect them.

Changing places

Around five million years ago, North and South America became joined by a bridge of land. Some South American mammals, such as sloths, glyptodonts and porcupines, began to move north, while northern mammals, such as rabbits, horses and big cats, began spreading south.

★ *Megatherium* was a giant sloth that lived on the ground.

The North American porcupine originally came from South America.

Dying out

Not long after North and South America became joined, many species of South American mammals died out. Experts used to think that this happened because the mammals of the south could not compete with the northern mammals. However, many southern species were already disappearing by the time the northern mammals arrived in the south.

Doedicurus was a glyptodont with a viciously spiked tail.

Hapalops was a tree-climbing sloth.

Changes in the weather

No one knows why so many South American mammals became extinct. However, around the time that North and South America joined together, the weather all over the world became very changeable. Some southern mammals may have died out because, unlike the mammals of the north, they were not used to changes in their climate.

★ *Glyptodon* was the size of a small car.

MAMMALS

73

The Elephant's Story

The earliest ancestors of today's elephants were long-bodied, pig-like creatures that lived in the swamps of Africa around 40 million years ago. They wallowed around in the water, feeding on soft-leaved plants.

The early elephant Moeritherium spent most of its life in the water.

Trunks and tusks

Over millions of years, the early elephants became taller. This made it hard for them to reach down to the plants that they ate. Gradually, their upper lips and noses grew longer and developed into a short trunk.

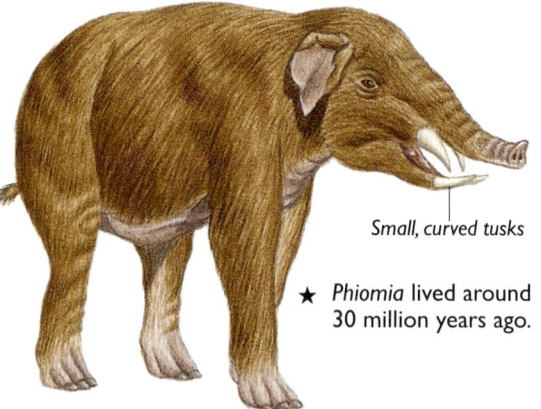

Small, curved tusks

★ *Phiomia lived around 30 million years ago.*

The elephants used their trunks to suck up water and shovel plants into their mouths. They also grew curved tusks which helped them to scoop up their food.

Extraordinary elephants

Many different kinds of elephants evolved in Africa, Asia, Europe and America, and some of them had teeth, tusks and trunks that grew in strange shapes. However, around five million years ago, an elephant called *Stegodon* evolved which looked very similar to elephants today.

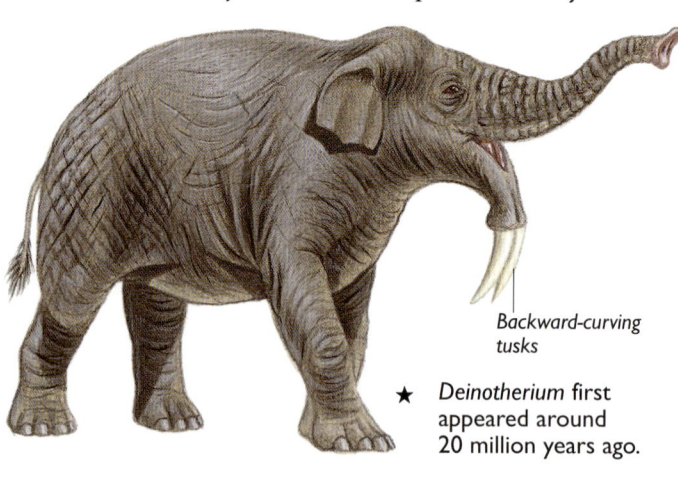

Backward-curving tusks

★ *Deinotherium first appeared around 20 million years ago.*

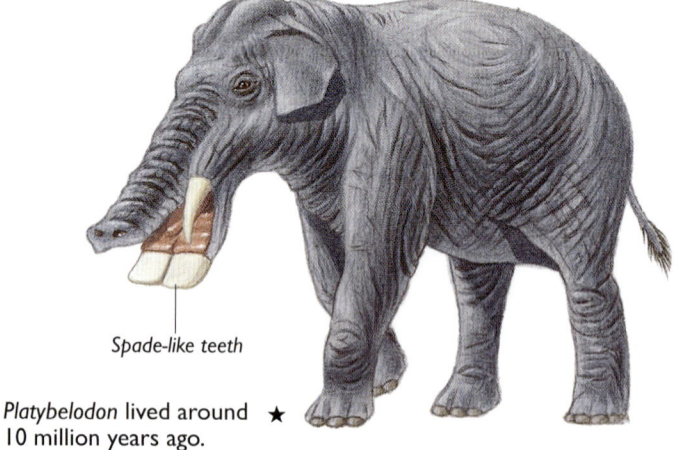

Spade-like teeth

Platybelodon lived around 10 million years ago. ★

★ *Stegodon evolved around 5 million years ago.*

Mammoths drowned in tar

Around six million years ago, a group of enormous elephants, called mammoths, appeared. Mammoths measured up to 4.5m (15ft) tall, and had very long, curved tusks.

Fossils of mammoths and other animals have been found at La Brea, near Los Angeles in the USA. Around 15,000 years ago, there were several pits filled with tar in this area. The tar became covered with rainwater, and many animals thought the pits were drinking pools. Hundreds of creatures became stuck in the tar and drowned.

Vulture

Mammoths come to the pool to drink.

Wolves and wild cats feed on any animals that have drowned.

This picture shows a tar pit at La Brea.

Elephant ancestors

Around 4,000 years ago, the mammoths died out. This may have happened because the weather became too warm for them or because they were hunted by humans. Two groups of elephants survived in Africa and Asia. They were the ancestors of today's elephants.

African elephants like these are descended from elephants that lived in Africa about four million years ago.

MAMMALS

Animals of the Ice Age

Several times in the history of the Earth, large parts of the world have been buried under thick sheets of ice. Each time, the ice has stayed frozen for thousands of years, and these long, freezing periods are known as ice ages.

The last ice age

The last ice age began around 100,000 years ago and ended around 10,000 years ago. During this time, large areas of land in the northern half of the world were covered in ice.

This map shows the world during the last ice age.

■	Areas covered in ice
■	Frozen lands where animals could live

Frozen mammoths

Sometimes, animals fell into ponds which later froze solid. The animals' bodies were trapped in ice and could not rot away, so they were preserved for thousands of years. Several woolly mammoths have been found in the ice of Siberia, in northern Russia. Some of these mammoths were covered with hair, and some still had their last meal preserved in their stomachs.

This baby mammoth was discovered in the ice of Siberia in 1977.

Woolly mammoths

Living on the edge

At the start of the last ice age, many animals moved to warmer areas, but some stayed in the frozen lands near the edge of the ice sheets. Very cold places where the ground is always frozen are known as tundra. The animals of the tundra grew thick coats to keep themselves warm. Most of them ate mosses, lichens and small bushes, but some were hunters.

This scene shows some of the animals that lived in the tundra.

The Arctic hare's white coat helps it to hide in the snow.

The Arctic fox is a cunning hunter.

Reindeer use their large horns to defend themselves against meat-eaters.

Between the ice ages

The last ice age was one of a series of ice ages that began two million years ago. In between these freezing periods, the weather became very warm. Thick forests grew where the ice sheets had been, and animals that were used to the cold were forced to travel to cooler areas. Meanwhile, heat-loving animals, such as hippos and lions, were able to live in places as far north as Europe and North America.

Disappearing animals

At the end of the last ice age, around 10,000 years ago, many animals died out. No one knows exactly why this happened, but one reason must have been the change in the weather. Some animals, such as mammoths, were hunted by early humans, and this could be another reason why they disappeared.

Icy winds whistle across the tundra.

The woolly rhinoceros is covered with thick hair.

Lichens and mosses grow on rocks,

Musk oxen roam the tundra, searching for plants to eat.

Bears shelter in caves when the weather becomes very cold.

Small plants and bushes poke up through the snow.

MAMMALS

Apes and Monkeys

Apes, monkeys and humans all belong to a group of mammals known as primates. The first primates appeared on the Earth about 66 million years ago. They were small, squirrel-like creatures that scurried around in the trees.

Plesiadapis, an early primate

★

Sharp claws

Mesopithecus monkeys live in the treetops.

This monkey is teaching its young to climb.

Gigantopithecus is an enormous ape. It is around 2.5m (8ft) tall.

Gigantopithecus lives on the forest floor. It is too heavy to climb trees.

Fingers and toes

Gradually, some early primates began to change. Instead of claws, they grew fingers and toes with sensitive tips. Fingers and toes were useful for judging the thickness of branches and for holding onto them tightly.

Seeing in 3-D

Primates developed much better eyesight than most other mammals. Each of their eyes saw a different picture, and their brains put the pictures together to make a three-dimensional image. Seeing in 3-D helped primates to judge distances when they leaped from one branch to another.

Early monkeys and apes

By around 30 million years ago, some primates had evolved into the first monkeys and apes. Even the earliest monkeys were expert tree-climbers, and some monkeys developed long, curling tails for grasping branches. Apes were bigger and stronger than monkeys. They had broad chests, flexible shoulders and strong arms, which helped them to swing from tree to tree.

HUMANS

Learning to survive

Climbing and balancing are difficult things to do, and apes and monkeys evolved big brains to help them cope with life in the trees. They began to live in large groups, and to look after each other. They also spent a long time bringing up their babies and teaching them how to survive.

Climbing and walking

Over millions of years, different apes and monkeys learned to live in different parts of the trees, so that they could all find enough food to eat. Some even left the trees and started living on the ground.

When they were on the ground, some apes sometimes walked on two feet instead of crawling on all fours. This left their hands free for carrying food. However, they couldn't stand up straight, which made it hard to walk very far on two feet.

This monkey is cleaning another monkey's fur. This is called grooming.

This Dryopithecus ape is using its strong arms to swing between branches.

Monkeys and apes use their fingers and thumbs to make a tight grip.

This ape, called Sivapithecus, may have been able to walk for short distances on two feet.

Sivapithecus uses its hands to carry food.

On the ground, Dryopithecus walks on all fours.

Changing faces

Most early primates had long noses, or snouts, for sniffing out their food, and long, pointed teeth for nibbling fruit and insects. However, some later apes relied on their eyes instead of their noses to find food, so their snouts gradually became shorter. Their teeth also became shorter and flatter, so they could grind up the tough plants and grasses that grew on the ground.

HUMANS

79

Southern Apes

Over five million years ago, some apes in Africa started learning to walk upright. Apes that walk upright are called hominins. We are hominins too, but the earliest ones were very different from us. They were much shorter than us, and had small brains and ape like faces.

The earliest known hominin is called *Australopithecus*, which means "southern ape". It lived from around five million to a million years ago.

★ *Australopithecus* skull

Experts dig up new hominin bones all the time. The most famous set of bones is an *Australopithecus* skeleton from Hadar, in Ethiopia. The skeleton has been named "Lucy".

Finding footprints

At Laetoli, in Tanzania, experts have found a trail of *Australopithecus* footprints preserved in volcanic ash. This proves that Lucy and her friends had started walking upright.

The footprints at Laetoli

Swinging through trees

At first, *Australopithecus* spent a lot of time in the trees. It had long, curved fingers and toes, and long arms, which helped it to grip branches and swing between them. However, its knees were like ours, which shows that it could also walk upright.

Map of Africa

EUROPE
ASIA
AFRICA

★ Hadar
★ Olduvai Gorge
★ Laetoli
★ Sterkfontein

★ Some places where *Australopithecus* bones have been found

This picture shows a group of early *Australopithecus*.

The group lives at the edge of a thick forest.

Most Australopithecus are less than 1.5m (5ft) tall.

Walking on two feet leaves the hands free for carrying things.

Stones are useful for cracking open tough-skinned fruit.

Australopithecus has a hairy body and an apelike face.

Why did apes stand up?

Nobody is sure why some apes began walking upright, but one explanation is the weather.

Between seven and four million years ago, the Earth's climate got much cooler. In East Africa, the forests where *Australopithecus* lived began to disappear. It was harder to find fruit and leaves to eat, so *Australopithecus* had to travel farther to find food. Using two legs was less tiring than using four.

Standing upright also made it easier for *Australopithecus* to spot dangerous animals in the tall grass at the edge of the forest.

Different types

Eventually, *Australopithecus* seems to have evolved into several different types. Some are known as "gracile" (slender), while others are known as "robust" (large and strong). The "robust" *Australopithecus* had very powerful jaws, which allowed it to eat tough grasses and roots.

Some of the group are eating leaves and fruit from the trees.

Beyond the forest are large areas of grassland, called savannah.

Long, powerful arms

Standing upright, Australopithecus can see a wild cat lying in wait.

Long, curved toes and fingers for grasping branches

This group of Australopithecus has walked across the grassland to find food.

Some of the group use sticks to break open a termites' nest, so they can eat the insects.

HUMAN

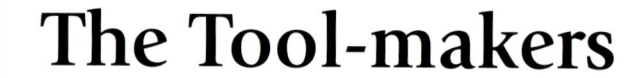

The Tool-makers

Around two and a half million years ago, a new species of hominin, called *Homo habilis,* evolved in Africa. For more than a million years, it lived alongside *Australopithecus* (see pages 80 and 81).

Homo habilis had a bigger brain than *Australopithecus,* and was more skilled. (Its name means "skilled man" in Latin.) It is sometimes known as "handy man" and is often thought of as the first human.

New skills

Australopithecus picked up sticks and stones and used them as tools, but *Homo habilis* could make its own tools. It made thin stone tools (called flakes) for cutting, and larger ones (called choppers) for smashing hard objects, such as nuts. These tools were made from flint, which is easy to shape.

★ Chopper

★ Flake

Shaping stones

Homo habilis made its tools by striking two rocks together. A long thin stone, called a hammerstone, was used to chip sharp flakes from a larger stone. This is known as stone knapping.

A group of *Homo habilis* making ★ and using tools

Chipping flakes from a stone

Hammerstone

Flake

Cracking nuts with a chopper

Sharpening sticks

Homo habilis probably made a wooden tool, called a digging stick, by sharpening one end of a branch with a stone flake. It may have used the sharpened sticks to dig up roots to eat.

Sharpening a stick with a stone flake

Digging for roots with a sharpened stick

Stealing meat

Although *Homo habilis* probably did no hunting, it did eat meat. Groups of *Homo habilis* used sharp stone tools to remove meat from the bodies of dead animals that they found. Their tools helped them to work fast, so they could get away before any wild animals attacked them.

A group of Australopithecus feeds on leaves. They cannot make tools for cutting meat.

This picture shows a group of *Homo habilis* stripping meat from a dead elephant.

These lions are coming to find food.

Large, sharp choppers are useful for smashing bone, to get at the soft marrow inside.

Vultures peck at the meat.

Stone flakes are used for slicing through meat.

The elephant died of old age.

This Homo habilis is taking away some meat to eat.

Starting to wander

Eating meat allowed *Homo habilis* to travel farther than *Australopithecus*. Because it no longer had to live so close to plants and fruit, it could explore wider areas. Its new diet also gave it more energy and helped its brain grow bigger.

HUMANS

The Coming of Fire

A million years after *Homo habilis* appeared (see page 82), a new hominin with an even bigger brain evolved in Africa. This species walked completely upright and is known as *Homo erectus*, which means "upright man" in Latin. *Homo erectus* people learned how to use fire, which gave them much more control over their lives.

Finding fire

Homo erectus people probably could not light fires themselves. Instead, they may have found fires that had started when lightning struck dry grass. They probably carried a burning branch away to a cave or a camp, then kept the same fire burning for days, or even weeks.

This picture shows *Homo erectus* people using fire in their cave.

Outside it is dark and cold.

Lightning has started a fire on the grassland.

People use burning branches to drive away wild animals.

These men have brought some meat to cook on the fire.

The wild cats are frightened of the fire.

Safe and warm

Fire kept *Homo erectus* people warm at night. It could also be used as a weapon against dangerous animals, which were scared away by the blaze.

Cooking food

Homo erectus people discovered that meat and plants were tastier when they were heated, and they began to cook their food. Cooked food is easier to chew, so their teeth and jaws gradually became smaller. As they ate more meat, their bodies grew stronger and taller, and their brains became bigger.

Lighting the darkness

By keeping a fire burning, *Homo erectus* people could see clearly after it got dark. This meant that, unlike earlier hominids, they did not have to go to sleep when the sun went down, but could continue working at night.

Better tools

Homo erectus people used fire to make better tools. They hardened the ends of wooden spears by holding them in the flames, and heated stones to make them easier to shape. They made the heated stones into tools called hand axes, which had very sharp edges.

★
Hand axe

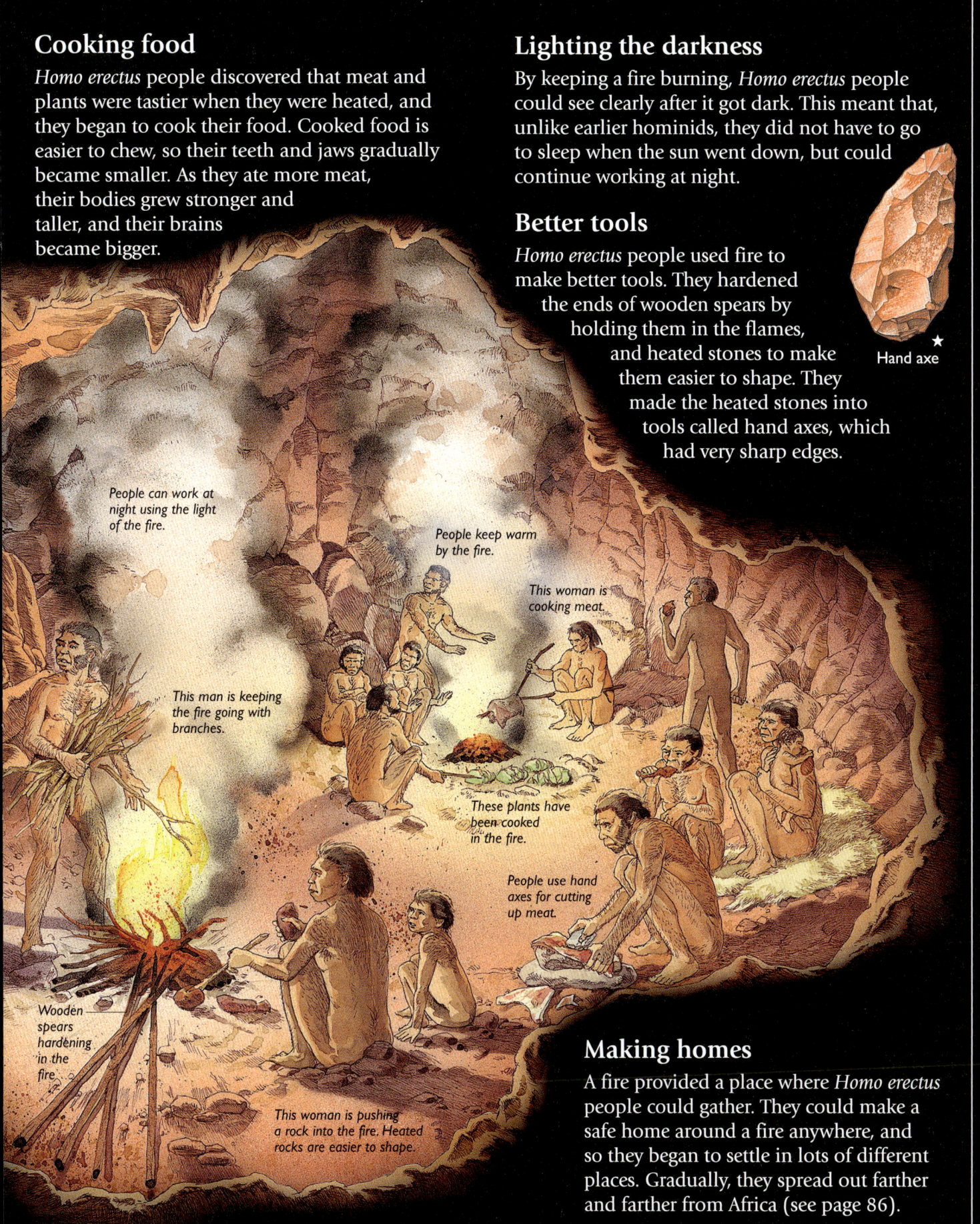

People can work at night using the light of the fire.

People keep warm by the fire.

This woman is cooking meat.

This man is keeping the fire going with branches.

These plants have been cooked in the fire.

People use hand axes for cutting up meat.

Wooden spears hardening in the fire.

This woman is pushing a rock into the fire. Heated rocks are easier to shape.

Making homes

A fire provided a place where *Homo erectus* people could gather. They could make a safe home around a fire anywhere, and so they began to settle in lots of different places. Gradually, they spread out farther and farther from Africa (see page 86).

HUMANS

85

The First Explorers

For over three million years, hominids lived only in eastern and southern Africa. This changed around 1.8 million years ago, when *Homo erectus* people began to move into new areas.

Out of Africa

Gradually, *Homo erectus* people spread out, until they had explored most of Africa. Some groups moved slowly east and eventually reached Indonesia and China.

Life in a Chinese cave

One group settled in a large cave near Zhoukoudian, in China. *Homo erectus* people lived there for 250,000 years.

This scene shows Homo erectus people in the Zhoukoudian cave.

Map showing how *Homo erectus* **spread**

ENGLAND
FRANCE ★ Terra Amata
SPAIN
Zhoukoudian ★
CHINA
AFRICA
INDONESIA

➡ *Possible route of Homo erectus*

Skulls and antlers

The people at Zhoukoudian ate meat from deer and horses, which they may have hunted. They made stone tools by hammering rocks with deer antlers, and also made drinking bowls from deer skulls.

Bowl made from a deer skull ★

★ Part of a deer antler used as a hammer

Animal skins keep people warm outside.

Firewood

This man is using a deer antler as a hammer.

This man is shaping a deer skull into a drinking bowl.

This girl is drinking water from a deer skull.

Discovering Europe

Homo erectus people probably arrived in Europe about 500,000 years ago. They moved around from place to place, hunting, fishing and gathering plants to eat. Eventually, they reached as far west as Spain and as far north as England.

Life on the coast

Some groups of *Homo erectus* people returned each year to stay in the same place. One group stayed every spring at a place called Terra Amata, on the south coast of France, where they may have built shelters from branches. They used wooden spears to hunt animals and catch fish.

Using fire

Homo erectus people could use fire to keep themselves warm. This meant they could move out of Africa, and into cooler areas. Their fires also kept wild animals away, so fewer people were killed, and their numbers started to grow.

Why did they travel?

Experts think that *Homo erectus* people had to travel to find enough food, because there were more people to feed. They hunted wandering animals, and the animals may have led them to new places.

This picture shows *Homo erectus* people hunting deer at Terra Amata.

People stay near streams, where they can find fresh water to drink.

Catching fish

Fish and meat are cooked on the fire.

Hunters use wooden spears and sharpened rocks.

HUMANS

87

Hunters of the Ice Age

By around 400,000 years ago, a new kind of people evolved. These new people had bigger brains than earlier people, and are known as *Homo neanderthalensis*, or Neanderthals.

They are named after the Neander Valley in Germany, where their bones were first found. Neanderthals appeared in Europe and western Asia during an ice age, when a large part of the Earth was covered in ice and snow (see page 76).

Big and clever

For a long time, people thought Neanderthals were unintelligent, apelike creatures, but experts now think differently. Neanderthals had strong, muscular bodies and a ridge of bone above their eyes, but otherwise they were very like us. Some of them had brains that were bigger than ours.

Finding food

In the long, frozen winters of the ice age, it was hard to find plants to eat, so Neanderthals ate a lot of meat. They stripped meat from dead animals that they found, and they also hunted animals, such as horses and reindeer.

Hunting with fire

Mammoths and rhinos were too dangerous to approach but, like all animals, they were scared of fire. Sometimes, Neanderthal hunters chased these huge animals with burning branches and forced them over the edge of a cliff. The animals were killed, and the hunters could then remove the meat from the dead bodies.

This scene shows Neanderthal hunters chasing mammoths over a cliff.

The hunters shout and wave their arms to frighten the mammoths.

Ridge of bone

Large jaw

Short, stocky body

Wooden spear

Burning branches

Knotted animal skins

The Neanderthals' strong bodies help them to cope with the cold.

This man has been wounded by a mammoth.

The mammoths are terrified by the fire and the men's shouts.

Keeping warm

During the freezing winters, Neanderthals needed warm clothes to keep out the cold. They probably made simple tunics by knotting animal skins together. Neanderthals often sheltered in caves, but out in the open they may have made shelters from branches and animal skins.

New tools

Neanderthals made better tools than earlier people. They had different tools for hunting, cutting food, and shaping wood. They also used their powerful jaws as extra tools, for tearing meat from animal bones and for cleaning animal skins.

HUMANS

89

Early Families

Neanderthals were more intelligent than earlier people, and they developed a more organized way of life. This helped them to survive in the freezing cold of the ice age. They worked together in family groups and cared for anyone in their family who was sick or injured.

Helping the injured

Hunting wild animals was very dangerous, and injuries were common. Some men were so badly hurt that they could never hunt again. These men were probably looked after by their families for the rest of their lives.

Gifts for the dead?

Some experts think that the Neanderthals believed in life after death. Animal horns, stone tools and pollen from flowers have all been found in Neanderthal graves. These objects may have been placed in the graves as gifts to help dead people in the afterlife.

In this picture, a dead Neanderthal is being buried by his family and friends.

The man is buried near the back of a cave.

Deer antler to place in the grave

These people are placing gifts around the body.

Goat's horn

Flowers

Stone tools

Deer bones

This injured man is being helped by his brother.

The man's family have curled up his body.

Later, people will cover the body with soil.

Burying the dead

Neanderthals were the first people to bury their dead, instead of just leaving the bodies to decay. They dug a hole with sharpened sticks and stones, then laid the body carefully inside it.

Starting to talk

No one really knows when people started speaking, but some experts think that Neanderthals were the first people who learned how to talk. They probably only used simple words, with lots of hand signals as well.

Being able to communicate helped the Neanderthals to work together and to organize hunts. They were also able to warn each other of danger.

This scene shows Neanderthals running to warn their family that wolves are approaching.

Lots of people gather to bury the man.

The end of the Neanderthals

Around 40,000 years ago, the Neanderthals began to die out. It's thought this may have been caused by climate changes that made their way of life difficult, or by diseases caught from other types of early people.

But before Neanderthals died out, some of them met with other types of early people, and even had families with them. So although Neanderthals died out, a trace of them still survives in people today.

HUMANS

91

The First Modern People

Around 300,000 years ago, a new type of people evolved. This species – known as *Homo sapiens* (meaing "wise man") – evolved in East Africa. All modern humans are descended from these people and have the same rounded skulls, straight foreheads and small jaws with firm chins.

★
Skull of
Homo sapiens

This scene shows how a tribe of people may have lived 30,000 years ago.

Hunting and gathering

The first modern people lived by hunting animals and gathering plants to eat. They kept moving from one place to another to find food. People who live like this are called hunter-gatherers. Some hunter-gatherers returned to the same place at the same time each year, and stayed there until the food ran out, before moving on.

Working together

These early people could talk just as well as people can today. Talking helped them to work together in big groups, or tribes. Each tribe probably had a leader who organized hunts.

These people are using slings to kill sea birds.

Seal hunters

These people are collecting mussels and crabs to eat.

This boy is cleaning an animal skin with a stone scraper.

This old man passes on tips on hunting, survival and the clan's history.

This woman is sewing animal-skin clothes with a bone needle.

Tools with handles

By 40,000 years ago, people were making tools with handles. They made spears by fitting sharp stone blades into long sticks. They also carved pieces of bone into jagged blades and tied them to sticks, to make harpoons. Bone was used to make fish-hooks as well.

These hunters are bringing back some antelope they have caught.

Shelter made from branches and deer skins

This woman is making a basket from reeds.

Meat hanging up to dry

Dried meat can be stored for a long time without going bad.

Harpoons for catching fish and seals

Bone blade

These men are from a different tribe. They have come to trade stone blades for seashells.

Sewing clothes

People began to sew animal skins together to make clothes. They made needles from bone, and used thin strips of leather as thread.

Trading and talking

As they wandered from place to place, tribes of people traded tools and valuable objects with each other. People from different tribes told each other about their experiences and passed on information about new places.

The spirit world

People seem to have believed that the world was controlled by powerful spirits, or gods. They probably tried to contact these gods by holding religious ceremonies. Perhaps they asked the gods to help them with their hunting, or to protect dead people in the afterlife?

New Worlds

Experts believe that modern people, known as *Homo sapiens*, first evolved in East Africa and spread south over the continent. Around 85,000 years ago, a few groups left Africa and spread slowly across the rest of the world.

Spreading out

These explorers probably left Africa somewhere near the Red Sea. Groups moved further and further every few years. Gradually, they replaced earlier people, and by 30,000 years ago, they were the only humans left on Earth. Experts use DNA studies to show that all the people of the Middle East, Asia, Europe and the Americas are descended from these first few people to leave Africa.

Across the sea

Around 50,000 years ago, during the last ice age, groups of people set off in boats from Southeast Asia. They may have been searching for food, or for more land, or perhaps they were just exploring.

This picture shows people from Southeast Asia on a voyage to find new land.

Different routes

Some groups in Europe and Asia hunted wandering herds of animals, such as bison. The animals may have led them to new places.

Many groups followed rivers inland. Others followed the coast. Their remains were lost when sea levels rose, but experts can find the same DNA in people now living in the same areas.

Bison

The first Americans

At times, the sea level was so low that Asia and North America were connected by a stretch of dry land, called Beringia. Some time between 30,000 and 13,000 years ago, tribes may have followed the herds across Beringia from Asia into North America, while others followed the coast. They gradually moved south until they had occupied all of North and South America.

Finding Australia

During the ice age, the sea level was much lower than it is today. This meant that there were lots of little islands where voyagers could stop and rest. However, they still had to cross miles of water between islands, and many people must have been lost at sea. Eventually, some voyagers reached the shores of Australia. They were the first people who ever lived there.

Wooden paddle

Some of the boats are made from bamboo stems tied together with thin strips of bamboo.

Map showing the spread of modern people

ATLANTIC OCEAN

ARCTIC OCEAN

33,000 years ago

BERINGIA

EUROPE

ASIA
70,000 years ago

NORTH AMERICA
12,000 years ago

ATLANTIC OCEAN

PACIFIC OCEAN

AFRICA
150,000 - 100,000 years ago

85,000 years ago

INDIAN OCEAN

SOUTH AMERICA
Date uncertain

AUSTRALIA
50,000 years ago

The map shows when people may have arrived in different places.

Dry land at the time of the last ice age

→ Possible routes

Some people have stayed behind to settle on this island.

Canoes made from hollowed-out tree trunks are used for short journeys.

These people have just set out from an island where they spent the night.

Leather bag filled with food

HUMANS

95

The Mammoth-hunters

Around 30,000 years ago, during the last ice age, tribes of people arrived on the freezing plains of eastern Europe. These people quickly adapted to living in such a cold and empty place. They became experts at hunting the mammoths that wandered across the plains, and they made almost everything they needed from the mammoths' bodies.

Hunting mammoths

Like other people at this time, the mammoth-hunters used a weapon called a spearthrower, which allowed them to throw their spears much farther than before. This made it possible to attack dangerous animals, such as mammoths, from a safe distance.

Mammoth-bone huts

There were few hills or caves on the plains, so the mammoth-hunters had nowhere to shelter from the snow and wind. Because hardly any trees grew there either, people had no wood to build huts. Instead, the mammoth-hunters made their homes from mammoth bones and skins.

This picture shows some mammoth-hunters and their huts.

Animal furs keep the hut dry and warm.

People light fires by knocking two stones together.

Mammoth tusk

Mammoth jaw bone

This man is teaching children how to throw a spear.

Spearthrower made from bone

HUMANS

Music and dancing

The mammoth-hunters made some of the first musical instruments that we know about. They used mammoth skulls and shoulder bones as drums, and hollowed out small bones to make flutes.

People probably danced to the music. Dancing may have been a way of bringing everyone in the tribe closer together. It may also have been part of a religious ceremony.

Mammoth-hunters playing music and dancing

Flute made from a hollowed-out bone

People have sewn feathers onto their clothes for the dance.

Mammoth-skull drum

Warm clothes

In the winter, the mammoth-hunters wore warm leather clothes made from mammoth skins sewn tightly together. They also wore leather boots and fur mittens.

Shells and beads

Sometimes, people made strings of beads from shells and animal teeth, and used ivory from mammoth tusks to make bracelets. Burials have been found where the person's clothes have hundreds of beads sewn on in patterns, perhaps indicating their status. Tribe leaders may have had their own special decorations.

This man is making a stone knife.

These women are making necklaces from shells and animal teeth.

★ Beads made from shells and animal teeth

The First Artists

Around 35,000 years ago, people began to paint pictures on the walls of caves. Cave paintings have been found in many parts of the world, but the most famous ones are in France and Spain. Nobody knows why these pictures were created, but tribes may have used the painted caves for meetings and ceremonies.

Painting caves

The first paints were made by grinding soft rocks into a paste. Artists used their fingers to draw the outline of a painting. Then, they shaded in the picture by dipping a piece of animal fur in paint and pressing it onto the cave wall.

The first priests?

Sometimes, artists painted strange creatures that seem to be part human and part animal. These paintings may be portraits of early priests dressed as animals. Tribes may have held religious ceremonies in the caves where these figures were painted.

This picture shows the kind of ceremony that may have taken place in a painted cave.

This man is a priest.

Deer antler

Birds' feathers

Wolf's tail

The people are asking their gods for help with their hunting.

Painted animals

Most of the paintings show animals, such as bison, deer, horses and mammoths. People may have believed the animals were guiding spirits or that they would bring success in hunting.

HUMANS

Only deep, dark caves are used for painting.

Bull

Horse

Herd of deer

Mammoth

Bison

An artist made these shapes by placing his hand on the wall and blowing paint around it.

The cave is lit by burning animal fat in stone bowls.

Skin painted with red soil

Body painting

As well as painting on cave walls, people used bright red soil to decorate dead bodies before they were buried. They may also have painted themselves with sacred symbols before taking part in religious ceremonies.

Making models

Early artists carved small statues from ivory or bone. Many of the statues show women, who may represent goddesses, and others show animals.

Ivory model of a person with a lion's head

Baking clay

Around this time, artists also discovered how to harden clay by baking it. Clay models of people and animals have been found in eastern Europe.

The first calendars?

Experts have found pieces of bone and antler with lots of tiny shapes carved on them. The shapes were carved by early people, and they seem to show the changing shape of the moon at different times of the month. Perhaps these carvings were the first calendars?

HUMANS

99

From Hunting to Farming

Around 12,000 years ago, the last ice age began to come to an end. All over the world, the weather became warmer, and the ice melted away in many areas. Huge forests began to grow where the ice had been.

After the ice age ended, some big animals, such as mammoths, died out. People had to rely on hunting deer, wild pigs and other small animals.

Most people moved around to find food, staying in a different place each season. However, some tribes of people found places where they could hunt animals, catch fish and gather plants throughout the year. This meant that these tribes could settle down and live in the same place all the time.

Taming animals

During the last ice age, hunters took baby wolves back to their camps and looked after them. The wolves began to see people as their friends, and they became tame. The wolves' babies grew up to be tame as well, and eventually these animals became working dogs. Hunters used the dogs to help them find and kill wild animals. There may also have been attempts to tame horses.

This ice age carving seems to show a horse wearing a harness. This suggests that early people may have tamed horses.

This picture shows a tribe of hunters living in a forest.

These people are using sticks to knock down nuts from a tree.

This girl has taken some honey from a bees' nest.

These women are gathering fruit and berries.

Wooden bowl

People use stone axes to chop up wood.

Canoe made from a tree trunk

Fishing net made from vines

QUICKLINKS: For links to websites where you can find out more about how people began to farm and tame animals, go to **usborne.com/Quicklinks**

These men are hunting birds with bows and arrows.

Tents made from branches and animal skins

Bowstring made of animal gut

This wild pig was caught in a pit in the forest.

Tame hunting dogs

Arrow with a stone point

Feathers make the arrows travel straight through the air.

Keeping herds

Some people began to tame lots of different animals, and eventually tribes started keeping herds of sheep, goats and cattle. This meant that people always had meat to eat and milk to drink, as well as fur and skins to make clothes.

Starting to settle

Groups of early farmers settled near the fields where their crops grew. They built huts for themselves and shelters for their animals. This was the beginning of village life.

Growing crops

Around 10,000 years ago, some tribes in the Middle East began to plant seeds and grow crops, such as wheat and barley. Once they had discovered farming, people could grow their own food, as well as going hunting and fishing.

HUMANS

101

Detail from the golden throne of
the Egyptian pharaoh Tutankhamun

Looking at the Ancient World

This section of the book covers a period of about 10,000 years, starting with the very first farmers and ending with the collapse of the Roman Empire.

From villages to empires

Farming was discovered independently in different parts of the ancient world. Everywhere, the start of farming led to dramatic changes in the way people lived. Gradually, villages, towns and cities were built, writing was invented, and the first great civilizations appeared – in the Middle East, China, India and Europe, and in Central and South America.

A gold statue of a king from the ancient Hittite Empire

The ancient world was an age of warriors and empires. Across the globe a series of great empires rose and fell, and some of these produced leaders, buildings and writings that are still famous today. This period also saw the birth of most of the world's main religions.

Where did it happen?

To check which area of the world you are reading about, look at the bottom corner of each page. The different areas of the world are shown on the map below.

How do we know?

Amazingly, after so many thousands of years, some ancient buildings are still standing today, although most lie buried underground. Experts, called archaeologists, uncover the ruins and study the objects they find there.

Stonehenge, in southern England, still survives 5,000 years after it was built.

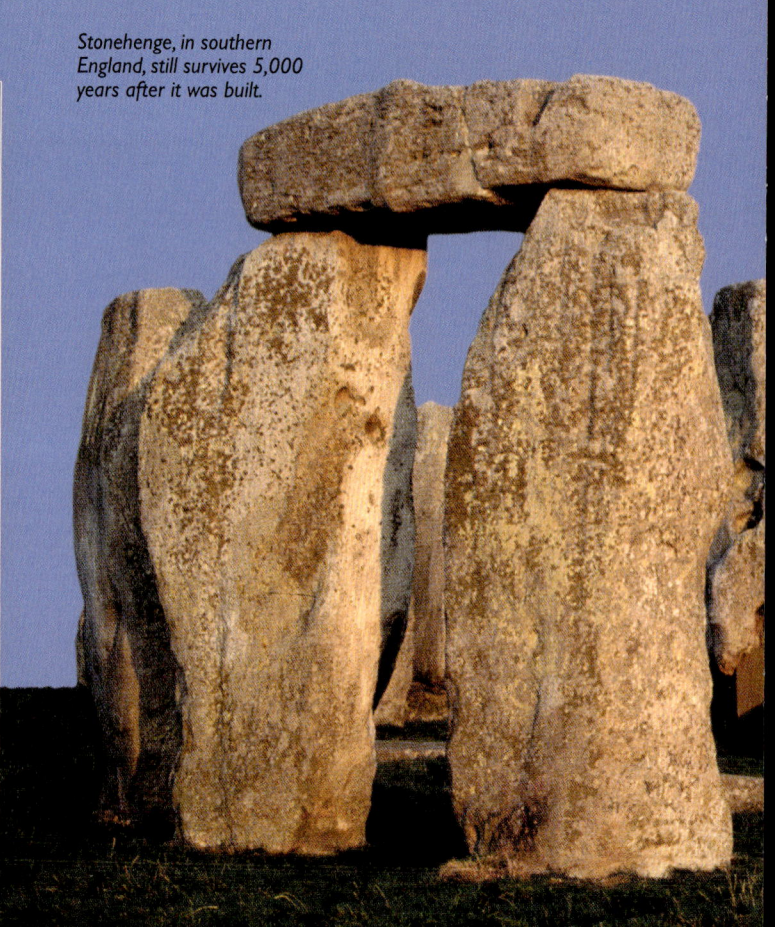

When did it happen?

Dates are often counted from before or after the birth of Christ. Dates before Christ's birth are shown by the letters "BC" (before Christ). For example, 50BC means 50 years before Christ was born. BC dates are counted back from 1BC, so 100BC is earlier than 50BC. There is a timeline across the bottom of each double page to help you see when events took place.

The letters "AD" show that an event happened after the birth of Christ. AD stands for *anno Domini*, which is Latin for "in the year of the Lord".

If a date has a letter "c." in front of it, this means that experts aren't sure exactly when the event took place. The "c." stands for *circa*, which means "about" in Latin.

QUICKLINKS: For links to websites where you can meet archaeologists and find out how they search for clues, go to **usborne.com/Quicklinks**

This model boat from an Egyptian tomb shows how ancient Egyptian boats were sailed and steered.

Wall paintings, like this one from the Roman town of Pompeii, show details of people's clothes and hair.

Objects from houses and tombs, such as weapons, tools, pots, furniture and fragments of cloth, give us valuable clues about how people lived in ancient times. Tombs and buildings may also contain statues, wall paintings and mosaics that show important people, or scenes from daily life.

Archaeologists also study the waste that ancient people threw away. Animal bones and seeds tell us what food people ate and what the climate and landscape were like at the time.

Ancient writing has been found on pieces of clay, on the walls of buildings and on scrolls of papyrus (a type of paper). These writings tell us about ancient rulers, laws and religious beliefs.

Ancient World Quicklinks

Quicklinks are links to specially selected websites with videos,
quizzes, homework resources and activities. Throughout this section, you
will see recommendations for websites where you can find out
more about the ancient world.

Here are some of the things you can do
at the sites we recommend:

★ Meet archaeologists and find out how they search for clues.

★ Explore the ruins of ancient Egyptian temples.

★ See the terracotta warriors buried with the first emperor of China.

★ Examine amazing artifacts made by the people of ancient Peru.

★ Visit a Roman fort and meet a Roman soldier.

To visit the websites, go to **usborne.com/Quicklinks**
and type "**WHE**" into the search box.

You can also download many pictures and maps in this book for
home or school use. Look for pictures marked with a ★.

This is the Sphinx at Giza, in Egypt. Behind it is the Great Pyramid, the largest stone building ever built.

The First Farmers

The very first people hunted wild animals, caught fish and gathered nuts, plants and berries to eat. It was thousands of years before people learned how to farm.

Farming probably began first in the Middle East around 10,000 years ago, in an area with rich soils and a wide variety of edible plants. It's sometimes called the Fertile Crescent.

Cutting wheat with a tool called a sickle

People noticed that seeds which had fallen on the ground grew into plants. They began to collect the seeds and plant them on purpose. The first crops grown like this were wild wheat and barley.

Around the same time, people learned how to tame animals. This meant that they always had plenty of meat, milk and wool. They could also use cattle for working in the fields.

These pots were made by early farmers.

Once people knew how to farm, they no longer needed to move around to hunt for food. They began to settle down in villages and learned how to make bricks from mud and clay to build homes.

In this picture of an early village, one house has been cut away to let you see inside.

Map of the Fertile Crescent

Çatal Hüyük

MEDITERRANEAN SEA

Jericho

Nile

RED SEA

Euphrates

Tigris

EUROPE · ASIA · AFRICA

Fertile Crescent

A wall protects the village from wild animals.

Clay for building a new house

Pots are baked hard in an oven, called a kiln.

Well

Making baskets

Making bricks from clay

Loom for weaving cloth

Pot for cooking

Making pots

Drying fruit

The roofs are made of poles covered with straw.

This man is tossing grain to separate it from the husk (the hard outside part).

Milking a goat

10,000BC · 5000BC · 4000BC · 3000BC

The First Towns

Slowly, small farming villages grew into towns. One of the oldest towns that has been found so far is at Jericho.

Jericho

The people of Jericho lived in small, round houses made of mud bricks.

A cutaway picture of a house in Jericho ★

Dead people were buried underneath the houses. Their skulls may have been put on display, as a way of showing respect.

Skull found at Jericho ★

Cowrie shells in place of eyes

Plaster filling

Jericho grew rich by trading with other communities, and people in the nearby villages became jealous. To protect themselves, the people of Jericho built a massive stone wall around the town.

Building the walls of Jericho

Çatalhöyük

Çatalhöyük (pronounced "chatal hoo-yook") was the largest of the early towns. Around 6,000 people lived there.

This cutaway picture shows part of Çatalhöyük. ★

Cattle and goats are kept for meat and milk.

When someone in Çatalhöyük died, the body was left outside to rot. The skeleton was buried under a bench in the house or in a shrine room, where the people prayed to their gods.

This picture shows a shrine room at Çatalhöyük.

Painted statue of a goddess

This priest is wearing a leopard skin.

Model of a bull's head with real horns

These priestesses have brought offerings of food and drink for the goddess.

Apple trees

People climb into the houses through a hole in the roof.

If enemies attack, the ladders are pulled up.

All the houses are joined together.

Clay bench covered with reeds

The houses have one main room.

The walls are made of mud bricks.

Fireplace

The Çatalhöyük people make clay sculptures of very large women. Some experts think that these are models of a great Mother Goddess.

Clay figure from Çatalhöyük

Important dates

c.10,000BC Farming begins in the Fertile Crescent.

c.8000BC Jericho grows into a wealthy town.

c.6250-5650BC Çatalhöyük is at its largest.

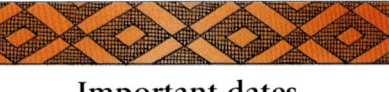

THE MIDDLE EAST

The First Cities

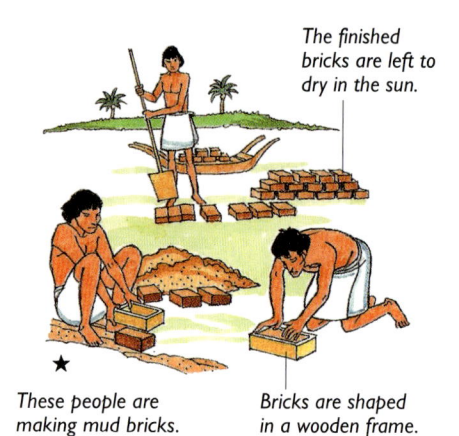

The finished bricks are left to dry in the sun.

These people are making mud bricks.

Bricks are shaped in a wooden frame.

EUROPE
ASIA
AFRICA

■ Mesopotamia
★ City-state

Euphrates
AKKAD
Tigris
SUMER
Uruk ★ ★ Lagash
★ Ur
Eridu ★
PERSIAN GULF

Map of Sumer

The flat land of Sumer was good for farming, but there was very little rain. Once a year, the two rivers flooded, soaking the dry ground. The Sumerians built ditches and canals, to store the water and carry it to the fields.

Farmers mending a canal

From around 5000BC, farmers settled in the wide valley between the Tigris and Euphrates rivers. This area became known as Mesopotamia, which means "the land between two rivers". Some of the world's first cities grew up in Sumer, in the southern part of Mesopotamia.

Farmers were soon able to grow more crops than they could eat. There was no need for everyone to farm, so some people had time to learn specialist skills, such as pottery and weaving.

At first, the Sumerians lived in houses made of reeds. Later, they learned how to make bricks from mud and straw.

Small farming villages gradually grew into huge walled cities, each with its own temple. Each city had a ruler who also had control of the farmland around the city. Cities organized like this are called city-states.

This picture shows part of the Sumerian city of Ur.

This huge, stepped platform is called a ziggurat.

Temple of Nanna, the moon god

A wall protects the city from attacks by other city-states.

The houses are built of mud bricks.

Marketplace

Houses for temple staff

These people are taking gifts up to the temple.

Temple courtyard

THE MIDDLE EAST

10,000BC   5000BC   4000BC   3000BC

The invention of writing

Farmers had to give part of their crop to the temple, and temple officials needed to know if a farmer had paid his share. Writing probably developed as a way of recording this information.

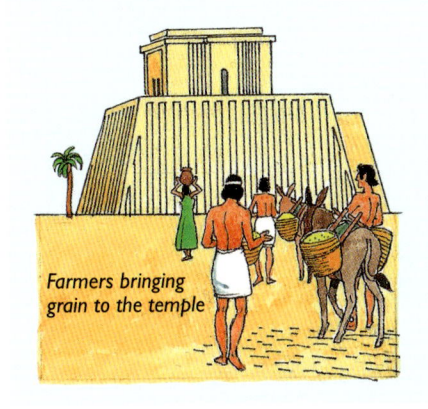

Farmers bringing grain to the temple

1 At first, people drew simple pictures of the objects they wanted to record. These pictures are called pictograms.

Object   Pictogram

2 The pictures were drawn one below the other on a piece of wet clay.

Reed pen

Piece of flattened clay

3 Later, people turned the clay around and wrote from side to side. This stopped them from smudging the pictures they had already drawn.

Picture turned sideways

4 Because of the shape of the reed pen, the pictures gradually changed into wedge-shaped symbols, which we call cuneiform writing. Cuneiform means "wedge-shaped".

Cuneiform writing

Orchard of date palms

Fields of barley and wheat

A canal joins the city to the Euphrates.

This is one of the city's two ports.

Trading ships

These boys are on their way to school.

Potter's workshop

This cutaway picture shows a house in a Sumerian city.

These men are drinking beer through metal tubes.

This boy is picking dates.

Stairs lead up to the roof.

Wooden railing

The walls are whitewashed.

The house is built around a central courtyard.

Reed mat

Bedroom

Kitchen

2000BC   1000BC   500BC   AD1   AD500

THE MIDDLE EAST

Crafts and Trade

There was no stone, metal or strong wood in Sumer, so all these things had to be brought in from other lands. In exchange, the Sumerians sold grain and wool, as well as the pots and metal objects they made in their workshops.

Sumerian traders sailed along canals and rivers into the Persian Gulf and beyond. They traded with merchants from as far away as the Mediterranean Coast in the west and the Indus Valley in the east.

In this picture, merchants are trading at a busy Sumerian market.

Metalwork

The Sumerians were skilled metalworkers, and made beautiful objects from gold, silver and copper.

Gold dagger and sheath

Stone is floated down the river on wooden rafts.

Wood from the mountains in the north

This trading ship has just come back from the Persian Gulf.

Wine jars

This man is selling vegetables.

This trader has brought back a cargo of gold, copper, ivory and semi-precious stones.

A man called a scribe lists the goods as they are unloaded.

Basket of grain

Jar of oil

Rolls of cloth

This trader has come from Syria.

These merchants are setting off on a trading expedition.

This man is selling fish.

Pots and wheels

Sumer had plenty of clay for making pottery. Pots were shaped by hand until around 3500BC, when the potter's wheel was invented.

Pots are baked hard in an oven called a kiln.

Potters at work ★

Pots are shaped on a wheel.

Boys mix the clay with their feet.

Stone carving

Sculptors carved small stone statues of people praying. People believed that if they placed a statue in the temple, the statue would pray for them.

★ *Stone statue of a temple official*

People soon realized that wheels could be attached to carts or chariots, and used for getting around. A donkey pulling a cart could carry three times as much as it could on its back.

★ *Wheel from a Sumerian chariot*

10,000BC	5000BC		4000BC	3000BC

Kings and War

Each city in Sumer was run by a group of noblemen. In times of war, they chose a leader who ruled until the war was over. As wars became more frequent, the war-leaders ruled for longer periods of time. In the end, they became kings who ruled for life, and handed power down to their sons.

This mosaic shows Sumerian soldiers in battle. ★

Sumerian soldier wearing a cloak and helmet

This is one of the enemy prisoners. He will be killed or sold as a slave.

Chariot

Donkeys

This soldier is about to throw his spear.

This is the charioteer. He drives the chariot.

Body of an enemy soldier

Royal tombs

The early kings and queens of the city of Ur were buried in large pits filled with amazing treasures. The tombs also contained the bodies of dozens of guards and servants, who had taken poison and died to be with their rulers.

The tomb of Queen Shudu-ad of Ur

Two oxen and four grooms

The soldier's long hair fitted in here.

★ Golden helmet from one of the tombs at Ur

Queen Shudu-ad

Ten ladies wearing golden headdresses

Wooden chest

Gaming board

Wooden sledge

Five guards

Stone tomb chamber

Gold, silver and copper bowls

Sargon of Akkad

Sargon came from Akkad, the land just north of Sumer. He was a skilled soldier and had control of a huge army. He conquered the whole of Sumer and Akkad, creating the world's first empire.

★ Sargon of Akkad

The Akkadian Empire lasted nearly 200 years until it was destroyed by a tribe called the Gutians.

Gutian tribesmen

The end of Sumer

The King of Ur won back the Sumerians' land and, for a short time, he ruled all of Sumer and Akkad. Around 2000BC, Sumer was invaded by people known as the Amorites. The land split up into many small states, and later became part of the Babylonian Empire (see page 132).

Important dates

c.5000BC Farmers settle in Sumer.
c.3500BC The wheel is invented. The first cities are built.
c.3300BC Picture writing is invented.
c.3100BC Cuneiform writing is used.
c.2500BC The royal tombs are built at Ur.
c.2350-2150bc Sumer is part of the Akkadian Empire.
c.2100bc The King of Ur rules Sumer and Akkad. The ziggurat at Ur is built.
c.2000bc The Amorites invade.

THE MIDDLE EAST

2000BC　1000BC　500BC　AD1　AD500

113

Farmers of the Nile Valley

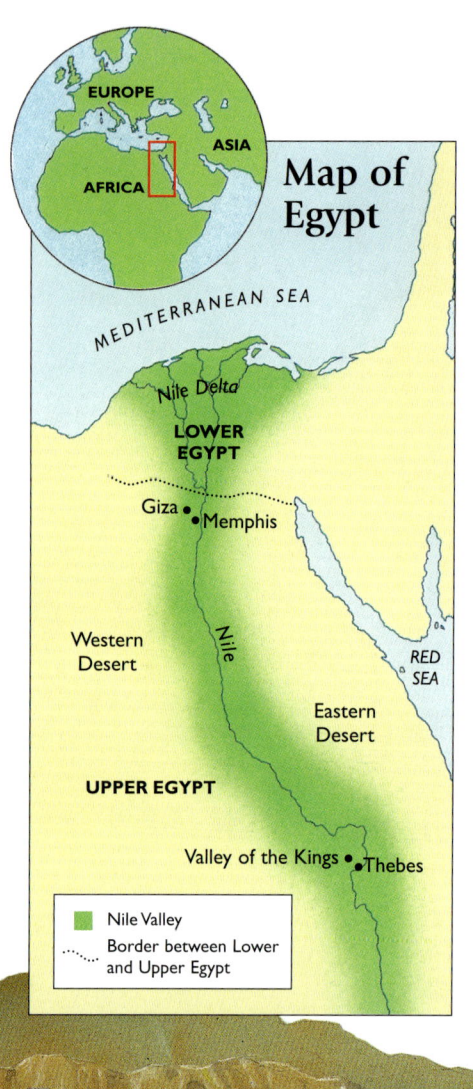

Map of Egypt

EUROPE

ASIA

AFRICA

MEDITERRANEAN SEA

Nile Delta

LOWER EGYPT

Giza • •Memphis

Western Desert

Nile

RED SEA

Eastern Desert

UPPER EGYPT

Valley of the Kings • •Thebes

Nile Valley

Border between Lower and Upper Egypt

Ancient Egypt was a long, narrow country which stretched along the Nile Valley. It was surrounded on both sides by desert.

Villages grew up along the Nile, because the land on either side of the river was good to farm. Every spring, melted snow from the mountains south of Egypt flowed into the Nile, and in July the river flooded. After several months, the water level fell, leaving behind rich, fertile soil.

Gradually, the farming villages of the Nile Valley joined together to form larger communities. By around 3100BC, there were two separate kingdoms, called Lower Egypt and Upper Egypt.

The two kingdoms fought a battle, which was won by King Menes of Upper Egypt. Lower and Upper Egypt became one country, and Menes built a capital city at Memphis for the new, united land.

★ This carving shows the king of Upper Egypt defeating the ruler of Lower Egypt.

This house has been badly damaged in a flood.

The best fields are nearest the river.

This pole with a bucket is called a shaduf. It lifts water into the fields.

Fishing boats

These men are using sickles to cut the wheat.

Donkeys are used for carrying grain.

Children collect any grain the men have missed.

Ditches and canals store floodwater and carry it to the crops.

AFRICA

10,000BC   5000BC   4000BC   3000BC

Crops

The Egyptians grew peas, beans, onions, garlic, leeks, cucumbers, grapes, melons, pomegranates, figs and dates. Grapes and pomegranates were made into wine.

★ Wine was made by stamping on the grapes to squeeze out the juice.

The main crops were wheat and barley, which were used to make bread and beer. People sometimes added honey or garlic to their bread to make it more tasty.

Animals

Egyptian farmers kept cattle, sheep, goats, pigs, geese, ducks and pigeons. Cattle were used to work in the fields, as well as for meat. Egypt had very little grassland, so cows were often kept in stalls.

Wooden model of a cow stall

The farmer's year

While the land was flooded, no work could be done in the fields. In November, after the floodwater had gone down, the farmer prepared his fields and planted his crops. In the spring, the whole family helped with the harvest. Then, the farmer mended the ditches that carried water to the fields, ready for the next year's flood.

This tomb painting shows an Egyptian farmer working in the fields. His wife is scattering seeds on the ground.

This scene shows farmers harvesting their crops.

This monkey has been trained to pick dates.

Cows trample on the grain to separate it from the stalks. This is called threshing.

These women are winnowing - tossing the grain to separate it from the husk (the hard outside part).

Granary for storing grain

AFRICA

Mummies and Pyramids

Experts divide Egyptian history into three main periods of time, called the Old Kingdom, the Middle Kingdom and the New Kingdom. The information on these two pages comes from all three periods.

Mummies

The Egyptians tried to stop dead bodies from decaying, because they thought this would allow the dead person to go on living in the Next World. These specially preserved bodies are called mummies.

These pictures show how a mummy was made.

1 The brain and internal organs were taken out and put in jars called canopic jars.

Canopic jar

Natron

2 The body was covered with a salt, called natron, to dry it out. Then, the insides were stuffed with linen, natron, sawdust and sweet-smelling spices.

3 The body was wrapped in bandages. Lucky charms, called amulets, were placed between the layers.

Anubis mask

★ 4 A mask was put over the mummy's face. A priest dressed as Anubis, god of the dead, prayed over the body.

Coffins

Lid of outer coffin

Lid of inner coffin

Funeral mask

Mummy

Inner coffin

Outer coffin

★ A mummy inside a nest of coffins

The first coffins were simple wooden boxes. Later, in the New Kingdom, mummies were put in a nest of two or three human-shaped coffins, one inside the other. These coffins were often brightly painted.

Tomb treasure

The tombs of rich Egyptians were filled with everything the dead person might need in the Next World. Kings were buried with amazing treasures, but robbers soon broke into the tombs and stole the treasure, so very little has been found.

★ This golden funeral mask belonged to the boy-king, Tutankhamun.

The pyramids

During the Old and Middle Kingdoms, the Egyptians built huge pyramids as tombs for their kings, or pharaohs. There are over 30 pyramids in Egypt, but the most famous ones are at Giza, where three pharaohs and their chief wives are buried.

Khafre will be buried in this pyramid.

This is the mortuary temple. A priest will come here every day to bring food and drink for the spirit of the dead pharaoh.

The smooth sides are meant to look like the rays of the sun.

This is the Great Pyramid. Khafre's father, Khufu, is buried here.

This picture shows the two largest pyramids at Giza, just after the death of the pharaoh Khafre.

These tombs, called mastabas, are for important noblemen.

These small pyramids are for the queen and the pharaoh's other wives.

A huge statue of the Sphinx guards the pyramids. It has a human head and a lion's body.

The Great Pyramid

The Great Pyramid is the largest stone building ever built. It is 147m (482ft) high and contains over two million stone blocks.

This picture shows ★ the inside of the Great Pyramid.

The outside is covered with a smooth casing of limestone.

Pharaoh's burial chamber

Chamber

Chamber

Grand gallery

Corridor

A passageway links the valley temple to the mortuary temple.

In the valley temple, priests will prepare the pharaoh's body for burial.

A funeral boat brings Khafre's body from his palace at Memphis.

Later tombs

In the New Kingdom, the pharaohs were buried in tombs cut deep into the rock in a hidden valley, called the Valley of the Kings. Although the tombs were hard to find, almost all of them were robbed. The tomb of Tutankhamun was the only one that escaped.

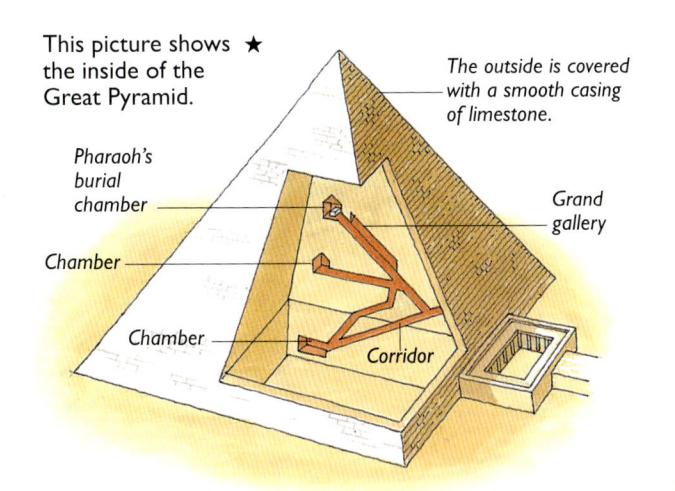

A funeral procession to the Valley of the Kings

Important dates

c.5000BC Farming begins in the Nile Valley.

c.3100BC King Menes unites Upper and Lower Egypt.

c.2686BC The Old Kingdom begins.

c.2180BC The Old Kingdom ends in famine and civil war.

c.2040BC Egypt is reunited. The Middle Kingdom begins.

c.1720BC Egypt is invaded by people called the Hyksos. The Middle Kingdom ends.

AFRICA

2000BC   1000BC   500BC   AD1   AD500

Cities of the Indus Valley

The land in the Indus Valley was good for farming, and the river flooded every year, just like the rivers in Sumer and Egypt. Farmers used the floodwater to help them grow more food.

Soon, there was no need for everyone to farm, so some people could do other jobs. People built towns, learned new crafts and started to trade.

By around 2500BC, there were over a hundred towns and cities in the Indus Valley. The two largest were Mohenjo-daro and Harappa.

Map of the Indus Valley

EUROPE
ASIA
AFRICA

Harappa
Indus
Mohenjo-daro
Lothal
INDIA
ARABIAN SEA

Area where the Indus Valley people lived

The Great Bath

The Great Bath at Mohenjo-daro

Inside the fortress at Mohenjo-daro was a large bathhouse. Priests or rulers may have bathed here before religious ceremonies.

This statue probably shows an ★ Indus Valley priest or ruler.

The city of Mohenjo-daro

Like other Indus Valley cities, Mohenjo-daro was carefully planned. In the middle was a walled fortress, which was built on a huge, man-made hill. Another wall surrounded the city.

This picture shows a typical street in Mohenjo-daro. Part of one house has been cut away to let you see inside.

The houses are built of mud bricks.

The house is built around an open courtyard.

In the summer, people sleep on the roof.

Bedroom

Well

Kitchen

The toilet is connected to a drain that runs under the street.

Oxen are used for pulling carts.

The streets are completely straight.

These men are cleaning the drain.

The Great Granary

Farmers in Mohenjo-daro had to give part of their crop to the city. The grain was stored in a huge granary inside the fortress, so it could be used if there was a bad harvest and food was short.

Grain is stored up here.

Platform for loading grain

A farmer brings his crop of wheat and barley.

The Great Granary at Mohenjo-daro

The walled fortress contains the city's most important buildings.

This woman is buying cotton for a new dress.

This man is selling beads.

Crafts

Potters made cooking pots, storage jars, drinking cups and objects such as children's toys.

Indus Valley pot

The head moves when this wire is pulled.

Toy pig

Toy ox

Beads for necklaces and bracelets were made from gold, clay and semi-precious stones.

Bead necklace

The farmers of the Indus Valley were the first people to grow cotton and weave it into cloth.

Picking cotton

Stoneworkers made carved seals with writing and pictures of animals on them. Traders may have had their own personal seal, which they used to stamp their name onto pieces of clay.

Carved stone seal of a humped bull

So far, no one has been able to read the Indus Valley writing.

Trade

We know that the Indus people traded with Sumer because their pottery and beads have been found there. They also sold wood, cotton and spices.

A trading ship sets sail from the port at Lothal.

The end of a civilization

From around 1800BC, the Indus Valley civilization began to collapse, but no one is sure why.

People may have ruined their farmland by growing too many crops and cutting down too many trees. There may have been quarrels between cities leading to violence. The climate may also have changed, so people did not have enough water.

Whatever the reason, people began leaving the cities and moved back to the countryside.

Important dates

c.3500BC Farmers settle in the Indus Valley.

c.2500-1800BC The Indus Valley civilization is at its most successful.

c.1500BC Cities are abandoned.

SOUTH ASIA

2000BC　　　　　　　　　500BC　　　　　ADI　　　　AD500

Europe's First Villages

Thousands of years ago, Europe was much colder than it is today, and in the north the land was covered in ice. When the weather warmed up, plants and trees were able to grow again, and wild animals roamed the forests.

Red deer

Wild boar

People relied on hunting animals and collecting wild plants to eat. They set up camps where they could find food, and moved on when the seasons changed and the food ran out.

Early Europeans

In some places, there was so much food all year that people could settle down. At Lepenski Vir, people built a village on the banks of the Danube, where there was always plenty of fish to catch.

★ Sculpture of a fish's head from Lepenski Vir

Map of Europe

Skara Brae

Sweet Track

Danube

Lepenski Vir

ATLANTIC OCEAN

MEDITERRANEAN SEA

MALTA

EUROPE
ASIA
AFRICA

Farmers of the forests

Around 6000BC, life in Europe began to change, as farming spread from the Middle East. In the thick forests that covered most of Europe, farmers cut down trees to make space for fields, and used the wood to build houses.

This picture shows an early European farming village. One house has been cut away to let you see inside.

Vegetables are grown here.

This man is thatching a roof with reeds.

Waste is thrown into a pit.

Making and decorating clay pots

Pigs feed on acorns in the forest.

These boys are collecting hazelnuts.

These men are making a willow fence.

People use stone axes to chop wood.

10,000BC   5000BC   4000BC   3000BC

Stone shelters

★ Inside a house at Skara Brae

The early Europeans built their houses from whatever they could find nearby. At Skara Brae in the Orkney Islands there were hardly any trees, so people built houses of stone. They even had stone furniture.

Home and dry

In marshy areas, people built long wooden walkways so they could move around easily from one village to another. The Sweet Track in southwestern England stretched for 1.8km (just over a mile).

Farmers on the Sweet Track

Stone temples at Tarxien

Some early farmers worked together to create buildings from massive blocks of stone. At Tarxien on the island of Malta, people built temples where they sacrificed animals to their great Mother Goddess.

In western Europe, stone tombs were built and covered with huge mounds of earth. Each tomb had several chambers and had room for up to 40 bodies.

Inside a stone tomb

People live in longhouses up to 45m (148ft) long.

Pasture for cattle

Fields of wheat and barley

A pig roasting on a spit

The roof has caught fire.

Sheep pen

Living area

Part of the wall is plastered with mud.

The walls are made of split logs.

The animals live in one end of the house.

Important dates

c.6000-5000BC	Fishing people live at Lepenski Vir.
c.6000-4000BC	Farming spreads across most of Europe.
c.4500BC	People begin building stone tombs.
c.3800BC	The Sweet Track is built.
c.3500BC	The first temple is built at Tarxien.
c.3100BC	Skara Brae is built.

EUROPE

2000BC	1000BC	500BC	AD1	AD500

121

The Monument Builders

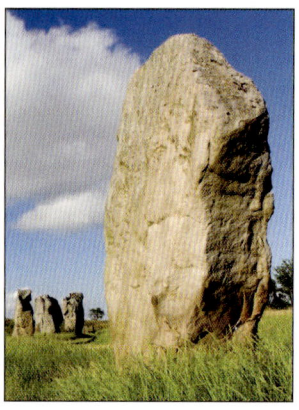

Standing stones at Avebury in southern England

Around 3200BC, people in northwestern Europe began building great circles and lines of standing stones. They also stuck wooden poles in the ground to make circles called wood henges, but most of these have rotted away.

Some experts believe that these mysterious stone monuments were used as giant outdoor calendars, while others believe they were used to glorify the dead.

Map of Europe

SCANDINAVIA

NORTH SEA

BALTIC SEA

ATLANTIC OCEAN

Avebury

Stonehenge

EUROPE

ASIA

AFRICA

★ Amber

- ● Stone circle
- ▲ Tin mine
- ■ Areas where amber was found

Building Stonehenge

Stonehenge in southern England is the most spectacular of all the stone circles. It was built in stages over a period of more than a thousand years, and was finally finished around 2200BC.

This picture shows Stonehenge being built.

The arches are called trilithons. This means "three stones" in Greek.

The stones fit neatly into each other.

The stones across the top are called lintels.

These stones are called uprights.

Logs are used to support the stone.

Deep hole

Some stones weigh as much as 370 people.

Soil is carried away in baskets.

These men are hauling a stone into position.

EUROPE

10,000BC   5000BC   4000BC   3000BC

Mastering metal

Some people in Europe were using copper over 6000 years ago. Later, people learned how to make bronze by mixing copper with tin. Bronze weapons and tools were much harder than copper ones, and were very valuable.

Gold and bronze model of the Sun on a horse-drawn chariot

Trading for tin

The tin needed to make bronze was only found in a few places in Europe (see map), so most people had to trade for it. The people of Scandinavia traded amber from the shores of the Baltic Sea for the metals they needed.

Bronze figure from Scandinavia ★

Tombs and treasure

The monument builders believed in life after death, and buried people with the weapons and tools they would need in the Next World. The tombs of wealthy people were filled with bronze swords and daggers, as well as beautiful golden objects.

Golden cup ★

A tomb called a round barrow

Important people were buried in round stone tombs covered with a great mound of earth. Each tomb held just one body. These tombs, called round barrows, are often found near stone circles.

The stones are dragged from a quarry 32km (20 miles) away.

Each stone is tied to a wooden sled.

Logs are used as rollers.

These lumps fit into holes made in the lintel.

The lintel is lifted up gradually on a platform of logs.

Layers of logs are slipped under the lintel one at a time.

Heavy stones are used to pound holes in the lintels.

Men stand on this platform to help put the lintel in place.

Wooden lever

These men are digging a hole for the next stone.

Digging tools are made of bone and deer antlers.

Important dates

c.5000BC People in northwestern Europe begin building stone circles.

c.3200BC Metalworkers in Europe make bronze.

c.3500-2200BC Stonehenge is built.

EUROPE

| 2000BC | 1000BC | 500BC | AD1 | AD500 |

123

Palaces and Legends

The Minoans lived on the island of Crete in the Mediterranean Sea. Their way of life slowly grew into the first great civilization in Europe.
The Minoans take their name from King Minos, who is said to have ruled the island.

★ Wall painting of a Minoan woman

The legend of King Minos

According to a Greek legend, the god Zeus fell in love with a beautiful princess called Europa. He turned himself into a bull and swam to Crete with the princess on his back. King Minos of Crete was one of Princess Europa's sons.

This painting of Europa and Zeus is taken from a Greek vase.

Map of Crete

★ Palace

EUROPE · ASIA · AFRICA

GREECE

Thera

MEDITERRANEAN SEA

Knossos · Mallia

Phaestos · CRETE · Zakro

The palace at Knossos

Each of the main towns on Crete was built around a huge palace, but the one at Knossos was the largest. It had over a thousand rooms, which were linked by corridors, staircases and courtyards.

Farmers bring grain to the palace storerooms.

The storerooms are at ground level.

Shafts like this let in the light.

Throne room

The roofs are made of wood.

The central courtyard is used for religious ceremonies.

The walls are built of limestone.

Wooden pillars hold up the roof.

The queen's bathroom

This picture shows the palace at Knossos. Part of the building has been cut away to let you see inside.

| 10,000BC | 5000BC | 4000BC | 3000BC |

QUICKLINKS: For links to websites about the enormous palace at Knossos and the myth of the Minotaur, go to **usborne.com/Quicklinks**

Storerooms

Farmers had to give some of their produce to the palace, where it was kept in the storerooms. Some of it was used to feed court officials and to pay the palace craftworkers. The rest was traded abroad.

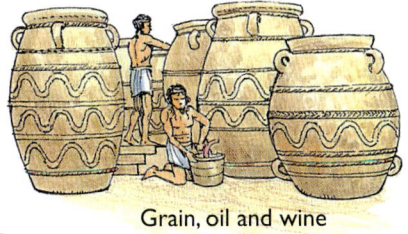

Grain, oil and wine were stored in huge earthenware jars.

Painted walls

★ Fresco of a group of dolphins

The palace walls were decorated with bright paintings called frescoes. A fresco is a picture which is painted on a wall while the plaster is still damp. The Minoans painted vivid scenes of palace life, plants and animals.

The throne room

The most impressive room has walls painted with plants and mythological creatured called griffins. It still contains a decorated marble seat, so it was thought to be the king's throne room, but it may really have been used for religious ceremonies.

This is the brightly painted "throne room" at Knossos.

The legend of the Minotaur

According to legend, the Minotaur was half-bull and half-man, and lived in a huge maze under the palace at Knossos. A young Greek prince called Theseus set out to kill it. The daughter of King Minos gave Theseus a magic sword and a ball of thread. As he went deeper into the maze, Theseus unwound the thread, leaving a trail behind him. He used the sword to kill the monster and then followed the thread back to the outside world.

Theseus prepares to kill the Minotaur.
★

These carved shapes are meant to look like bulls' horns.

Over 30,000 people live in and around the palace.

Parts of the palace are three or four floors high.

EUROPE

Life on Crete

Most people on Crete were farmers. They kept animals, such as cattle, sheep, goats and pigs, and grew wheat, barley, vegetables, plums, grapes and olives. People also ate a lot of fish, which they caught in the sea around the island.

Wall painting of a fisherman holding his catch of mackerel

Travel and trade

The Minoans were skilled sailors. They had a large fleet of ships and sailed all around the eastern Mediterranean. Minoan merchants sold pottery, grain, wine and olive oil, and brought back gold, silver, jewels, ivory and linen. They were successful traders and became very rich.

Minoan pots ★

Writing

Once the Minoans began to store goods and trade with other lands, they needed to keep a record of who owned what. At first they used pictograms (picture writing), but later they invented a form of writing which experts call Linear A. So far, no one has been able to understand what it says.

Stone tablet ★
carved with
Linear A writing

This picture of a busy Minoan town gives an idea of what life on Crete was like.

The houses are built of stone.

Wooden beams make the walls stronger.

A trading ship returning from Egypt

In the summer, people sleep on the roof.

Stairs leading to the roof are inside here.

The family lives upstairs.

This man is selling meat.

Olives, plums and grapes

This house belongs to a potter.

Downstairs there is a storeroom, a kitchen and the potter's workshop.

Fish, crabs and octopus for sale

Donkeys carry goods around the island.

These pots are for sale.

10,000BC   5000BC   4000BC   3000BC

Bull-leaping

The Minoans enjoyed an extremely dangerous sport known as bull-leaping. Highly trained acrobats grasped the horns of a charging bull and somersaulted over its back. The bull was sacred to the sea god, so bull-leaping may have been part of a religious ceremony.

This wall painting shows a ★ team of bull-leapers.

Religion

The Minoans did not build huge temples. Instead, they prayed and made offerings to their gods and goddesses in special rooms inside the palaces, or at small outdoor shrines.

Ash from the volcano on the island of Thera falls on Crete.

People try to escape as the buildings collapse.

An earthquake makes the palace walls crumble.

The end of the Minoans

Around 1450 BC, there was a major disaster on Crete. The palaces were badly damaged, but no one is sure exactly how this happened. Around this time, a volcano on the nearby island of Thera erupted. This may have caused an earthquake or a giant tidal wave, which wrecked the Minoans' towns. Falling ash from the volcano may have ruined their farmland.

A disaster like the one shown here may have helped bring the Minoan civilization to an end.

At around the same time, Crete was invaded by people known as the Mycenaeans, who came from Greece (see pages 128 to 131). The Minoans never really recovered and their civilization was replaced by that of the Mycenaeans.

Shrine

These priestesses are going to worship at a shrine.

Statue of a goddess

The double axe, a religious symbol

Musicians

This calf will be sacrificed.

This priestess is carrying offerings of wine and oil.

Important dates

c.6000 BC	Farmers settle on Crete.
c.2500 BC	Towns begin to grow up.
c.1900 BC	The first palaces are built. Picture writing is used.
c.1700 BC	The palaces are destroyed by an earthquake.
c.1700-1450 BC	The palaces are rebuilt. Crete is at its most powerful.
c.1650 BC	Linear A writing is used.
c.1450 BC	The palaces are destroyed. The Mycenaeans invade. The Minoan civilization gradually dies out.

EUROPE

2000BC	1000BC	500BC	ADI	AD500

Palaces and Tombs

Map of the Mycenaean world

Around 1600BC, the country now called Greece was divided into small kingdoms. Each kingdom was made up of a walled city and the land around it. The people who lived in Greece at this time became known as Mycenaeans, because Mycenae was the most important kingdom.

Mycenaean kings lived in magnificent palaces which contained offices, workshops and storerooms, as well as the king's private rooms. The most important room was the great hall, called the megaron.

This picture shows a feast in the megaron (great hall) of a Mycenaean palace.

★ Wall painting of a Mycenaean lady

The city of Mycenae

★

Palace

Windows up here let in light and let out smoke.

The ceiling and floor are brightly painted.

Wooden pillars hold up the roof.

Roast pig

The king sits on a raised platform.

Lyre

Circular fireplace

Grapes and figs

Bread is eaten with olive oil or honey.

This servant is pouring out wine.

A poet sings about the king's bravery in battle.

Pottery drinking cup

Mycenaean pots

Workshops

Metalworkers, potters and weavers worked for the king and had their workshops in the palace. Some of the things they made were traded abroad.

Offices

Scribes kept a record of all the goods stored in the palace. They wrote on clay tablets and used a form of writing which we call Linear B.

★ Clay tablet

Mycenaean scribes at work

Linear B writing

Bathrooms

One palace had a room with a built-in bathtub. The bathtub had no drain, so the water had to be scooped out with a jug and poured away.

Jar of perfumed oil

Stone bathtub

Stone step

★

The bathroom in the palace at Pylos

Early tombs

The early kings of Mycenae and their families were buried in deep pits, called shaft graves. The graves were protected by a circular stone wall.

A circle of graves at Mycenae

Each grave is marked by a stone slab.

A cutaway picture of a shaft grave

The shaft is 12m (40ft) deep.

Body

Tomb treasure

Mycenaean tombs were filled with gold and silver ornaments, goblets, swords and daggers. Shaft graves were difficult for robbers to break into, so a lot of this treasure has survived.

★ This golden funeral mask was found in a shaft grave at Mycenae.

Beehive tombs

The later Mycenaean kings were buried in huge, beehive-shaped tombs, called tholos tombs. These tombs were built under great mounds of earth.

This cutaway picture of a tholos tomb shows a king's funeral.

Priests and priestesses bring offerings of food and wine.

The inside is covered with gold rosettes.

These sheep will be sacrificed.

Musicians

The doorway is decorated with carved green and red stones.

The king's body is surrounded by treasure.

EUROPE

| 2000BC | | 1000BC | 500BC | AD1 | AD500 |

129

Warriors and Traders

War was an important part of Mycenaean life. Kings and nobles trained as warriors, skilled metalworkers made weapons from bronze, and poets told about the bravery of soldiers in battle.

Vase showing Mycenaean warriors

Hunting

When nobles were not at war, they used their chariots for hunting. They killed wild boar and used the tusks to decorate the helmets they wore in battle.

★ Hunting wild boar

When a city went to war, the king led his army into battle. He and his nobles rode in fast chariots, while the ordinary soldiers marched on foot.

In this picture, the king of the city of Mycenae is leading his army to war.

★

People cheer as the soldiers pass by.

The city walls are built of huge blocks of stone.

This is the Lion Gate. It is the main entrance to Mycenae.

Helmet covered with boars' tusks

Some warriors wear a bronze suit to protect them.

This huge rectangular shield is called a tower shield.

Some shields are shaped like a figure eight.

The chariots are made of wood and oxhide.

The king wears a helmet decorated with a horn.

Foot soldier

The shields are made of oxhide stretched over a wooden frame.

The invasion of Crete

Around 1450BC, Mycenaean warriors sailed to Crete and took control of the palace at Knossos. They also took over the Minoans' sea trade and became the leading traders in the eastern Mediterranean.

Mycenaean warships

Trade

Mycenaean traders sailed to places as far apart as Egypt and Italy. They bought ivory and precious metals in exchange for wine, olive oil, and objects such as weapons, pots and bowls.

The siege of Troy

Around 1250BC, the city of Troy (in modern Turkey) was destroyed. A famous tale is told about this real event.

According to the legend, Paris, prince of Troy, fell in love with Helen, the beautiful wife of a Mycenaean king. Paris took Helen off to Troy, so the angry Mycenaeans attacked the city and kept it surrounded for ten years.

One day, they left a huge wooden horse outside the walls of Troy and pretended to sail away. The Trojans thought the horse would bring them luck and dragged it into the city.

Mycenaean soldiers climbing out of the wooden horse ★

That night, Mycenaean soldiers, who were hiding inside the horse, climbed out. They opened the city gates and let in the rest of their army. Troy was destroyed and Helen was reunited with her husband.

The end of the Mycenaeans

From around 1250BC, there were many bad harvests. Some of the Mycenaeans attacked each other's cities, and stole cattle and crops. Some may even have left Greece to search for new homes, and their cities were gradually abandoned.

This scene shows part of a busy Mycenaean trading port.

This ship is being unloaded after a trip to the eastern Mediterranean.

Gold from Egypt

Ivory from Syria

Copper from Cyprus

Bronze swords and daggers

Silver bowl

Gold drinking cup

Jars of wine and oil

These things will be loaded onto a ship and sold on the next trip abroad.

Important dates

c.2000BC	The Mycenaeans settle in Greece.
c.1600-1200BC	The Mycenaeans are rich and powerful.
c.1450BC	Knossos is taken over.
c.1250BC	Troy is destroyed.
c.1200BC	The cities are gradually abandoned.

EUROPE

| 2000BC | 1000BC | 500BC | AD1 | AD500 |

The Empire of Hammurabi

Map of Hammurabi's Empire

Around 2000BC, the lands of Sumer and Akkad were invaded by desert people known as Amorites. They took control of several cities, including Babylon. Each city was then ruled by a different Amorite family.

Amorite invaders

Around 1792BC, a young man called Hammurabi became King of Babylon. He fought the other Amorite kings and conquered the whole of Sumer and Akkad, creating a powerful empire.

★ This picture of King Hammurabi is based on a stone carving.

Hammurabi's laws

Hammurabi put together one set of laws and punishments for all the people in his Empire. These laws were carved on a stone pillar for everyone to see.

These pictures show some of Hammurabi's laws.

If a surgeon carried out an operation that killed a patient, he had his hand cut off.

If an architect built a house that collapsed and killed someone, he was put to death.

A man who owed money to someone could lend him his wife as a slave.

Gods and legends

Priests told how the god Marduk saved the world from a terrifying sea monster.

The Babylonians had many different gods, but Marduk was the most important one. Some people believed that Marduk created the world by building a huge raft on the ocean and pouring dust on top of it.

The end of the Empire

After Hammurabi died, his Empire grew weaker. Around 1595BC, the city of Babylon was raided by the Hittites, and the Empire collapsed. (To find out what happened in Babylon later on, see pages 150 and 151.)

Important dates

C.2000BC The Amorites invade.
C.1792-1750BC King Hammurabi rules Babylon and creates the Babylonian Empire.
C.1595BC The Hittites raid Babylon, and the Empire collapses.

THE MIDDLE EAST

10,000BC	5000BC	4000BC	3000BC

The Hittite Empire

EUROPE
ASIA
AFRICA

Hittite Empire

Hattusa

A N A T O L I A

KINGDOM OF MITANNI

SYRIA

Kadesh

MEDITERRANEAN SEA

EGYPT

Map of the Hittite Empire

In around 2000BC, the Hittite people settled in Anatolia (in modern Turkey). By around 1650BC, they had all joined together to form one kingdom, with a capital city at Hattusa.

Warriors

The Hittites were tough warriors. They rode into battle in war chariots and carried iron weapons, which were stronger than the bronze weapons used by their enemies.

In this scene, Hittite warriors are leaving the city of Hattusa to go to war.

★

Kings and wars

The greatest Hittite king was Šuppiluliuma I. He invaded Syria, destroyed the nearby Kingdom of Mitanni and built up a powerful empire.

The Hittites and the Egyptians were bitter enemies. They fought a fierce battle at Kadesh, which neither side won. The two countries later made peace.

★ Gold statue of a Hittite king

Gods

The Hittites had many gods, including one named Tarhunna. People believed he controlled the weather.

Tarhunna holding a flash of lightning

The end of the Hittites

Around 1195BC, the Empire was attacked by raiders (see page 141). Some Hittites survived in Syria, but the Empire collapsed.

This gateway is called the Lion Gate.

Stone tower

There is a tunnel under the city wall, so soldiers can rush out and surprise the enemy.

City wall

Tunnel

The city is surrounded by a massive stone wall.

Iron helmet

Spear tipped with iron

This man drives the chariot.

Archers march on foot.

Wicker shield

Leather tunic covered with metal plates

The chariot is big enough to carry three men.

Important dates

c.2000BC The Hittites settle in Anatolia.

c.1650BC Hattusa is the capital of the Hittite kingdom.

c.1350-1322BC King Šuppiluliuma I rules.

c.1285BC The Battle of Kadesh

c.1195BC The Hittites are defeated by invaders.

THE MIDDLE EAST

BABYLONIANS

HITTITES

2000BC   1000BC   500BC   AD1   AD500

The Egyptian Empire

Around 1650BC, Egypt was invaded by people called the Hyksos. They had horses and chariots, and easily defeated the Egyptian soldiers who fought on foot. The Egyptians gradually learned how to use chariots and later drove the Hyksos out of Egypt. Then, they began to invade nearby lands and quickly built up a large empire.

Egyptian painting showing a horse and chariot

Warrior pharaohs

The Egyptians were led into battle by their pharaohs (kings), who were skilled soldiers. The greatest warrior pharaoh was Thutmose III, who led his army to war 17 times. During his rule, the Egyptian Empire was at its largest.

The most dangerous of Egypt's enemies were the Hittites. Pharaoh Ramesses II fought against them for over 30 years. The two countries finally made peace, and Ramesses married a Hittite princess.

EUROPE

ASIA

AFRICA

HITTITE EMPIRE

CYPRUS

SYRIA

Wine and oil came from Crete.

CRETE

MEDITERRANEAN SEA

LIBYA

SINAI

Nile

Timber, silver, tin, slaves and horses came from the eastern Empire.

Donkeys carried copper and turquoise from Sinai.

RED SEA

Salt, dates, reeds and cattle came from water holes in the desert.

NUBIA

Map of the Egyptian Empire

Egypt

Egyptian Empire in 1450bc

The map shows the goods that Egypt bought from other lands.

Gold, copper, amethysts, slaves and cattle came from Nubia.

Statue of Thutmose III

★

Trading trips

An Egyptian trading ship at Punt

★

Myrrh tree

The Egyptians had their own gold mines and could use the gold to buy the things they needed. They traded with other lands in their Empire and beyond (see map above). Some traders even went as far as Punt, a place on the east coast of Africa. There, they bought valuable myrrh trees, which were used to make sweet-smelling incense.

Fan made of ostrich feathers

Pharaoh   Queen

Paintings on the walls show scenes of life in Egypt.

Courtier

A scribe notes down the gifts people have brought.

Copper from Sinai

Gifts of wine and oil for the pharaoh

These Syrians are bowing very low.

One of the pharaoh's two viziers (advisers)

Officials

A herdsman from Sinai

Exotic fruit

Ostrich eggs

Golden rings

Ivory

Visitors from Nubia

Leopard skin

Pet baboon for the queen

★

In this scene, visitors are bringing gifts to the pharaoh's court. Some pillars have been taken out to show more of the throne room.

The pharaoh's court

People came from all over the Empire to the pharaoh's court. They brought goods to trade and rich gifts for the pharaoh. The gifts were a kind of tax, called tribute, that all conquered people had to pay. Some foreign rulers even sent their daughters to marry the pharaoh, who had many wives.

Travel

There were few roads in Egypt, as they would have been washed away by floods each year. The easiest way to travel was by boat along the Nile. Trading ships also sailed to ports on the Red Sea and in the eastern Mediterranean.

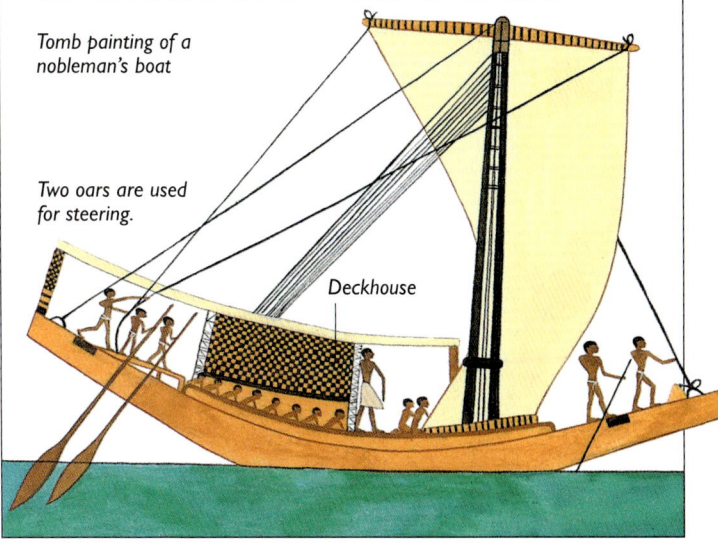

Tomb painting of a nobleman's boat

Two oars are used for steering.

Deckhouse

AFRICA

2000BC		1000BC	500BC	AD1	AD500

Temples and Gods

The Egyptians had many different gods and goddesses. Most of them were linked with a special animal or bird, and they were often shown in paintings and carvings with the head of that animal or bird. This made them easy to recognize.

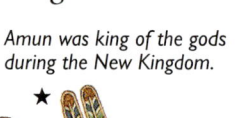

Here you can see some Egyptian gods and goddesses.

★ Ma'at, goddess of truth and justice

Osiris, ruler of the dead ★

★ Taweret, a female hippopotamus, looked after pregnant women and babies.

Thoth, god of wisdom and writing, had the head of an ibis (a kind of bird). ★

Amun was king of the gods during the New Kingdom.

    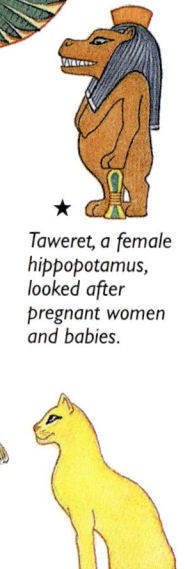

★ Ra, the sun god, was sometimes shown with a hawk's head.

★ Anubis, god of the dead, had a jackal's head.

Horus, the son of Isis and Osiris, was god of the sky. He had a falcon's head.

Isis, the sister and wife of Osiris, was goddess of crafts.

Bast, the cat ★ goddess

This temple at Abu Simbel in Nubia was carved out of solid rock.

The Egyptians built many huge, stone temples along the banks of the Nile. They believed that their gods and goddesses lived in these temples.

Inside each temple was a statue of the god who lived there. Every morning, priests woke the god, washed the statue, dressed it, gave it food and prayed to it.

Ordinary people did not normally go inside the temple. They only saw the statue of the god on festival days, when it was taken out and carried around the town.

This is the festival of Bast, the cat goddess. The procession is just leaving the temple.

Priests and priestesses lead the way.

This priest is burning incense.

These bulls will be sacrificed.

Statue of Bast

Shrine

Golden boat

Dancers   Musicians

Attached to the temple were craft workshops, a library and a school, and many different people worked there.

Some people who worked in the temple

Scribe (his job was to read and write for everyone else)

Sculptor

Carpenter

Potter

Weaver

Paper is very expensive, so the boys write on pieces of pottery.

The teacher is a scribe.

A temple school

A few boys from rich families went to the temple school to learn how to read and write. Older boys could study history, geography, religion, languages, mathematics and medicine. Girls did not go to school. They were taught at home by their mothers.

Writing

The Egyptians wrote in pictures or signs, which we call hieroglyphs. Scribes wrote on special paper, called papyrus, which was made from reeds. Ink was made in solid blocks and had to be mixed with water.

Papyrus

Block of ink

Wooden pens

★

This is a monument to the sun god. It is called an obelisk.

The temple walls are covered with carvings, paintings and hieroglyphs.

Hieroglyphs (picture writing)

Statue of the pharaoh (king)

Life at Home

Egyptian houses were built of bricks made from a mixture of mud and straw. The bricks were shaped in a wooden frame and were then left to dry in the sun. Most houses only had one or two rooms, but rich people lived in large, luxurious villas.

This huge villa belongs to a rich nobleman. He is receiving visitors in the reception hall. Part of the house has been cut away to let you see inside. ★

The servants live here.

Grapevines

Wine press

Grain store

The walls are plastered and painted white.

The gatekeeper lives here. He keeps out unwelcome visitors.

The family gives parties in the central hall.

These children are playing a board game on the roof.

Reception hall

Bedroom

Brightly painted pillars

People offer gifts to the gods at this shrine.

Parties

Rich Egyptians often gave large parties with lots of food and drink. Guests were entertained by musicians, singers, dancers, jugglers and acrobats. Servants put cones of perfumed fat on the guests' heads. As the fat melted and ran down their faces, it cooled them down and made them smell nice.

Perfumed fat

This Egyptian painting shows guests, dancers and musicians at a party.

10,000BC	5000BC	4000BC	3000BC

Games

The Egyptians had several types of board games, such as the two shown on the right, but no one is sure how they were played. Children played with balls, spinning tops, dolls and animals made from wood or pottery.

★ Hounds and jackals

★ Senet

★ Toy dog

This handle opens the dog's mouth.

★ Hippo made of painted pottery

★ *Children enjoyed ball games.*

Cattle pens

Well

Fish pond

Shade to keep off the sun

Walled garden

The end of the Egyptian Empire

The last great warrior pharaoh was Ramesses III. He defended Egypt against raiders known as the Sea Peoples (see page 141).

After Ramesses died, the Empire grew weaker. Civil war broke out and Egypt was invaded by the Assyrians, then by the Nubians and later by the Persians.

In 332BC, Egypt was conquered by Alexander the Great (see pages 160 and 161). After Alexander's death, the country was ruled by the Ptolemy family, who were descended from one of his generals.

In 32BC, Rome went to war with Egypt. The Egyptians were defeated and Queen Cleopatra, the last Ptolemy ruler, killed herself. Egypt then became part of the Roman Empire.

Cleopatra

Sports

The most popular sports were hunting and fishing. Noblemen hunted water birds and river animals, such as hippos and crocodiles. People also enjoyed wrestling, fencing and energetic games, such as tug-of-war.

This picture of a tug-of-war comes from an Egyptian wall painting.

Hunting a hippo from a reed boat

Important dates

c.1650BC	The Hyksos invade Egypt. The Middle Kingdom ends.
c.1550BC	The Hyksos are driven out. The New Kingdom begins.
c.1450BC	The Egyptian Empire is at its largest.
c.1280BC	Ramesses II makes peace with the Hittites.
c.1175BC	The "Sea Peoples" attack.
c.1070BC	The New Kingdom ends in civil war.
671BC	The Assyrians invade.
525BC	The Persians invade.
332BC	Alexander the Great conquers Egypt.
30BC	Egypt becomes part of the Roman Empire.

AFRICA

2000BC   1000BC   500BC   ADI   AD500

The People of Canaan

Map of Canaan

Map showing EUROPE, ASIA, AFRICA, HITTITE EMPIRE, Ebla, Ugarit, CYPRUS, Byblos, MEDITERRANEAN SEA, CANAAN, PALESTINE, EGYPT

The land of Canaan lay at the eastern end of the Mediterranean Sea. The people of Canaan were farmers and traders, who lived in many small kingdoms. Each kingdom had a walled city with villages and farmland around it.

The walled city of Ebla

The huge cedar trees which grew in the north were very valuable, and Canaan became rich. It was fought over constantly by empire builders, such as the Egyptians and the Hittites. From around 1550BC, most of Canaan was ruled by Egypt.

Cedar tree

Trade

Canaanite merchants set sail from ports such as Byblos and Ugarit. They traded all around the eastern Mediterranean.

In this picture, a Canaanite merchant is getting ready to set off for Egypt.

A scribe lists all the goods that are to be loaded onto the ship.

These slaves will be sold to an Egyptian nobleman.

This cedarwood will be used to build boats in Egypt.

Merchant

Jar of olives

Ivory box

Brightly dyed cloth

Golden cups and vases

Jar of oil

Wine jars

Gods

The Canaanites had many gods, but the most powerful one was Baal, the god of rain, storms and war. His wife, Astarte, was the goddess of love.

★ Statue of Baal

Priests sacrificed animals at hilltop shrines.

Writing

The Canaanites invented an alphabet with just 27 letters. It was much easier to use than Egyptian or Sumerian writing, which had hundreds of signs.

Clay tablet carved with Canaanite writing

Invasions

Between 1195BC and 1190BC, Canaan was invaded by the Sea Peoples (see opposite page). Some Sea Peoples settled in the south, but the Canaanites kept control in the north.

10,000BC   5000BC   4000BC   3000BC

Raiders of the Mediterranean

The "Sea Peoples" were actually many different groups of people, who probably came from Greece, the Greek islands and southwestern Turkey. Around 1195BC, troubles at home forced them to look for somewhere else to live, and they invaded the eastern Mediterranean.

An army of Sea Peoples destroyed the Hittite Empire, then some of them sailed south, attacking towns on the coast of Canaan. Others made their way on foot.

Sea Peoples on the move

Women and children travel in carts.

Around 1190BC, the Sea Peoples attacked Egypt. They fought on land and sea, and were defeated in a fierce battle off the coast of Egypt.

The Philistines

After their defeat, the Sea Peoples scattered around the Mediterranean. One group, called the Peleset, settled in southern Canaan which was later named Palestine after them. In the Bible, they are known as Philistines.

The Philistines had strong iron weapons which helped them to conquer nearby peoples, such as the Hebrews (see pages 142 and 143).

★ Philistine coffins were made of pottery.

This picture shows the sea battle between the Sea Peoples and the Egyptians.

Egyptian archers fire arrows from the beach.

The Sea Peoples fight with spears or swords.

This ship has been overturned.

This tribe is called the Sherden. They wear helmets decorated with horns.

The Sea Peoples' ships have a bird's head at each end.

Leather tunic

The Egyptians fight with spears or bows and arrows.

The Egyptians ram one of the Sea Peoples' ships.

Many of the Sea Peoples are drowned.

Important dates

c.1550-1200BC Most of Canaan is ruled by the Egyptians.

c.1400BC The Canaanites invent the first alphabet.

c.1195BC The Sea Peoples defeat the Hittites.

c.1175BC The Egyptians defeat the Sea Peoples.

c.1150BC The Philistines settle in southern Canaan.

THE MIDDLE EAST

CANAANITES

SEA PEOPLES

2000BC   1000BC   500BC   AD1   AD500

The Hebrew Kingdoms

The early Hebrew tribes wandered along the edges of the desert near the land of Canaan. Unlike most people in ancient times, they believed in only one god. They thought he would look after them if they obeyed him.

The early Hebrews lived in tents.

The great escape

You can read about the Hebrews in the Old Testament of the Bible. One famous story tells how they were forced to work for the kings of Egypt. Led by a man called Moses, they escaped across the desert into Canaan.

The Hebrews' escape from Egypt is known as the Exodus.

Map of Israel

EUROPE
AFRICA
ASIA
PHOENICIA
MEDITERRANEAN SEA
Jerusalem • CANAAN
EGYPT

- Kingdom of Israel at the time of David and Solomon
- Philistine lands

Conquering Canaan

The Hebrews probably arrived in Canaan around 1250BC. After many battles, they won some land and settled down to farm.

★ This cutaway picture shows the house of a Hebrew farmer.

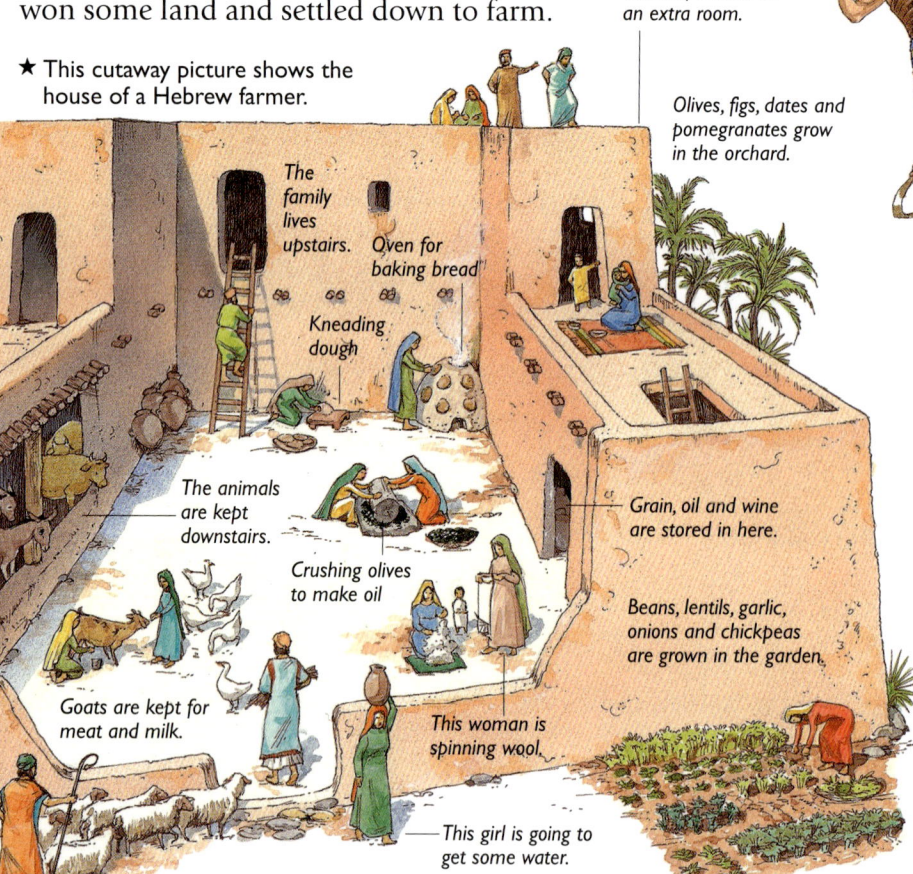

The roof is used as an extra room.

Olives, figs, dates and pomegranates grow in the orchard.

The family lives upstairs.

Oven for baking bread

Kneading dough

The animals are kept downstairs.

Crushing olives to make oil

Goats are kept for meat and milk.

Grain, oil and wine are stored in here.

Beans, lentils, garlic, onions and chickpeas are grown in the garden.

This woman is spinning wool.

This girl is going to get some water.

Fighting the Philistines

The Hebrews had to fight to defend their land against the Philistines who had settled on the coast. The Hebrews chose a man called Saul to be their king and lead them into battle, but the hero of the war was a boy called David. The Bible tells how he killed the Philistines' strongest warrior with a stone hurled from a sling.

★ David kills the Philistine warrior Goliath.

King David

David became king when Saul died. He defeated the Philistines and united the Hebrews into one kingdom, called Israel. He captured Jerusalem and made it his capital city.

King Solomon

David's son, Solomon, set up trade links with other lands, such as Phoenicia, and made Israel rich and powerful. He used part of his wealth to build a great temple in Jerusalem for his people's god.

This cutaway picture shows Solomon's temple in Jerusalem.

Outside Solomon's temple was a bronze basin filled with holy water.

Phoenician craftworkers ★ helped the Hebrews to build the temple.

The temple is built of limestone.

The walls are lined with cedarwood from Phoenicia.

This room is called the Holy of Holies. The High Priest comes in here once a year.

The walls are covered with gold.

Bronze pillar

Porch

Storerooms for temple treasure

Main hall

Golden lampstand

Offerings of grain are burned on this altar.

This box is called the Ark of the Covenant. Inside it are stone slabs carved with sacred laws called the Ten Commandments.

The Ark is guarded by two golden statues.

Two kingdoms

After Solomon's death, quarrels broke out between the north and the south. The country split into two kingdoms, Israel in the north and Judah in the south.

The end of the Hebrew kingdoms

In 722BC, the Assyrians invaded Israel and took control. The Israelites later rebelled and many were taken to Assyria as slaves. Judah was conquered by the Babylonians, who destroyed Jerusalem and took the Judeans prisoner. The Judeans, who became known as Jews, were allowed to return home after the Babylonian Empire collapsed.

The people of Judah were taken to Babylon as slaves.

Important dates

c.1250BC	The Hebrews arrive in Canaan.
c.1020BC	Saul becomes king.
c.1000-965BC	King David rules. The Philistines are defeated.
c.965-928BC	King Solomon rules. The temple is built.
c.926BC	The kingdom splits in two, Israel and Judah.
722BC	The Assyrians invade Israel.
587BC	The Babylonians destroy Jerusalem. The people of Judah are taken prisoner.

THE MIDDLE EAST

| 2000BC | 1000BC | 500BC | ADI | AD500 |

Traders from Phoenicia

The Phoenicians were descended from the Canaanites, who lived at the eastern end of the Mediterranean Sea (see page 140). From around 1200BC, they became the most successful traders in the ancient world.

Cities by the sea

The main Phoenician trading ports were the cities of Tyre, Sidon and Byblos. The cities were protected by strong walls and each one had its own king, who lived in a luxurious palace.

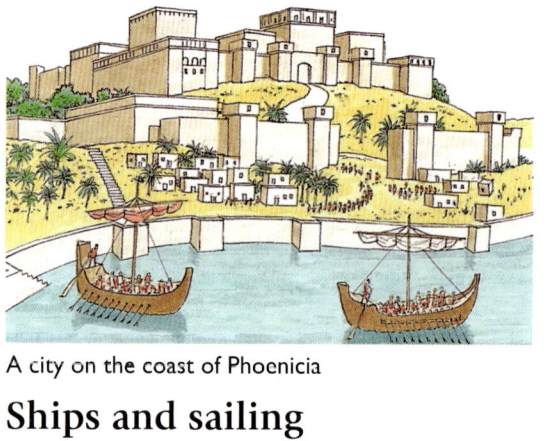

A city on the coast of Phoenicia

Ships and sailing

The Phoenicians were expert sailors. Their sturdy trading ships sailed all over the Mediterranean and beyond, probably even reaching the British Isles. One expedition sailed all the way around Africa.

Crafts

★ Glass bead

Skilled craftworkers made objects for traders to sell abroad. The Phoenicians were known for their fine ivory carvings and their beautiful glass bottles and beads.

★ Ivory carving

Purple people

The Phoenicians used a shellfish, called a murex, to make an expensive purple dye. The name "Phoenician" comes from a Greek word meaning "purple men".

★ Murex shell

The ship is steered from the back using two huge oars.

This trading ship is about to set sail for Spain.

Cargo is stored below the deck.

Jars of cedar oil, wine and spices

This picture shows a ship being loaded with cargo at a busy Phoenician trading port.

Phoenician cedarwood

This merchant wants to buy some cloth.

Salt from North Africa

Ivory from Egypt

Copper from Cyprus

Rolls of purple cloth

Glass bottles are packed inside pottery jars to keep them safe.

Map of the Phoenician world

▨	Phoenicia
▨	Areas where the Phoenicians settled
→	Trade route
⇢	Exploration route

EUROPE
ASIA
AFRICA

TO THE BRITISH ISLES
TO WEST AFRICA
SPAIN
CORSICA
SARDINIA
IBIZA
Carthage
AFRICA
Rome
ITALY
SICILY
MALTA
GREECE
CRETE
MEDITERRANEAN SEA
CYPRUS
Byblos
Sidon
Tyre
EGYPT
Nile

A warship sails ahead to protect trading ships from pirates.

A warship with two rows of oars is called a bireme.

The ship is made of cedarwood and pine.

This is the merchant who owns the ship.

The city of Carthage

Merchants set up trading posts and colonies around the Mediterranean. The most famous one was Carthage on the north coast of Africa. Stories say it was set up by a Phoenician princess called Dido, who tricked the local African ruler into giving her enough land to build a city.

The port at Carthage

Writing

The Phoenicians invented a simple alphabet with just 22 letters. It gradually developed into the alphabet we use today.

Part of the Phoenician alphabet

Phoenician letters	B	Y	L	W	Y	Φ
Modern letters	H	K	L	M	N	Q

The end of the Phoenicians

Although the Phoenicians became part of the mighty empires of Assyria, Babylon and Persia, their way of life survived until they were conquered by Alexander the Great in 332BC. The city of Carthage remained powerful for another 200 years, but was totally destroyed by the Romans in 146BC.

Roman soldiers destroying Carthage

Important dates

c.1200-1000BC The Phoenicians become rich and powerful.

c.814BC Carthage is built.

c.701BC Phoenicia is conquered by the Assyrians.

332BC Phoenicia is conquered by Alexander the Great.

146BC Carthage is destroyed by the Romans.

THE MIDDLE EAST

2000BC   1000BC   500BC   AD1   AD500

145

The Assyrians at War

In early times, the Assyrians lived in a small area of farmland by a river called the Tigris. Around 2000BC, they were taken over by invaders who made Assyria into a kingdom.

The Assyrians were warlike people. They often attacked the surrounding lands, but were always beaten back. Finally, led by a series of strong kings, they conquered the nearby kingdoms and built up a huge empire.

Map of the Assyrian Empire

Assyria

Assyrian Empire at its largest in 663BC

EUROPE

ASIA

AFRICA

MEDIA

Nineveh • • Nimrud
Ashur •

Euphrates

Tigris

• Babylon

MEDITERRANEAN SEA

PERSIAN GULF

EGYPT

Cruel conquerors

Conquered people had to pay heavy taxes to the Assyrian king, and anyone who refused to pay was brutally punished. Cities that rebelled were attacked.

The man in this carving is paying his taxes by giving a camel.

Attacking a city

The Assyrians were experts at attacking cities. They kept the city surrounded, so no one could escape. Then, they battered down the walls and captured the city.

In this scene, the Assyrians are attacking a rebel city.

A messenger brings news of a rebellion in another city.

Going to war

Every year, the mighty Assyrian army set out to conquer new lands. Soldiers had to travel great distances before going into battle.

This picture shows the Assyrian army crossing a river.

Most of the army is made up of foot soldiers.

Chariots are rowed across in small boats.

Soldiers swim across holding onto inflated goatskins.

Shield-bearer   Archer

Driver

Each chariot carries three soldiers.

These soldiers are blowing up goatskins to make floats.

10,000BC   5000BC   4000BC   3000BC

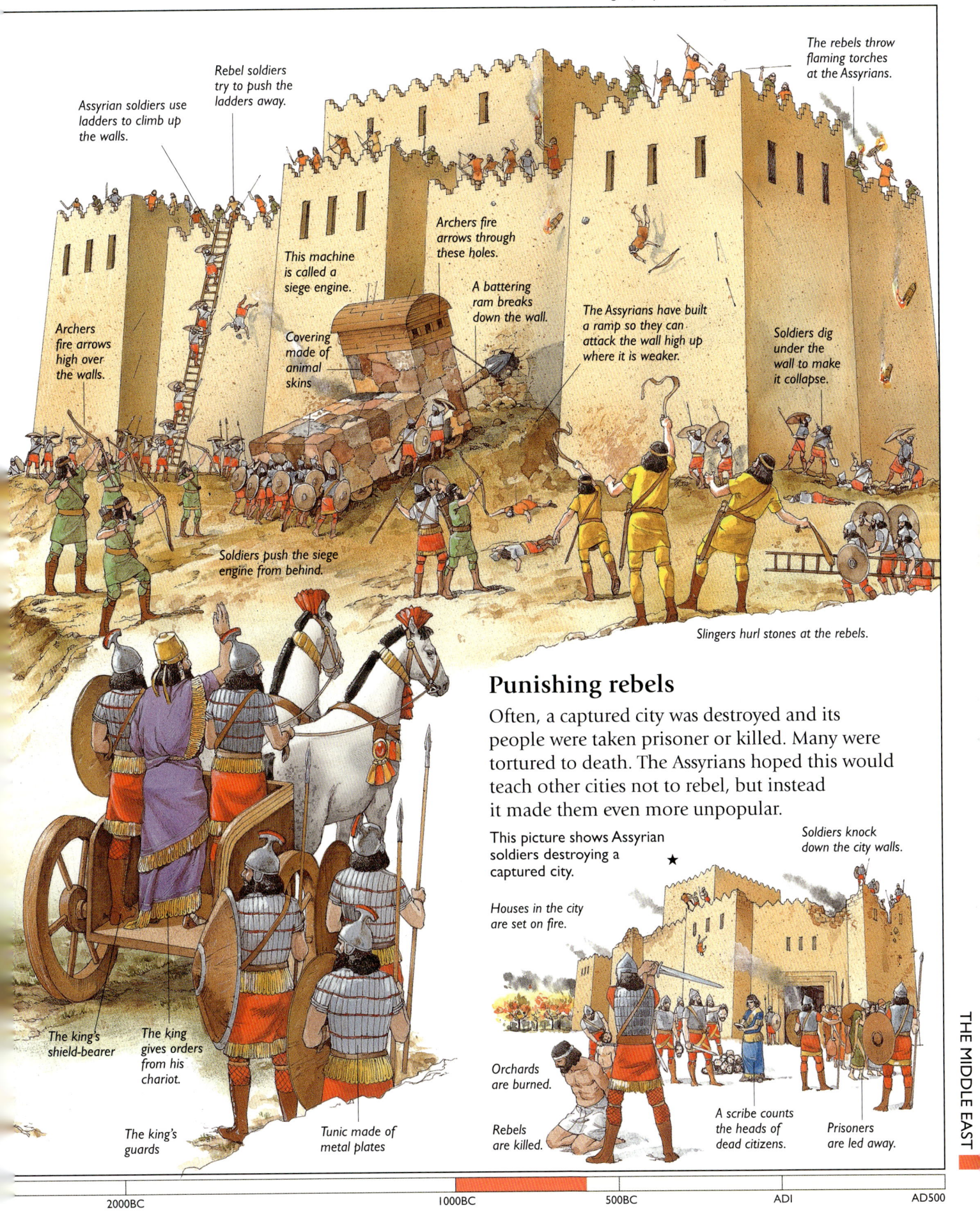

Assyrian soldiers use ladders to climb up the walls.

Rebel soldiers try to push the ladders away.

The rebels throw flaming torches at the Assyrians.

Archers fire arrows through these holes.

This machine is called a siege engine.

A battering ram breaks down the wall.

The Assyrians have built a ramp so they can attack the wall high up where it is weaker.

Soldiers dig under the wall to make it collapse.

Archers fire arrows high over the walls.

Covering made of animal skins

Soldiers push the siege engine from behind.

Slingers hurl stones at the rebels.

The king's shield-bearer

The king gives orders from his chariot.

The king's guards

Tunic made of metal plates

Punishing rebels

Often, a captured city was destroyed and its people were taken prisoner or killed. Many were tortured to death. The Assyrians hoped this would teach other cities not to rebel, but instead it made them even more unpopular.

This picture shows Assyrian soldiers destroying a captured city.

Houses in the city are set on fire.

Soldiers knock down the city walls.

Orchards are burned.

Rebels are killed.

A scribe counts the heads of dead citizens.

Prisoners are led away.

THE MIDDLE EAST

2000BC   1000BC   500BC   ADI   AD500

147

The Assyrians at Home

Most people in Assyria were farmers. They dug ditches to carry water to their fields and grew barley, sesame, grapes and vegetables. Farmers also kept sheep, goats and cattle.

An Assyrian farmer at work

Wooden pole

Stone weight

A machine called a shaduf lifts water into the fields.

Leather bucket

Gods and spirits

The Assyrians believed that their land belonged to Ashur, their chief god. They had many other gods and goddesses, and also believed in evil spirits.

Mighty kings

Assyrian kings thought that they were chosen by the gods to rule Assyria and conquer new lands. They gave themselves grand titles, such as "King of the Universe". The king also served the gods by building temples and leading religious festivals.

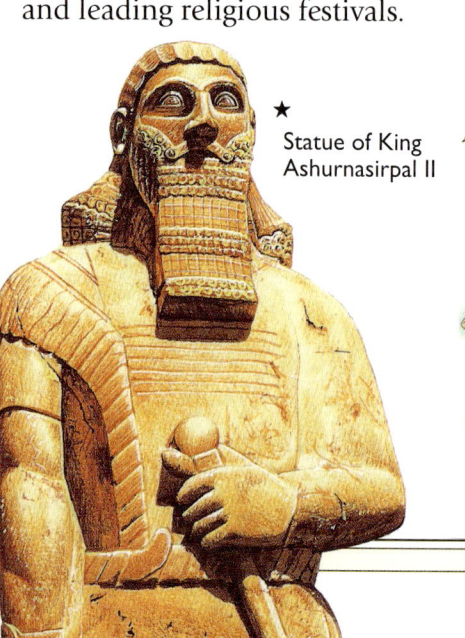

★ Statue of King Ashurnasirpal II

Cities and palaces

The Assyrians built magnificent cities with beautiful palaces and temples. Their first capital city at Ashur was named after their god. Later, King Ashurnasirpal II built a new capital city at Nimrud.

The throne room in Ashurnasirpal's palace at Nimrud ★

An opening in the ceiling lets in light.

The statue has a human head and the body of a winged lion.

A messenger brings news from around the Empire.

This is one of the two statues that guard the entrance to the throne room.

A servant holds a canopy over the king.

A scribe takes notes.

By the time of Ashurbanipal, the last great Assyrian king, the capital had been moved to another new city at Nineveh.

This picture shows King Ashurbanipal and his queen in the palace garden at Nineveh.

Double flute

Harp

The king's dogs

Lotus flowers grow in the pool.

Musicians

Libraries

The palace at Nineveh had a library filled with hundreds of clay tablets, which King Ashurbanipal collected from around the Empire. There were tablets on history, religion, mathematics and medicine.

An Assyrian library

Each clay tablet is covered in writing.

Lion hunting

When Assyrian kings were not at war, they hunted lions to show off their skill and bravery. The lions were kept in special parks so that the king could hunt whenever he wanted.

King Ashurbanipal in his hunting park

Soldiers use their shields to stop the lions from escaping.

The king is about to kill a lion with his spear.

The lions are kept in cages.

Grapevines keep off the sun.

Servants fan the king and queen to keep them cool and chase away flies.

Cakes made of honey and figs

The king lies on a couch.

Burning incense perfumes the air.

The furniture is decorated with gold and ivory.

The end of the Empire

In the end, the Assyrian Empire became too big to control. People rebelled and the Empire began to break up. In 612BC, the people of Babylon and nearby Media joined together to attack Assyria. The cities of Ashur and Nineveh were completely destroyed and the Empire collapsed.

Median soldier

Important dates

c.2000BC	Assyria becomes a kingdom.
c.1000-663BC	The Assyrians build up a powerful empire.
883-859BC	King Ashurnasirpal II rules. Nimrud is built.
704-681BC	King Sennacherib improves the city of Nineveh.
669-631BC	King Ashurbanipal rules.
612-609BC	The Babylonians and the Medes attack Assyria. The Empire collapses.

THE MIDDLE EAST

2000BC	1000BC	500BC	AD1	AD500

The City of Babylon

Pottery head of a
Kassite priestess

Babylon first became powerful under its great
king Hammurabi (see page 132). When his
Empire collapsed, the city was taken over by a
tribe called the Kassites, who ruled peacefully
for many years.

After around 7911BC, Babylon became part of the
Assyrian Empire. The people of Babylon often
rebelled against the Assyrians, who eventually
attacked and destroyed the city.

In 626BC, a Babylonian general called
Nabopolassar made himself King of Babylon.
He joined with the people of nearby Media
to defeat the Assyrians. He and his son,
King Nebuchadnezzar II, rebuilt
Babylon and made it one of the
richest cities in the world.

This picture shows the
city of Babylon during
the New Year Festival.

This stepped tower is
called a ziggurat. It was
built by Nebuchadnezzar
for the god Marduk.

Shrine

Priests live here.

The king's
throne room

The king's
palace

These gardens
are known as the
Hanging Gardens
of Babylon.

Nebuchadnezzar built the
gardens for his wife, because
she missed the green
hills of her homeland.

This gateway is called
the Ishtar Gate. It
is named after the
goddess Ishtar.

The gate is
covered with
bright blue tiles.

An avenue called
the Processional Way
leads into the city.

Pictures
of bulls
and dragons

A statue of the god
Marduk is carried to a
shrine outside the city.

People watch the
procession from
the battlements.

THE MIDDLE EAST

| 10,000BC | 5000BC | | 4000BC | | 3000BC |

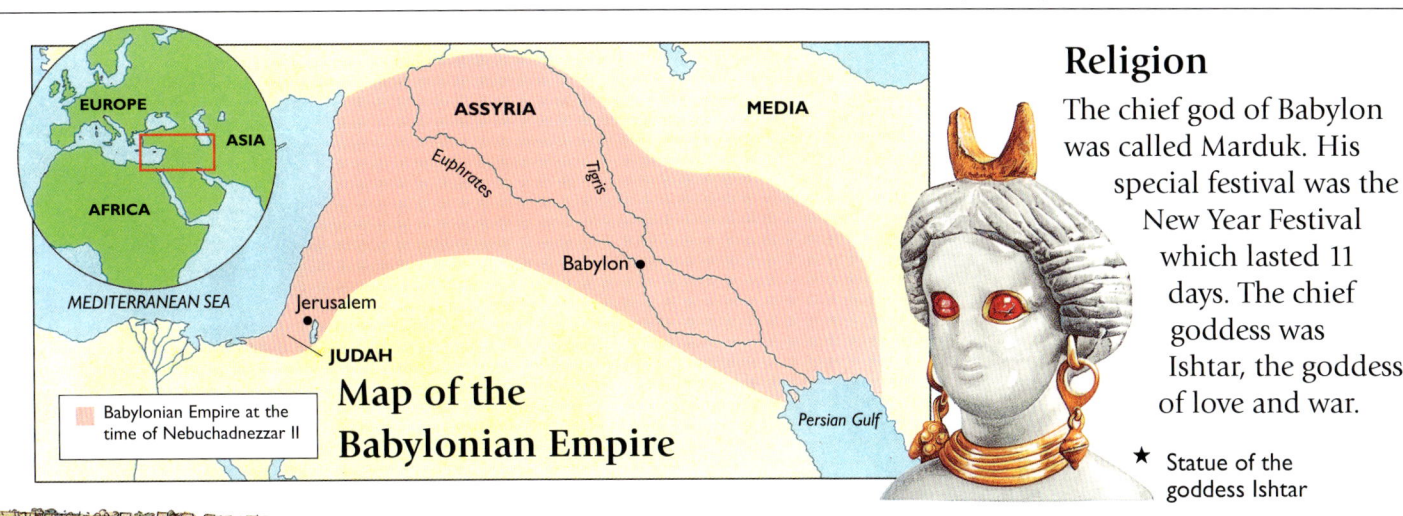

EUROPE
ASIA
AFRICA
MEDITERRANEAN SEA
ASSYRIA
Euphrates
Tigris
MEDIA
Babylon
Jerusalem
JUDAH
Persian Gulf

Babylonian Empire at the time of Nebuchadnezzar II

Map of the Babylonian Empire

Religion

The chief god of Babylon was called Marduk. His special festival was the New Year Festival which lasted 11 days. The chief goddess was Ishtar, the goddess of love and war.

★ Statue of the goddess Ishtar

Building an empire

King Nebuchadnezzar II fought many wars and built up a large empire. One of his most famous wars was against the people of Judah. When they rebelled, he destroyed Jerusalem, their capital city, and took thousands of them to Babylon as slaves.

Machinery carries water to the top of the Hanging Gardens.

Water runs down the terraces and keeps the soil wet.

Telling the future

The Babylonians believed that they could tell the future by looking at the insides of dead animals. Priests had clay models which showed them what to look for.

Clay model of a sheep's liver

★

The end of Babylon

In 539BC, Babylon was captured by an army from Persia (modern Iran) and became part of the powerful Persian Empire (see pages 152 and 153).

The main part of the city is surrounded by two massive walls.

Important dates

c.1595-1155BC	The Kassites rule Babylon.
c.911BC	Babylon becomes part of the Assyrian Empire.
689BC	Babylon is destroyed.
626-605BC	King Nabopolassar rules. The Assyrians are defeated.
605-562BC	King Nebuchadnezzar II rules. Babylon is rebuilt.
539BC	Babylon becomes part of the Persian Empire.

THE MIDDLE EAST

2000BC   1000BC   500BC   AD1   AD500

The Power of Persia

Persia is the old name for the country we now call Iran. Around 1300BC, the area was invaded by two tribes known as the Medes and the Persians. They set up two kingdoms, Media in the north and Persia in the south.

Frieze showing Persian soldiers

In 550BC, King Cyrus II of Persia defeated the Medes, took over their lands and built up a huge empire. Later, under King Darius I, the Persian Empire grew to become the largest the world had ever seen.

The Royal Road

Darius built good roads across the Empire, so that messengers could travel more quickly. The Royal Road stretched 2700km (1680 miles) from Sardis in the west to the capital city at Susa.

Mede

Persian

EUROPE

ASIA

AFRICA

SCYTHIA

BLACK SEA

GREECE

CASPIAN SEA

BACTRIA

Sardis

MEDIA

MEDITERRANEAN SEA

Babylon

Susa

ELAM

EGYPT

Persepolis

PERSIAN GULF

INDIA

RED SEA

Map of the Persian Empire

☐ Persia
☐ Persian Empire at its largest
— Royal Road

★ Persian armlet made of solid gold

Running the Empire

King Darius collected taxes from conquered people all over the Empire and became fabulously rich. He allowed people to keep their religion and way of life, as long as they paid their taxes.

Darius divided his vast Empire into regions, each one run by a local ruler called a satrap. Officials kept an eye on the satraps and made sure they stayed loyal to the king.

This picture shows King Darius receiving visitors in his throne room.

Canopy

Officials

Burning incense perfumes the air.

Prince Xerxes, the king's son

King Darius

A satrap (local ruler) greets the king.

Guards

A messenger arrives at an inn along the Royal Road.

10,000BC   5000BC   4000BC   3000BC

Persepolis

Darius used some of his wealth to build a magnificent palace at Persepolis. During the New Year Festival, officials from every part of the Empire came to the palace with gifts for the king.

This picture shows people arriving at Persepolis for the New Year Festival.
★

This is the Great Hall, where the king receives his visitors. It can hold 10,000 people.

The tops of the pillars are carved in the shape of bulls.

Inside, the Great Hall is decorated with gold, silver, ivory and ebony (a dark wood).

Staircase covered with carvings

This man has brought a camel from Bactria.

An African carrying ivory

This Indian is carrying pots of gold dust.

A Babylonian with gifts of gold and silver bowls

A Mede shows people where to wait.

Guards

This man is from Elam. He has brought a lion cub for the king.

Visitors wait outside in the courtyard.

A Scythian brings cloth and a golden armlet.

Persian officials

Religion

The Persians followed the teachings of a prophet called Zarathustra (or Zoroaster), who taught that there was only one god. Fire was holy, and priests (called Magi) kept a sacred fire burning.

Priests carried twigs to feed the sacred fire.

The end of the Persian Empire

For many years, Persia was at war with Greece. The Persians won some battles, but were eventually beaten back. (You can find out more about these wars on page 155.)

After the death of Darius's son, King Xerxes I, the Empire grew weaker. In 331BC, Persia was conquered by Alexander the Great (see pages 160 and 161).

Important dates

c.1300BC	The Medes and the Persians settle down.
c.700-600BC	The kingdoms of Persia and Media are set up.
559-530BC	Cyrus II rules Persia.
550BC	Cyrus defeats the Medes.
522-486BC	Darius I rules Persia. The Empire is at its largest.
490-479BC	The Persians are at war with Greece.
486-465BC	Xerxes I rules Persia.
331-330BC	Persia is conquered by Alexander the Great. Persepolis is burned.

THE MIDDLE EAST

2000BC   1000BC   500BC   ADI   AD500

153

The Greeks at War

Map of Greece

EUROPE
ASIA
AFRICA

HELLESPONT
AEGEAN SEA
GREECE
Plataea
Marathon
Athens
Salamis
Olympia
Sparta
MEDITERRANEAN SEA

Soldiers and armies

All the city-states had their own army, and they were often at war with each other. Heavily armed foot soldiers, called hoplites, were the most important part of an army.

Spear
Horsehair crest
Bronze helmet
Shield of bronze, wood and leather
Bronze and leather breastplate
Sword
Bronze leg guard (called a greave)

A Greek hoplite ★

This picture shows a group of hoplites (foot soldiers) charging at the enemy.
★

Hoplites fight in closely packed rows. A block of soldiers is called a phalanx.

Flute music helps the men keep in step with each other.

Soldiers at the front lower their spears.

If this soldier is killed, the man behind him will take his place.

The soldiers are protected by a wall of overlapping shields.

After the Mycenaean civilization collapsed (see page 131), life in Greece was hard. People had to spend all their time growing food and forgot many of the skills they had learned, such as writing. This period of time is called the Greek Dark Ages.

★
Greek trading ship

From around 800BC, the Greeks began to trade with other lands and became richer. They lived in small city-states with their own rulers and customs. Each city-state was made up of a city and the farmland around it. The two most important states were Athens and Sparta.

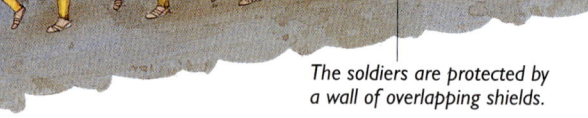

Sparta

The fiercest warriors in Greece came from Sparta. All Spartan men were full-time soldiers who spent their lives training and fighting. Boys were taken from their mothers at the age of seven to begin their training. Girls had to keep fit, too, so that they would have strong, healthy babies.

Bronze statue of a Spartan warrior
★

Statue of a Spartan girl in a running race

The first marathon

In 490BC, the Persians invaded Greece. The Greeks fought back and defeated them in a fierce battle at Marathon. A runner carried the good news over 32km (20 miles) to Athens, and then died of exhaustion. The modern marathon race is named after this famous event.

The first marathon runner

The Persians fight back

In 480BC, the Persians attacked again. They built a bridge of boats tied together with ropes, and crossed the stretch of water known as the Hellespont. Then, they marched into Greece and destroyed the city of Athens.

The Persian army crossing the Hellespont

Victory for Greece

The Greeks won a great sea battle near the island of Salamis. They trapped the Persian fleet in a narrow channel of water and wrecked over 200 Persian ships. The Greek army finally defeated the Persians in a huge land battle at Plataea.

This picture shows the sea battle between the Greeks and the Persians at Salamis.

A ship with three rows of oars is called a trireme. All the ships in this picture are triremes.

In a battle, the sail and mast are taken down and stored here.

This ship has been rammed and is sinking.

Each ship is rowed by 170 oarsmen.

The Persian ships are decorated with a dragon's head.

The ships are steered using two oars at the back.

Archers hide behind a row of shields.

Greek archer

Greek hoplites throw spears at the Persians.

A bronze ram smashes into the side of the Persian ship.

The Greek oarsmen row at full speed.

The painted eyes are meant to scare the enemy and help the ship see where it is going.

EUROPE

2000BC   1000BC   500BC   AD1   AD500

Life in Ancient Greece

Although the Greeks were almost always at war, they managed to create one of the greatest civilizations in history. The time from 500BC to 350BC is known as the Classical Period.

Life at home

While Greek men went out to work, shop and meet their friends, women stayed at home. They ran the household, looked after the children and supervised the slaves.

The house in this cutaway picture belongs to a rich Greek family.

This picture shows a dinner party in the andron (dining room).

★

Slaves serve the food.

Men wear a robe called a himation.

Musicians

Slices of roast wild boar

Wine mixed with water

Barley bread

Fried octopus

The roof is made of pottery tiles.

The women's room is called the gynaeceum.

★

The bedrooms are upstairs.

Wooden balcony

Well

Cobbled courtyard

The men eat in a room called the andron.

Each morning, the family meets for prayers around the altar.

The slaves are cooking dinner in the kitchen.

Bathroom with a terracotta bathtub

This picture shows women in the gynaeceum, where they spend most of their time.

★

Women weave tapestries to hang on the walls.

This girl is spinning wool.

Mirror

Jar of perfume

Women wear a robe called a chiton.

School

Boys from rich families started school when they were seven years old. They learned reading, writing, mathematics, music, poetry, athletics and dancing. Girls stayed at home and were taught by their mothers.

Vase painting of a boy learning to read

The Olympic Games

Athletics was a popular pastime for men in ancient Greece, and competitions were held all over the country. The most important was the Olympic Games. The Games were held every four years at Olympia, as part of a festival for Zeus, the king of the gods.

Discus thrower

The main events at the Olympic Games were running, jumping, boxing, wrestling, horse racing, chariot racing, discus and javelin throwing. In one race, men had to run wearing a bronze helmet and leg guards and carrying a heavy shield.

Athlete with helmet, shield and leg guards

Horse race

Drama

The first great plays in the world were written by the ancient Greeks. The plays were performed as part of religious festivals to please the gods. These festivals lasted several days and there was a prize for the best play.

This picture shows a play being performed.

★ Greek actors wore painted masks to show what sort of character they were playing.

A crane is used so that actors playing gods can fly through the air.

This wall has been painted with scenery for the play.

All the actors are men, but some of them are dressed as women.

An actor dressed as a bird

Padded costume

Stage

This circular area is called the orchestra.

A group of actors, known as the chorus, performs songs and dances to explain what is happening on stage.

The judges sit in special seats at the front.

This altar is used for offerings to Dionysus, the god of wine and pleasure.

The audience sits on stone seats built into the hillside.

EUROPE

2000BC   1000BC   500BC   AD1   AD500

The City of Athens

After the wars with Persia, the Greeks were afraid that the Persians might attack again. Led by the city of Athens, many of the Greek city-states joined forces to defend themselves, and Athens built up a strong navy.

★ Perikles

Trade in Athens increased, and the city became rich and powerful. Perikles, Athens' greatest leader, used this new wealth to rebuild the city.

This picture shows the marketplace (or agora) in the middle of Athens. ★

This is the temple of Athene, the goddess of wisdom and war. It is called the Parthenon.

Religious processions enter through this gateway.

This hill is called the Acropolis.

A road called the Sacred Way leads up to the Acropolis.

This building, called a stoa, contains shops. The shops sell gold, spices and silk cloth.

These slaves are for sale.

Men come to the agora to meet their friends.

Jugglers entertain the crowds.

Hot food is sold here.

People from other cities can change their money at the banker's table.

This man is selling wool and linen cloth.

Fruit and vegetable stall

An official checks the weight of some olives.

People come from all over Greece to buy Athenian pottery.

Meat is displayed on a marble slab to keep it cool.

Pottery lamps

Women come to get water from the fountain.

People buy honey to sweeten their food.

Olive oil for burning in lamps

Men usually do the shopping.

This farmer has brought eggs and cheese to sell.

Flowers for sale

EUROPE

| 10,000BC | 5000BC | | 4000BC | | 3000BC |

158

Power to the people

In Athens, all free men had a say in how the city was run. They met once every ten days to discuss new laws, and took decisions by voting. This type of government is called democracy, which means "rule by the people". Women, foreigners and slaves were not allowed to vote.

A politician making a speech to the men of Athens

Beautiful buildings

The Greeks built magnificent temples from gleaming white marble. Most temples had a triangular-shaped roof held up by rows of columns (pillars). All over the world, people have copied the style of Greek buildings.

Greek columns were built in three different styles.

★ Doric   ★ Ionic   ★ Corinthian

This is the Parthenon in Athens, a Greek temple which was built in the Doric style.

Science and learning

★ Plato

Greek thinkers asked themselves questions about how people should behave. Two of the most famous, Socrates and Plato, lived in Athens.

★ Socrates

Scientists tried to explain how the world worked. They studied plants, animals, the human body, the Sun and the stars.

One astronomer found out that the Earth moves around the Sun.

Scholars, such as Pythagoras, discovered rules that are still used in mathematics today.

Manuscript showing Pythagoras' ideas about triangles

A Greek called Herodotus wrote the first proper history book in the world. It was about the Persian Wars.

Herodotus interviewed survivors of the Persian Wars.

War with Sparta

Some of the Greek city-states grew worried that Athens had become too powerful and, in 431 BC, war broke out between Athens and Sparta. The other city-states joined in, and the war (called the Peloponnesian War) lasted 27 years. Athens was finally defeated, but all the city-states were left weak and exhausted.

Vase painting of Greek soldiers

EUROPE

| 2000BC | 1000BC | 500BC | AD1 | AD500 |

Alexander the Great

The Greek city-states kept on fighting each other even after the Peloponnesian War was over. They were too busy to see what was happening in the kingdom of Macedonia to the north.

★ King Philip II of Macedonia

The Macedonian king, Philip II, had built up a strong army of well-trained soldiers. He began to conquer the Greek city-states and, by 338BC, he controlled all of Greece. Soon after this, Philip was murdered and his 20-year-old son, Alexander, became king.

Alexander on his horse Bucephalus ★

Map of Alexander's Empire

■ Alexander's Empire at its largest
➡ Alexander's route

Alexander's conquests

Alexander was a brave soldier and a brilliant commander. He led his army on a journey of over 32,000km (almost 20,000 miles), creating the largest empire in the ancient world. Today, he is known as Alexander the Great.

Part of a mosaic showing Alexander in battle

1 Alexander attacked the port of Tyre, using rocks fired from catapults on boats. It took months to capture the city.

2 The Egyptians welcomed Alexander. At Siwa, a desert oasis, he was greeted as the son of the Egyptian god Amun.

3 The Persians were defeated by Alexander In 331BC. His army later captured the palace of Persepolis and set it on fire.

4 In India, Alexander defeated a king called Porus, whose army rode on hundreds of war elephants.

Alexandria

Alexander built new Greek-style cities all over his Empire and named many of them after himself. The most famous is Alexandria in Egypt. Scholars came to Alexandria from all over the Greek world to study and discuss new ideas. Many things were invented there, including the first lighthouse in the world.

This picture shows the lighthouse at Alexandria. ★

Statue of Zeus, king of the gods

The lighthouse, known as the Pharos, was one of the seven wonders of the ancient world.

A fire is kept burning at the top.

Bronze mirrors reflect the light. It can be seen 50km (30 miles) away.

Carts filled with wood for the fire are pulled up a ramp inside the lighthouse.

The second level has eight sides.

The first level has four sides.

Inside are rooms for the lighthouse workers and guards.

A causeway links the lighthouse to the mainland.

The base is built of massive stone blocks. The rest is made of marble.

A trading ship returning from the Black Sea

Alexander's death

Alexander had to return from India because his exhausted troops refused to go any farther. Soon after reaching Babylon, he caught a fever and died. He was just 33 years old.

Statue of Alexander wearing a lion skin ★

After Alexander

After Alexander's death, his generals fought each other for control of the Empire. Antigonas took Greece and Macedonia. Ptolemy won Egypt, where his family ruled for the next 300 years. The rest was taken by Seleucus and became known as the Seleucid Empire. In the end, all three kingdoms were conquered by the Romans.

Egyptian carving of Ptolemy

Important dates

c.1100-800BC	The Greek Dark Ages
c.776BC	The first Olympic Games
c.508BC	Democracy begins in Athens.
490-479BC	The Persian Wars
461-429BC	Perikles leads Athens.
447-438BC	The Parthenon is built.
431-404BC	The Peloponnesian War
338BC	Philip II of Macedonia takes control of Greece.
336-323BC	Alexander rules Greece and builds up his Empire.
323-281BC	Alexander's generals fight. The Empire splits up.
146BC	Greece becomes part of the Roman Empire.

EUROPE

2000BC   1000BC   500BC   AD1   AD500

Riders of the Plains

Among the many peoples who roamed across the plains of central Asia was a group of horsemen known as the Scythians. By around 700BC, they had moved into the land north of the Black Sea, conquering the people who lived there.

Scythian horseman

Map of the Scythian world

EUROPE

ASIA

AFRICA

BLACK SEA

GREECE

PERSIAN EMPIRE

MEDITERRANEAN SEA

Scythian lands

Areas where the Greeks settled

★ Scythians in battle

Bloody battles

Scythian warriors were skilled at fighting on horseback. They were excellent archers, but also fought with spears and battle-axes. After a battle, they used the skulls of their dead enemies to make drinking cups.

Life on the move

The Scythians bred horses and kept herds of cattle and sheep. They were nomadic people – always on the move, looking for grass where their animals could graze. They lived in tents which they could pack up and carry with them.

In this picture of a Scythian camp, one tent has been cut away to let you see inside.

This slave is an Assyrian soldier who was captured in battle.

This woman is cooking a beef stew.

The tents are made of felt.

The larger tents have two or three rooms inside.

This girl is doing embroidery.

Carved wooden table

The inside is lined with bright wall hangings.

Carpets and cushions make the tent comfortable.

Copper cooking pot

This woman is sewing felt shapes onto cloth to make a wall hanging.

This boy is drinking horse's milk.

Bowls are made of leather, clay or wood.

Dead and buried

When a Scythian chief died, he was buried with his most precious possessions under a huge mound (called a kurgan). A year later, 50 men and horses were killed and placed around the mound.

This scene shows the funeral procession of a Scythian chief.

A mound (or kurgan) like this will be built over the chief's tomb.

Golden comb from a Scythian tomb

The horses wear elaborate headdresses.

Golden harness

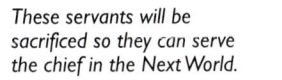
These servants will be sacrificed so they can serve the chief in the Next World.

The chief's horses will be killed and buried with him.

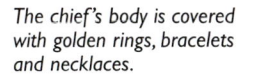
The chief's body is covered with golden rings, bracelets and necklaces.

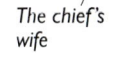
The chief's wife

People shave their heads and cut themselves to show their grief.

The men use horses to round up their cattle and sheep.

This boy is learning to use a bow and arrow.

In the winter, people wear warm clothes made of wool, fur, felt or leather.

Sheepskin coat

These men are going hunting for deer and hares.

Quiver containing arrows

This man is making leather from animal skins.

This man is making a new bow.

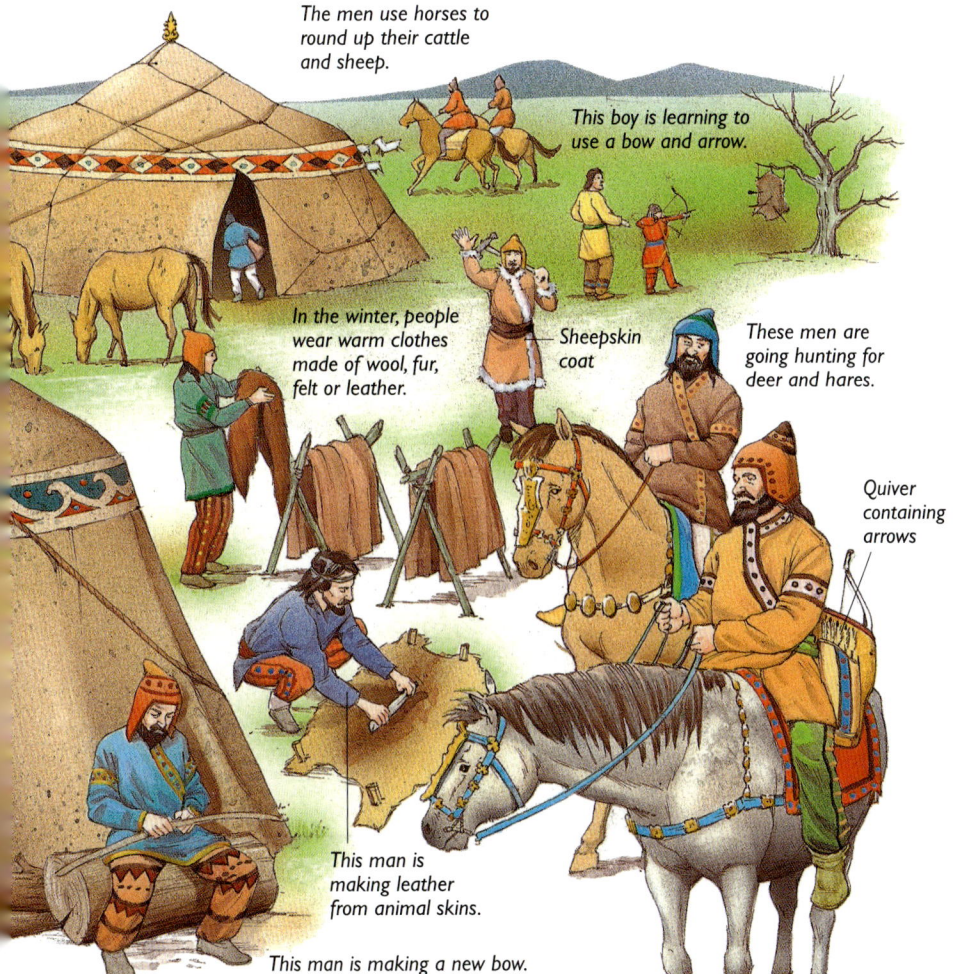

Wealth and weakness

The Scythians sold wheat grown by farmers whose lands they had conquered. They traded with the Greeks and bought precious metals from merchants in central Asia. They also taxed traders passing through their lands and became very rich.

Around 300BC, the Scythians' power began to weaken, and they were eventually conquered by King Mithridates who ruled the land south of the Black Sea.

Important dates

c.700-600BC	Scythian warriors raid nearby lands.
514BC	The Scythians fight off an attack by the Persians.
c.400-300BC	The Scythians are rich and successful.
110-106BC	The Scythians are defeated.

EUROPE

2000BC		500BC	ADI	AD500

The People of Early China

ASIA

Early Chinese pot

Yellow

Yangtze

YELLOW SEA

Area ruled by the Shang kings

Map of China

China is surrounded by mountains, deserts and seas, and for thousands of years it was cut off from the rest of the world. The way of life that grew up there was quite different from life anywhere else in the ancient world.

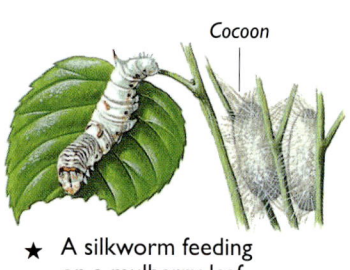

Cocoon

★ A silkworm feeding on a mulberry leaf

The cocoons are rinsed in hot water to loosen the threads.

A woman blows on the fire to keep it hot.

★ Unwinding thread from silk cocoons

Silk and silkworms

Silk thread is made by silkworms (a type of caterpillar), who spin it into cocoons to protect themselves while they turn into moths. The Chinese were the first to learn how to unwind the thread from the cocoons and spin it into fine silk cloth.

The first farmers

Around 7000BC, people began farming along the banks of the Yellow River. They grew millet (a type of grain), fruit, nuts and vegetables, and kept pigs, dogs and chickens. Along the Yangtze River, where it was warmer and wetter, people grew rice.

A farmer planting rice shoots

The first Chinese farmers built villages, used stone tools for working in the fields and made beautiful painted pots.

This picture shows an early Chinese ★ farming village. Part of one house has been cut away to let you see inside.

A ditch protects the village from wild animals.

These men have been out hunting and fishing.

Pig pen

Millet is stored in underground pits.

Village meeting house

A hole in the roof lets out smoke from the fire.

Thatched roof

The houses are built partly underground.

The walls are made of wood plastered with mud.

10,000BC   5000BC   4000BC   3000BC

The Shang kings

By around 1600BC, a large part of China was ruled by a family (or dynasty) of kings called the Shang. When a king died, he was buried in a huge pit filled with precious objects. People and animals were sacrificed and placed in the pit with him.

This scene shows the funeral ceremony of a Shang king. ★

These servants have been sacrificed so they can serve the king in the Next World.

Horses are led down a ramp into the burial pit.

The king's body

Bronze pots and carved jade ornaments

The king's chariot and horses are buried beside him.

After the ceremony, slaves will fill the pit with soil.

Kings and nobles

Around 1046BC, the Shang kings were conquered by people called the Zhou. The new Zhou kings allowed noble families to own land in return for their loyalty and help in times of war.

A Zhou noble in his war chariot

As the nobles became more powerful, the Zhou kings began to lose control. Nobles set up their own small kingdoms and fought each other constantly to try to win more land.

Confucius

A thinker called Kong Qiu (known in the West as Confucius) lived during this troubled time. He taught that war would only end when people knew the right way to behave. People should obey their rulers, and rulers should be kind to their people.

Confucius

Mastering metal

Craftworkers in Shang China learned how to make weapons and containers from bronze. People used elaborate bronze cauldrons to prepare food and wine for their dead ancestors, who they thought were gods.

Bronze cauldron

Writing on bones

Writing in China began around 1400BC. To help them tell the future, priests carved questions on bones called oracle bones. They heated the bones until they cracked, and then "read" the pattern made by the cracks to find the answers to their questions.

Early Chinese writing

★ Oracle bone

| 2000BC | | 1000BC | 500BC | ADI | AD500 |

THE FAR EAST

China's First Emperor

Qin Shi Huangdi

By around 480BC, China was made up of seven kingdoms which were constantly at war with each other. By 221BC, the kingdom of Qin (pronounced "chin") had conquered all the others, and the King of Qin controlled a huge empire. He called himself Qin Shi Huang, which means "First Emperor of China".

This picture shows part of the Great Wall of China.

The wall is 3460km (2150 miles) long.

Watchtower

A Chinese noble

The Great Wall of China

Qin Shi Huang had a massive wall built to protect his Empire from attacks by northern tribes (later called the Huns). The Great Wall was made by joining together smaller walls put up by earlier rulers. It has been strengthened since, and is still the biggest man-made structure in the world.

Controlling the nobles

To prevent nobles from rebelling against him, Qin Shi Huang forced them to move to the capital city, Xianyang, where he could keep an eye on them. Weapons belonging to the nobles' armies were taken away and melted down.

★ This scene shows the Great Wall being built.

Soldiers up here guard the workers from enemy attacks.

The top is paved with stones or bricks.

The wall is made of soil and rubble.

The outside is covered with stone slabs.

Scaffolding made of bamboo poles

Peasants and criminals are forced to work on the wall.

This man is supervising the work.

Basket of stones

If a worker dies, his body is built into the wall.

A low wall (or parapet) protects soldiers from enemy arrows.

People travel along the wall.

If enemies attack, a fire is lit on top of the tower to warn other soldiers.

10,000BC   5000BC   4000BC   3000BC

Map of China

- Empire of Qin Shi Huangdi
- The Great Wall

ASIA

Yellow

Xianyang

YELLOW SEA

Yangtze

Uniting the Empire

Qin Shi Huang built new roads and canals to link the different parts of his Empire. He also made everyone use the same type of coins and the same weights and measures. This made it much easier for people to trade with each other.

Chinese coins

To make sure that his orders could be understood by everyone, Qin Shi Huang introduced a standard form of writing throughout the Empire.

This Chinese symbol means "by order of the emperor".

Punishing protestors

Qin Shi Huang believed that people were evil and had to be forced to obey the law. Anyone who disobeyed was brutally punished. He ordered the burning of any books that did not agree with his ideas, and scholars who protested were thrown into a pit and buried alive.

This picture shows the burning of the books.

Scholars are thrown into a pit.

The terracotta army

When Qin Shi Huang died in 210BC, he was buried in a huge tomb guarded by an army of over 7,500 life-size model warriors. The warriors were made of terracotta (a type of pottery) and carried real weapons. It is said that crossbows were set to fire automatically at anyone who tried to break into the tomb.

Terracotta warriors standing guard around the emperor's tomb

The face of each warrior is different.

THE FAR EAST

| 2000BC | | 1000BC | 500BC | ADI | AD500 |

The Han Dynasty

Soon after the first emperor died, rebellions broke out and the Empire collapsed. In 202BC, a soldier called Liu Bang took control of the country and made himself emperor. He was the first of a dynasty (family) of emperors called the Han, who ruled China for the next 400 years.

Wooden model of a Han noble

Official business

An official with his attendants

The Han emperors had lots of officials to help them run their Empire. The officials collected taxes, looked after roads and canals, and made sure that everyone obeyed the law.

Tough tests

Anyone who wanted to be an official had to take exams. People were asked questions on ancient poetry and the teachings of the thinker Confucius.

Officials taking an exam

This scene shows part of Ch'ang-an, the capital city of the early Han emperors.

★

Watchtower

This house belongs to a rich noble.

Tiled roof

A procession of court officials

The wooden walls are painted with lacquer to make them waterproof.

The sloping roof keeps rain off the walls.

Traders sell food at market stalls.

Officials make sure that traders charge fair prices.

Rich people are sometimes carried around in a litter.

The noble and his family relax in the garden.

In the winter, the windows are covered with waxed paper.

Acrobats

Goldfish pond

This farmer has brought pigs and geese to sell at the market.

Important officials travel in horse-drawn carriages.

THE FAR EAST

10,000BC   5000BC   4000BC   3000BC

168

The Silk Road

Around 130BC, Chinese merchants began to travel across Asia to trade with merchants in the West. Camels carried Chinese silk, spices and precious stones along a route known as the Silk Road, which stretched all the way from China to the Mediterranean Sea.

★ Chinese silk banner

Map of China

Tombs and treasure

Han tombs were filled with everything the dead person might need in the Next World, such as clothes, food, medicines, cups and bowls. One prince and his wife were buried in suits made of jade (a hard, green stone). People thought this would stop the bodies from rotting away.

Wooden bowl covered with shiny lacquer

The jade burial suit of Princess Tou Wan

The suit is made from over 2,000 pieces of polished jade linked together with gold wire.

Wars and quarrels

The Han emperors fought to defend the Empire against tribes of Huns from the north, and eventually defeated them. The Huns gave up attacking China and moved away to the west.

However, quarrels between the royal family and their courtiers weakened the power of the emperor. In AD220, the last Han emperor gave up his throne, and the Empire fell apart.

Important dates

c.7000BC	Farming begins in China.
c.4000BC	Rice farming begins.
c.2700BC	Silk making begins.
1600-1046BC	The Shang dynasty
c.1400BC	Writing on oracle bones
1046-221BC	The Zhou dynasty
c.722-481BC	The Zhou kings lose power. The nobles fight each other.
551BC	Confucius is born.
481-221BC	Seven kingdoms are at war (the Warring States Period).
221-210BC	Qin Shi Huang rules as China's first emperor.
202BC-AD220	The Han dynasty
c.AD1-100	Buddhism spreads from India (see page 174).
c.AD100	Paper is invented.

Inventions

The Chinese were the first people to make paper. They dipped a bamboo screen into a mixture of pulped tree bark, plants and rags. A thin layer of pulp was left to dry on the screen.

Making paper ★

Bamboo screen

Pulp

Chinese scientists invented many other things that are still used today, such as the compass, the wheelbarrow, and the ship's rudder (used for steering).

If the earth shakes, a ball falls into the toad's mouth, showing the direction of the earthquake.

Chinese machine for detecting earthquakes ★

THE FAR EAST

The People of Ancient Japan

★ Jomon vase

From around 14000BC to 1000BC, the people of Japan lived by hunting, fishing and collecting nuts and berries to eat. There was so much food around that they did not think of farming. This long period of time is called the Jōmon Period.

Map of Japan

ASIA

SEA OF JAPAN

JAPAN

PACIFIC OCEAN

■ Yamato area where the first emperors lived

Tombs and warriors

The early emperors were buried in stone tombs under enormous keyhole-shaped mounds of earth. Small clay models of warriors were placed around the mound to guard it.

This picture shows the tomb of an emperor.

The keyhole-shaped burial mound is 485m (1590ft) long.

This picture shows a typical Jōmon village. ★

The thatched walls of the houses are held up by branches.

These hunters have caught a wild boar.

This girl is collecting shellfish.

This man is trying to catch a tuna fish.

Gateway

The mound is surrounded by water.

This woman is coiling strips of clay to make a pot.

People wear animal skins.

This woman is cooking dinner.

Fishbones and old shells are thrown in a heap.

★ Tomb model (or haniwa) of a Yamato warrior

New skills

Bronze bell

Around 1000BC, settlers moved to Japan from the mainland of Asia. They brought new skills with them, such as rice farming and metalworking, and lived in groups each ruled by a chieftain.

The first emperors

From around 250BC, one group gradually gained power over the rest, until they became the first emperors of Japan. They ruled from a central area called Yamato. During their rule, many new ideas, such as writing, were brought over from China.

The Japanese believed their emperors were descended from the Sun Goddess.

Important dates

c.14000–1000BC	People hunt and fish for food (the Jōmon Period).
c.1000BC–AD250	Rice farming and metalworking begin (the Yayoi Period).
c.AD250–500	Emperors take control of central Japan.
c.AD450	Writing is introduced from China.

QUICKLINKS: For links to websites with virtual tours of Petra, an ancient city carved out of rock, go to **usborne.com/Quicklinks**

The Riches of Arabia

The deserts of Arabia are among the hottest and driest places on earth. Only a few people lived there, roaming around from one water hole to another.

Desert people lived in tents.

Around 1000BC, people learned how to tame camels, which meant they could travel farther across the desert.

Camels can travel for up to eight days without water.

Kingdoms of the south

Along the south coast of Arabia, where there was more rain, rich kingdoms grew up. The most famous is Sabaea. Its capital city, Marib, had a huge dam to control the water supply.

The Bible tells how the Queen of Sabaea (or Sheba) visited King Solomon of Israel.

Map of Arabia

Trade route

Sweet smells

In the southern kingdoms, two special types of bushes grew. Their sap was used to make frankincense and myrrh (types of sweet-smelling incense).

Collecting sap to make incense

Incense was burned in religious ceremonies all over the ancient world as an offering to the gods. It was also used to make perfumes and medicines.

An Egyptian priest burning incense

Arab traders with their camels

Routes to riches

Merchants from India brought spices and jewels to ports on the south coast of Arabia. Arab traders carried these goods to Egypt or the Mediterranean, and sold them at a great price.

The city of Petra

At the northern end of the trade routes was the kingdom of Nabataea. Its capital city, Petra, was built in a narrow valley surrounded by rocky cliffs.

This is the treasury in Petra, which is carved out of solid rock.

Important dates

c.1000BC	The Arabs tame camels.
c.500BC-AD100	Sabaea is at its most powerful.
c.100BC-AD106	Nabataea is rich and powerful.

THE MIDDLE EAST

ARABS				
2000BC	1000BC	500BC	AD1	AD500

171

Life in Ancient Africa

Kushite pots

Thousands of years ago, the Sahara Desert was an area of grassland and lakes. The people who lived there hunted wild cattle, giraffes, rhinos and hippos. Then, around 6000BC, the Saharan people learned how to tame animals and began to herd cattle rather than hunt them.

Saharan rock painting of herdsmen with their cattle ★

Map of Africa

- ■ Area where the Nok people lived
- → Route of the Bantu people

By 3400BC, dry weather had turned the grassland into desert. The Sahara Desert split Africa in two, and life north of the Sahara developed very differently from life in the south.

The kingdom of Kush

For hundreds of years, the kingdom of Kush in the Nile Valley was ruled by the Egyptians. Around 1000BC, the Kushites broke free and later went on to conquer Egypt themselves.

Egyptian picture of a Kushite prisoner of war

Until around 590BC, the capital city of Kush was at Napata. Then, a new capital was built at Meroë where there was better farmland. The people of Meroë mined iron, which they used to make weapons and tools. They grew rich by trading with India and the lands around the Mediterranean.

The kings and queens of Meroë were buried under steep-sided pyramids. ★

Nok sculptors made life-size pottery heads. ★

The Nok people

By around 500BC, the Nok people of West Africa had learned how to use iron. They melted it down in clay furnaces and shaped it into strong tools. These tools helped them to become successful farmers.

This picture shows Nok people using a furnace. ★

Inside are layers of iron ore and charcoal for fuel.

Liquid iron collects in a pit under the furnace.

Bellows pump air inside to keep the furnace hot.

Air pipe

AFRICA

| 10,000BC | 5000BC | 4000BC | 3000BC |

The spread of farming

Most Africans south of the Sahara hunted wild animals and gathered plants to eat, but the Bantu tribes of West Africa were farmers. Thousands of years ago they began to move south and east looking for new land. By AD500, they had reached the southern tip of Africa, and farming had spread to most of the continent.

A cutaway picture of a Bantu house ★

The inside is plastered with clay.

This man is making farming tools from iron.

Framework of wooden poles

Layers of clay and thatched grass

The floor is raised on wooden logs.

Doorway

The riches of Axum

Around AD100, the kingdom of Axum grew up on the Red Sea coast. Axum became rich by trading with Arabia, India and parts of the Roman Empire. Merchants from other lands stopped at the port of Adulis on their way to and from India.

This scene shows merchants at the port of Adulis.

A ship loaded with spices from India

These monkeys will be taken abroad and sold as pets.

Frankincense and myrrh from Arabia

African slaves for sale

This Axumite merchant is selling African ivory, gold and emeralds.

Cloth from the Roman Empire

Jars of wine and oil from Rome

Standing stones

The kings of Axum used some of their wealth to build magnificent palaces and tall stone towers. Each tower marked the tomb of a king.

★

The huge tower shown here was carved from a single block of stone.

A Christian king

Around AD320, missionaries brought the Christian religion to Axum, and King Ezana of Axum became the first Christian king in Africa. (See pages 192 and 193 for more about Christianity.)

Axumite gold coin ★

The cross is used as a Christian symbol.

Important dates

c.6000BC	People in the Sahara tame cattle.
c.3400BC	The Sahara grasslands have turned to desert.
c.1600-1000BC	The kingdom of Kush is ruled by Egypt.
c.750-664BC	Kushite kings conquer and rule Egypt.
c.590BC	Meroë becomes the capital city of Kush.
c.500BC-AD200	The Nok people are at their most successful.
c.AD500	The Bantu people have spread through Africa.
c.AD100-700	The kingdom of Axum is rich and powerful.
c.AD330-350	King Ezana rules Axum.

AFRICA

The Ideas of India

Around 1500BC, groups of settlers began to arrive in the Indus Valley (in modern Pakistan). Gradually, they spread out across northern India and settled down. This was the start of an era known as the Vedic period.

From hymns to Hinduism

Vedic priests sang hymns to their many gods. Hymns were passed on by word of mouth as the people had no writing. Many years later, they were written down in holy books called the Vedas. These writings became very important in the Hindu religion, which is the main religion in India today.

★ Shiva the destroyer, one of the many Hindu gods

A class of their own

People were divided into different classes according to their jobs. Later, children always belonged to the same class as their parents. This way of grouping people was known as the caste system.

Priests and scholars

Warriors and kings

Merchants and farmers

Workers

★ The four main groups in the caste system

Siddhartha in his chariot

The beginning of Buddhism

The Buddhist religion was started by an Indian prince called Siddhartha Gautama. One day, when he was out riding in his chariot, Siddhartha came across sickness, old age and death for the first time.

Siddhartha was very upset by what he saw and decided to find a way to escape suffering and live in peace. He left his palace and became a wandering holy man.

Siddhartha as a holy man

After many years, Siddhartha realized that people suffer because they want things and only care about themselves. Because of this understanding, he became known as the Buddha, which means the "enlightened one". People listened to the Buddha teaching, and his ideas spread.

★ Statue of the Buddha's head

Indian war elephants

Map of India

INDIA

Indus

Ganges

• Sanchi

• Ajanta

ARABIAN SEA

BAY OF BENGAL

ASIA

AFRICA

■ Maurya Empire at its largest

The Maurya Empire

By 500BC, northern India was made up of many small kingdoms. In 321BC, a warrior named Chandragupta Maurya seized one of these kingdoms and went on to conquer most of India, creating the Maurya Empire. The Empire was at its largest under Chandragupta's grandson, Ashoka.

A Buddhist emperor

For 11 years, Ashoka fought to make his Empire bigger. Then, in one battle, so many people were killed that he decided to become a Buddhist and give up fighting. Ashoka promised to rule his people with kindness, and had his promises carved on stone pillars all over his Empire.

★ These lions decorated the top of one of Ashoka's pillars.

Painting and poetry

After Ashoka's death, the Empire grew weaker, and in the end it split up. India was not united again until AD320, when a new family of emperors called the Guptas took over.

The Gupta Empire is famous for its beautiful painting and sculpture. Classical Indian music and dance developed during this time, and the poet Kalidasa wrote about nature and love.

Part of a wall painting from the Buddhist cave temples at Ajanta

During Ashoka's rule, many Buddhist monasteries and monuments were built. Huge stone domes, called stupas, were built at places connected with the Buddha's life.

The Great Stupa at Sanchi ★

Buddhist monks   Gateway   Carvings show scenes from the Buddha's life.   Stone railing

Important dates

c.1500-600BC	The Vedic period.
c.560-480BC	Siddhartha Gautama (the Buddha) lives.
327-325BC	Alexander the Great tries to conquer north India (see pages 160 and 161).
321BC	Chandragupta Maurya sets up the Maurya Empire.
272-231BC	Ashoka is emperor.
185BC	The Maurya Empire collapses.
AD320-535	The Gupta Empire

SOUTH ASIA

2000BC	1000BC	500BC	AD1	AD500

The First North Americans

People first arrived in North America at least 15,000 years ago, and probably much earlier. At that time, a large part of the Earth was covered in ice and snow. America and Asia were joined by a bridge of land and ice. The first North Americans walked across from Asia or followed the coast.

Hunting a mammoth

At first, people roamed around hunting large animals, such as mammoths, horses and bison, but by 8000BC most of these animals had died out. Hunters had to find smaller animals, and relied more on picking wild plants to eat.

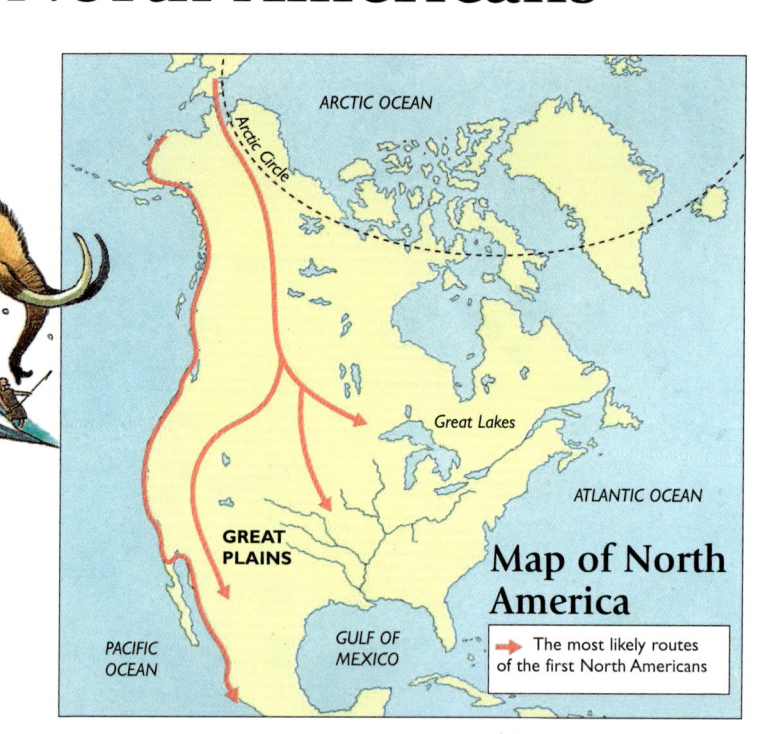

Map of North America

The most likely routes of the first North Americans

Plums

Rosehips

A prickly pear

A gourd

Wild plants

People spread out across the plains, woodlands, mountains, deserts and icy wastes of North America. They began to settle down, and a different way of life grew up in each of these areas.

These men are cutting up a dead bison.

★ This picture shows people of the Great Plains hunting bison.

Hunters of the Plains

Bison were one of the few large animals that did not die out, and the people of the Great Plains hunted them for their meat and skins. The skins were scraped clean and made into clothes and tents.

Scraping a bison skin

This man has just thrown his spear.

Some bison are killed with spears.

The hunters are disguised as wolves.

The bison are being chased over the edge of a cliff.

NORTH AMERICA

10,000BC   5000BC   4000BC

Ivory knife used for cutting snow

QUICKLINKS: For links to websites about peoples of North America and where they settled, go to **usborne.com/Quicklinks**

Hunters of the Arctic

The people who settled in the far north had to survive in the freezing lands of the Arctic. They caught fish, and hunted walrus and seals. In winter, they used blocks of snow to build shelters called igloos.

A cutaway picture of an igloo ★

Clear ice window

Blocks of solid snow stuck together with softer snow

This tunnel stops cold air from getting inside.

Wooden sled

Desert peoples

In the deserts of the southwest, people lived by hunting small animals and collecting nuts, seeds and wild fruits. Later, some people learned to grow corn, beans and squashes.

This scene shows a group of desert people known as the Basketmakers. ★

This boy is picking fruit from a cactus plant.

Baskets for carrying water are lined with gum from plants.

Babies are carried in backpacks called cradleboards.

This woman is weaving a basket from twigs.

The houses are built partly underground.

These men have caught some rabbits.

Woodland peoples

In the eastern woodlands along the Ohio River, people hunted deer, caught fish and collected berries. They also grew plants, such as beans, gourds and sunflowers. This way of life is known as the Adena culture.

A cutaway picture of an Adena house ★

Smoke hole

Bark roof

The walls are made of twigs woven together.

The Adena culture, and the Hopewell culture that came after, are famous for the huge earth mounds they built. Some of the mounds were pyramid-shaped, but others were shaped like animals.

The Great Serpent Mound is 217m (712ft) long.

The Hopewell culture traded with other peoples from the Great Lakes to the Gulf of Mexico, bringing back copper, shells and alligator teeth, which were used to make necklaces and ornaments.

Carved copper bird

Important dates

c.15,000-8000BC	Early North Americans hunt large animals.
c.8000-1000BC	People spread out and learn new ways of life.
c.2500BC	People settle in the Arctic.
c.500BC-AD100	The Adena culture
c.100BC-AD500	The Hopewell culture
c.AD50-500	Late Basketmakers

2000BC   1000BC   500BC   ADI   AD500

NORTH AMERICA

SOUTH AMERICA: c.2000BC–AD500

QUICKLINKS: For links to websites where you can examine amazing artifacts made by the people of ancient Peru, go to **usborne.com/Quicklinks**

The People of Ancient Peru

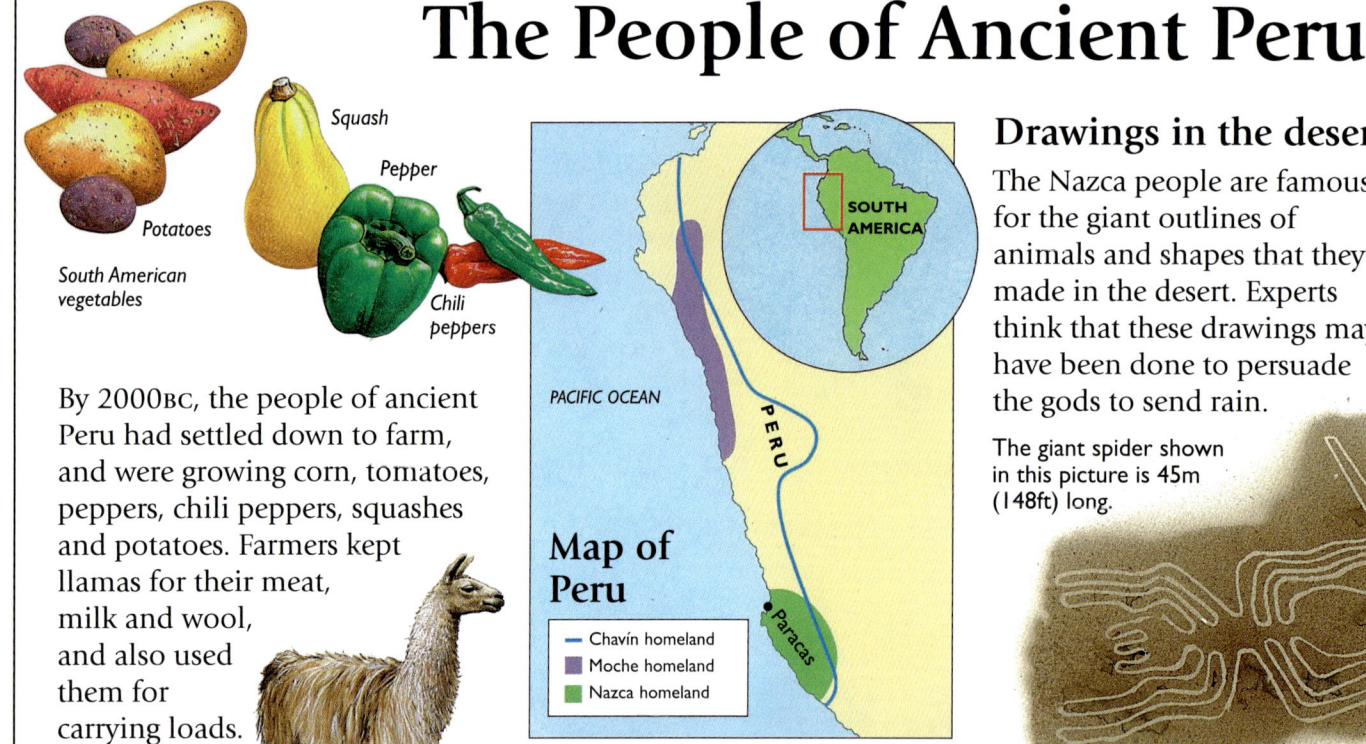

South American vegetables

Squash

Pepper

Chili peppers

Potatoes

By 2000BC, the people of ancient Peru had settled down to farm, and were growing corn, tomatoes, peppers, chili peppers, squashes and potatoes. Farmers kept llamas for their meat, milk and wool, and also used them for carrying loads.

Llama

PACIFIC OCEAN

PERU

Map of Peru

— Chavín homeland
— Moche homeland
— Nazca homeland

Paracas

SOUTH AMERICA

Drawings in the desert

The Nazca people are famous for the giant outlines of animals and shapes that they made in the desert. Experts think that these drawings may have been done to persuade the gods to send rain.

The giant spider shown in this picture is 45m (148ft) long.

Gods and gold

Around 900BC, the Chavín people created the first civilization in South America. They were skilled stoneworkers and built huge temples filled with sculptures and carvings of their snarling, animal-like gods. The Chavín were also the first people in the Americas to make things from gold.

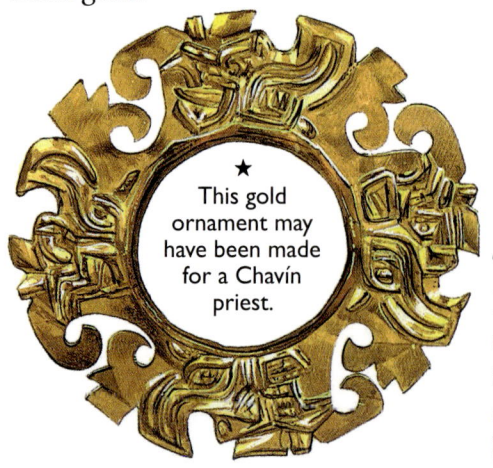

★ This gold ornament may have been made for a Chavín priest.

Cloth pictures

★ Paracas embroidery

The Paracas people of southern Peru were skilled at weaving and embroidery. When someone died, the body was placed in a basket and was wrapped in layers of beautifully embroidered cloth.

Priests and pottery

In the north, the Moche people were ruled by powerful warrior-priests. They conquered nearby tribes, and often sacrificed prisoners of war to their gods. The Moche are famous for making pots in human shapes.

A pot in the shape of a ★ Moche warrior

Important dates

c.2000BC	The people of Peru first grow corn.
c.900-250BC	The Chavín people
c.800-100BC	The Paracas people
c.100BC-AD800	The Nazca people
c.AD100-800	The Moche people

THE AMERICAS

10,000BC   5000BC   4000BC   3000BC

QUICKLINKS: For links to websites where you can see giant Olmec stone heads and other artifacts, go to **usborne.com/Quicklinks**

Corn plant

The Olmecs

The Olmecs lived on a swampy plain beside the Gulf of Mexico. They had no farm animals to provide them with meat, so growing crops was very important. Corn was the main crop, but farmers also grew beans, squashes, chili peppers and avocados.

Gods and games

By around 1200BC, the Olmecs had begun building a series of temples to their gods at a place called San Lorenzo. Later, San Lorenzo was destroyed and a new place of worship was built at La Venta.

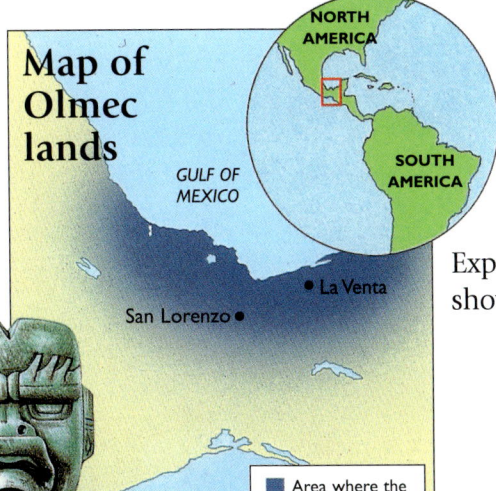

Map of Olmec lands

NORTH AMERICA

SOUTH AMERICA

GULF OF MEXICO

La Venta

San Lorenzo

PACIFIC OCEAN

■ Area where the Olmecs lived

★ Carving of the Olmecs' jaguar god

Huge heads

The Olmecs are best known for the massive stone heads that they carved. Some of these are almost 3m (10ft) high. Experts think that the heads may show different Olmec rulers.

This huge stone head was carved from a single block of stone.

This picture shows a religious ceremony at La Venta.

Some experts think this mosaic shows the face of the jaguar god.

The mosaic has just been finished.

Priest

Blocks of green stone

Blue clay

The mosaic is buried immediately, because it is too holy to look at.

As part of their religion, the Olmecs played a sacred ball game. Players used a hard rubber ball and wore helmets to protect their heads. Some of the players may have been sacrificed at the end of the game.

Olmec ball-players

★

The end of the Olmecs

Around 400BC, the temples at La Venta were abandoned. The Olmecs died out, but their way of life influenced many of the people who came after them (see pages 180 and 181).

Important dates

c.1200BC San Lorenzo is built.
c.900BC San Lorenzo is destroyed.
c.400BC La Venta is abandoned.

THE AMERICAS

Ancient Cities of the Americas

The city of Teotihuacán (in modern Mexico) was the biggest ancient city in the Americas. People began building it around 100BC, and by AD500 it was the sixth largest city in the world.

In the middle of Teotihuacán was the Citadel, where the rulers of the city lived in splendid palaces. Most other people lived in large apartment buildings, which had room for several families.

The rain god of Teotihuacán

Crafts

Craftworkers in Teotihuacán shaped pots and figures from clay, carved ornaments from polished stones and shells, and made tools and weapons from obsidian (a hard glassy rock).

Clay figure from Teotihuacán ★

Trade

Teotihuacán was an important trading city. In the marketplace, merchants traded pottery and obsidian tools for seashells, sweet-smelling incense and the beautiful tail feathers of the quetzal bird. The feathers were used to decorate the clothes of rich people.

Quetzal bird

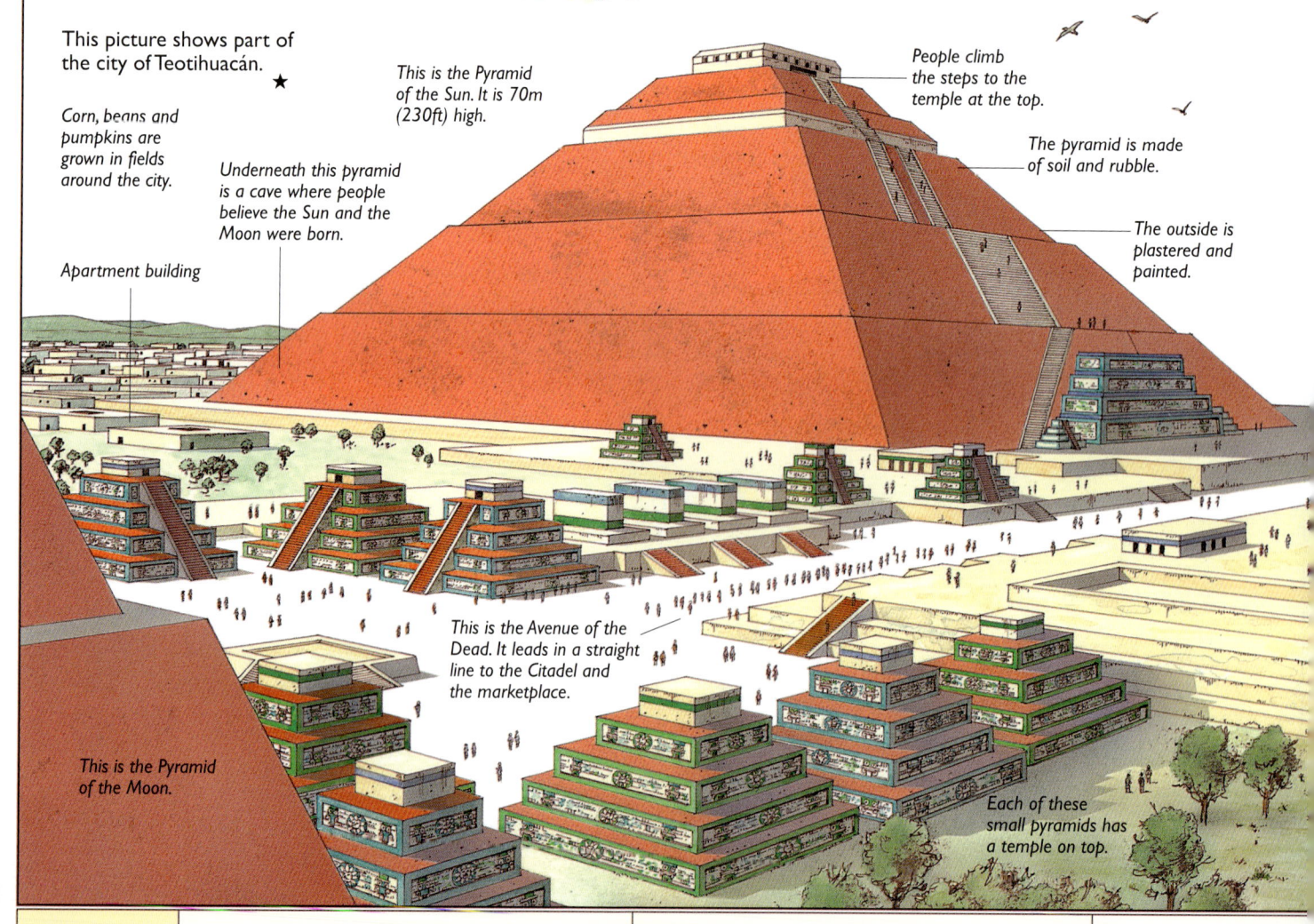

This picture shows part of the city of Teotihuacán. ★

Corn, beans and pumpkins are grown in fields around the city.

Underneath this pyramid is a cave where people believe the Sun and the Moon were born.

This is the Pyramid of the Sun. It is 70m (230ft) high.

People from all over Central America come to worship at the city's temples.

People climb the steps to the temple at the top.

The pyramid is made of soil and rubble.

The outside is plastered and painted.

Apartment building

This is the Avenue of the Dead. It leads in a straight line to the Citadel and the marketplace.

This is the Pyramid of the Moon.

Each of these small pyramids has a temple on top.

10,000BC	5000BC		4000BC	3000BC

Cities in the jungle

The spectacular stone cities of the Maya people lay deep in the Central American rainforest. Mayan cities were built around a complex of squares, temples, palaces and ball courts (where people played a sacred ball game). The buildings were covered in carvings of Mayan gods and kings.

These men are carving a giant stone pillar.

Map of Central America

Land of the Maya

NORTH AMERICA
SOUTH AMERICA
GULF OF MEXICO
Teotihuacán
MEXICO
• Palenque
PACIFIC OCEAN

This is the Temple of Inscriptions in the Mayan city of Palenque.

Words and numbers

The Maya invented a writing system using picture signs (or glyphs) and wrote in books made of bark paper. Experts are just beginning to understand what this writing means.

Part of a Mayan book

Zero   One   Five

The Maya used three symbols to write all the numbers. They were using the number "zero" hundreds of years before anyone else thought of the idea.

Twelve

Blood, war and sacrifice

The Maya had many gods, and thought they could please them by making offerings of human blood. One way of doing this was to pull a string of thorns through a hole in the tongue.

Carving of a queen offering blood ★

The kings of the different Mayan cities were often at war with each other. They fought for power and riches, and took prisoners to sacrifice to their gods.

Feather headdress
Jaguar skin
★ *Mayan warrior*

Important dates

c.300BC   The Maya begin building stone cities.

c.100BC–AD250   Teotihuacán is built.

c.AD250-900   The Maya are at their most successful.

c.AD500   Teotihuacán is rich and powerful.

c.AD750   Teotihuacán is destroyed in a fire.

THE AMERICAS

2000BC   1000BC   500BC   AD1   AD500

The Celtic Tribes

The people known as Celts were made up of many different tribes, but they all had a similar language and way of life. This way of life had grown up near a place called Hallstatt (in modern Austria) by around 800BC.

The Celts gradually spread out across most of Europe, settling in the lands they conquered. One group even settled as far away as Asia Minor (modern Turkey).

Celtic statue of a boar, a symbol of strength

Map of the Celtic world

- ■ Celtic homeland
- ■ Areas where the Celts settled

EUROPE · ASIA · AFRICA

IRELAND · BRITAIN · GAUL · Hallstatt

ATLANTIC OCEAN · BLACK SEA

Rome · ASIA MINOR

MEDITERRANEAN SEA · Delphi

Life at home

Wherever the Celts settled, they set up farms and small villages. Their houses were built of wood or stone and had one big room inside, where the family cooked, ate and slept.

This cutaway picture shows a typical Celtic house. ★

Thatched roof

The house is built around a frame of wooden posts.

Wool is woven into brightly patterned cloth.

This woman is cooking a wild boar stew.

This girl is grinding grain to make flour.

Jar of grain

Barrel of beer

The walls are made from wattle-and-daub (twigs covered with mud and straw).

Straw mattress

Iron cooking pot

Celtic crafts

The Celts were highly skilled metalworkers. They used iron to make strong weapons and tools, and created beautiful objects from bronze, silver and gold.

A gold neckband, called a torc ★

This bronze shield was found in the Thames in London. ★

Barrel for catching rainwater

This man is chopping wood for the fire.

The skull of a dead enemy

Animal skins are hung across the doorway to keep out the cold.

These boys are playing with dice.

Forts and fighting

The Celts were fierce warriors and their tribes often fought each other. They built large hilltop forts to protect their women, children and animals from attacks by enemies.

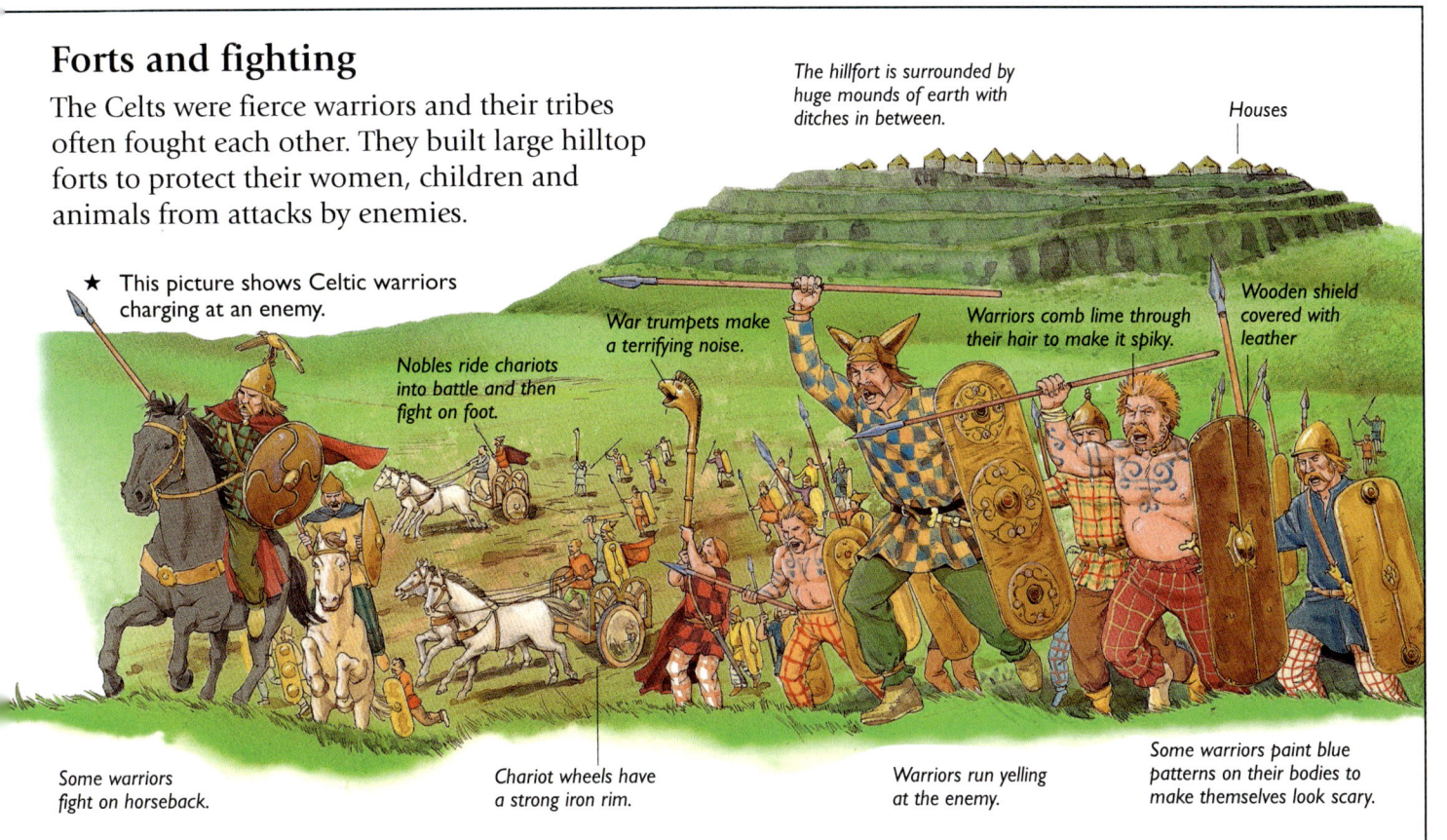

The hillfort is surrounded by huge mounds of earth with ditches in between.

Houses

★ This picture shows Celtic warriors charging at an enemy.

War trumpets make a terrifying noise.

Nobles ride chariots into battle and then fight on foot.

Warriors comb lime through their hair to make it spiky.

Wooden shield covered with leather

Some warriors fight on horseback.

Chariot wheels have a strong iron rim.

Warriors run yelling at the enemy.

Some warriors paint blue patterns on their bodies to make themselves look scary.

Feasts

Warriors held great feasts to celebrate their victories in battle. They were entertained by poet-musicians, called bards, who recited poems about the brave deeds of Celtic heroes.

A Celtic feast

A bard chanting a poem

Harp

This is the chieftain (leader) of the tribe.

Flagon of wine

A pig roasting on a spit

Religion

A druid dropping a sword into a sacred pool

The Celts believed that some of their gods lived in streams, rocks and trees. Priests, called druids, threw precious objects into rivers and lakes as gifts to the gods. Sometimes, they sacrificed animals or humans.

Roman conquerors

As the Roman Empire grew, the Celts fought hard to defend their lands. However, they were no match for the mighty Roman army, and in the end most of them were conquered. The Celtic way of life only survived in Ireland and in remote parts of Scotland and Wales.

Important dates

c.800BC The Celtic way of life first appears.

c.390BC The Celts destroy part of Rome.

c.279BC The Celts attack and rob the Greek temple at Delphi.

c.278BC The Celts reach Asia Minor.

58-51BC The Roman general Julius Caesar conquers the Celts in Gaul (modern France).

AD43 The Romans invade Britain.

EUROPE

2000BC   1000BC   500BC   AD1   AD500

The Rise of Rome

The city of Rome began as a small farming village by a river called the Tiber. As time passed, more villages were built and eventually they joined together to form a city.

An early village in the Tiber Valley

The story of Romulus

According to a Roman legend, the city was set up by a man named Romulus. As babies, he and his twin brother Remus had been left to die near the Tiber. They were found by a wolf, who fed them until they were rescued by a shepherd.

★

Statue of the wolf feeding Romulus and Remus

When the twins grew up, they decided to build a city on the banks of the Tiber, but they had a violent quarrel. Romulus killed his brother and named the city after himself. Tradition says this happened in 753BC.

Map of the Roman Republic

SPAIN
Carthago Nova
NORTH AFRICA
CORSICA
SARDINIA
MEDITERRANEAN SEA
ITALY
Rome
Carthage
SICILY
EUROPE
ASIA
AFRICA

■ Roman lands in 218BC
■ Carthaginian lands in 218BC
→ Hannibal's route

The Roman Republic

Until around 509BC, Rome was ruled by kings. Then, the last king was driven out of the city and Rome became a republic. The Roman Republic was ruled by the Senate, a group of men (called senators) who came from the city's most important families. Led by the Senate, the Romans gradually conquered all of Italy.

Coin showing the Senate House

This picture shows a meeting of the Senate. Part of the seating has been cut away.

Senators wear a toga (robe) with a purple stripe.

Each year, some senators are chosen by the people to do special jobs.

This senator organizes entertainment, such as chariot races. He is very popular.

★

This senator is a judge. He is making a speech about a new law.

Guard

These two men are in charge of the Senate this year. They are called consuls.

Conquering Carthage

In 264BC, a series of wars broke out between the Romans and the people of Carthage in North Africa. Both sides fought fiercely over who should control trade around the Mediterranean Sea.

The Carthaginians invaded Italy ★ in 218BC. This picture shows them crossing the Alps.

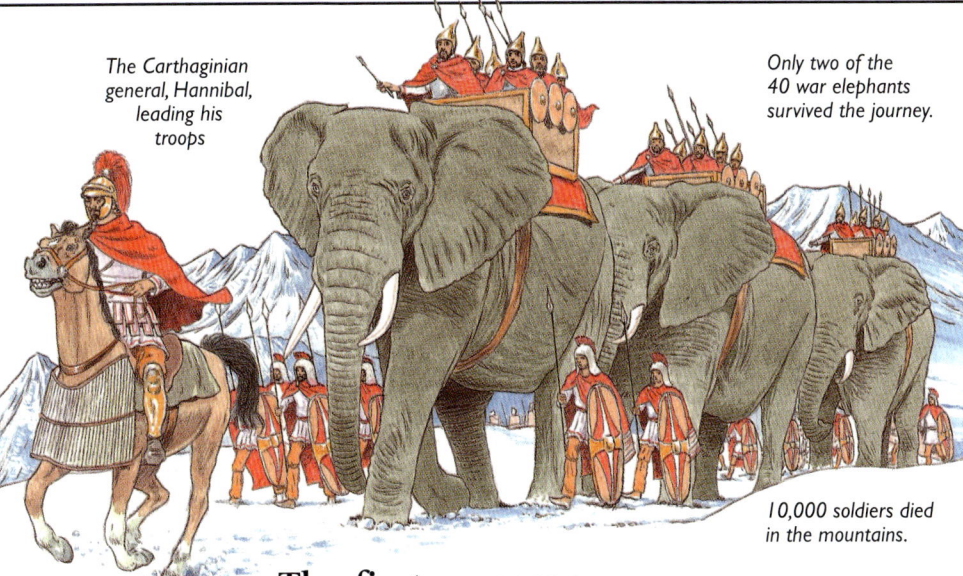

The Carthaginian general, Hannibal, leading his troops

Only two of the 40 war elephants survived the journey.

10,000 soldiers died in the mountains.

The wars between Rome and Carthage are known as the Punic Wars. They ended in 146BC when Carthage was completely destroyed. The Romans took over the Carthaginian lands and went on to conquer all the kingdoms around the Mediterranean.

The first emperor

After Julius Caesar died, there were more struggles for power. In 31BC, Caesar's great-nephew, Octavian, defeated his rival, Mark Antony, and won control of Rome. Octavian took the name Augustus, which means "respected one". He became Rome's first emperor.

Blazing buildings and boats in the port at Carthage

Statue of the Emperor Augustus ★

Augustus is shown wearing the uniform of a Roman general.

Julius Caesar

As the Romans won more land, the senators argued over how things should be run. Rival groups of senators used the army to help them fight for power. In 49BC, a general called Julius Caesar marched with his army to Rome and seized power. Caesar brought peace, but some senators grew worried that he planned to make himself king, so they stabbed him to death.

Julius Caesar

★

EUROPE

| 2000BC | | 1000BC | 500BC | AD1 | AD500 |

The Roman Army

By the time Augustus became emperor, Rome controlled most of the land around the Mediterranean Sea. Over the next 150 years, the Romans conquered even more land, creating a vast empire that stretched from Britain to the Middle East. The Empire was at its largest in AD117 during the rule of the Emperor Trajan.

Emperor Augustus ★

★ Emperor Trajan

The Romans won wars because they had a strong, well-organized army, and their soldiers fought in highly disciplined groups. A group of 80 soldiers was called a century, centuries were grouped into cohorts, and ten cohorts made up a legion.

A Roman legionary (foot soldier) ★

Javelin

Iron helmet

Breastplate made of metal strips

Sword

Tunic

Leather sandal studded with nails

Wood and leather shield

During the Republic, any man who owned land could be asked to fight for a while. By the time of the emperors, most soldiers were well-trained professionals, who made the army their career.

Roman Empire at its largest

EUROPE
ASIA
AFRICA

ATLANTIC OCEAN

Nîmes

ITALY

Rome

Pompeii

BLACK SEA

MEDITERRANEAN SEA

Map of the Roman Empire

Attacking a city

The Romans were determined fighters and even conquered cities that were very well defended. They surrounded a city so no one could escape, and then used clever techniques to force their way in.

This scene shows the Roman army attacking a walled city.

A wooden siege tower is wheeled into position.

Soldiers move around under a roof of shields. This is called a tortoise.

Soldiers have built a ramp over uneven ground.

The tower is covered with strong metal plates.

Soldiers climb up inside a siege tower.

A drawbridge is lowered over the wall so the soldiers can run across into the city.

Any survivors inside the city will be captured and sold as slaves.

Houses are set on fire by flaming arrows.

Defenders shoot arrows from the city walls.

Soldiers dig under the walls to make them collapse.

Battering rams smash the walls.

Men operate the battering ram from inside.

Large catapults hurl heavy stones at the walls.

Smaller catapults fire metal bolts at the enemy.

These men are specialist archers from the Middle East.

The men have built a covered walkway so they can approach the walls safely.

On the road

To keep the Empire under control, soldiers had to be able to move quickly to wherever they were needed. A network of good roads was built linking every part of the Empire. On these roads, soldiers could march over 50km (30 miles) a day.

Soldiers on the move

Camps and forts

At the end of a long day's march, the soldiers had to build a camp for the night. The next morning, the camp was packed up and the army moved on. At the borders of the Empire, where soldiers were needed all the time, permanent stone forts were built.

Soldiers building a temporary camp

Leather tents

Fence

Rampart (earth mound)

Ditch

EUROPE

| 2000BC | 1000BC | 500BC | AD1 | AD500 |

187

Life in a Roman Town

The Romans took their way of life to all the lands they conquered. Each area, or province, of the Empire was run by a governor who made sure that people paid their taxes, obeyed Roman laws and respected Roman gods.

Statue of Jupiter, king of the gods

Retired Roman soldiers settled down to farm the land they had conquered, settlements grew up near Roman camps and forts, and new towns were built all over the Empire.

Roman towns were very well planned. They had many fine public buildings, such as temples and baths, as well as houses, apartment blocks, shops and restaurants.

This scene shows a busy Roman town. Some of the walls have been cut away to let you see inside the buildings.

Temple

Public bathhouse where people wash, swim and relax

The top floors are made of wood and often catch fire.

Firefighters use buckets of water to put out the fire.

Tiled roof

Most people live in large apartment blocks, called insulae.

Poorer families live in small rooms at the top.

Toilets are connected to underground drains.

School

Graffiti

Richer people have large, comfortable rooms.

There are shops at street level.

People get water from the fountain.

Bakery

Butcher's shop

Stepping stones for crossing the street

10,000BC   5000BC   3000BC

A life of luxury

While most townspeople lived in crowded apartment blocks, rich people had spacious houses with shady gardens. The houses were beautifully decorated inside. Some even had central heating under the floors and their own water supply.

This picture shows the reception hall (or atrium) of a Roman house. ★

Mosaic floor made of tiny pieces of stone

Rainwater collects in a pool.

This huge aqueduct, near the French town of Nîmes, is 49m (160ft) high.

Waterworks

Roman towns needed lots of fresh water to supply public baths, fountains and toilets. A system of pipes and channels (called aqueducts) took water to where it was needed. Engineers built tunnels and bridges to carry the water pipes across hills and valleys.

Buried treasure

Pompeii in southern Italy was a large, wealthy town. In August AD79, the nearby volcano Mount Vesuvius erupted. Pompeii was buried under clouds of ash and rivers of scorching gas and rock. Experts have since dug through the ash to uncover the town, giving us an amazing picture of everyday life in Roman times.

There are no drains upstairs, so people throw their waste onto the street.

Slaves for sale

Sick people buy medicines and magic spells from the pharmacist.

Apartments have no stoves for cooking, so people buy hot food from snack bars.

Slaves do most of the shopping.

Shoes for sale

Rich people are carried around in litters.

Wall painting from a house in Pompeii

EUROPE

2000BC	500BC	ADI	AD500

Fun and Games

Wealthy Romans had lots of free time because they had slaves to do all the work for them. There were so many slaves working in Rome that many poorer Romans could not find jobs. To keep them happy, the emperor handed out free food and put on spectacular shows, called "the games".

A young Roman slave

Gladiator shows

Most gladiators were slaves or criminals, who were made to fight to entertain the crowds. At the end of a fight, the spectators decided if the loser should live or die. Thousands of gladiators were killed in this brutal sport.

Fights took place in huge stone stadiums, called amphitheatres. The biggest of these was the Colosseum in Rome, which held 50,000 people. Sometimes, the arena was flooded, so that gladiators could take part in sea battles.

This cutaway picture shows a sea battle in the Colosseum. ★

A huge awning can be hung from these poles to give shade for the spectators.

This picture shows two types of gladiators. ★

Trident

This net is used by the gladiator to tangle his opponent.

This gladiator carries a net and trident.

This gladiator is more heavily armed.

Poorer people sit higher up.

Women watch from behind this wall.

Slaves and foreigners stand right at the top.

The floor of the arena is waterproofed with wood and canvas.

Rich Romans sit in the best seats at ground level.

EUROPE

10,000BC · 3000BC

190

Chariot races

A driver and horses in a chariot race

The reins are wound around the driver's body.

Racing chariots are very light for extra speed.

The most popular of the games were the chariot races, which were held at a racetrack called a circus. The races were exciting to watch but were very dangerous, as drivers were often thrown off and killed.

There are four teams. Drivers wear red, blue, green or white to show which team they belong to.

Pastimes

As well as going to the games, Romans enjoyed relaxing in the public parks and gardens. They played board games and also liked gambling games.

Board game

Coins and dice for gambling

Children had seesaws, swings, kites, hoops, marbles and dolls to play with.

Sometimes, they rode around in small carts pulled by geese.

Wooden dolls

Drama

The first Roman plays were copied from Greek ones and were quite serious. By the time of the emperors, people preferred watching comedies. The shows gradually became more and more spectacular, with lots of music, dancing and special effects. Some actors became so popular that they were mobbed by their fans.

Mosaic showing a child in a toy cart

Concrete (a Roman invention) makes the walls very strong.

The stone seats are supported by arches.

The outside is decorated with marble pillars and statues.

There are 80 entrances, so people can get in and out quickly.

Roman actors in their costumes ★

Important dates

753BC	The city of Rome is set up, according to legend.
c.509BC	Rome becomes a republic.
264BC	The Punic Wars start.
146BC	The Romans destroy Carthage.
49BC	Julius Caesar takes control of Rome.
27BC	Augustus becomes the first Emperor of Rome.
AD72-80	The Colosseum is built.
AD117	The Roman Empire is at its largest.

EUROPE

| 2000BC | 1000BC | 500BC | AD1 | AD500 |

The Spread of Christianity

The Christian religion began with a Jew called Jesus, later known as Jesus Christ. You can read about his life and teachings in the New Testament of the Bible.

Mosaic showing Jesus as a shepherd

The life of Jesus

Jesus was born in Judea, a small province in the Roman Empire. At around the age of 30, he chose 12 men to be his disciples (followers) and began preaching. News spread that he could perform miracles, and crowds of people came to hear him.

This mosaic shows Jesus bringing a dead man back to life. ★

Jesus's teachings

Jesus taught that it was more important to love God and serve others than to obey the Jewish law. He said that people should stop doing wrong and make a fresh start, so that they could be part of God's kingdom.

Map of the Christian world

→ Paul's journey to Rome
† Christian churches in AD100
■ Areas that were strongly Christian by AD300

BLACK SEA
Rome
GREECE
ASIA MINOR
Tarsus
MALTA
MEDITERRANEAN SEA
Jerusalem
JUDEA
RED SEA

EUROPE
ASIA
AFRICA

Paul of Tarsus

Jesus's death

Jesus's teachings upset the Jewish religious leaders, and the Romans were afraid that his ideas might lead to a rebellion in Judea. He was arrested in Jerusalem and was crucified (nailed to a cross to die).

Ivory carving of Jesus on the cross ★

REX IVD

Spreading the word

After Jesus died, his teachings were spread by his followers, who said that he had risen from the dead. Paul of Tarsus took the Christian message to Asia Minor (modern Turkey), to Greece and even to Rome.

On his way to Rome, Paul was shipwrecked off the coast of Malta.

Hard times

Christianity spread quickly around the Roman Empire. Some emperors saw the Christians as rebels because they refused to worship Roman gods, and thousands were arrested, tortured and killed.

Many Christians were thrown to the lions for public entertainment.

To avoid being arrested, Christians often had to meet in secret. In Rome, they met in the catacombs, a series of tunnels under the city that were used as burial places.

Secret symbols

Christians used secret signs to show other Christians that they shared the same faith. One of these was the Chi-Ro sign ✸.

★

Portrait of a Christian family with the Chi-Ro sign

The Chi-Ro sign was made up of the first two letters of the word "Christ" in Greek. It has been found carved on tombs, statues and doorways, and on the walls of the catacombs.

Christian emperors

The Emperor Constantine was the first Roman ruler to accept the Christian faith. After seeing a cross of light in the sky, he sent his army into battle with the Chi-Ro sign on their shields. Constantine won the battle and later became a Christian.

Constantine riding into battle

Constantine gave christians the freedom to worship openly, and helped to spread Christianity across Europe. He built the first great Christian churches, and gave Christians special privileges. Finally, in AD391, the Emperor Theodosius made Christianity the official religion of the Roman Empire.

This scene shows a group of Christians in the catacombs.

★

The ashes of dead people are stored in clay jars.

There are over 900km (560 miles) of tunnels.

The walls are painted with scenes from the Bible.

Christians meet to pray and to worship God.

Important dates

c.5BC	Jesus Christ is born.
c.AD29	Jesus Christ is crucified.
AD45-58	Paul travels around Asia Minor and Greece.
AD58-60	Paul travels to Rome.
AD312	The Emperor Constantine makes Christianity legal.
AD391	Christianity becomes the official religion of the Roman Empire.

THE MIDDLE EAST

2000BC	1000BC	500BC	ADI	AD500

The Fall of Rome

Around AD200, the power of the Roman Empire began to weaken. The Roman armies started to choose their own emperors, and fighting broke out between different groups of soldiers. At the same time, the Empire was attacked by tribes from the northeast, known as Germani. The Romans called these people "barbarians".

A Germanic ★
warrior

A throwing-axe, called a francisca

Map of the barbarian invasions

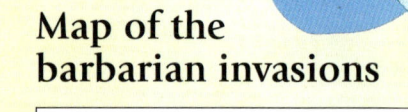

■ Western Roman Empire	➡ Burgundians
■ Eastern Roman Empire	➡ Alemanni
➡ Angles, Saxons, Jutes	➡ Lombards
➡ Franks	➡ Visigoths
➡ Vandals	➡ Ostrogoths

ATLANTIC OCEAN

BLACK SEA

Constantinople

•Rome

MEDITERRANEAN SEA

EUROPE

ASIA

AFRICA

Defending the Empire

In AD284, a general called Diocletian became emperor. To defend the Empire against the barbarians, he reorganized the army and made it bigger. Diocletian realized that the Empire was too big for one person to control, so he split it in two. He ruled the eastern half himself, while the western half was ruled by a general called Maximian. Each emperor had a deputy to help him rule.

★

Statue of Diocletian and Maximian with their two deputies

The Emperor Constantine

When Diocletian retired, there were more struggles for power. In AD312, Constantine became Emperor of the West. Later, he took control of the East as well, reuniting the Empire.

Constantine moved the capital of the Roman Empire to the town of Byzantium on the Black Sea. He rebuilt Byzantium, filled it with treasures from around the Empire and renamed it Constantinope, after himself.

★ A later mosaic of Constantine holding a model of Constantinople

Asian invaders

Lasso

Hun warriors in battle ★

Around AD370, eastern Europe was invaded by people from central Asia, known as the Huns. As the Huns moved across Europe, they pushed the Germanic tribes off their land and into the Roman Empire.

Peace at a price

The Romans allowed some Germanic tribes, such as the Visigoths, to settle inside the Empire, as long as they helped to fight off other barbarians.

Visigoth settlers

Rome in ruins

In AD395, the Roman Empire split permanently into East and West, and from then on waves of barbarians swept across the Western Empire (see map). The city of Rome was attacked by the Visigoths in AD410, and by the Vandals in AD455.

This scene shows Vandal warriors wrecking Rome.

Many Romans are killed.

The end of the Empire

In AD476, a Visigoth chief called Odoacer made himself King of Italy, and the Western Empire came to an end. The Eastern Empire, with its capital at Constantinople, lasted for another thousand years.

Treasures are stolen.

Buildings are set on fire.

Statues are smashed.

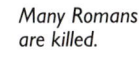

Important dates

AD286 Diocletian splits the Roman Empire in two.

AD312 Constantine becomes Emperor of the West.

AD324 Constantine reunites the Empire.

c.AD370 The Huns arrive in Europe.

AD395 The Roman Empire splits permanently in two.

AD410 Rome is attacked by the Visigoths.

AD455 Rome is destroyed by the Vandals.

AD476 The Western Empire ends.

EUROPE

500BC   AD1   AD500

Part of a 15th-century tapestry showing a scene from the Hundred Years' War

Looking at the Medieval World

In this section of the book, you can find out what was happening all over the world from around 500 to around 1500. This time in history is known as the medieval period, or the Middle Ages.

A changing world

By the year 500, the Roman Empire had collapsed and tribes of people were roaming through Europe, looking for places to live. Over the next 500 years, these people settled down and created kingdoms of their own. Most of the kingdoms were led by strong Christian rulers, who encouraged art and learning, but also fought each other for land.

Meanwhile, in Arabia, the new religion of Islam was born, and great empires flourished in Africa, Asia and the Americas. For centuries, these empires were isolated from Europe, but by the end of the Middle Ages, European explorers were sailing to distant lands.

Pearls

Ruby

Pepper

Cardamom

Garnet

European explorers and traders brought back jewels and spices like these from the empires of the East.

When and where?

Important events and their dates are shown in boxes. If a date has a letter "c." in front of it, this means that experts aren't sure exactly when the event took place. (The "c." stands for *circa* which means "about" in Latin.)

To see which period of time you are reading about, take a look at the timeline at the bottom of each page. You can also check the bottom corner of the page to find out which area of the world you are in. The different areas of the world are marked on the map below.

This is a statue of Charlemagne, a great early Christian ruler.

Medieval works of art, such as paintings and carvings, often show important people and great events. These works of art can also reveal fascinating details about daily life.

Manuscripts like this show the skill of the monks who illustrated them.

In many parts of the medieval world, people wrote things down in handwritten books, called manuscripts. Scholars recorded events of the time, explorers described their travels, and inventors explained their ideas. Government officials kept records of taxes, laws and trials, while writers produced poems and stories based on real life.

How do we know?

Many buildings and objects have survived from medieval times, giving a vivid impression of life in the Middle Ages.

Other medieval buildings are now in ruins, or even buried underground. Experts, called archaeologists, uncover buried buildings and objects, and also use computer technology to help create a picture of how things used to look.

The carved head shown here is part of a ruined Mayan temple at Chichén Itzá, in Central America.

199

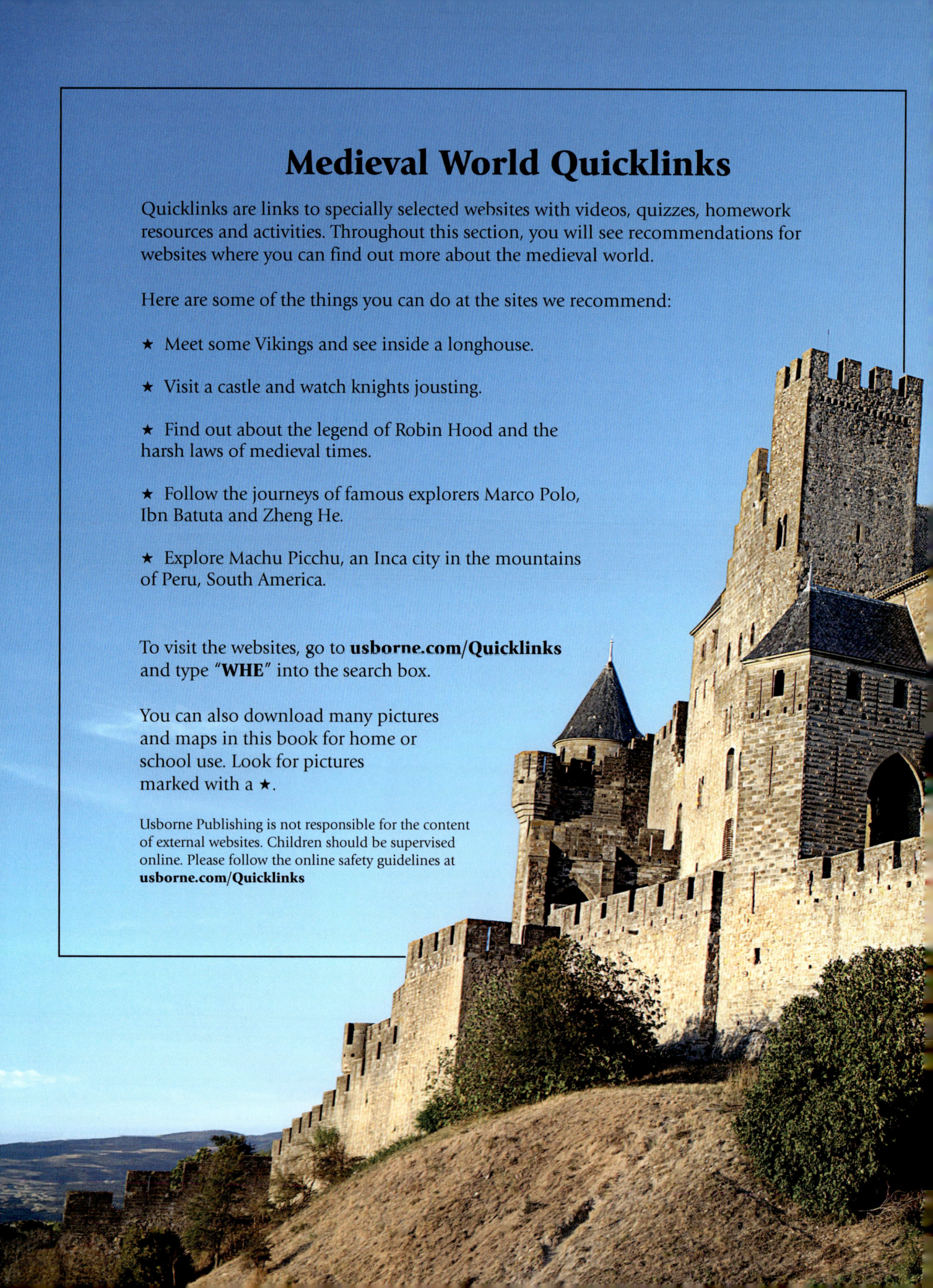

Medieval World Quicklinks

Quicklinks are links to specially selected websites with videos, quizzes, homework resources and activities. Throughout this section, you will see recommendations for websites where you can find out more about the medieval world.

Here are some of the things you can do at the sites we recommend:

★ Meet some Vikings and see inside a longhouse.

★ Visit a castle and watch knights jousting.

★ Find out about the legend of Robin Hood and the harsh laws of medieval times.

★ Follow the journeys of famous explorers Marco Polo, Ibn Batuta and Zheng He.

★ Explore Machu Picchu, an Inca city in the mountains of Peru, South America.

To visit the websites, go to **usborne.com/Quicklinks** and type "**WHE**" into the search box.

You can also download many pictures and maps in this book for home or school use. Look for pictures marked with a ★.

These are the ramparts of the French city of Carcassonne, an important fortress in the Middle Ages.

The Byzantine Empire

By the year 400, the Roman Empire had split into two parts. The Empire in the west was attacked by warlike tribes and collapsed in 476, but the Empire in the east survived for another thousand years. The eastern Empire was known as the Byzantine Empire because its capital city, Constantinople, was originally called Byzantium.

Map of the Byzantine Empire

SPAIN · Rome · ITALY · GREECE · Constantinople · MEDITERRANEAN SEA · NORTH AFRICA

EUROPE · ASIA · AFRICA

- Byzantine Empire at the start of Justinian's reign
- Land won by Justinian

★ *Mosaic of the Byzantine Emperor Justinian*

Justinian's Empire

In the 6th century, the Byzantine Emperor Justinian won back many of the lands that had once been part of the Roman Empire. Under him, the Byzantine Empire was larger than it would ever be again.

Running the Empire

Justinian's dream was to create a great Christian empire. With the help of his wife, Theodora, he set up a new system of laws, and gave orders for many churches to be built. Priests, artists and merchants all visited his palace.

Justinian's palace in Constantinople

Emperor Justinian · Empress Theodora · Canal · Priest · Court lady · Merchants from North Africa visit Justinian's court. · Visitors grovel in front of the emperor. · Palace guard

EUROPE

500   600   700   800   900

Byzantine art

Byzantine artists were famous for their delicate embroidery and ivory carvings. They also created huge, glittering mosaics and painted dramatic religious portraits, called icons.

Silk embroidery

An icon of the Virgin Mary and Child

Defending the Empire

The Byzantines fought constant battles against Muslim Arabs and Turks. They were threatened by tribes from the north, and even had to fight against Crusaders from western Europe, who were supposed to be on their side (see page 241).

The end of the Empire

After Justinian's death, the Empire became smaller and smaller, and by 1400 only the land around Constantinople was left. In 1453, an army of Ottoman Turks attacked the city. After six weeks of fighting, the Byzantines surrendered and their Empire collapsed.

This picture shows the Ottomans' final attack on Constantinople.

Religious split

Christians in the Byzantine Empire developed their own style of church building and held services in Greek, instead of Latin. The Byzantine Church was led by the Patriarch in Constantinople.

Justinian built the Cathedral of Saint Sophia in Constantinople. (It was later turned into a mosque.)

After many quarrels between the Patriarch and the Pope (the head of the Church in the west), the Byzantine Church split away from the Church in the west.

The Byzantine soldiers are weak and exhausted.

The Ottoman troops have powerful cannons.

Important dates

395	The Roman Empire is divided in two.
476	The Roman Empire in the west collapses.
527-565	Justinian reigns as Byzantine emperor.
1054	The eastern Church splits from the western Church.
1204	Crusaders capture Constantinople.
1261	The Byzantines drive out the Crusaders.
1453	The Ottoman Turks conquer Constantinople.

EUROPE

1100   1200   1300   1400   1500

THE BARBARIANS: c.500-800

*QUICKLINKS: For links to websites where you can examine elaborate treasures made by Visigoths and Franks, go to **usborne.com/Quicklinks***

The Barbarian Kingdoms

The Romans first used the name "barbarian" to describe the tribes of warriors who invaded their Empire from the northeast. The barbarians swept across Europe destroying the Roman Empire, but, by around 500, they had begun to settle down in their own independent kingdoms.

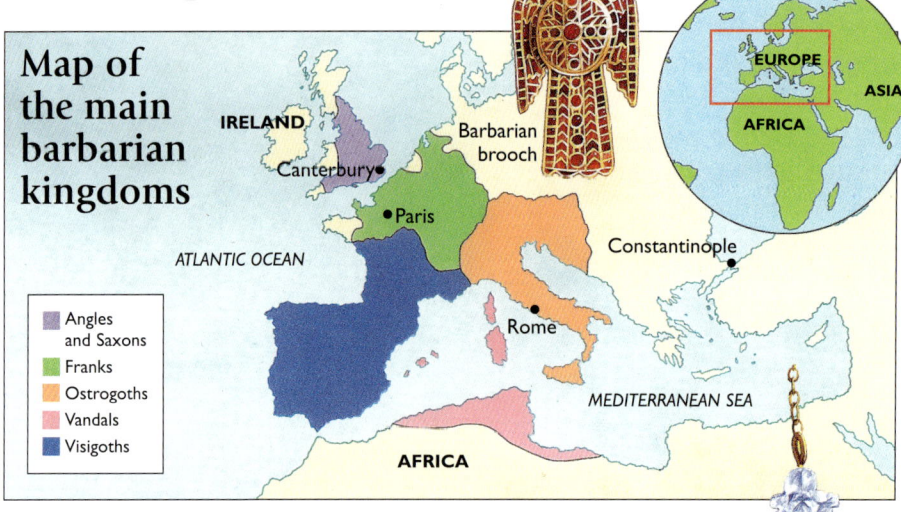

Map of the main barbarian kingdoms

- Angles and Saxons
- Franks
- Ostrogoths
- Vandals
- Visigoths

IRELAND · Canterbury · Paris · ATLANTIC OCEAN · Barbarian brooch · Constantinople · Rome · MEDITERRANEAN SEA · AFRICA

EUROPE · ASIA · AFRICA

A barbarian warrior charging into battle

Barbarian villages

The barbarians wanted to be rich like the Romans, but in fact they destroyed the Roman way of life. Most barbarians lived in small farming villages and let the Roman cities fall into ruins.

The kingdom of the Franks

The largest barbarian kingdom belonged to the Visigoths, but the most successful was created by Clovis, leader of the Franks. He made his capital in Paris, and started a line of kings known as the Merovingian dynasty, which lasted until 751.

Clovis and his queen Clothilda, painted by a later artist ★

Barbarian treasures

Some of the barbarians were very skilled at metalwork. They made elaborate swords and drinking cups, as well as beautiful crowns and brooches for their kings and chiefs.

Visigoth crown ★

A barbarian village

Animals and people share the same houses.

A strong fence keeps out enemies and wild animals.

The chief's house is used for meetings.

Important dates

429-533	Vandal kingdom in North Africa
c.450-1066	Angles and Saxons rule parts of Britain.
456-711	Visigoth kingdom in Spain
481-511	Clovis rules over the Franks.
493-555	Ostrogoth kingdom in Italy
c.500-843	Frankish kingdom in France and Germany

EUROPE

500	600	700	800	900

QUICKLINKS: For links to websites where you can zoom in on beautifully illustrated medieval manuscripts, go to **usborne.com/Quicklinks**

Return to Christianity

A pagan god

Most barbarians were pagans who did not believe in Christ. Wherever they settled, churches were abandoned. By around 500, Christianity had almost disappeared in many parts of Europe.

Spreading the message

The leaders of the Church in Rome and Constantinople decided to send out monks to teach the Christian religion. Monks were also sent from Ireland, which had not been invaded by barbarians. Slowly, the barbarians became Christians, and churches and monasteries were built all over Europe.

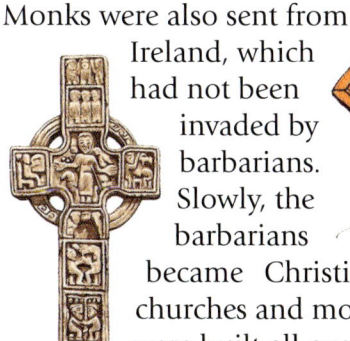

Irish missionaries

Irish monks set up carved crosses near their monasteries.

Augustine and the Angles

A monk called Augustine was sent from Rome to preach to the Angles of southeast Britain. Thousands of Angles became Christians and their leader, King Ethelbert, made Augustine the first Archbishop of Canterbury.

Augustine preaching to the Angles

Queen Bertha is already a Christian.

King Ethelbert

Monks and manuscripts

Most barbarians could not read or write, but the monks made sure that learning did not die out. They kept holy books in their monasteries and made beautiful copies of them. These handwritten books, called manuscripts, were often beautifully illustrated.

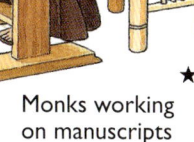
Monks working on manuscripts

An illustration from a manuscript called the *Book of Kells*

The Rise of Islam

In the year 610, a man called Mohammed started to teach a new religion in Arabia. The religion became known as Islam, and its followers were called Muslims.

Arabia in Mohammed's time

Mohammed's message

Mohammed said that people should obey Allah, the one true god. He taught Muslims to pray five times a day, to give money to the poor, and to go without food and drink during daylight hours in the month called Ramadan.

Muslims going on a pilgrimage

Mohammed also said that all Muslims should try to go on a pilgrimage (religious journey) to Mecca, the holy city of Islam.

Mosques

Muslims pray in beautiful buildings called mosques. They are called to prayer by a man called a muezzin who stands in a tower called a minaret. Pictures of animals and people are not allowed in mosques. Instead, mosques are decorated with patterned tiles and beautifully carved religious texts.

This picture shows Muslims praying ★ in the courtyard of a mosque.

These towers are called minarets.

This is the mihrab. It shows the direction of Mecca.

The crescent is a symbol of Islam.

This is the minbar. A man called an imam preaches from here.

Muslims must wash in this fountain before they pray.

These people are praying. They kneel on prayer mats, facing Mecca.

This is the inner courtyard of the mosque.

The Koran

Muslims believe that Mohammed received many messages from Allah. Mohammed's followers wrote down these messages in a holy book, called the Koran.

Decorated pages from the Koran

The spread of Islam

Mohammed began preaching in Mecca, but rich merchants drove him out of the city and in 622 he escaped to Medina. In 624, an army from Mecca attacked the Muslims in Medina. Mohammed and his followers fought bravely and won the Battle of al Badr. After this victory, many people in Arabia became Muslims.

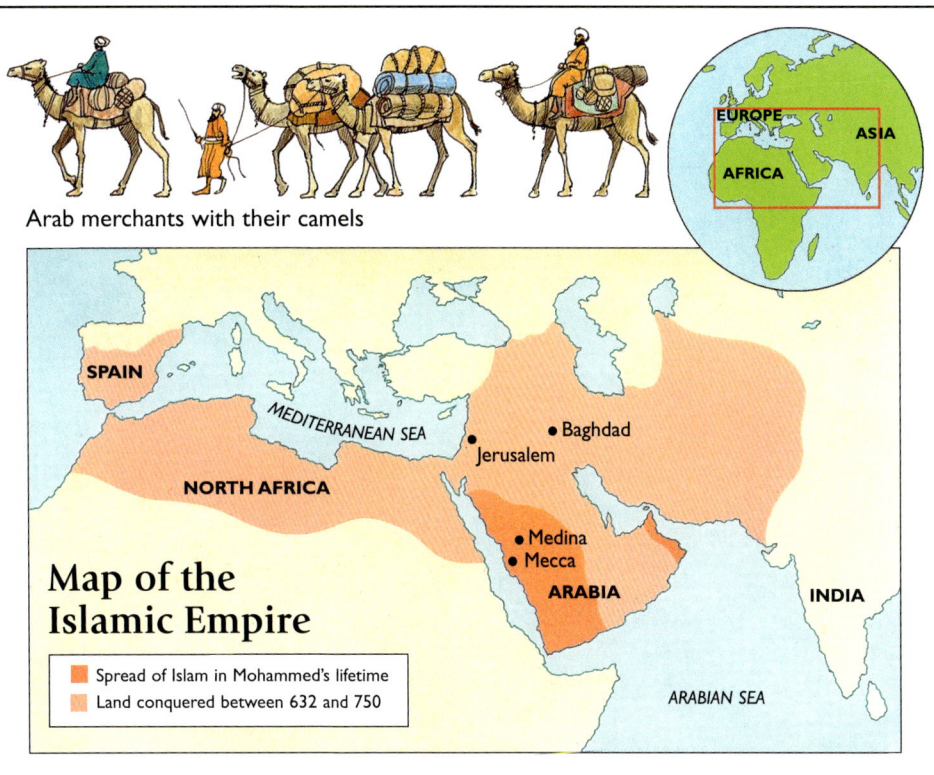

Arab merchants with their camels

Map of the Islamic Empire

- Spread of Islam in Mohammed's lifetime
- Land conquered between 632 and 750

A scene from the Battle of al Badr

Conquering caliphs

After Mohammed's death in 632, the Muslims were ruled by a series of leaders, called caliphs. The caliphs fought many battles to spread their religion. By 750, they had built up a vast Islamic Empire, stretching from northern India in the east to Spain in the west.

A caliph's army fighting a battle

Building mosques

Everywhere the caliphs conquered, they built mosques where people could pray. The Dome of the Rock in Jerusalem is part of a mosque that was built 50 years after the Arabs captured the city.

The Dome of the Rock in Jerusalem

The dome stands inside the Al-Aqsa mosque.

Traders and towns

The religion of Islam was spread by traders as well as soldiers. Arab merchants made journeys throughout the Empire and beyond, and, wherever the traders met, new Muslim towns grew up.

THE MIDDLE EAST

1100 1200 1300 1400 1500

The Arab World

In 750, an Arab family called the Abbasids became the new caliphs (rulers) of the Islamic Empire (see map on page 207). The people of the Empire were united by the religion of Islam, and many of them spoke Arabic.

Arabian wealth

The Abbasid caliphs collected taxes from people all over the Empire. They became fabulously rich and lived a life of luxury in a beautiful palace in Baghdad (in modern Iraq).

A caliph having a massage

Learning

The Arabs were keen to learn from other people's ideas. They collected books from all over the world and kept them in libraries. Arab scholars studied works from ancient Greece, Persia, India and China, and translated them into Arabic. They also wrote many books of their own and taught students in universities.

A scholar teaching students

City life

Arabian cities were busy and crowded, but they were also well organized. People prayed and studied in mosques, and washed in public baths. Souks (markets) sold a variety of goods, local and imported.

This picture shows an Arabian city street.

Many of the houses have three floors.

The streets are very narrow.

The upper part of the house is specially for women and children. It is called the harem.

Most of the houses are covered in white plaster. This helps to keep them cool.

An awning protects the goods from the sun.

There are baskets for sale at this stall.

This man is selling spices.

This trader is selling brass bowls and trays.

Women wear veils to cover their faces.

Donkey carrying carpets

Carpet seller

THE MIDDLE EAST

Medical instruments

Medicine and science

Arab doctors learned about diseases and performed difficult operations. Scientists discovered how to make steel and how to make drugs from chemicals.

A water clock

Every half hour, the bird whistles.

The falcon drops a ball into the dragon's mouth.

The ball falls through the dragon's body and into the elephant.

The elephant driver beats his drum.

Inventors built amazing clocks, and engineers designed elaborate machines that were used to water fields.

This man is buying silk.

Sailing and exploration

Arab merchants sailed to China, Africa and India, and explorers set off on long journeys to distant lands. Sailors and explorers used special instruments to help them find their way.

★ An Arab sailing ship, called a dhow

A sailor using an instrument, called an al Kemal.

Astronomy

Astronomers studied the sky at night and made maps of the stars. These maps helped sailors and explorers to find their way across seas and deserts.

Arab astronomers at work

Arabic numbers

From India, the Arabs learned a simple way of writing numbers, including zero. Until then, most people had used Roman numbers, which were very complicated and had no zero. The numbers that we use today are based on Arabic numbers.

0 1 2 3 4 5 6 7 8 9

Arabic numbers from zero to nine

The end of the Islamic Empire

Although the Abbasid caliphs called themselves the rulers of the Islamic world, their Empire was divided by the end of the 8th century. Separate kingdoms grew up in Spain, Egypt and India, and religious quarrels split the people of the Empire.

In 1055, an army of Turks captured Baghdad. The Turks controlled the caliphs until 1258, when a Mongol army invaded Baghdad, and killed the last caliph.

Important dates

c.570-632	Mohammed lives in Arabia. Most of Arabia is converted to Islam.
632-850	The first caliphs create a vast Islamic Empire.
750-1258	The Abbasid caliphs rule the Islamic Empire.
1055	The Turks take control of the caliphs.
1258	The Mongols conquer Baghdad. The Islamic Empire ends.

THE MIDDLE EAST

1100   1200   1300   1400   1500

Vikings at Home

A Viking farmer sowing seeds

The Vikings came from Sweden, Norway and Denmark (see map on page 212). Their name probably means "pirate" and they were fierce raiders and fighters. In their own lands, the Vikings were farmers, fishermen and craftworkers.

Farm life

Many of the Vikings were farmers. They grew crops and vegetables, and kept cows, pigs, chickens and goats. They also hunted wild animals.

Crafts

The Vikings were great metalworkers and carvers. They made elaborate weapons and necklaces, and beautiful carved objects.

Viking chesspiece ★

Viking homes

Thatched roof

Chest for storing clothes

The chief and his wife sleep in this bed.

Smoke hole

Wall hanging

This woman is weaving cloth at a loom.

Wooden frame

Carved door frame

This man is bringing wood for the fire.

In the winter, some animals are kept inside.

Toilet

Wall made from cane

★ This picture of a Viking longhouse has been cut away so you can see inside.

This boy looks after the pigs.

Most Vikings lived in large homes, called longhouses. Each longhouse belonged to a chief, and all the families who worked for the chief ate and slept in his house.

500	600	700	800	900

Death and burial

The Vikings buried people with food and treasure to take with them to the next life. Sometimes, a great warrior was buried on a ship, which might be burned at sea or buried under a mound. It was thought the ship went to Valhalla, a kind of heaven where only warriors could go.

This picture shows a Viking ship burial.

Grave marked by stones in the shape of a ship

Gravestone with carved letters, called runes

Mourners

Weapons

Chest full of treasure

The dead warrior is covered by a tent (shown cut away here).

The warrior's slave girl and animals are killed and buried with him.

Valhalla

People believed that dead warriors fought all day and feasted all night in Valhalla, the home of their chief god, Odin. Beautiful maidens, called Valkyries, looked after the warriors.

A feast in Valhalla

Valkyrie

Dead warrior

The chief god, Odin, outside Valhalla

Viking feasts

The Vikings held rowdy feasts to celebrate their battles. Musicians played harps and pipes, and poets (called skalds) recited long poems and daring deeds.

A Viking feast

Skald (poet)

EUROPE

Vikings Abroad

Viking longship

Viking homeland
Lands where the Vikings settled
Viking routes

GREENLAND

ICELAND

NORWAY SWEDEN

FINLAND

DENMARK

IRELAND

BRITAIN

ATLANTIC OCEAN

FRANCE

NEWFOUNDLAND

Indigenous Americans

SPAIN

ITALY

Arab traders

NORTH AFRICA

Baghdad ●

Map of the Viking world

The Vikings did not have enough land for everyone to farm, so around 790 some of them started to leave their homeland. Fierce raiders attacked the coast of Europe, explorers searched for new territory, and traders and settlers sailed to distant lands.

★
Viking raider

Raiders

For over 300 years, Viking raiders terrorized the people of Europe. Ferocious warriors arrived in swift warships, called longships. Then, they fought their way inland, robbing towns and villages as they went.

This picture shows a raid on a village. Part of the church has been cut away so you can see inside.

The raiders invaded large areas of Britain, Ireland, France and Italy. Later, some of them settled in these places.

Around 1100, the raids came to an end. By that time, many of the Vikings had become Christians and their people were much less violent.

Many people are killed.

Raiders steal treasure from churches and homes.

EUROPE

500   600   700   800   900

212

Explorers

Daring adventurers and traders sailed over seas and up rivers. When they could not sail any farther, the crew carried their boat, or dragged it on logs, to the next river.

Statue of Leif Ericson

Eric the Red explored Greenland. His son, Leif Ericson, went farther west and reached America. The land he found, called Vinland, was probably modern Newfoundland.

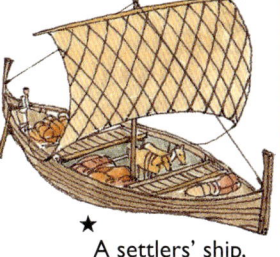

Explorers dragging their boat overland

Settlers

Boatloads of Viking settlers arrived in the newly discovered and conquered lands.

In northern France, the Vikings were called Normans (northmen) and in eastern Europe they were known as the Rus (redheaded people). The areas where they lived became known as Normandy and Russia.

A settlers' ship, called a knorr

Some Vikings settled in Iceland and Greenland. Others even went to live in Vinland (in America), but Indigenous Americans attacked their homes and they soon fled back to Greenland.

Indigenous Americans attacking Vikings

Viking longships arrive swiftly and silently.

A lookout makes sure that it is safe to land.

The crew lower their sail and row ashore.

Some raiders seize animals and food.

This barn has been set on fire.

Some warriors take women as slaves.

Some people try to hide.

A few people manage to escape.

Traders

Viking merchants traded in Europe and beyond. Some adventurous traders even reached the Arab city of Baghdad. The Vikings sold swords, fur and ivory (from walrus tusks). In return, they bought silk, precious stones, carvings, and beautiful objects made from gold and silver.

This eastern statue was found in Viking lands.

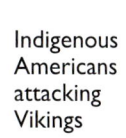

Important dates

c.790 The Viking raids begin.
c.830-900 Frequent raids on the British Isles and France.
c.860 The Vikings settle in Russia.
c.900-911 The Vikings settle in Normandy.
c.983-986 The Vikings start a colony in Greenland.
c.1000 Leif Ericson reaches North America.
c.1100 The Viking raids end.

1100   1200   1400   1500

EUROPE

213

Anglo-Saxon England

A Saxon ship arriving in Britain

Around the year 400, tribes of Angles, Saxons and Jutes began arriving in Britain from Denmark and northern Germany.

These people were later known as Anglo-Saxons, and the land where they settled was called "Angle land", or England. By 600, England was divided into seven kingdoms, each ruled by a warrior king.

Map of the Anglo-Saxon kingdoms

EUROPE
ASIA
AFRICA

SCOTLAND
IRELAND
NORTH SEA
ENGLAND
WALES
ENGLISH CHANNEL

— Border of the Danelaw in 878
Northumbria
Mercia
East Anglia
Essex
Kent
Sussex
Wessex

The map shows the kingdoms in 800.

Thanes, churls and slaves

The Anglo-Saxon kings ruled over nobles (called thanes), farmers (called churls) and slaves. Thanes and churls were free, but they had to fight for their king. Slaves were owned by their masters.

A slave serving a thane at a feast

Buried treasure

Some Anglo-Saxon kings were buried in ships, surrounded by their treasures. Helmets, weapons and jewels have all been found in the ship graves of Anglo-Saxon kings.

★ This helmet was found in a ship grave in East Anglia.

Village life

Most Anglo-Saxons lived in villages, although some of the villages grew into small towns. The men worked in the fields and went out hunting and fishing. The women cooked, made clothes and looked after the hens and pigs. Some villagers were potters, blacksmiths and carpenters.

★ This picture shows part of an Anglo-Saxon village.

Shepherd

Weaving shed

These women are weaving and spinning wool.

This man is using a pole lathe to help him make a wooden bowl.

He pushes a pedal to make the wood turn as he carves it.

Blacksmith

Fighting the Danes

Around 800, armies of Danes (Vikings from Denmark) began to invade England. By 874, they had conquered all the kingdoms except Wessex. King Alfred of Wessex drove the Danes out of his kingdom and won back Sussex, Kent and Mercia, which all became part of Wessex.

King Alfred fighting a Danish invader

Alfred the Great

King Alfred agreed that the Danes could settle in the eastern part of the country, called the Danelaw, while he ruled the rest of England (see map). Alfred built strong, walled towns and set up a navy. He made fair laws and encouraged art, religion and learning. Later, he became known as Alfred the Great.

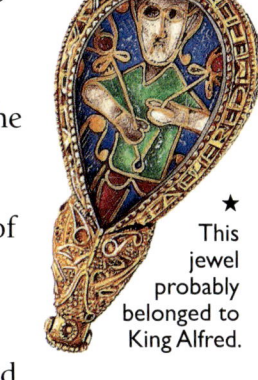

★ This jewel probably belonged to King Alfred.

Anglo-Saxons and Danes

In 924, Alfred's grandson, Athelstan, became king of all of England, but in 1013 the Danes invaded again. England was ruled by Danish kings for 30 years before the Anglo-Saxons regained control of their country.

Coin showing Cnut, King of England and Denmark

The end of the Anglo-Saxons

Edward the Confessor became King of England in 1042. He was a religious man who rebuilt Westminster Abbey. When Edward died in 1066, Harold Earl of Wessex was crowned king. He defeated a Viking army at Stamford Bridge, but he was soon defeated by the Normans, who conquered England (see page 218).

★ Edward the Confessor

Wooden fence   Thatched roof   Houses are built from planks of wood.

Well   Hen house

A thane lives in this hall. He holds feasts for all the villagers here.

Oven

Bread

Women cook soup in a cauldron.

Slaves roast a pig on a spit.

Musicians and jugglers arrive for the feast.

A fowler (bird catcher) brings birds for the feast.

Important dates

c.410-520 Angles, Saxons and Jutes settle in England.

c.600 England is divided into seven kingdoms.

867-874 The Danes invade England.

871-899 Alfred is King of Wessex.

924-939 Athelstan rules England.

1013-1042 Danish kings rule England.

1042-1066 Edward the Confessor is King of England.

1066 The Normans conquer England.

FRANCE: c.770-840

QUICKLINKS: *For links to websites where you can find out more about Charlemagne and his Empire, go to* **usborne.com/Quicklinks**

Charlemagne's Empire

In 768, a young prince called Charles was crowned King of the Franks and inherited most of the land that is now France. (See page 204 for more about the Franks.) He was a brilliant soldier and a keen Christian, and he became known as Charlemagne, which means "Charles the Great".

Map of Charlemagne's Empire

EUROPE
ASIA
AFRICA

Aachen

WESTERN KINGDOM
EASTERN KINGDOM
MIDDLE KINGDOM

■ Lands inherited by Charlemagne
■ Lands conquered by Charlemagne
— Borders between kingdoms in 843

Stained-glass portrait of Charlemagne ★

Building an empire

Charlemagne wanted to create a new Christian empire as large as the Roman Empire had been. For over 30 years, he fought for land, insisting that any non-Christians he conquered should join the Church. On Christmas Day 800, the Pope crowned him "Emperor of the Romans".

★
Pope Leo III crowning Charlemagne as Emperor of the Romans

Religion and learning

Charlemagne paid for churches and monasteries to be built all over his Empire. He encouraged scholars, artists and craftworkers to come and work in Aachen, where he had his palace.

Charlemagne's splendid palace at Aachen

After Charlemagne

Charlemagne's Empire did not last long after his death. By 843, the Empire had split into three kingdoms, and each kingdom was ruled by a member of Charlemagne's family. The three rulers fought against each other and their kingdoms became very weak.

Important dates

768 Charlemagne becomes King of the Franks.

773-804 Charlemagne builds up his Empire.

800-814 Charlemagne is emperor.

843 Charlemagne's Empire is split into three kingdoms.

EUROPE

FRANCE
GERMANY

500   600   700   800   900

The Holy Roman Empire

By 900, all three parts of Charlemagne's old Empire were in danger. Vikings had invaded the Western and Middle kingdoms, and tribes of Magyars (from present-day Hungary) were attacking the Eastern kingdom.

Otto the Great

In 955, Otto I, King of the Eastern kingdom (now part of Germany), beat the Magyars at the Battle of Lechfeld. The Magyars were pagans who did not believe in Christ, and the Pope was so pleased by Otto's victory that he crowned him "Holy Roman Emperor".

Map of the Holy Roman Empire

Rome

SICILY

■ Frederick II's Empire
■ The Pope's lands

Emperor Otto's crown

Emperors and popes

After Otto, all the German kings had the title of "Holy Roman Emperor". They used their bishops to help them rule the Empire and had many quarrels with the popes over who was more powerful. (see page 232).

The Wonder of the World

Emperor Frederick II inherited the kingdom of Sicily from his mother and ruled his Empire from there. Known as "the Wonder of the World", he kept wild animals, and welcomed astrologers and Muslim scholars to his court.

★ Emperor Frederick II

The Battle of Lechfeld ★

Magyar horseman

German horseman

Magyar foot soldier

German foot soldier

Important dates

955	The Battle of Lechfeld
962-973	Otto I is emperor.
1220-1250	Frederick II is emperor.
1250-1273	The Empire is weak.
1273-1291	Rudolf of Habsburg is emperor. He starts a new family of emperors.

EUROPE

1100   1200   1300   1400   1500

THE NORMANS: c.1060-1200

QUICKLINKS: For links to websites about the Norman invaders and the death of King Harold at the Battle of Hastings, go to *usborne.com/Quicklinks*

The Norman Conquests

The Normans were descendants of the Vikings who had settled in Normandy during the 900s. Like their Viking ancestors, the Normans were great sailors and warriors who were hungry for more land.

Norman ships

King Harold ★
of England

Map of the Norman conquests

☐ Norman lands in 1130

ATLANTIC OCEAN

EUROPE

ASIA

AFRICA

ENGLAND

Hastings

NORMANDY

FRANCE

MEDITERRANEAN SEA

ITALY

SICILY

Invading England

Duke William of Normandy believed he should be King of England because of a promise made to him by the previous English king, Edward the Confessor. In 1066, William sailed to England and fought King Harold of England at Hastings. The Normans were victorious and Harold was killed in battle.

Italy and Sicily

The Normans also invaded southern Italy and the island of Sicily. In 1130, a Norman count became King of Sicily. For the next 60 years, the Normans ruled the island and the southern part of Italy.

Norman horsemen fighting English foot soldiers at the Battle of Hastings ★

Mosaic of Roger II, the first Norman King of Sicily

Ruling England

William was crowned the new King of England. He built castles all over the country and gave land to powerful nobles who promised to obey him.

Norman soldiers outside a castle

King William ★
the Conqueror

Important dates

1060-1130 The Normans gradually conquer Sicily and southern Italy.

1066 The Normans conquer England and Duke William becomes king.

1130-1204 The Normans are kings of Sicily.

EUROPE

500   600   700   800   900

Edward III

The Hundred Years' War

After the Normans had conquered England, the French and English kings fought many wars over who owned land in France. The longest of these was the Hundred Years' War. It began when Edward III of England claimed that he should be King of France.

Edward III and the Black Prince

Edward and his son, the Black Prince, won a famous battle at Crécy, seized the town of Calais and captured the French king at Poitiers. By 1360, the English had won a lot of land in France (see map), but over the next 40 years, they lost most of it.

Henry V

In 1415, King Henry V of England captured Harfleur and won the Battle of Agincourt. Henry planned to be the next King of France, but the French king's son refused to accept this, and fighting broke out again.

This picture shows the start of the Battle of Agincourt.
★

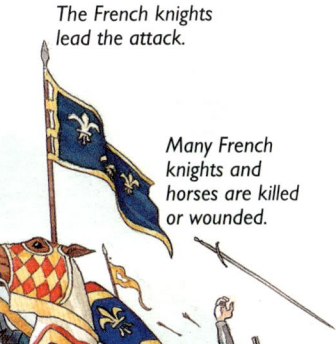

The Black Prince

Land ruled by England in 1360

Borders of France

Jeanne d'Arc

In 1429, the French made a comeback. Led by a peasant girl called Jeanne d'Arc, they drove the English out of Orléans. The English burned Jeanne to death, but the French continued to win back land. In 1453, a French army captured Bordeaux, and the war ended.

Jeanne d'Arc

The French knights lead the attack.

Many French knights and horses are killed or wounded.

English archers shoot at the French knights.

Wooden stakes protect the English.

Important dates

1337 The Hundred Years' War begins.

1346 The English win the Battle of Crécy.

1415 The English win the Battle of Agincourt.

1429 Jeanne d'Arc drives the English out of Orléans.

1453 The Hundred Years' War ends.

EUROPE

Kings, Nobles and Peasants

Life was very organized in medieval Europe. People were divided into four main groups and each group had different jobs to do. This way of life is now called the feudal system.

King

Nobles

Knights

Peasants

★ This diagram shows the four main groups in the feudal system.

Knights

Nobles gave land to their knights as payment for their help in battle. Knights trained for war and fought for nobles and kings.

A knight training for war

Peasants

Peasants farmed the land of the knights, nobles and kings. In return, the landowners protected the peasants from enemy attacks. (To find out more about peasants, see pages 226 and 227.)

Part of a medieval calendar, showing peasants working in a noble's fields

Kings

At the top of the feudal system was the king. He owned all the land in a country, made the laws and led the country's army.

A king being crowned

Nobles

The king gave large areas of land to his nobles. In return for this land, the nobles promised to fight for the king and to provide him with knights for his army.

★ A noble promises to serve and obey his king. This promise is called "paying homage".

The people rebel

In spite of their promises to serve and obey, nobles sometimes rebelled against their king, and peasants led revolts against their lords.

King John and his barons

King John of England was a strong king with a fierce temper. He kept his nobles (called barons) under tight control, but in 1215 they rebelled. The barons made John sign an agreement called Magna Carta. This said that the king had to talk to a council of barons and bishops before he made any big decisions.

King John

The birth of Parliament

In 1275, English knights and townsmen joined the barons and bishops in a new council, known as Parliament. Over the next hundred years, several councils like this were created to control the kings of Europe.

A meeting of the English Parliament

The Peasants' Revolt

In 1381, hundreds of English peasants rebelled against the landowners. They were provoked by the introduction of a new tax called the Poll Tax, and they wanted freedom from working for their lords. Led by Wat Tyler, they marched to London and rioted in the streets. King Richard II met the rebels and promised to help them, but later he punished them.

★ This picture shows the peasants rioting in London.

Peasants break into the Tower of London.

Houses are set on fire..

These men are stealing from a rich merchant's house.

These people are wrecking a lawyer's house.

This prisoner has been released from jail.

Some people are murdered.

Nobles and merchants try to escape.

Wat Tyler leads the peasants through the streets.

Important dates

1215 King John signs Magna Carta.

1275 The English Parliament starts to meet regularly.

1381 The Peasants' Revolt

EUROPE

1100   1200   1300   1400   1500

Knights, Soldiers and War

Foot soldiers defending a castle

During the Middle Ages, people had to be prepared for war at any time. Kings and nobles built castles to protect themselves from their enemies, knights and foot soldiers trained for war, and armies fought battles at home and abroad.

Defending a castle

A castle could be attacked by foreign invaders or by an enemy lord. Castles were designed to be extremely strong and easy to defend.

This picture shows an army attacking a castle.

Guards throw rocks over the battlements.

Castle guards pour boiling oil through here.

Archers fire arrows through these slits.

Soldiers use a siege tower to climb into the castle.

The drawbridge is pulled up to keep out enemies. (It has been cut away to let you see behind it.)

Some daring soldiers climb a siege ladder.

The portcullis is made of iron. It can be raised and lowered.

Battering ram

Some soldiers have built a bridge from planks and branches.

Pike

Catapult

Rock

Moat

This man is using a longbow.

Becoming a knight

Only boys from noble families could become knights. First, a boy worked as a page in a castle, learning how to ride and fight. Then, he became a squire and looked after a knight. When the squire had proved that he was a brave warrior, he was knighted by a king or a noble.

★ A noble knighting a squire

- Morning star
- Metal helmet
- Chain mail made from linked metal rings
- Shield with coat of arms

★ Mounted knight

This is the pennant (flag) of the lord of the castle.

Stones from the catapult have damaged the castle walls.

This extra shelter was built just before the battle.

Soldiers use wicker shields to protect themselves.

Slingshot catapult

Rocks for the catapult

This man is loading a crossbow.

Knights in battle

Knights fought on horseback, using swords, lances (long poles), axes, and vicious weapons called morning stars. Each knight wore a symbol, called a coat of arms, to show which family he belonged to.

Foot soldiers

Foot soldiers served their lord by guarding his castle and fighting for him. They fought with daggers, pikes (long spears), bows and arrows.

Medieval bowmen

EUROPE

| 1100 | 1300 | 1400 | 1500 |

223

Living in a Castle

Kings and nobles lived in castles with their families, their servants and their soldiers. In times of peace, the lord of the castle managed his lands, kept law and order, and held feasts and tournaments.

This cutaway picture shows the central keep (tower) of a castle.

★

These guards are looking out for enemies.

This bedroom belongs to the lord and his lady.

This is a private room for the lord's family. It is called the solar.

Watchtower
Keep
Inner bailey (courtyard)
Moat
Gatehouse
Outer bailey (courtyard)
Drawbridge

★ Plan of a castle

Chapel

This man is baking bread in an oven.

The castle guards eat here.

Well

Dungeon

Great hall

Stables

Garderobe (toilet)

Kitchen

Blacksmith

Knife grinder

Entrance

Food is kept cool in the storeroom.

Doves are kept in the dovecote.

Hunting

Kings and nobles often went hunting in the countryside around their castles. They rode on horseback with packs of hounds, and hunted deer, wild boar, bears and wolves.

King John hunting deer in a forest

Falconry

Falconry was a popular sport in the Middle Ages. Lords and ladies had their own falcons and hawks, which were trained by falconers to catch small animals and birds.

Falconers

Pastimes

Nobles and their families enjoyed dancing, singing and playing musical instruments. They played games, such as chess, and ladies worked on fine embroidery.

A game of chess

Feasting

Lavish feasts were held in the great hall of a noble's castle. ts served rich food and wine, jesters told jokes, and minstrels played their instruments and sang. Many different courses were served, and a feast could last for hours.

This picture shows a feast in a castle. ★

This is the high table. The most important guests sit here.

The lord and lady sit under a canopy.

The guests eat with their fingers.

This man tastes the lord's food, to make sure it has not been poisoned.

Musicians will play their trumpets when the next course arrives.

Roast swan

Boar's head

This dessert is called a subtlety. It is made mainly from marzipan.

Slices of stale bread are used for plates.

Salted fish on a pewter dish

Jester

Minstrel

Tournaments

Tournaments, or mock battles, were often held in the castle grounds. The most popular sport at a tournament was jousting. In a joust, two knights charged at each other and each knight tried to knock his opponent to the ground.

This knight has dropped his lance and his shield.

The horses are called destriers.

★ Knights jousting at a tournament

EUROPE

225

Living in a Village

During the Middle Ages, most people lived in villages. A knight, known as the lord of the manor, owned all the land around a village and the peasants had to earn the right to farm some of his land. Some peasants were freemen, who paid money or food for their land, but others, called villeins, had to work part-time for their lord.

A peasant sowing seeds

This picture shows a medieval village.

The fields are divided into strips.

A nobleman lives in this castle.

The lord of the manor lives in the manor house.

The lord of the manor is going hunting.

This is the pound where stray animals are kept. Their owners must pay to get them out.

The villagers keep their animals on a piece of land called a common.

Village green

This man is locked in the stocks as a punishment.

This man is fishing.

Stable

Inn

Well

Blacksmith

Carpenters

This man is cutting wheat with a sickle.

Farming

Most villages had three large fields. One was planted with wheat and one with barley. The third field was left fallow (unplanted), so it would be fit for planting the next year. Each field was divided into strips for different families to farm. A family would have several strips in each of the three fields.

These people are taking wool, eggs and cheese to sell in a nearby town.

Other jobs

All the villagers worked on the land, but some, like the miller and the blacksmith, did other jobs as well. People gave them food in return for their work.

EUROPE

500   600   700   800   900

Village homes

Peasants lived in simple cottages with bare floors and no glass in the windows. They had to share their home with their animals.

The miller grinds the villagers' grain in this windmill.

This cottage has been cut away so you can see inside. ★

Food for the winter is stored in the roof.

Hole for smoke

Thatched roof

Timber frame

Church

Priest's house

Thatcher

People sleep on straw mattresses.

Tools

Stable

Cooking pot

Stone fireplace

Clothes chest

The walls are made from wattle-and-daub (twigs covered with mud and straw).

This woman is spinning wool.

Vegetable garden

Beehives

Food

A medieval picture of a woman milking a cow

Each house had a big garden where peasants grew vegetables, fruit and herbs, and kept bees and chickens. Housewives made cheese from their cows' milk, to eat and to sell. Fish was cheap, but meat was an expensive treat.

Fairs

At least once a year, a fair was held on the village green. Merchants came to buy and sell goods, people played games and held wrestling matches, and entertainers amused the crowds.

Acrobats

These men are wrestling.

Juggler

★ A village fair

This man has trained a bear to dance.

EUROPE

Living in a Town

This picture shows part of a medieval town.

By the year 1100, small towns were starting to appear all over Europe. Many of these towns were built beside a castle. People living in a town paid rent to the lord of the castle, but they did not have to work for him and they could choose how to earn their living.

A medieval town

Castle

Town wall

Wine merchant's house

Church

Cloth merchant's shop

Farmers bring food and wool to the market.

Marketplace

People throw waste into the streets.

Brewer

Beggar

This is the potter's workshop. His family lives upstairs.

Inn

Drain

The streets are very dirty.

Craftworkers

Many craftworkers set up workshops in the towns. They made useful things, such as clothes, pots and pans, which they sold to the townspeople and to farmers who visited the towns.

Dyers dyeing cloth

Merchants

Merchants sold wool, wood and iron to the craftworkers. They also sold luxury goods from foreign lands, such as silk, jewels, wine and spices.

A wine merchant's boat

Other jobs

Bakers, butchers and brewers provided food and drink for the townspeople. Innkeepers ran taverns, and priests and doctors came to work in the towns.

Town visitors

Farmers and traders came to the towns to buy and sell goods. Everyone who visited a town had to pay money, called a toll, before they were allowed in.

Poor people live in cottages.

Houses often burn down.

This is the guildhall, where members of the guilds meet.

Water-carrier

Baker's shop

Shoemaker's workshop

Guilds

Craftworkers who made the same things began to group together in special clubs, called guilds. The guilds made sure that everyone made high-quality goods and that prices and wages were fair. Merchants also had guilds to make sure that they traded fairly.

★
Blacksmiths' guild badge

Joining a guild

Most members of guilds were men. Before a man could join a guild, he had to work for seven years as an apprentice to a master craftsman. Then he made his "masterpiece". If it was good enough, he joined the guild as a journeyman. Only a few journeymen became masters.

A master testing his apprentices

Holy days and mystery plays

On special holy days, the guilds put on plays for the people of the town. Sometimes, they performed a long series of plays based on Bible stories. These plays became known as mystery plays, because they were produced by craftworkers, and the medieval word for craft was "maisterie".

★
A scene from a play of Saint George and the dragon

A play of the Last Judgment

This wagon is called a pageant.

Angel

Guild sign

Demon

The mouth of Hell

| 1100 | 1200 | 1300 | 1400 | 1500 |

Traders and Towns

By the 1300s, people in Europe could buy luxuries such as silk, jewels, sugar and spices. The merchants of Europe traded with Arab and Turkish merchants, who sold goods from places as far away as India, Africa and China.

Jewels, silk and spices from the East

Trade fairs

Several times a year, merchants from all over Europe met at trade fairs to buy and sell goods. The towns where the fairs were held became very rich.

A bishop blessing a trade fair

Mighty merchants

Medieval merchants employed workers to make goods, such as cloth, and paid for splendid buildings to be built in their towns. The leading merchants of a town met in a group, called a council, and made decisions about the way their town was run.

The cloth merchants of Bruges paid for this market hall.

Merchant bankers

As trade increased, many people needed to borrow money to buy goods. A group of merchants from Lombardy in northern Italy created the first bank, and other Italians soon set up banks all over Europe.

Merchant bankers counting money

Buying freedom

At first, townspeople paid rent to their local lord, but, as the towns grew richer, people wanted to be independent. In many towns, the people bought a document called a charter from their lord. The charter was stamped with the lord's seal to show that he had handed over his rights to the townspeople.

★ A seal on a town charter

City-states

Some great cities in Italy and Germany had their own rulers who lived in palaces and made laws for their cities. These independent cities were known as city-states.

Venice was one of the richest city-states.

The Hanseatic League

Some of the busiest trading towns in Europe were grouped around the North Sea and the Baltic Sea. These towns formed a club, or hanse, later known as the Hanseatic League. By 1350, there were over 70 towns in the league. All the towns helped each other and followed strict trading rules.

This picture shows a busy port in a Hanseatic town.
★

NORWAY • Stockholm

SWEDEN

• Visby

NORTH SEA • Riga

DENMARK

BALTIC SEA

RUSSIA

Lübeck • Danzig
• Rostock
Hamburg
Bremen •

HOLY ROMAN EMPIRE

• Bruges
• Cologne

Map of the main Hanseatic towns

This ship is sailing to England.

This ship is carrying Chinese silk and jewels.

Rich merchant's house

Merchants store their goods in warehouses.

Wine

Some goods are sold at market stalls.

Crane

The merchant ships are called cogs.

Bales of wool

Chests of spices

Traders bring furs from Russia.

A clerk records the goods as they are loaded.

Wood and grain are loaded onto this ship.

Small boats called lighters take goods to the quay.

Wood from Norway

1100	1200	1300	1400	1500

EUROPE

The Power of the Popes

★ Mosaic of a medieval pope

In the Middle Ages, religion played a vital role in the lives of every person in Europe. The head of the Church was the Pope, who lived in Rome. The popes had many bitter power struggles with the kings and Holy Roman Emperors. (See page 217 to find out more about the Holy Roman Empire.)

Popes and Emperors

The popes and the Holy Roman Emperors both wanted to control all the bishops in the Holy Roman Empire. This led to fierce arguments. In 1077, Pope Gregory VII made Emperor Henry IV wait barefoot in the snow for three days, before he would forgive him.

Pope and king

A French king, known as Philip the Fair, argued with Pope Boniface VIII over the king's right to collect taxes from lands owned by the Church. In 1303, Boniface announced that he had supreme power over all other rulers. This made Philip so angry that he took Boniface prisoner.

Pope Boniface

★ King Philip the Fair

Popes in France

In 1309, a French pope moved to Avignon in southern France. The popes stayed in France for a hundred years, and, for part of this time, rival popes ruled in Rome. Some countries followed the Avignon Pope and others supported the Pope in Rome (see map). This split in the Church was called the Great Schism.

This picture shows a procession in the city of Avignon.

Map of Europe

Followers of the Pope in Avignon
Followers of the Pope in Rome
Mostly followers of the Pope in Rome

The Pope's palace

People beg the Pope for his blessing.

The Pope is carried on a throne.

City merchants

Nuns

Monks

Bishops

These men, called cardinals, advise the Pope.

Priest

Bishop

500   600   700   800   900

Enemies of the Church

In the Middle Ages, it was very dangerous to behave differently from the way the leaders of the Church expected. Anyone who questioned the Church's teachings was punished severely, people who acted strangely were accused of witchcraft, and Jews were cruelly persecuted.

Persecuting Jews

Jewish people had to wear special clothes so they could be recognized. They were attacked and killed all over Europe, and driven out of England, France and Spain.

Jewish clothing

Trying witches

Suspected witches were given very unfair trials, such as trial by water. If they floated, they were guilty, and if they sank, they were innocent.

A suspected witch

Hounding heretics

People who questioned the teachings of the Church were called heretics. The popes sent out monks, called inquisitors, to find heretics and persuade them to change their minds. If they refused, they were tortured or killed.

Heretics being burned to death

Crusaders and Cathars

Crusader knights attacking a Cathar city

The Cathars were people who believed that the world was evil. Their ideas spread rapidly through southern France and this frightened Pope Innocent III. Innocent started a war, called the Albigensian Crusade, which did not end until all the Cathars were wiped out.

The Crusaders built this cathedral at Albi after they had defeated the Cathars.

Preacher power

Jan Hus was a Czech preacher who attacked the power of the Pope and said that people should read the Bible for themselves. He was arrested and burned to death as a heretic. After his death, his supporters, called Hussites, rebelled against the Pope and the Holy Roman Emperor. The fighting lasted for 17 years and the Hussites won many towns in eastern Europe.

Jan Hus being led to his death

Important dates

1210-1229	The Albigensian Crusade
c.1230	Popes begin to use inquisitors.
1290	Jews are driven out of England.
1306	Jews are driven out of France.
1309-1417	Popes in Avignon
c.1372-1415	The life of Jan Hus
1378-1417	Popes in Avignon and Rome (the Great Schism)
1419-1436	The Hussite wars
1492	Jews are driven out of Spain.

EUROPE

1100   1200   1300   1400   1500

Building a Cathedral

A bishop

Medieval bishops and archbishops gave orders that vast cathedrals should be built to show the glory of God. Most cathedrals took over a century to build. They were beautifully decorated with carvings, statues and stained-glass windows.

This picture shows a cathedral being built. ★

Stories in glass

Stained-glass windows in cathedrals and churches showed scenes from the Bible. Preachers used these pictures to teach people who could not read.

Window showing ★ a scene from the story of Noah's Ark

Spire

Wooden scaffolding

A machine called a winch lifts blocks of stone.

The roof is covered with sheets of lead.

Sometimes, workers fall and are killed.

The master mason tells the workmen what to do.

Stone cutters

Stone carver

Sculptors

Workshop

Carpenters make benches for priests to sit on.

These men are mixing mortar (cement).

The architect is showing the bishop a stained-glass window.

500   700   800   900

EUROPE

234

Going on a Pilgrimage

A pilgrim

During the Middle Ages, many Christians went on religious journeys called pilgrimages. They became pilgrims to show their love for God, and because they hoped that God would forgive their sins and cure their diseases.

Pilgrim routes

Pilgrims journeyed to holy places, called shrines, where saints were buried or sacred objects were kept. Many people made the journey to Jerusalem or Rome, and pilgrims flocked to Compostela in Spain, to visit the shrine of Saint James, the patron saint of pilgrims.

★
Saint James

Canterbury pilgrims

In England, pilgrims went to Canterbury to pray at the grave of Saint Thomas Becket, an archbishop who was murdered by the knights of King Henry II.

The murder of Thomas Becket

Pilgrims' tales

Although the pilgrims' journeys were difficult and dangerous, they could also be fun. In the medieval poem *The Canterbury Tales*, pilgrims tell each other stories as they travel along.

This picture shows pilgrims on their way to Canterbury.
★

Pilgrims stop at inns to eat and sleep.

Monks   Nuns

Sometimes, robbers attack the pilgrims.

This man is telling a story.

Sick child

Some people sing hymns.

This man is selling badges to pilgrims.

Rich people ride on horseback.

A priest preaches to the pilgrims.

This woman hopes that she will be cured.

This man is barefoot to show that he is sorry for his sins.

EUROPE

Monks and Monasteries

A monk and a nun

Many Christians in the Middle Ages chose to serve God by becoming monks or nuns. They lived apart from the rest of the world in monasteries for men, and convents for women. Monks and nuns prayed regularly, followed strict rules, and had special work to do each day.

This picture shows a monastery. Some of the walls have been cut away so you can see inside.

Monks wash in the lavatorium.

All the monks eat together in the refectory.

Kitchen

Visitors stay in the guesthouse.

Orchard

Vegetable garden

Monks care for sick people in the hospice.

Well

Monks copy manuscripts in the scriptorium.

This house belongs to the abbot, the head of the monastery.

Beehives

Meetings are held in the chapter house.

Monks praying together in their chapel

Becoming a monk

Monks had to promise to give up everything they owned, to obey their abbot (chief monk), and not to get married. Before a man made these promises, he joined the monastery as a novice, learning its rules and getting used to its way of life.

Monks splitting wood

Saint Benedict's rules

Medieval monks followed rules that were written by Saint Benedict in the 6th century. He said that monks should pray, study, and work hard in the fields. They should eat plain food, wear simple clothes (called habits) and look after the sick and the poor.

EUROPE

500	600	700	800	900

Monks sleep in the dormitory.

Some monks work in the fields.

The monastery is surrounded by a wall.

This walkway is called a cloister.

Chapel

Altar

These poor people are coming to ask for food.

Fishpond

Healing the sick

The monks grew herbs in their monastery gardens and used them to treat people who were sick. They kept careful records of which herbs worked, and became experts at making medicines.

Monks using herbs to make medicines ★

Making manuscripts

Unlike most people in the Middle Ages, many monks could read and write. They made handwritten books, called manuscripts, and decorated them with pictures and patterns.

★ A decorated letter in a medieval manuscript

Wealth and power

Rich people gave money and land to the monks, and many monasteries became very wealthy. Some monks stopped living a simple life, and instead of praying and working hard, they spent their time running their lands, and enjoying a life of luxury.

A monk greedily helps himself to a drink.

EUROPE

237

Art in the Middle Ages

Most men and women in medieval Europe couldn't read, but they learned a lot by looking at pictures. People learned about Christianity from the paintings, carvings and stained-glass windows in their local church, and preachers used these images to illustrate their teachings.

Pictures in churches

Medieval churches were filled with images. Even the smallest churches had vivid paintings on their walls and simple carvings inside and out. Large churches and cathedrals were decorated with stunning stained-glass windows, delicate carvings and striking statues.

Painted statue ★ of a German Christian princess

★
This window, which shows a coward running away from a rabbit, teaches people to be brave.

Curious carvings

Medieval carvers did not always show religious subjects. High up on church walls, they carved mischievous characters and monsters in stone. Some carvings on the outsides of churches had water spouts sticking out of their mouths. These carvings are known as gargoyles.

★ Carving of a monster

EUROPE

| 500 | 600 | 700 | 800 | 900 |

Art for the rich

Wealthy lords and ladies owned their own prayer books and Bibles, which were written by hand and beautifully illustrated. They also hung splendid tapestries on the walls of their castles. Many tapestries showed scenes of castle life.

A huntsman from a tapestry

Golden treasures

Goldsmiths made elaborate objects, such as crowns, goblets, and crosses, and decorated them with precious jewels.

★ Decorated top of a bishop's staff (stick)

Inspiring images

This 14th-century painting shows the Virgin Mary and Jesus surrounded by angels in heaven. It was probably displayed on an altar (table) in a private chapel.

Skilled artists painted beautiful religious pictures on wooden panels. These paintings, known as altarpieces, stood on an altar (table) in a church or chapel, and inspired people to worship.

The artists did not try to make their pictures realistic. Instead, they aimed to create an impression of heaven, by painting glowing scenes with glittering golden backgrounds.

EUROPE

| 1100 | 1200 | 1300 | 1400 | 1500 |

The Crusades

By the 1060s, an area known as the Holy Land (roughly between the Mediterranean Sea and the Jordan river) was controlled by Muslim Turks. They threatened Christian visitors and attacked the Christian Byzantine Empire. When the Turks beat the Byzantines at the Battle of Manzikert (see page 252), Christians felt their religion was in danger.

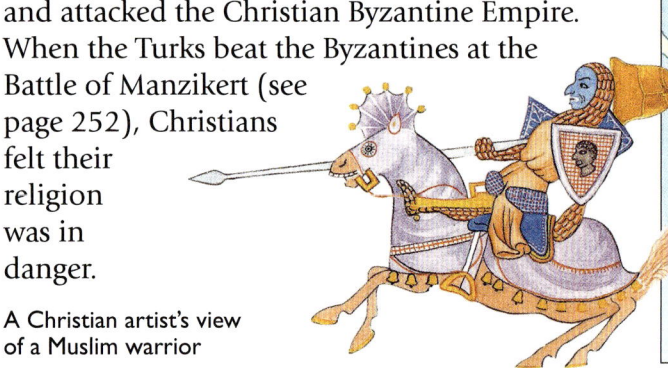
A Christian artist's view of a Muslim warrior

Map of the Holy Land

▪ Crusader lands of Outremer

Constantinople

TURKEY

Edessa

THE HOLY LAND

Acre

MEDITERRANEAN SEA

Jerusalem

NORTH AFRICA

EUROPE · ASIA · AFRICA

Salah ad-Din Yusuf ibn Ayyub

The call to battle

After the Turks' victory, the Byzantine Emperor asked the Christians of western Europe for help. In 1095, Pope Urban II preached a sermon in France. He urged Christians from all over Europe to go on a crusade, or holy war, to drive the Muslims out of the Holy Land.

Pope Urban preaching his famous sermon in France

The First Crusade

Nobles from France, Germany and Italy gathered their armies together and set off for the Holy Land. It took them three years to reach Jerusalem, but in 1099 they captured the city and the surrounding lands. The Crusaders called these lands Outremer, which means "the kingdom across the sea".

The Muslims fight back

After the First Crusade, many Crusaders went home, leaving Outremer weak. Muslims seized the town of Edessa, and a Second Crusade failed to win it back. Under brave leader Salah ad-Din Yusuf ibn Ayyub (Saladin) the Muslims recaptured Jerusalem.

In this scene, an army of crusaders is trying to capture a walled city.

Muslim soldiers fighting fiercely

The Third Crusade

The Third Crusade was led by the rulers of England, France and Germany. They won many battles, and captured the city of Acre, but they did not win back Jerusalem.

Crusaders fighting Muslims ★ during the Third Crusade

Crusaders ride heavy horses that are good at charging.

Muslim warriors ride lightweight horses, so they can attack swiftly.

Richard the Lion Heart, King of England, leads his army.

Crusader knights

Groups of knights who were also monks were formed to fight the Muslims. The main groups were the Knights Templar, the Teutonic Knights and the Knights Hospitaller.

A Knight Templar

The end of the Crusades

Three more Crusades set out in the next hundred years. In 1229, the Muslims agreed that the Christians could take back Jerusalem, but this agreement did not last. The Muslims continued to win back land and in 1291 they conquered Acre, the last Crusader city.

Important dates

1071	The Battle of Manzikert
1096-1099	The First Crusade
1099	The Crusaders capture Jerusalem.
1147-1149	The Second Crusade
1187	The Muslims recapture Jerusalem. The Third Crusade
1191	The Crusaders capture Acre.
1202-1204	The Fourth Crusade
1204	The Crusaders capture Constantinople.
1229	The Crusaders control Jerusalem.
1244	The Muslims recapture Jerusalem.
1291	The Muslims recapture Acre. The Crusades end.

The Fourth Crusade

The Fourth Crusade only went as far as Constantinople, the capital of the Byzantine Empire. Although the Crusaders were supposed to be on the same side as the Byzantines, they attacked their city and stole many of its treasures. The Crusaders ruled Constantinople for nearly 60 years.

This picture shows Saint Mark's Cathedral in Venice. The four bronze horses were stolen from Constantinople.

THE MIDDLE EAST

| 1100 | 1200 | 1300 | 1400 | 1500 |

The Black Death

In 1347, a ship returned to Italy from Asia, bringing with it a terrible plague (disease). The plague was called the Black Death because of the deadly black swellings it caused. In six years, it swept across Europe, killing roughly one in every three people.

A sick sailor being carried ashore

Map of Europe

The map shows when the Black Death reached different parts of Europe.

Areas not affected by the Black Death

RUSSIA 1353
BRITAIN 1348
POLAND 1350
1349
1348
1347
FRANCE
ATLANTIC OCEAN
SPAIN
EUROPE ASIA AFRICA

Fatal fleas

The Black Death was spread by bloodsucking fleas that lived on rats, and by airborne germs, but no one realized this. People tried to stop the plague from spreading, but nothing worked.

People burning the clothes of the dead

Punishment from God

Many people thought that God had sent the Black Death as a punishment for their sins. A group of men, called the Flagellant Brothers, tried to stop the disease by whipping their bodies to punish themselves. They went from town to town and actually helped to spread the plague.

This picture shows ★ a town infected with the Black Death.

The owners of these houses have escaped to the country.

Thieves steal food from empty houses.

The dead are taken away in carts.

Infected houses are marked with a cross.

Some Brothers whip themselves.

A group of Flagellant Brothers walks through the town.

Rats run through the streets.

This doctor is trying to protect himself by wearing a leather mask.

EUROPE

500   600   700   800   900

QUICKLINKS: For links to websites about the legend of Robin Hood and harsh laws in medieval times, go to **usborne.com/Quicklinks**

Criminals and Outlaws

Life in medieval Europe could be dangerous and violent. Thieves lurked in towns, robbers lay in wait on lonely roads, and quarrels sometimes led to deadly fights.

Catching criminals

Groups of men took turns being watchmen in their towns and villages, but everyone had the right to catch a criminal. Anyone who saw a crime take place could chase after the wrongdoer, calling out to others to join in. This noisy chase was called a "hue and cry".

This picture shows a hue and cry in a village.

Wrongdoers are kept in this lock-up (prison).

The village watchmen join in the chase.

The pig's owner has started the hue and cry.

This man has stolen a pig.

Public punishments

Most punishments were carried out in public, to make people frightened of breaking the law. Wrongdoers could be locked in the stocks, or dragged through the streets and whipped, and people who committed serious crimes were put to death in front of large crowds.

Harsh laws

There were many harsh laws in the Middle Ages, but some of the most hated were the forest laws. These laws allowed kings and nobles to hunt deer on their own lands, while any peasant who killed a deer was severely punished, and could even be put to death.

Outlaws

Sometimes, people ran away to escape punishment. These runaways became outlaws and lived in forests. They had no rights and it was not a crime to kill them. Many stories have been written about the famous English outlaw Robin Hood, but no one knows if he really existed.

A criminal being dragged through the streets

Statue of ★ Robin Hood

Kingdoms of the Celts

Celtic archer

By the year 500, barbarian tribes ruled most of Europe (see page 204), but some people, called the Celts, managed to stay independent. The Celts in Brittany remained separate from France until 1532, and the Welsh, Scots and Irish all fought to stay free of England.

Controlling Wales

The English kings wanted to control the princes who ruled Wales, so they gave land on the Welsh borders to powerful English nobles. These nobles, called marcher lords, kept the Welsh out of England, but also won Welsh lands for themselves.

Stained-glass portrait of a marcher lord

Welsh princes

Prince Llywelyn the Great united the Welsh princes and married the King of England's daughter. His son, Gruffydd, was taken prisoner by the English, but his grandson, Llywelyn ap Gruffydd, was accepted as the Prince of Wales by the English king.

Gruffydd falling to his death from the Tower of London

The English triumph

Llywelyn ap Gruffydd gained control of most of Wales, but in 1276 King Edward I of England decided to fight the Welsh. Llywelyn was killed, Edward made his own son Prince of Wales, and the English built castles all over north Wales. After this, there were many Welsh rebellions, but none of them lasted for long.

Edward I naming his son Prince of Wales

Map of the Celtic kingdoms

Celtic Kingdoms

Marcher lords' lands in 1280

EUROPE, Asia, Africa

ATLANTIC OCEAN

SCOTLAND

Bannockburn

IRELAND

Dublin

ENGLAND

WALES

FRANCE

BRITTANY

This picture shows a Welsh army attacking an English castle.

The castle has high, strong walls.

English archers

Some English soldiers throw rocks.

Many of the Welsh are killed.

Welsh soldiers clamber up the cliff.

EUROPE

500   600   700   800   900

Wallace of Scotland

Scotland had its own king, but in 1296 the Scots could not decide who should be their next king, so Edward I of England took over as ruler. This made the Scots furious, and a Scottish knight called William Wallace led them into battle against Edward. At first, Wallace was victorious, but later he was captured and killed.

Statue of ★
William Wallace

Most of the Scottish army are not trained soldiers.

Robert Bruce will lead his knights into battle.

Scottish knights

Scottish foot soldiers defend themselves with spears.

Bruce and Bannockburn

In 1306, Robert Bruce was secretly crowned King of Scotland. He defeated King Edward II of England at Bannockburn, and in 1328 Edward accepted that Scotland was an independent kingdom.

This picture shows the start of the Battle of Bannockburn.

The Scots have planted stakes in the ground.

The English knights charge at the Scots.

The ground is wet and marshy.

Some horses fall into pits dug by the Scots.

The English in Ireland

In 1160, an English noble, nicknamed Strongbow, went to help an Irish king fight against his rivals. Strongbow married the king's daughter and seized Dublin. This alarmed the English king who started a campaign to win Irish land for himself. By 1400, the English controlled eastern Ireland, but the Irish won back most of their land over the next hundred years.

Irish king

Irish warriors attacking an English army

Important dates

1170	Strongbow seizes Dublin.
1258-1282	Llywelyn ap Gruffydd is Prince of Wales.
1301	Edward II becomes Prince of Wales.
1314	Battle of Bannockburn
1328	Edward II accepts Scotland's independence.
1532	Brittany becomes part of France.

EUROPE

| 1100 | 1200 | 1300 | 1400 | 1500 |

The Rise of Burgundy

One of the most powerful nobles in medieval Europe was the Duke of Burgundy, who ruled over an area, called a duchy, in eastern France. When the Duke died in 1361, he left no son to inherit his land, so King Jean II of France made his youngest son, Philippe, the new Duke.

Duke Philippe and his descendants built up a huge duchy in France and Flanders (an area now made up of Holland, Belgium and northern France). The dukes collected taxes from cloth merchants, bankers and farmers, and became incredibly rich.

Supporters of the arts

The dukes of Burgundy paid artists and writers to produce works of art. The famous painter Jan van Eyck worked for the Burgundy family.

Map of Burgundy's lands

- Duchy of Burgundy in 1363
- Burgundian lands at their largest
- Border between French and Habsburg lands after 1493

The Arnolfini Marriage, by Jan van Eyck, was painted to celebrate the wedding of an Italian merchant who had settled in Flanders.

Quarrels in France

The dukes of Burgundy fought against the Duke of Orléans and his supporters, the Armagnacs. They also argued with the kings of France. In 1419, Duke Jean of Burgundy was murdered, probably on the orders of the French king's son. After this, Burgundy supported England in the Hundred Years' War against France.

Marie and Maximilian

In 1476, Duke Charles the Bold of Burgundy arranged for his only child, Marie, to marry Prince Maximilian Habsburg of Austria. The following year, Charles died in battle, and the French king seized some of his lands. For the next 20 years, Maximilian fought the French over Burgundy.

Maximilian Habsburg

Burgundy divides

Maximilian was crowned Holy Roman Emperor in 1493. In the same year, he and the French king agreed to divide Burgundy between them. The French took all the Burgundian lands in France, except for a small part of the original duchy. The rest of Burgundy joined the Holy Roman Empire.

EUROPE

500   600   700   800   900

The court of Burgundy

Magnificent feasts and dances were held in the castles of Burgundy. The knights and ladies of the Burgundian court wore extravagant clothes and had beautiful manners.

A dance in a Burgundian castle

The musicians play from the gallery (balcony).

This poet is waiting to present his work to the duchess.

Duke

Duchess

The duke's cup is held up high so no one can breathe on it.

This is the chancellor, who advises the duke.

Everyone at court wears fabulous clothes made from silk, satin, fur and velvet.

Important dates

1363-1404	Philippe the Good is Duke of Burgundy.
1410-1411	The Burgundians fight the Armagnacs.
1419	Jean the Fearless of Burgundy is murdered.
1477	Marie of Burgundy marries Maximilian Habsburg of Austria.
1477-1493	France and Austria fight over Burgundy.
1493	Maximilian Habsburg becomes Holy Roman Emperor. Burgundy is divided.

EUROPE

1100   1200   1400   1500

The Wars of the Roses

In 1455, a bitter struggle broke out between two branches of the English royal family. The opponents were the house (or family) of Lancaster and the house of York. Their struggle became known as the Wars of the Roses because both sides wore a rose emblem (or badge).

★ The white rose of York and the red rose of Lancaster

English royal family tree

- King Edward III
  - Edward the Black Prince
    - King Richard II
  - John of Gaunt, Duke of Lancaster
    - John Beaufort
      - John Beaufort
        - Margaret Beaufort
          - King Henry VII (also known as Henry Tudor)
    - King Henry IV
      - King Henry V
        - King Henry VI
  - Edward, Duke of York
    - Richard of Cambridge
      - Richard, Duke of York
        - King Edward IV
          - Elizabeth of York
          - King Edward V
          - Richard of York
        - King Richard III

Key:
- Plantagenets
- Lancasters
- Yorks
- Tudors

Lancaster weakens

King Henry VI came from the Lancaster family, but, unlike his father and grandfather, he was not a great warrior. He failed to stop the French from winning the Hundred Years' War and he could not control his nobles. He also suffered from mental health problems.

Henry VI

The struggle begins

In 1454, Parliament gave Richard, Duke of York, the right to rule on King Henry's behalf. The next year, a group of nobles, led by Henry's wife, refused to let Richard rule. The Yorkists and Lancastrians gathered their supporters and began to fight.

A Yorkist king

Edward IV's symbol was a white rose inside a sun.

After a series of battles, Henry VI escaped to Scotland, and Richard of York's son, Edward, was crowned King of England. Edward IV ruled for 22 years, but he struggled against the Lancastrians for the first 10 years of his reign.

Warwick the Kingmaker

The Earl of Warwick helped his cousin, Edward IV, become king, but later he supported Henry VI when he tried to be king again. Warwick became known as "the Kingmaker".

The Earl of Warwick plotting against King Edward IV

★

EUROPE

500   600   700   800   900

Richard III

Edward IV died when his oldest son, Edward, was 12 years old. Before Edward V could be crowned, his uncle, Richard of Gloucester, declared himself king. Few people dared to oppose Richard, and he was crowned Richard III.

Richard III

Princes in the Tower

Richard insisted that Edward and his brother should stay in the Tower of London. The boys were never seen again and many people thought that Richard had given orders for them to be killed.

The young princes, painted by a 19th-century artist

The end of Richard III

The Lancastrians were determined to get rid of King Richard. Their choice for a new king was Henry Tudor, a member of the Lancaster family. In 1484, Henry invaded England from France. He fought against King Richard at the Battle of Bosworth Field, and Richard was defeated and killed.

This picture shows Henry Tudor leading his troops to fight King Richard III.

There are about 4,000 men in Henry's army.

The Lancastrian nobles support Henry.

Henry Tudor

Many men join Henry's army.

Some Yorkist nobles have abandoned Richard and joined Henry's army.

The first of the Tudors

Henry Tudor was crowned King Henry VII of England. He united the families of Lancaster and York by marrying Elizabeth of York, daughter of Edward IV. The Wars of the Roses came to an end, and England was ruled by the Tudors until 1603.

Important dates

1422-1461	Henry VI is king.
1455	The Wars of the Roses begin.
1461-1483	Edward IV is king.
1483	Edward V becomes king, but is never crowned.
1483-1485	Richard III is king.
1485	The Lancastrians win the Battle of Bosworth Field. The Wars of the Roses end.
1485-1509	Henry VII is king.

1100   1200   1300   1400   1500

EUROPE

Mongol Invaders

A Mongol yurt

The Mongols were nomads (wandering people) who roamed the plains of central Asia. They lived in tents, called yurts or gers, and were always on the move, searching for grasslands where their animals could feed. In battle, the Mongols were cruel and bloodthirsty.

Genghis Khan

Around 1180, a young Mongol warrior called Temüjin began to lead daring raids on other Mongol tribes. He built up a powerful army and slowly brought all the tribes under his control. In 1206, the tribes named him Genghis Khan, though it's not certain what this means.

Genghis Khan

Building the Empire

Led by Genghis, the Mongols invaded northern China. Then, they swept eastward, killing thousands of people as they went. Genghis made laws for everyone in his Empire to obey, set up a messenger service, and encouraged trade.

After Genghis died, his sons and grandsons became khans (rulers). They won more land for their Empire in China, Europe and the Middle East.

This picture shows the Mongol army on the move.

This messenger is bringing news to the khan.

Map of the Mongol Empire

- ▨ Mongol lands before Genghis Khan
- ▨ Mongol Empire at its largest
- ▬ Border of Tamerlane's Empire

RUSSIA

MONGOLIA

Beijing

PERSIA

CHINA

JAPAN

PACIFIC OCEAN

INDIA

ARABIAN SEA

This yurt belongs to one of the khan's wives.

Camels carry heavy loads.

These are the warriors' spare horses.

This is one of the khan's generals.

Lance

Some warriors wear breastplates and shoulder guards.

Guards protect the khan.

The khan wears a golden robe.

Warriors use bows and arrows, curved swords and lances.

Mongol horsemen use high saddles and short stirrups.

Kublai Khan

★ Kublai Khan in Chinese dress

Kublai Khan was a grandson of Genghis Khan. He conquered all of China and made Beijing his capital city.

Kublai tried twice to invade Japan, but the Japanese resisted fiercely. He gave up trying to attack Japan when violent winds (called "kamikaze") wrecked his ships.

Japanese warriors attacking a Mongol warship ★

Timur

After Kublai's rule, the Mongol Empire fell apart. Family quarrels made its rulers weak and many of the conquered people fought back.

Then, in 1360, a Mongol leader called Timur began to build a new empire. Timur seized land in Persia, Russia and India, but the Empire did not last long after his death.

Timur ★

The khan's banner

This banner is made of horsetails. When they are in battle, the Mongols fly a banner of black horsetails.

The khan's yurt

Catapult

Larger yurts are pulled on carts. Smaller yurts are packed up and carried by animals.

The wheels of the cart need constant greasing with animal fat.

Teams of oxen pull the larger yurts.

These drummers beat their kettledrums when the army charges.

Important dates

1162 Temüjin is born in Mongolia.

1206 Temujin is given the name Genghis Khan.

1206-1227 Genghis Khan builds the Mongol Empire.

1259-1294 Kublai Khan rules.

1279 The Mongol Empire is at its largest.

1360-1405 Timur builds a new Mongol Empire.

1100   1200   1300   1400   1500

THE FAR EAST

251

Triumphs of the Turks

The Turks were wandering people who came from central Asia. Around 950, a tribe of Turks called the Seljuks began to sweep westward. They invaded the Islamic Empire which had become so weak that its ruler welcomed the Seljuks into his capital, Baghdad.

Seljuk warriors ★

Seljuks lived in tents called yurts.

Map of Seljuk lands

EUROPE
ASIA
AFRICA

TURKEY
Manzikert
SYRIA
Baghdad
Jerusalem
PERSIA
PALESTINE
CENTRAL ASIA

■ Seljuk lands at their largest
— Borders of the Islamic Empire
— Borders of the Byzantine Empire

Metal breastplate

Embroidered cloth

The Crusaders fight back

Some Seljuks attacked Christian visitors to the Holy Land, and many Christians felt that they should fight for the land where their religion began. The Pope called for a crusade (holy war) against the Seljuks, and by 1100 the Crusaders had conquered most of the Holy Land (see page 240).

Seljuks attacking Christians

Winning land

In the 1050s, the Seljuks began invading the Byzantine Empire. They defeated the Byzantines at Manzikert and won Turkey. Later, they also captured Syria and the Holy Land. Many Seljuks settled in their newly gained lands. They followed the Muslim religion and built elaborate mosques.

A Seljuk holy dancer, called a Mevlevi or whirling dervish

A Seljuk ★ mosque

Minaret (prayer tower)

The end of the Seljuks

By 1200, the Seljuks had split into small groups ruled by rival princes, and many Seljuk people rebelled against their leaders. When tribes of Mongols attacked them, the Seljuks were too weak to fight back. By 1300, the Mongols had conquered most of the Seljuk lands except Turkey.

Mongol soldiers

500   600   700   800   900

The rise of the Ottoman Empire

In 1301, a Turkish prince called Osman declared himself Sultan (king) of all the Turks. He built up an army and began to win land. The land won by Osman and his descendants was called the Ottoman Empire.

Osman I

Running the Empire

The Ottoman sultans were strong rulers as well as skilled soldiers. They made strict laws for their people, and built beautiful mosques, schools and baths in their cities.

A public bath built for a sultan

Map of the Ottoman Empire

BLACK SEA

Constantinople

TURKEY

Ottoman lands in 1301
Land won by Osman I
Ottoman Empire in 1500

The fall of Constantinople

The Ottomans gradually won land from the Byzantine people, and in 1453 they captured Constantinople, the capital of the Byzantine Empire (see page 203). Sultan Mehmed II rebuilt Constantinople, which he renamed Istanbul, and made it the capital of the Ottoman Empire.

This picture shows the Ottomans marching through Constantinople after their victory. ★

Some buildings are on fire.

Mounted soldiers

Sultan Mehmed

Guards

The Byzantine people are scared.

Prisoners of war

Many buildings have been damaged in the battle.

Janissaries (foot soldiers)

Musicians announce the arrival of the sultan.

Important dates

1055	The Seljuks enter Baghdad.
1071	The Seljuks defeat the Byzantines at Manzikert.
1099	The Crusaders capture parts of the Holy Land.
c.1200-1300	The Mongols invade the Seljuk lands.
1301-1326	Osman I is sultan.
1451-1481	Mehmed II is sultan.
1453	The Ottomans capture Constantinople.

THE MIDDLE EAST

1100 1200 1300 1400 1500

Kingdoms of Eastern Europe

During the 6th century, tribes of warriors from Asia began moving west into Europe. The warriors were pagans who did not believe in Christ, and the people of Europe were terrified of them.

The tribes created many warlike kingdoms in eastern Europe. Most of these kingdoms did not last long, but some of them later became powerful Christian countries.

Map of eastern Europe

BALTIC SEA

RUSSIA

LITHUANIA

Tannenberg

HOLY ROMAN EMPIRE

Prague

Lechfeld

EUROPE
ASIA
AFRICA

Crown of Charles IV of Bohemia

Poland
Hungary
Bohemia
Wallachia
Lands of the Teutonic Knights

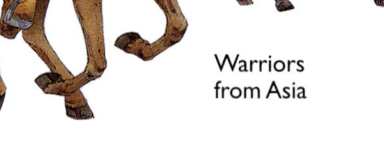

Warriors from Asia

Magyars in Hungary

In the 800s, a tribe called the Magyars conquered the area now known as Hungary. The Magyars fought fiercely to win more land, but in 955 they were beaten by the Germans at the Battle of Lechfeld (see page 217).

The Holy Roman Empire

After the Germans' victory, the Pope set up the Holy Roman Empire and made the German king its emperor (see page 217). The Pope relied on the emperor to defend Christian Europe against invading pagan tribes.

The kingdom of Hungary

In 975, the Magyar leader, Géza, became a Christian, and in 1001 the Pope accepted Géza's son, Stephen, as the first King of Hungary. Stephen was a keen Christian who was later made a saint. He created a peaceful kingdom with strong laws, and most of the Magyars became Christians.

This picture shows King Stephen leading a religious procession.
★

Churches have been built all over Hungary.

Bishops and priests accompany their king.

500   600   800   900

EUROPE

Count Dracula of Transylvania

Transylvania was part of the mountainous kingdom of Wallachia. In the 15th century, it was ruled by a count called Vlad Tepes, who was famous for his cruelty. Vlad put thousands of people to death by impaling (spearing) them on wooden stakes. He was given the nickname Dracula, which means "dragon's son".

Count Dracula

The kingdom of Bohemia

The kingdom of Bohemia (now part of the Czech Republic) was created by a tribe of Slavs in the 800s. It grew into a rich and powerful country. In 1355, the Pope made Charles IV of Bohemia the Holy Roman Emperor, and Charles moved the capital of the Empire to Prague.

The Teutonic Knights

The Christian kingdom of Poland was threatened by pagan Prussians in the north, so the Poles asked the Teutonic Knights for help. The Teutonic Knights were soldier-monks from Germany who had fought in the Crusades.

The Knights conquered the Prussians and seized their lands. Then, they tried to win more land in Poland, Russia and Lithuania. Eventually, they were beaten by the Poles, the Lithuanians and their allies at the Battle of Tannenberg.

This picture shows Teutonic Knights attacking a Prussian village.

Knights have set fire to the village.

Any Prussians who do not accept Christianity are killed.

Knights use rafts to cross the lake.

Some Prussians will be taken prisoner.

These Prussians are escaping into the forest.

Important dates

955 The Germans beat the Magyars at Lechfeld. The Pope creates the Holy Roman Empire.

1001 The Pope recognizes the Christian kingdom of Hungary.

1224-1239 The Teutonic Knights conquer the Prussians.

1355-1378 Charles IV of Bohemia is Holy Roman Emperor.

1410 The Teutonic Knights are defeated at the Battle of Tannenberg.

EUROPE

| 1100 | 1200 | 1300 | 1400 | 1500 |

The Rise of the Russians

Viking ship

Around the year 700, Vikings from Sweden began to travel down rivers into the area that is now western Russia. At first, the Vikings attacked the Slavs who were living there, but later they settled down and started to build towns.

Rurik the Rus

Around 862, a Viking leader called Rurik captured the Slavic city of Novgorod and the lands around it. Rurik's followers were called the Rus, from which we get the name Russian. The Russians won lots of land and, in 882, Kyiv became their new capital city.

The city of Novgorod

Map of Russian lands

- SWEDEN
- Neva
- Novgorod
- Lake Peipus
- Moscow
- Kulikova
- Kyiv
- Constantinople

Russian lands around 1000

Borders of the Khanate of the Golden Horde

Borders of Russia in 1505

EUROPE · ASIA · AFRICA

Vladimir the Saint

Vladimir became Prince of Kyiv in 978. He believed that he could turn people into Christians by forcing them to be baptized (washed in water as a sign of a new beginning). After his death, Vladimir was made a saint because so many of his people had become Christians.

Prince Vladimir

This picture shows Russian people being baptized.

Yaroslav the Wise

Vladimir's son, Yaroslav, made Kyiv into a rich and powerful city. He encouraged art and learning, created a strong government, and sent traders to Constantinople. Later, he became known as "Yaroslav the Wise".

Saint Sofia's cathedral in Kyiv, built in Yaroslav's reign

Soldiers force people into the water.

500	600	700	800	900

The Mongols arrive

The Russian rulers who came after Yaroslav were weak, and in 1240 Kyiv was captured by tribes of Mongols. They created a vast kingdom called the Khanate of the Golden Horde, and forced the Russian rulers to pay them large sums of money, called tribute.

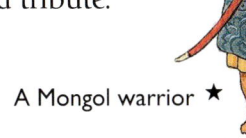

A Mongol warrior ★

Nevsky's victories

While the Tartars were invading the south, the Russians in the north defeated a Swedish army on the banks of the Neva, and drove back German invaders at Lake Peipus. Their leader, Alexander, became a hero. He was called "Nevsky" because of his victory at the Neva.

Nevsky leading his troops into battle
★

The growth of Moscow

Nevsky's son, Daniel, was crowned Prince of Moscow in 1280. Over the next 200 years, the princes of Moscow built up a powerful kingdom. Moscow became the most important city in Russia and, in 1328, the head of the Russian Church settled there.

Artists from Muscovy painted beautiful religious pictures, called icons.

The Mongols weaken

By the 1350s, the Mongols were fighting amongst themselves. Their kingdom split up, and in 1380 they were defeated by the Muscovites at Kulikova, in southern Russia.

Ivan the Great

The Mongols' power was finally broken by Prince Ivan III of Moscow. Ivan conquered the city of Novgorod and went on to win more land. In 1480, he declared himself Tsar (emperor) of all the Russians and refused to pay the Tartars any more tribute. He built many beautiful buildings in his capital city of Moscow.

Ivan the Great, first Tsar of Russia

The Cathedral of the Annunciation in Moscow, built in Ivan's reign ★

Important dates

c.700	The Vikings arrive in Russia.
c.862	Rurik creates a Rus kingdom.
1240	The Battle of the Neva
c.1250-1480	The Mongols rule southern Russia.
1380	The Battle of Kulikova
1480-1505	Ivan the Great rules Russia.

EUROPE

1100	1200	1300	1400	1500

The Struggle for Spain

In 711, an army of African Muslims crossed from North Africa into southern Spain. Spain had been ruled for 200 years by Visigoths (see page 204), but the Visigoths had become weak and were easily defeated by the new invaders.

Muslim warrior

Map of Spain

FRANCE

Córdoba

Granada

NORTH AFRICA

EUROPE
ASIA
AFRICA

— Border of al-Andalus in 1000
Aragon
Granada
León and Castile
Navarre
Portugal
Valencia

The map shows the main Spanish kingdoms in 1250.

Moving north

By 718, Muslim forces had conquered all of Spain except the mountainous kingdoms of the north. They also marched into France, but Charles Martel led an army of Franks against them. In 732, the Franks defeated the Muslim forces at the Battle of Poitiers, then they slowly drove them back into southern Spain.

Franks fighting Muslims

Muslim fighters

Franks

Learning and leisure

The people of al-Andalus were famous for their civilized way of life. They studied science, mathematics and astronomy, composed music, and wrote poetry. They also enjoyed playing games, such as chess.

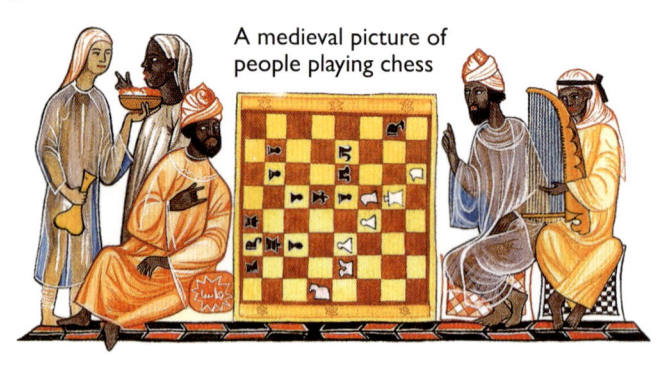

A medieval picture of people playing chess

The kingdom of al-Andalus

Muslim rulers created a kingdom of their own in Spain, called al-Andalus. They were great traders and builders and their capital, Córdoba, became one of the richest cities in Europe.

The Great Mosque at Córdoba

The rise of the Christian kingdoms

Around 1000, al-Andalus became weaker and began to split into separate kingdoms. At the same time, the Christian kingdoms in the north were growing stronger.
In 1037, León and Castile were united, and in 1139, the new kingdom of Portugal was created. Christian Spain was eventually united by the marriage of Isabella of Castile and Ferdinand of Aragon in 1469.

★ A king of León

EUROPE

500   600   700   800   900

The Christians fight back

For over 450 years, the rulers of the Christian kingdoms fought to drive the Muslims out of Spain. The Christians gradually moved south, conquering cities as they went. This long struggle to win back land is known as the "Reconquista".

This picture shows a Christian army marching into battle.

El Cid

The most famous soldier of the Reconquista was Rodrigo Diaz, known as El Cid, which means "the Lord". He led daring raids into Muslim lands and seized the kingdom of Valencia, which he ruled himself.

El Cid

The kingdom of Granada

By 1250, the Christians had won back all of Spain except the Muslim kingdom of Granada. One reason Granada survived so long was because its sultans (rulers) paid large sums of money, called tribute, to the kings of León and Castile. It was finally conquered in 1492.

A sultan of Granada

The Alhambra Palace in Granada

Battle tent called a pavillion

Foot soldiers with crossbows and axes

Mounted knights

Noblemen ride beside the army.

The nobles and knights are very richly dressed.

Drummer

Standard-bearer

Heralds blow trumpets.

Important dates

711   Muslim forces invade Spain.

c.730   Muslims rule most of Spain.

732   Charles Martel defeats Muslim forces at Poitiers.

c.1000   Muslim power in Spain starts to weaken.

1037-1492   The Christians win back Spain (the Reconquista).

1100   1200   1300   1400   1500

EUROPE

259

NORTH AFRICA: C.400-1500

QUICKLINKS: *For links to websites where you can visit Cairo and examine beautiful Fatimid art and architecture, go to* **usborne.com/Quicklinks**

Conquerors of North Africa

The land along the north coast of Africa was one of the richest parts of the Roman Empire, but in 429 it was invaded by the Vandals (see page 204). The Vandals forced the people of North Africa to pay very high taxes, and let many Roman cities fall into ruins.

Map of North Africa

Mosaic of a Vandal

MEDITERRANEAN SEA

NORTH AFRICA

Sahara Desert

TURKEY

SYRIA

• Cairo

EGYPT

ARABIA

EUROPE
ASIA
AFRICA

Muslim land in 1500
Border of Egypt

A Roman villa in North Africa

Byzantine rulers

In 533, the Byzantine Emperor Justinian drove the Vandals out of Africa. For the next 150 years, Byzantine rulers in North Africa tried to bring back the Roman way of life.

Coin showing the Emperor Justinian

Arab invaders

Arab forces invaded North Africa in 697, and by 750 it had become part of the Muslim Arab Empire. At first, North Africa was controlled by the Arab caliph (ruler), but slowly local rulers set up their own Muslim kingdoms.

Arab invaders

Fatimids in Egypt

In 969, a group of Muslims from Syria, the Fatimids, seized control of Egypt. They set up an independent kingdom and their capital city, Cairo, became very rich. The Fatimids ruled for 200 years until they were conquered by Arab leader, Salah ad-Din Yusuf ibn Ayyub (Saladin) (see page 240).

Cairo's city gates were built by the Fatimids.

Minaret (prayer tower)

Many merchants came to trade in Cairo.

Mamluks in Egypt

The descendants of Saladin stayed in power for 80 years, but in 1250 the Mamluks took over. They were Muslims who had once been slaves in Saladin's army. The most famous Mamluk leader was Sultan Baybars, who prevented tribes of Mongols from invading Egypt.

A Mamluk warrior

Important dates

429-533   The Vandals rule North Africa.

533-697   The Byzantines rule North Africa.

697   Arab invaders conquer North Africa.

750   North Africa is part of the Arab Empire.

969-1171   The Fatimids rule Egypt.

1250-1517   The Mamluks rule Egypt and defeat the Mongols at the Battle of Ain Jalut.

AFRICA

NORTH AFRICA
EAST AFRICA

500   600   700   800   900

EAST AFRICA: C.1000-1500

QUICKLINKS: For links to websites where you can explore Great Zimbabwe and the kingdom of Ethiopia, go to **usborne.com/Quicklinks**

Cities of East Africa

Around the year 1000, busy ports began to grow up on the coast of East Africa (see map). Merchants from Arabia, India and China sailed to these ports bringing tools, cloth, glass and china. In return, the Africans traded gold and ivory, iron and slaves, and even wild animals.

East Africans gave this giraffe to the Chinese emperor as a gift.

Stone bird from Great Zimbabwe

City of gold

People from all over southeast Africa brought gold to the city of Great Zimbabwe. The gold was collected in the city, then sent on to ports along the coast. The rulers of Great Zimbabwe became rich and powerful. They lived inside a walled fortress in the middle of the city.

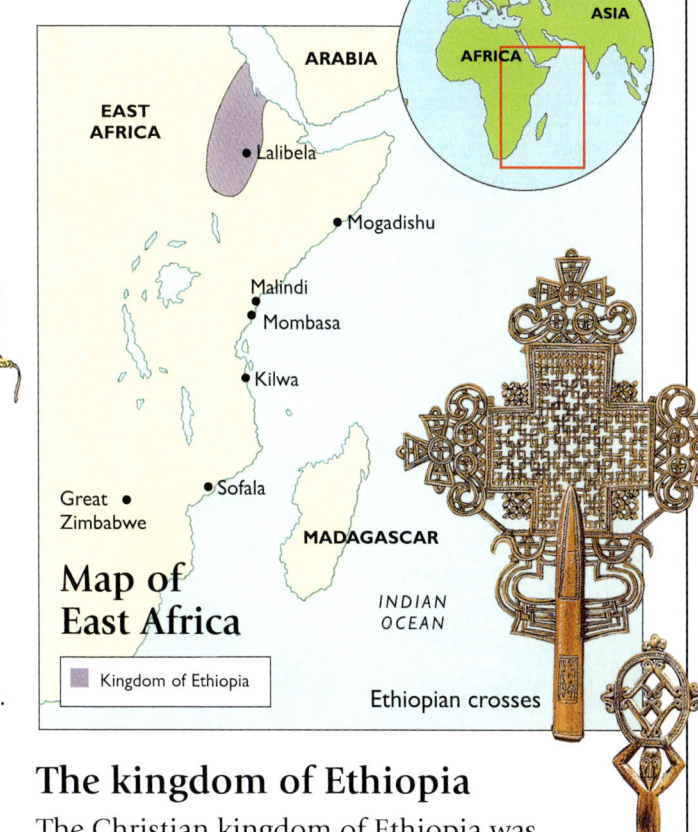

Map of East Africa

Kingdom of Ethiopia

ARABIA

EAST AFRICA

Lalibela

Mogadishu

Malindi

Mombasa

Kilwa

Great Zimbabwe

Sofala

MADAGASCAR

INDIAN OCEAN

Ethiopian crosses

The kingdom of Ethiopia

The Christian kingdom of Ethiopia was created around 1000. King Lalibela of Ethiopia believed that God had ordered him to carve churches out of rock. He built 11 churches which became very famous and the kingdom's main city was named after him.

One of King Lalibela's churches

This picture shows the fortress at Great Zimbabwe.

★

Religious ceremonies are held here.

The houses are made from clay and gravel, with grass roofs.

Strong outer wall made from granite blocks

Important dates

c.1000	The kingdom of Ethiopia is created.
c.1000-1200	Trading ports grow up on the east coast of Africa.
1200-1230	King Lalibela's churches are built in Ethiopia.
c.1350	Great Zimbabwe is at its largest.

AFRICA

| 1100 | 1200 | 1300 | 1400 | 1500 |

States of West Africa

By the year 800, Arab merchants from North Africa were crossing the Sahara Desert to trade with the people of West Africa. The West Africans grew rich by trading gold, slaves, and ivory from elephants' tusks, and many powerful states grew up (see map).

Arab merchants

Empires of gold

Between 300 and 1600, three great states rose and fell in the area south of the Sahara Desert. The Ghana Empire was followed by the Mali Empire and then by Songhai. Their people mined gold from rocks and their rulers became fabulously wealthy.

Rock with a crust of gold

Mansa Musa of Mali

The most famous West African ruler was Mansa Musa, head of the Mali Empire. He was a Muslim and a strict, but fair, ruler. He went on a pilgrimage (religious journey) to Mecca in Arabia, giving away presents of gold as he went.

This map shows Mansa Musa with an Arab merchant.

Map of West Africa

PORTUGAL

ATLANTIC OCEAN

NORTH AFRICA

Sahara Desert

Timbuktu

Niger

Igbo Ukwu

Congo

ARABIA

Mecca

EUROPE
ASIA
AFRICA

- ⬛ Benin
- ⬛ Ife
- ⬛ Kanem-Bornu
- ⬛ Kongo
- ⬛ Mali
- — Border of Ghana
- — Border of Songhai

The map shows the main West African states.

The city of Timbuktu

Timbuktu was one of Mali's most important cities. It had a large royal palace, a famous university, and many beautiful mosques. Muslim scholars from all over West Africa came to study at Timbuktu.

This picture shows part of the city of Timbuktu.

The city is surrounded by a high wall.

Poor people live in huts with no windows.

Rich people live in large houses with windows.

Well

All the houses are made from mud.

Rulers of the forest

By 800, there were several states in the forests around the mouth of the Niger. Most of the rulers of these states were also priests. A burial chamber at Igbo Ukwu, capital of the Nri kingdom, shows how priest-rulers were buried.

Cutaway picture of a ruler's burial chamber

The state of Ife

The forest state of Ife (pronounced "ee-feh") grew up around 1000. Its people were expert metalworkers who discovered a way of making figures from bronze. They made portraits of their past rulers and prayed to them.

★ Bronze head of a ruler from Ife

The kingdom of Benin

The richest forest state was Benin. Its craftworkers made delicate ivory carvings and spectacular bronze statues, and its ruler (called an Oba) lived in an enormous palace. Elaborate religious ceremonies were held at the palace.

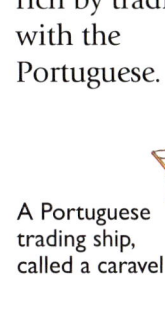

★ A drummer at the Oba's palace

The Portuguese arrive

In 1445, ships from Portugal reached the mouth of the Congo. Over the next 50 years, the Portuguese built trading towns along the West African coast. Some of the forest states, such as Benin, became very rich by trading with the Portuguese.

A Portuguese trading ship, called a caravel

Grain store

Marketplace

Mosque

African merchant

A servant holds a parasol to shade his master from the sun.

These men are carrying elephants' tusks.

Arab merchant

Farmers carry food to market.

Important dates

c.300-1200	Empire of Ghana
c.800-1911	Kingdom of Nri
c.850-1897	Kingdom of Benin
c.1000-1420	State of Ife
c.1200-1500	Empire of Mali
c.1312-1337	Mansa Musa rules Mali.
c.1350-1600	State of Songhai
c.1450	The Portuguese start trading in West Africa.

AFRICA

1100   1200   1300   1400   1500

Conquerors of Northern India

India split into small states around the year 550. These states were ruled by Hindu rulers – they followed the religion of Hinduism. The states of the south lasted for the next thousand years, but the states of the north were gradually conquered by Muslims.

An Indian ruler

Muslim invaders

Arab armies began invading northwest India in 711. Arab conquerors set up several peaceful Muslim kingdoms, but, around 1000, Mahmud of Ghazni led a series of savage raids on India from Afghanistan. Almost 200 years later, another Afghan, Muhammud of Ghor, conquered most of northern India. He killed hundreds of Indians and destroyed many Hindu temples.

Map of India

- **Sultanate of Delhi around 1300** (green)
- **Border of the Chola Empire** (orange line)
- **Empire of Vijayanagar around 1500** (pink)

Sultans of Delhi

In 1206, Qutb ud-Din Aibak, a Turkish soldier, took control of northern India and made himself Sultan (king) of Delhi. The sultans ruled for the next 300 years. They were great builders, but cruel rulers.

Sultan Aibak built this tower to celebrate his victories.

Mongol raiders

In 1398, the Mongol leader Timur led a savage attack on the city of Delhi. The Mongols massacred most of the people of Delhi and left the sultans very weak.

Indian troops fighting Afghan invaders

Hindu temple

The Afghans ride swift horses.

The Afghans surround the Indians.

The Indian war elephants move very slowly.

SOUTH ASIA

500   600   700   800   900

States of Southern India

The Hindu rulers of southern India lived in beautiful palaces surrounded by towering temples. Holy men, called Brahmins, helped the kings to govern, and hundreds of servants worked in the palaces and temples.

This picture shows an Indian ruler and his court. ★

Hindu temple

Servants fan the king.

King

Brahmins (holy men) advise the ruler.

Musicians

Dancers perform a sacred dance.

The Chola Empire

One of the most successful southern states was Chola. Its rulers built up a great empire and sent merchants to Arabia and China. Chola craftworkers were famous for their graceful bronze statues.

Chola statue ★ of a Hindu god

Vijayanagar fights back

Around 1300, the Muslim sultans of Delhi began to attack southern India. They won land rapidly until 1336 when two brothers created the new Hindu empire of Vijayanagar. The new empire's army soon defeated the Muslims, and Vijayanagar became the most powerful state in the south.

Buddhist teachers

Although the rulers of southern India were Hindus, they allowed Buddhist monks to set up universities and teach their religion. Buddhism spread from India all over Southeast Asia, and many Chinese Buddhists came to study in India.

Buddhist monks in Sri Lanka

Important dates

711	Arabs start to invade northern India.
886-1267	The Chola rulers control most of southern India.
1001-1026	Mahmud of Ghazni leads raids on northern India.
1193	Muhammud of Ghor conquers northern India.
1206-1526	The sultans of Delhi control most of northern India.
1336-1565	The Empire of Vijayanagar is successful.
1398	The Mongols invade northern India.

SOUTH ASIA

1100   1200   1300   1400   1500

Kingdoms of Southeast Asia

Traders from India began arriving in Southeast Asia during the 2nd century. The local people learned about the Indian way of life, and set up small kingdoms like the ones in India. By the 800s, there were several powerful kingdoms on the mainland and islands of Southeast Asia.

Map of Southeast Asia

■	Pagan kingdom
■	Sukhothai kingdom
■	Khmer empire
■	Champa kingdom
■	Srivijaya kingdom
■	Sailendra kingdom

Courtiers kneeling before a king of the Sukhothai kingdom

Hindus

The Hindu religion spread from India throughout Southeast Asia, and the kings built magnificent temples where their people could worship Hindu gods. The people also prayed to their kings, who they thought of as gods.

People bringing gifts to a Hindu temple

Statue of the Buddha ★ from the Sukhothai kingdom

Buddhists

Around the year 300, Buddhist monks from India brought their religion to Southeast Asia. Buddhism was popular, but it did not destroy the Hindu religion, and most of the kingdoms had temples for Hindus as well as for Buddhists.

Warring kingdoms

The kings of Southeast Asia were often at war with each other. Sometimes, warriors sailed over seas or along rivers to make surprise attacks on another kingdom.

Warriors from the Champa kingdom rowing up a river

The Khmer empire

The greatest empire in Southeast Asia was ruled by the Khmers. Their capital city, Angkor, housed half a million people and was built close to a lake. The people of Angkor dug reservoirs to hold floodwater from the lake, and their farmers used the water to grow rice all through the year.

This picture shows a procession in the city of Angkor.

This temple is called Angkor Wat. The Khmer imperial family lives here with its servants and priests.

Priests study the stars from the side towers.

Gifts for the gods are stored here.

Crocodiles swim in the moat.

Princess

Prince

Guards

Warriors on war horses

The ruler is treated like a god.

Temple dancers

Priests

Musicians

States collapse

By 1400, the Khmer rulers had become weak. Many of their people rebelled against them, and in 1431 Angkor was conquered by an army from the Sukhothai kingdom. By 1600, all the great states had been replaced by smaller ones.

Important dates

c.100-1600 The Champa kingdom
c.700-900 The Sailendra kingdom
c.700-1300 The Srivijaya kingdom
c.800-1400 The Khmer empire
c.1000-1300 The Pagan kingdom
c.1200-1500 The Sukhothai kingdom

THE FAR EAST

1100   1200   1300   1400   1500

Dynasties of China

In 581, a ruling family (or dynasty) called the Sui took control of China. The Sui emperors built a network of canals, which made it much easier for merchants to travel around the country.

A Sui emperor's canal boat

The Tang dynasty

In 618, a new dynasty, called the Tang, took over. The Tang emperors ruled China for 300 years and created an empire that stretched from Korea to Turkestan. The capital of the Tang Empire was the splendid city of Ch'ang-an – now called Xi'an. Nearly two million people lived within its walls.

★ A Tang emperor

Map of China

TURKESTAN

TO THE WEST

Beijing

Ch'ang-an

KOREA

SOUTH CHINA SEA

ASIA

AUSTRALIA

Tang Empire
Border of the Song Empire
Border of the Ming Empire
Silk Road

This picture shows part of the city of Ch'ang-an. ★

The city is divided into walled areas called wards.

Pagoda (Buddhist tower)

Emperor's palace

Merchants sell silk, tea and spices.

Beggar

Food stall

Potter's workshop

A poet reciting his poems

Farmers bring food to market.

These gates are locked at night.

Foreign merchants visit the city.

Canal

Merchant's boat

| 500 | 600 | 700 | 800 | 900 |

THE FAR EAST

Tang inventions

During the Tang period, the Chinese discovered how to make gunpowder and a kind of fine pottery now called china. They also began to print on paper, using wooden stamps.

At first, gunpowder was only used for fireworks.

The Song dynasty

By 900, the Tang emperors had beome very weak, and in 960 the Song family took control of China. Under the Song emperors, the Chinese had little contact with the outside world, but they continued to produce beautiful china and paintings.

Song artists often painted scenes from daily life.

The Ming dynasty

In 1368, a Buddhist monk called Zhu Yuanzhang led a rebellion against the Mongols and started the Ming dynasty. The Ming emperors built up a strong army and encouraged trade, exploration and art. They ruled from Beijing, which became one of the world's greatest cities.

★

Ming china is famous for its delicate patterns.

Adventurous traders

★

A Chinese trading ship, called a junk

Chinese merchants sailed as far away as Africa and also journeyed overland on a route known as the Silk Road. Traders on the Silk Road took silk, china and paper to the Middle East and Europe.

Mongol invaders

In 1211, Mongol fighters began to invade China. In 1279 the Mongol leader, Kublai Khan, became emperor (see page 53) starting the Yuan dynasty. Kublai Khan was visited by Marco Polo, a merchant from Venice, who wrote about his travels in China.

Marco Polo at Kublai Khan's palace

Marco Polo brings gifts.

Kublai Khan

Guards

Chinese courtiers

Important dates

581-618 The Sui dynasty
618-907 The Tang dynasty
960-1279 The Song dynasty
1275-1292 Marco Polo visits China.
1280-1368 The Yuan dynasty
1368-1644 The Ming dynasty

THE FAR EAST

1100   1200   1300   1400   1500

Land of the Samurai

By the year 500, Japan was governed by powerful rulers. Some admired the way the Chinese emperors ruled, and from 710 they built their capital city, at Nara, to look like the Chinese city of Ch'ang-an. (See pages 268 and 269 to find out more about China.)

Chinese-style pagoda at Nara

The emperor's court

In 784, Emperor Kanmu moved his court to Heian (modern Kyoto), where he lived in luxury, cut off from ordinary people. Many clever women lived at the court and one of these courtiers, Murasaki Shikibu, wrote the world's first novel, called *The Tale of Genji*.

The emperor and his courtiers at Heian

Map of Japan

ASIA
AUSTRALIA
CHINA
SEA OF JAPAN
KOREA
JAPAN
Heian
Nara
PACIFIC OCEAN

Shinto and Buddhism

Shinto was the local religion of Japan. Its followers believed in spirits that lived in rocks, trees and streams. Around 600, Buddhist monks from China and Korea brought their religion to Japan. Buddhism spread fast, but Shinto did not die out.

Entrance to a Shinto shrine

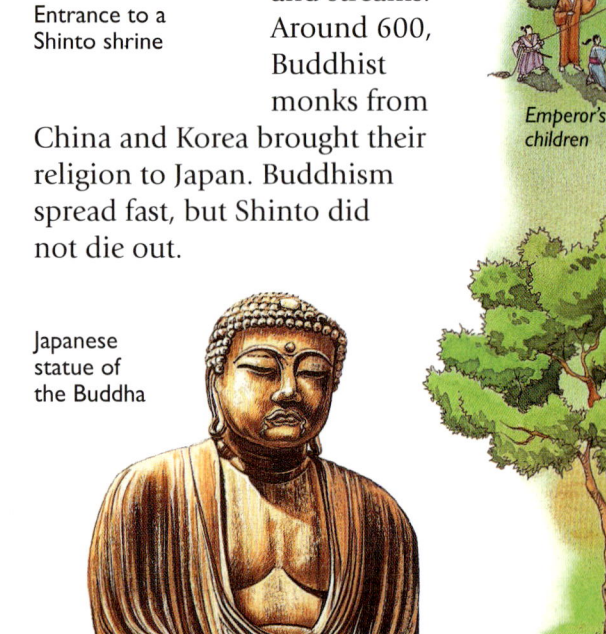

Japanese statue of the Buddha

Buddhist pagoda

Emperor's palace

Nursemaid

Emperor's children

Buddhist priests

Tea house

Lily pond

Emperor

A poet reads his poem aloud.

Emperor's advisers

Musicians

Servants bring food.

These court ladies accompany the empress.

Courtiers drink tea.

Empress

Nobles and shoguns

The emperors gradually gave away land to noble families. At first, the Fujiwara family were very powerful, but in 1192 the Minamatos gained control of Japan. The emperor made Minamato no Yoritomo the first shogun, or military commander. For the next 700 years, shoguns were the real rulers of Japan.

Minamato no Yoritomo, the first shogun

Samurai armies

The shoguns relied on local lords to rule the country. Each lord had an army of warriors, called samurai. The samurai fought fiercely for their lord and were willing to die for him. They also drove away foreign invaders, such as the Mongols (see page 251).

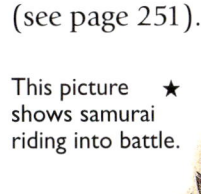

★ This picture shows samurai riding into battle.

Lance

Some samurai wear masks.

Horned helmet

Short sword

Long sword

Samurai ride strong mountain horses.

Stone-headed arrows

Leather breastplate

Straw sandal

Noh plays

Actors performed dramas, called "Noh" plays, to entertain noble families. The actors were all men, and wore masks to show what sort of characters they played. A Noh play combined music, singing, dancing and poetry.

★ Noh masks

Jobs in Japan

Rice farmers working in flooded fields, known as paddy fields

Most Japanese people were rice farmers who worked on their lord's land. Others worked as fishermen, miners, paper-makers, silk-makers, sword-makers and carpenters. Farmers and craftworkers took their goods to sell in the towns.

Sword-makers sharpening blades

Important dates

500	Powerful rulers control most of Japan.
710	Nara becomes the capital of Japan.
794	Heian becomes the capital of Japan.
858-1160	The Fujiwaras control Japan.
1192	Minamato no Yoritomo becomes the first shogun.
1274-1281	The Mongols try to invade Japan.

THE FAR EAST

1100   1200   1300   1400   1500

Explorers and Sailors

RUSSIA

Venice

Fez

Mecca

ARABIA

AFRICA

INDIA

Beijing

CHINA

Nanking

Ch'ang-an

Marco Polo brought back ginger from China.

PACIFIC OCEAN

INDIAN OCEAN

INDONESIA

Map of explorers' routes

- → Hsuan-tsang's route
- → Marco Polo's route
- → Ibn Batuta's main journeys
- → Cheng Ho's main voyages

Ibn Batuta sailed in a boat called a dhow.

Travel in the Middle Ages was very difficult and dangerous, but a few brave explorers set out on amazing jouneys. Although traders had reached Africa, India and China, these countries were almost completely unexplored.

Ibn Batuta's dream

Ibn Batuta's dream

Ibn Batuta was a wealthy Muslim from Tangier in North Africa. When he was 21, he went on a pilgrimage (religious journey) to Mecca, in Arabia. On the way, he dreamed that a huge bird was carrying him over the Muslim world and beyond. This dream inspired him to spend his life exploring.

A lifetime of travel

An Indian sultan welcoming Ibn Batuta

Ibn Batuta's first journey took him to Arabia, southern Russia and India. Then, he sailed to China. On his second great expedition, he explored parts of Africa. Ibn Batuta covered over 120,000km (75,000 miles) during his 30 years of travel.

Xuanzang goes west

In the 7th century, a Buddhist monk called Xuanzang made the long and dangerous journey from Ch'ang-an in China to northern India. He spent 16 years visiting Indian monasteries and temples. Then, he returned to China with hundreds of manuscripts and statues.

Xuanzang

Marco Polo goes east

Marco Polo left Venice for China when he was 17. He journeyed overland for three and a half years with his father and uncle. The Polos were welcomed by the Mongol emperor, Kublai Khan (see page 269) at his court. Marco Polo stayed in China for 17 years, before sailing back to Venice.

He told many stories about the sights he had seen and the legends he had heard.

★ Marco Polo told a story about a man-monster with a single foot.

Zheng He's voyages

A Chinese explorer named Zheng He went on seven great voyages to Indonesia, Arabia and Africa. He sailed with over 300 ships (called junks), and brought back amazing treasures, such as gold, ivory and wild animals.

This picture shows Zheng He returning to China from Africa.

The Chinese emperor waits to welcome Zheng He.

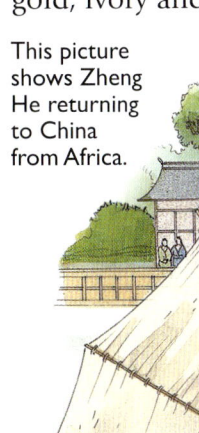

Merchants, priests and translators all went on the voyage.

Zheng He

Important dates

c.628-645 Xuanzang's travels
1271-1295 Marco Polo's travels
c.1325-1355 Ibn Batuta's travels
1405-1433 Zheng He's voyages

THE WORLD

1100   1200   1300   1400   1500

The People of the Pacific

Map of the Pacific

SOUTHEAST ASIA

NORTH PACIFIC OCEAN

INDIAN OCEAN

AUSTRALIA

SOUTH PACIFIC OCEAN

POLYNESIA

EASTER ISLAND

NEW ZEALAND

Breadfruit

Coconut

Sweet potato

Pacific fruit and vegetables

From aound 5,000 years ago, settlers from East and Southeast Asia began arriving in the islands of the Pacific Ocean. They were skilled sailors who studied the winds, stars and ocean currents to find their way around. Very slowly, the settlers spread out. By around 900, they had reached as far east as Easter Island.

Island life

Most of the Pacific islanders lived in small groups ruled by powerful leaders. They went fishing, gathered fruit, grew vegetables, and kept pigs, dogs and chickens. The islanders believed in many gods and offered them sacrifices.

This picture shows a Pacific island village.

Coconut palm

These people are setting out to find new land.

Settlers' ship

Roof made from coconut palm leaves

Wall made from the trunks of coconut palms

Canoe

Visitors from other islands trade shells and feathers.

People use leaves as plates.

Women weaving baskets

This man is trying to spear a fish.

Men carving a statue

AUSTRALASIA

500   600   700   800   900

Big heads

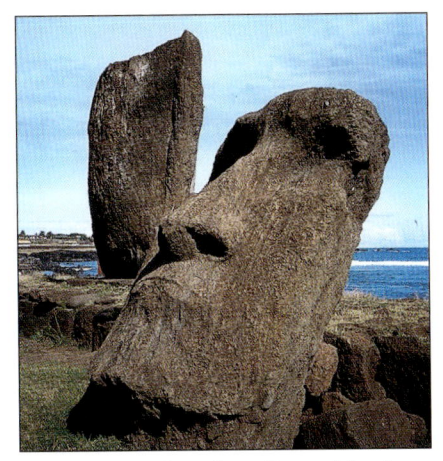

Carved heads (moai) on Easter Island

The people of Easter Island carved over 900 huge stone heads called moai, and stood them on platforms all around the coast. These statues were probably meant to represent powerful chiefs. Some are over 12m (40ft) tall.

Banana plant

This man is planting sweet potatoes.

Tower built for a god

These people are bringing offerings to one of their gods.

Māori settlers

Around 1320, a large group of people set sail from the islands of Polynesia and reached New Zealand. They called themselves the Māori. At first, they fished, gathered fruit, and hunted large birds. Later, they grew vegetables. By 1500, the Māori had become very warlike.

Māori leader ★

Beliefs and stories

Māori people believed in many gods and spirits and shared stories about their ancestors. They also believed that certain people and places were sacred – these were called tapu, or taboo.

Carved pendant showing Tiki, an ancestor ★

The first Australians

People arrived in northern Australia around 65,000 years ago. They and their descendants are known as Indigenous Australians. They arrived in simple boats from East Asia and slowly spread out over Australia. They mainly lived by gathering plants and hunting animals. Hunters used tools such as boomerangs to catch their prey.

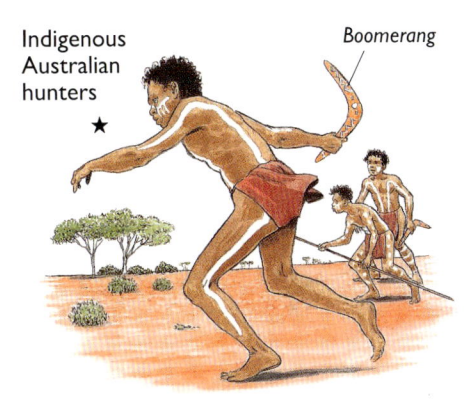

Indigenous Australian hunters ★

Boomerang

Many cultures

Over time, Indigenous Australians developed many different languages and cultures in the different parts of Australia where they lived. Some shared stories of spirits and magical animals such as the Rainbow Serpent.

Painting of the Rainbow Serpent

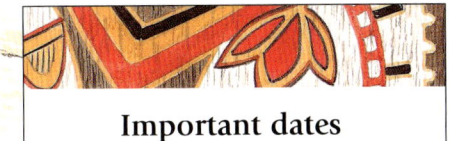

Important dates

c.900 Settlers reach Easter Island.

c.1350 The Māori reach New Zealand.

c.1250-1500 The Easter Islanders build huge stone heads.

AUSTRALASIA

NORTH AMERICA: c.700-1500

QUICKLINKS: *For links to websites about Indigenous North Americans, from Inuit peoples to Mississippians, and their ways of life, go to* **usborne.com/Quicklinks**

Indigenous North Americans

Inuits

The peoples of North America had many different ways of life. In the frozen north, Inuit peoples hunted seals; some lived in igloos. In woodlands, people hunted deer, and gathered nuts and berries. The peoples of the northwest survived mainly by fishing, and the peoples around the Great Plains grew corn and hunted buffalo. Other ways of life began in the deserts of the southwest and around the Mississippi River.

Indigenous people of the Woodlands

Map of North America

- Inuit peoples
- Woodland peoples
- Northwest peoples
- Mississippians
- Puebloans

HUDSON BAY

Great Plains

ATLANTIC OCEAN

• Cahokia

Mississippi

Pueblo Bonito

PACIFIC OCEAN

GULF OF MEXICO

Mississippian towns

Around 900, the farmers of the Mississippi Valley began to build towns. In the middle of the towns were groups of flat-topped mounds. The biggest town, Cahokia, had over a hundred mounds. Chiefs were buried under the mounds with pots, carvings and jewels.

Clay bottles made by Mississippian potters

This picture shows a town in the Mississippi Valley. One house has been cut away so you can see inside. ★

Temple

Chief's house

Priests

Earth mound

Central square

Grain store

Hunters

The chief is carried by his servants.

Potter's house

Pueblo people

Around 750, some people in the southwest began to build villages with rooms stacked one above the other. Villages built like this were called pueblos, and the people who lived in them are known as Puebloans.

In this picture of a pueblo, one house has been cut away to show what is happening inside. ★

This woman is repairing a wall.

Weavers make cotton clothes and rugs.

People use ladders to reach their roofs.

The walls are made from dried mud, called adobe.

Dried meat

Women grind corn.

Farmers grow corn, beans and cotton.

Clay pots are baked in ovens called kilns.

Potters make and decorate pots.

During the day, people work and eat on the roofs of their houses.

Trading towns

Towns grew up in places where the Puebloan people met to trade with each other and with people from other tribes.

Kiva (sunken room)

Pueblo Bonito ★

The town of Pueblo Bonito was built inside a deep valley and surrounded by a vast network of roads. It housed around 1200 people in 800 rooms. In the middle of the town were several sunken rooms, called kivas. These rooms were used for religious ceremonies and meetings.

Puebloan crafts

Carvers made ornaments from polished stone, weavers made clothes from brightly dyed cotton, and potters made jugs and pots that were covered with bold patterns.

Painted figure from a Puebloan pot ★

Puebloan jug ★

Pierced pots

Elaborately decorated pots with pierced holes were placed in the graves of Puebloan leaders.

Burial pot ★

Important dates

c.750 Puebloans begin to build villages.

c.900 Mississippians begin to build towns.

c.1300 Puebloans abandon their towns and villages.

c.1500 Mississippians abandon their towns.

NORTH AMERICA

1100   1200   1300   1400   1500

Priest's knife ★

The Aztec Empire

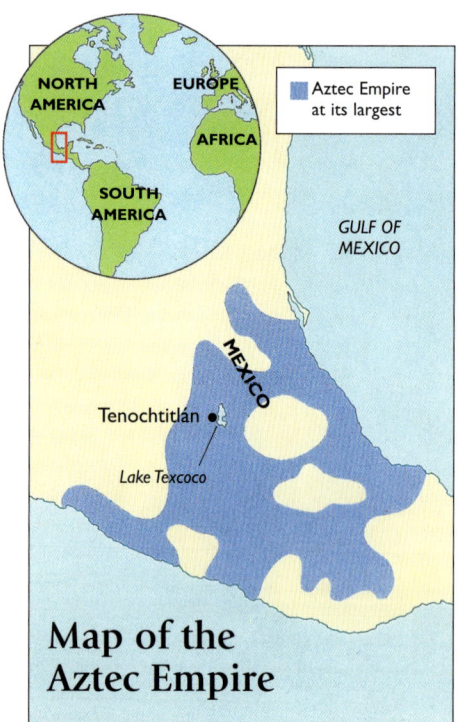

| Aztec Empire at its largest |

NORTH AMERICA
EUROPE
AFRICA
SOUTH AMERICA

GULF OF MEXICO

MEXICO

Tenochtitlán

Lake Texcoco

Map of the Aztec Empire

This picture shows part of the city of Tenochtitlán.

The Aztecs were wandering, warlike people who arrived in central Mexico around 1300. They settled on an island in Lake Texcoco and started to build the village of Tenochtitlán. Over the next 200 years, Tenochtitlán grew into a great city and the Aztecs built up an empire around it.

The city on a lake

Tenochtitlán spread over a group of islands at the edge of Lake Texcoco. In the middle of the city was a beautiful square, filled with temples where priests held ceremonies.

Sacrifices to the sun

The Aztecs believed that their sun god, Huitzilopochtli, might die unless they kept him strong. To keep him alive, they fed him human hearts. Priests cut out their victims' hearts, then hurled the bodies down the temple steps.

Aztec priests making human sacrifices

Temple of Huitzilopochtli, god of the sun and war

Lake Texcoco

People live in small, flat-roofed houses.

Temple of Tlaloc, the rain god

King's palace

Temple of the sun

Victims' heads are stored on skull racks.

Temple of Quetzalcoatl, the serpent god

People play a religious ball game in this court.

In this school, boys learn to be priests.

A carved wall surrounds the central square.

THE AMERICAS

500   600   700   800   900

The Aztec year

It was important for the Aztecs to know when to hold their festivals. They divided the 365 days of the year into 18 months of 20 days each. The remaining 5 days were believed to be unlucky.

The outer rings of this calendar stone show the days of the year.

Aztec wars

The Aztec army fought constant wars against surrounding tribes. They forced the defeated tribes to give them food and treasure, and took thousands of prisoners to be sacrificed to their gods.

Aztec eagle knight ★

Floating fields

Farmers filled huge baskets with earth and floated them on lakes. In these floating fields, they grew corn, beans and chili peppers.

An Aztec god protecting a corn plant

Bird attacking the corn   Corn plant   God of planting and spring

Crafts

Many Aztecs worked as potters, weavers and carpenters. Sculptors carved huge statues, and craftworkers made beautiful objects from gold and feathers.

Gold pendant

The end of the Empire

In 1519, the Spanish soldier Hernan Cortés arrived in Mexico determined to conquer the Aztecs. The Aztecs were terrified by the Spanish guns and horses. Some thought that Quetzalcoatl, the serpent god, had come back to earth.

Mask of Quetzalcoatl

At first, Cortés did not attack the Aztecs, but in 1521 he invaded Tenochtitlán and conquered its people. After this defeat, many Aztecs died from European diseases and their way of life soon disappeared.

The defeat of the Aztecs

Spanish troops arrive on horseback.

Spanish soldiers fire guns at the Aztecs.

Important dates

c.1300   The Aztecs arrive in the Valley of Mexico.

c.1325   The Aztecs start to build Tenochtitlán.

1420s   The Aztecs begin to conquer the surrounding tribes.

c.1500   The Aztecs control the Valley of Mexico.

1521   Cortés conquers the Aztecs.

Canoe

Bridges link plots of land.

Raised roads join the city to the mainland.

Merchants trade goods in the market.

Feathered costume

★ Aztec warrior

Shield made from feathers

1100	1200	1300	1400	1500

The Maya and the Toltecs

The Maya people lived in small kingdoms in the rainforests and plains of Central America. They were ruled by powerful kings who were also priests and warriors.

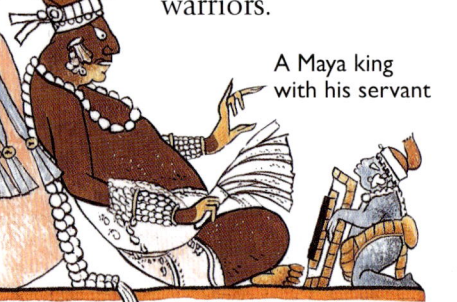

A Maya king with his servant

Gods and kings

The Maya believed in many gods and gave them gifts of human blood. They also believed that their kings had godlike powers. Maya kings were buried under temples and people prayed to them as gods.

This jade mask was found in the tomb of a Maya king. ★

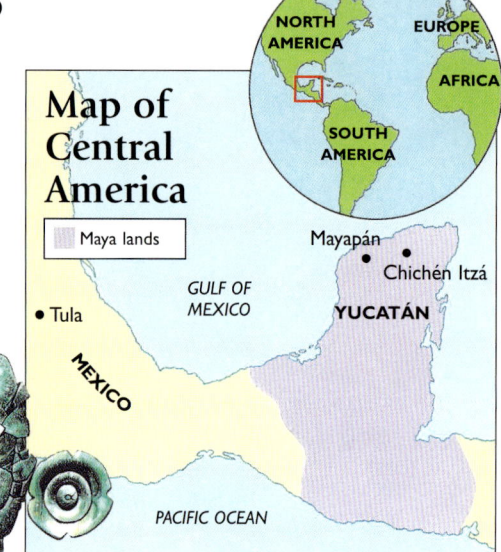

Map of Central America

Maya lands

Mayapán

Chichén Itzá

GULF OF MEXICO

YUCATÁN

Tula

MEXICO

PACIFIC OCEAN

NORTH AMERICA
EUROPE
AFRICA
SOUTH AMERICA

Cities of stone

Each Maya kingdom had a splendid capital city built from stone. The king lived in the city with his nobles, warriors and priests. Farmers from the country brought food to the city and came to watch the spectacular ceremonies that were held there.

This picture shows a ceremony in a Maya city.
★

The king offers sacrifices at the top of the steps.

The temples are covered in painted carvings.

Farmers watch the ceremony.

Musicians

Priests and warriors

The people are asking their gods for a good harvest.

Nobles dance and sing.

These prisoners of war will be sacrificed to the gods.

Game of life and death

Young warriors played a fast-moving ballgame which was meant to symbolize the battle between life and death.

This picture shows ★ the Maya ballgame.

Helmet

Players hit a rubber ball with their arms, knees and hips.

Padded belt

Arm guard

Knee guard

Counting the days

Astronomer-priests studied the stars and invented several types of calendars. One included an accurate 365-day calendar. Calendars were written out using signs for words and numbers, and were used to track movements of the Sun, Moon and planets, and plan religious ceremonies.

Part of a Maya calendar

Dots, dashes and curved lines show dates.

Carving of a Toltec warrior

The rise of the Toltecs

Around 850, most of the Maya people moved north into an area known as the Yucatán. Meanwhile, in Mexico, the Toltecs were becoming powerful. The Toltecs controlled Mexico from their capital at Tula. They were warriors, traders and craftworkers.

Tula and Chichén Itzá

There are some interesting similarities between buildings at the Toltec city Tula and the Maya city of Chichén Itzá. Experts aren't sure whether Toltecs and Maya borrowed ideas from each other's cultures, or whether they worked together to build them.

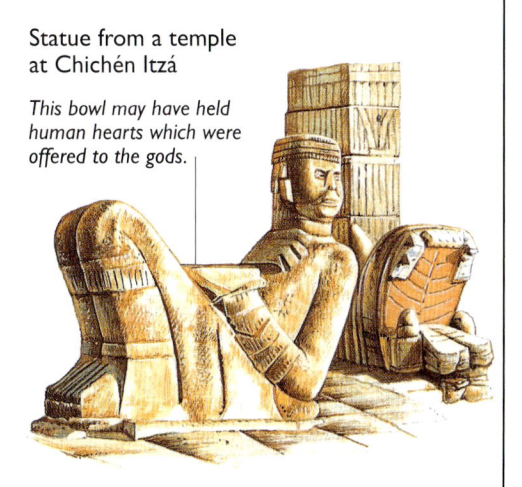

Statue from a temple at Chichén Itzá

This bowl may have held human hearts which were offered to the gods.

Scatter and collapse

In the 1100s, invading tribes drove the Toltecs out of Mexico towards Maya territories. By 1160, tribes from the north began invading Chichén Itzá. The Toltecs scattered, and the Maya moved to new cities, but by 1500, Maya kingdoms had shrunk to just a few small towns.

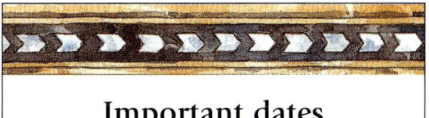

Important dates

c.600 The Maya are at their most successful.

c.850 The Maya abandon their cities in the south.

c.900-1000 The Toltecs are powerful in Mexico.

c.1100 The Toltecs are driven toward Maya lands.

c.1160 Chichén Itzá is invaded and Maya and Toltecs leave.

c.1500 The Maya live in just a few small towns.

THE AMERICAS

1100   1200   1300   1400   1500

Empires of the Andes

The strip of land between the Andes Mountains and the Pacific Ocean was home to several tribes, but one of the most powerful groups was the Chimú. Around 1100, the Chimú people began to conquer other tribes and started building up an empire.

★ Gold knife showing a Chimú noble

The city of Chanchan

Part of the Chimú city of Chanchan

By 1200, the Chimú ruler and his nobles controlled a large empire from their capital city at Chanchan. Potters, weavers and goldsmiths all worked in the city, and farmers brought in food from the surrounding countryside.

— Fish design

Chimú pottery jar

Chimú painting of a man with a serpent

The rise of the Incas

The Incas lived in a small mountain kingdom around the city of Cuzco, but in 1438 their ruler, Pachacuti, set out to win more land. The Incas defeated the Chimú and won large areas of land in the south, creating an empire that stretched along most of the Pacific coast.

Inca warriors ★

— Mace

Sling

Painted shield

— Leg band made from feathers

Keeping count

The Inca Empire was very well organized and everyone had some kind of work to do. People were fed when food was short, and cared for when they were sick. To make sure the Empire ran smoothly, officials kept records on knotted cords, called quipu.

Quipu ★

NORTH AMERICA

AFRICA

SOUTH AMERICA

Chanchan

Machu Picchu

Cuzco

SOUTH AMERICA

PACIFIC OCEAN

Andes Mountains

Map of the Chimú and Inca Empires

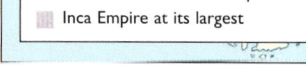 Border of the Chimú Empire
 Inca Empire at its largest

Cities of stone

Even though they had no wheeled vehicles or metal tools, the Incas built amazing cities from stone. The cities had temples, observatories and palaces, as well as ordinary homes.

The mountain city of Machu Picchu ★

On the road

A network of roads linked all the parts of the Inca Empire. These roads were used by farmers, traders, messengers and soldiers. The emperor made frequent journeys through his lands to make sure that all his people stayed loyal to him.

This picture shows an Inca emperor on a journey through his empire.

Farmers have built terraces so they can grow crops on the mountainside.

Bridge made from reeds

Traders take food to market.

Soldiers march to war.

Storehouse for food

People can stay overnight in these rest houses.

Farmers grow peppers, chilies, corn and potatoes.

A new messenger will take the bag to the next rest house.

A messenger hands over a bag containing quipu.

The emperor is carried on a throne.

Llamas carry heavy loads.

Royal guard

Priest

Young girls sing and dance.

Musicians play for the emperor.

The end of the Incas

In 1532, a band of Spanish soldiers, called conquistadors, attacked the Incas. Led by Francisco Pizarro, they captured and killed the Inca emperor. This was a great blow to the Incas, and within a few years the Empire collapsed.

Important dates

c.1100	The Chimú start to build their Empire.
c.1300	The Incas settle around Cuzco.
1438-1471	Pachacuti is Emperor of the Incas.
1438-1525	The Inca Empire grows.
1476	The Incas conquer the Chimú Empire.
1532	Spanish conquistadors attack the Incas.
c.1540	The Inca Empire ends.

SOUTH AMERICA

1100   1200   1300   1400   1500

Artists of Italy

Around 1350, artists and thinkers in northern Italy became very interested in the art, architecture and learning of ancient Greece and Rome. They began to try out new ideas based on what they had learned. This movement is known as the Renaissance, which means "rebirth".

Patrons

Princes, popes and merchants paid money to artists, architects and writers and encouraged them to create works of art. Rich people who supported artists were known as patrons.

★
Medal showing Lorenzo de' Medici, a famous patron

Florence and the Medicis

The most powerful patrons of the Renaissance were the Medicis, a family of bankers from Florence. The Medicis encouraged artists and scholars to work in their city, and many new ideas were first tried out in Florence.

This picture shows the main square in Florence.

The signori (city rulers) live and meet in this palace.

Nobles

Priests

These men, called signori, run the city. Every two months, new signori are chosen.

Beggar

Rich cloth merchant

Children of the Medici family

Lorenzo de' Medici leads a procession through the city to welcome visitors from Rome.

EUROPE

500   600   700   800   900

Architects

Architects designed buildings with pillars, rounded arches and domes. This style of building was created by the Greeks and Romans and is called classical architecture.

Florence Cathedral ★

One of the first examples of the new classical style was the dome of Florence Cathedral, designed by the architect Brunelleschi.

This covered area is called a loggia. People hold meetings here.

Primavera, by the painter Sandro Botticelli, shows a legend about the coming of Spring.

Painters

Inspired by Greek and Roman art, painters tried to make their pictures look as lifelike as possible. They discovered that things in the distance look smaller than things that are close up. They used this effect, called perspective, to give their pictures a feeling of depth. Before the Renaissance, artists in Europe painted mainly religious pictures, but by 1400 the artists of Italy had become much more adventurous. As well as religious pictures, they painted portraits, landscapes, recent events, and scenes from Greek and Roman legends.

Sculptors

Sculptors copied Greek and Roman statues and used real people as models for their work. They even examined dead bodies to find out how bones and muscles worked. The statues of the Renaissance looked lifelike, strong and graceful.

★ Statue of David, a famous character in the Bible, by the sculptor and painter Michelangelo

Scholars discussing new ideas

An architect showing some plans to his patron

Lawyers

An artist sketching a building

EUROPE

1100	1200	1300	1400	1500

Ideas and Inventions

By the 1400s, many people were studying the works of the ancient Greeks and Romans. These works made them realize how much human beings could achieve, and started a new belief in human ability. This belief, called humanism, spread all over Europe, as artists, writers and scientists tried out new ideas.

Scientists and inventors

During the Renaissance, people started to ask new questions about the world. They carried out scientific experiments and studied plants, animals and humans. Inventors worked on new ideas for clocks, weapons, telescopes, water pumps and other machines.

This picture is based on a design for a flying machine by Leonardo da Vinci.

The flying machine would have been too heavy to get off the ground.

Frame made from beech wood

Wings made from heavy silk

Rope used for steering

These pedals make the wings flap up and down.

Education

Before the Renaissance, only priests were educated, but during the 1400s this began to change. Boys from wealthy families went to school, and rich girls were taught at home by tutors. Pupils studied the writings of the Greeks and Romans, as well as music, art and foreign languages.

Boys at school

Leonardo da Vinci

Leonardo da Vinci was a perfect example of a well-educated Renaissance man. He was an artist, an inventor, an architect and a musician. He made detailed drawings of animals and people, and created designs for amazing machines.

Leonardo da Vinci

Drawings of the human body by Leonardo da Vinci

Leonardo cut up human bodies, so that he could draw and study them.

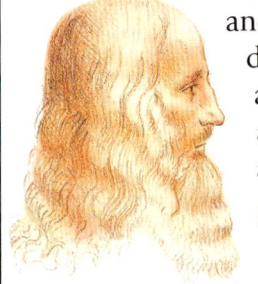

EUROPE

500   600   700

286

Alchemists

Some learned people in Renaissance Europe worked as alchemists. They tried to find a way to turn ordinary metal into gold, and some even thought that they could create a magic potion that would give people eternal life. Alchemists learned how to make chemicals and invented lots of scientific equipment.

An alchemist's laboratory

Flasks of boiling chemicals

This man is using scales to weigh powder.

The alchemist follows instructions in a manuscript.

Hourglass used for timing experiments

This boy is grinding powder with a pestle and mortar.

Writers and thinkers

Poets began to write about human feelings, and thinkers discussed how countries should be run. An Italian called Niccolò Machiavelli wrote a book called *The Prince*, which said that a ruler should always do what was best for his kingdom, even if it meant being cruel and ruthless.

Niccolò Machiavelli

The birth of printing

In the 1450s, a German named Johannes Gutenberg invented a machine called a printing press, which printed books a page at a time. Until then, all books in Europe had been copied by hand.

Wooden press

Paper

Metal letters arranged in a block and covered with ink

★ A printing press

Page from an early printed book

Soon, printing presses were set up all over Europe. Books were produced quickly and cheaply, and this helped to spread the new ideas of the Renaissance thinkers and scientists.

Important dates

c.1350 The Renaissance begins in Italy.

1452-1519 Life of Leonardo da Vinci

1455 Johannes Gutenberg produces the first printed book, a copy of the Bible.

1469-1527 Life of Niccolò Machiavelli

EUROPE

1100   1200   1300   1400   1500

Voyages of Discovery

NEWFOUNDLANDS

NORTH AMERICA

ATLANTIC OCEAN

Columbus's ship, the Santa Maria

CHINA

INDIA

PACIFIC OCEAN

AFRICA

PACIFIC OCEAN

SOUTH AMERICA

INDIAN OCEAN

Map of voyages

- → Bartolomeu Dias
- → Vasco da Gama
- → Christopher Columbus
- → Amerigo Vespucci
- → John Cabot

Compass used by sailors

Large areas of the world were completely unknown to the people of medieval Europe. European explorers and traders had reached North Africa, India and China, but had yet to reach America.

This map, made in 1489, shows how some people saw the world at that time.

Finding a way east

By the 1450s, traders in Europe were desperate to find a way to the East by sea. Silks and spices from India and China were in great demand, but they had to be carried overland on long and dangerous journeys.

Henry the Navigator

Prince Henry of Portugal, known as Henry the Navigator, was convinced that ships could reach India by sailing south around Africa.

Henry the Navigator

He persuaded Portuguese explorers to sail south, even though they believed that the southern seas were boiling hot and filled with monsters. Henry paid for nearly 20 expeditions along the west coast of Africa.

Early artist's view of a sea monster ★

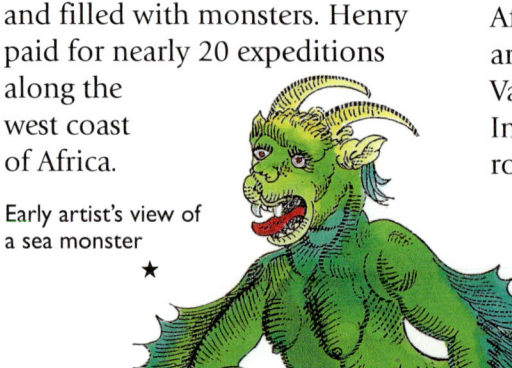

Sailing around Africa

In 1487, a storm blew the ship of a Portuguese explorer, Bartolomeu Dias, around the southern tip of Africa.

Part of a map showing a ship sailing around southern Africa

After this, other ships sailed around Africa, and in 1498 Vasco da Gama reached India by this route.

500   600   700   800   900

Christopher Columbus

Most people in the Middle Ages knew that the world was round. An Italian captain, named Christopher Columbus, was sure that he could reach China by heading west and sailing all the way around the world. He persuaded the King and Queen of Spain to pay for his voyage.

Columbus's ships wait in the port.

The Santa Maria

This picture shows Columbus leaving Spain. ★

The Niña   The Pinta

Sailors check their food supplies for the voyage.

Columbus   King Ferdinand of Spain   Queen Isabella   Courtiers

Columbus finds land

After five weeks, Columbus arrived in the West Indies, a group of islands close to Central America. Columbus thought that he had reached the East, but people soon realized that he had reached an exciting new land. They called this land the New World.

Columbus arriving in the West Indies

Some Native Americans give the sailors presents.

Columbus   The sailors carry weapons.

Sailors planting a cross

Amerigo Vespucci

In 1499, another Italian, Amerigo Vespucci, reached the mainland of America. Vespucci sailed down the coast of South America as far as the Amazon River. America was named after him in 1507.

Amerigo Vespucci

John Cabot

In 1497, an expedition set out from England, led by an Italian captain called John Cabot. Cabot crossed the Atlantic Ocean in search of India, but instead he reached Newfoundland, off the coast of North America.

The Spanish flag

Important dates

c.1420-1460 Henry the Navigator encourages Portuguese expeditions.

1487 Bartolomeu Dias sails around Africa.

1492 Christopher Columbus reaches the West Indies.

1497 John Cabot reaches Newfoundland.

1498 Vasco da Gama sails to India.

1499 Amerigo Vespucci reaches South America.

THE WORLD

1100   1200   1300   1400   1500

19th-century painting of workers shaping steel in a forge

THE LAST 500 YEARS

Looking at the Last 500 Years

Between the years 1500 and 2000, life changed dramatically in most parts of the world. At first, this transformation happened gradually, but by the 1800s people's lives were changing fast, and in the 20th century things really gathered speed.

Changing journeys

Moving from place to place in the 1500s was very slow and difficult, and journeys didn't get much easier for 300 years. Travel started to change in 1804, when the first steam train was built. Around 80 years later, the motor car was invented, and by the 1960s planes could cross the globe in hours, and spacecraft had taken astronauts to the Moon. By the end of the 20th century, unmanned spacecraft had reached most of the planets in our solar system.

Fighting for freedom

During the 16th century, a few powerful rulers governed large areas of the world, and ordinary people had very little say in how their countries were run. This began to change in the 1700s, when new ideas of rights for all spread through Europe and America. Rebels struggled to gain more freedom, and gradually more and more people won the right to vote for their country's leaders. Today, people are still fighting for freedom in many parts of the world.

This is a scene from the time of the French Revolution in 1789. It shows people setting off to join the revolutionaries.

The American Henry Ford made motor cars that lots of people could afford. Here he is in one of his cars, around 1920.

Science and technology

Daily life in the 1500s was extremely hard, but over the next 500 years new discoveries and inventions slowly changed people's lives. Advances in medicine meant that people lived much longer, while new machines made everyday tasks faster and easier. In the 20th century, cars, computers and television transformed the way that many people lived.

World views

Most people in 1500 had no idea what the world looked like and many still believed that the Earth was flat. Gradually, over the next 500 years, scientists and explorers built up a picture of the globe. Today, satellites can take photographs of the Earth from space, and people can see television pictures of places all over the world.

This is the Hubble Space Telescope. It allows scientists to see farther into space than they ever have before.

QUICKLINKS: *For links to websites where you can discover how historians investigate the past, go to* **usborne.com/Quicklinks**

Where did it happen?

There are maps throughout the book to show you exactly where things happened. You can also check which area of the world you are reading about by looking at the bottom corner of each page. The different areas of the world are shown on the map below.

NORTH AMERICA

EUROPE

ASIA

Middle East

South Asia

Far East

AFRICA

SOUTH AMERICA

AUSTRALASIA

This is the diary of Anne Frank, a young Jewish girl who described her life in hiding during the Second World War.

How do we know?

Historians study history by collecting lots of different kinds of evidence. They piece this evidence together to create a picture of what happened in the past.

Letters and diaries give first-hand accounts of things that happened in the past, newspapers contain the news and views of the time, and government records provide many useful facts and figures. Maps give a clear idea of which parts of the world were known and explored, while scientific papers and notebooks describe experiments and discoveries.

Since the 1860s, photography has provided a vivid record of events all over the world. Historians who study the 20th century use film and sound recordings to help with their research, and also interview people about their memories and experiences.

Many buildings and objects have survived from the last 500 years, and these provide valuable clues about the way people lived and worked. Paintings, drawings and statues show famous people and events, and reveal fascinating details of daily life.

Many historians have studied film showing the murder of the US President John F. Kennedy in 1963. Here you can see the President and his wife minutes before he was shot.

The Last 500 Years Quicklinks

Quicklinks are links to specially selected websites with videos, quizzes, homework resources and activities. Throughout this section, you will see recommendations for websites that will bring the history of the last 500 years to life.

Here are some of the things you can do at the sites we recommend:

★ Explore the Palace of Versailles in France and the Taj Mahal in India.

★ Walk down a street in 1660s New Amsterdam, now known as New York City.

★ Follow the triangle of trade and explore the lives of enslaved Africans.

★ Discover famous speeches by Emmeline Pankhurst, Martin Luther King and other history makers.

★ See early computers and try a quiz about how computers work.

To visit the websites, go to **usborne.com/Quicklinks** and type "**WHE**" into the search box.

You can also download many pictures and maps in this book for home or school use. Look for pictures marked with a ★.

Usborne Publishing is not responsible for the content of external websites. Children should be supervised online. Please follow the online safety guidelines at **usborne.com/Quicklinks**

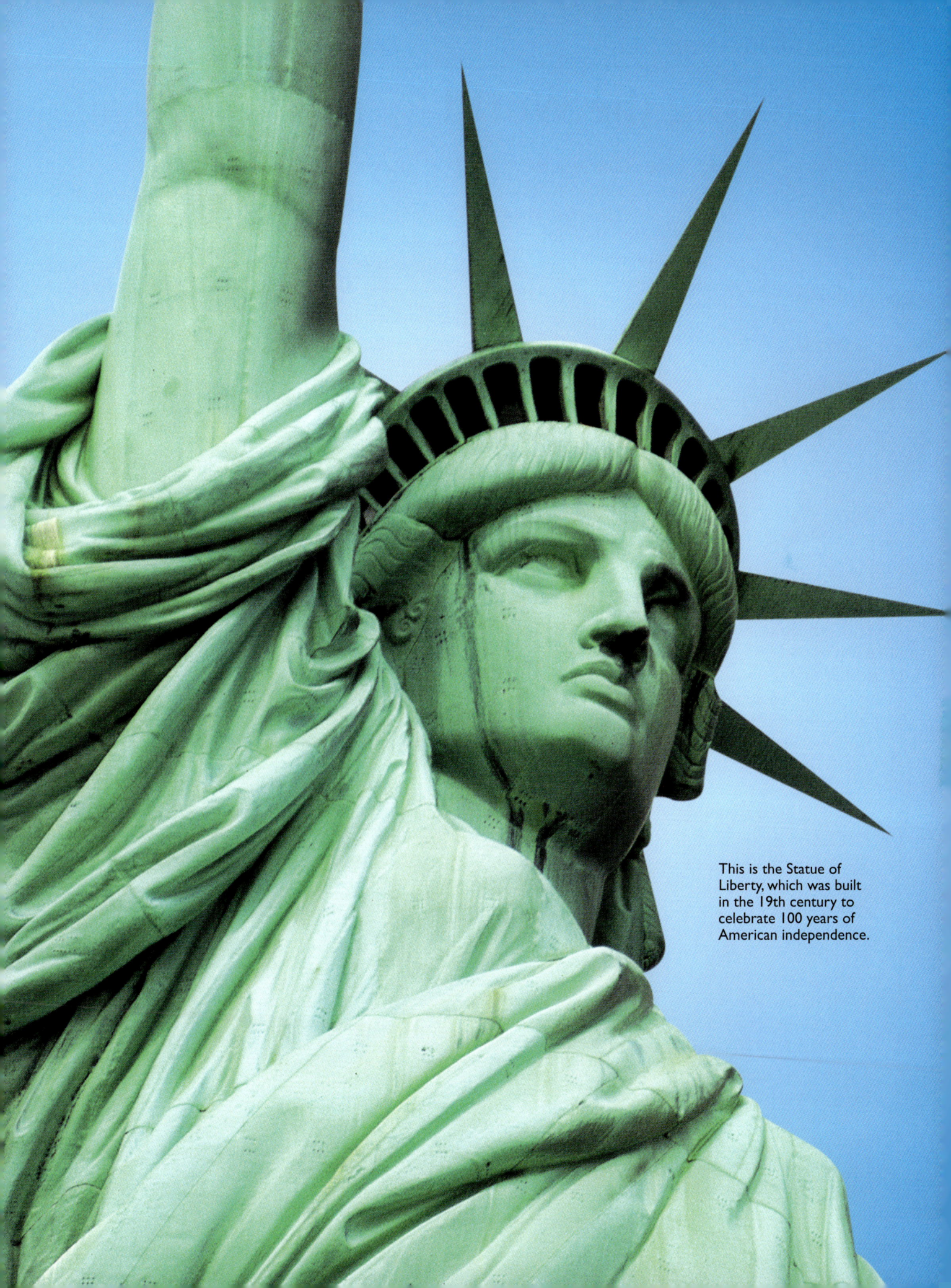

This is the Statue of Liberty, which was built in the 19th century to celebrate 100 years of American independence.

Exploring the World

The 16th century was a very exciting time for explorers. After Christopher Columbus arrived in America in 1492, people dreamed of finding treasure in the exotic New World. They also hoped they would find new routes to the rich trading countries of China and India.

Spices and jewels from India

Around the world

The Portuguese explorer Ferdinand Magellan discovered a route around South America into the Pacific Ocean. Magellan died during the voyage, but one of his captains, Sebastian del Cano, continued sailing west until he reached Europe. This was the first voyage around the world and it proved that the Earth was round.

Magellan's ship Vittoria as shown by an artist of the time

Exploring Canada

Jacques Cartier, a French explorer, sailed along the east coast of what is now Canada, searching for a new route to China. Later, he canoed up the Saint Lawrence River, and reached a small village which he named Montreal.

Sailing northwest

An English expedition led by Martin Frobisher tried to reach China by sailing around the top of Canada. Frobisher believed he had found a way around Canada, but in fact he had only sailed into a bay.

Sailing northeast

A Dutch sea captain named Willem Barents hoped to find a route to India by sailing northeast past Norway. His ship became trapped in ice in the Arctic Ocean, but he managed to build a shelter, and stayed there until the ice melted.

ARCTIC OCEAN

Barents hunted polar bears on the ice of the Arctic Ocean.

NORWAY

AFRICA

INDIAN OCEAN

INDIA

CHINA

AUSTRALIA

Map of voyages

→ Magellan's route	→ Frobisher's route
→ Del Cano's route	→ Drake's route
→ Cartier's route	→ Barents' route

THE WORLD

296

Spanish conquerors

Spanish soldiers, known as conquistadors, arrived in Central and South America, determined to win land and gold. They defeated the Aztec and Inca people who lived there, and destroyed their powerful empires.

★ A gold Aztec ornament

Sailing and stealing

Sir Francis Drake of England was a skilled sailor and a daring pirate. He sailed all the way around the world, stealing treasure from Spanish ships as he went.

A miniature portrait of Sir Francis Drake

Along the Amazon

A Spanish explorer, Francisco de Orellana, sailed along the entire length of the Amazon River in South America. His boat was often in danger from fast-flowing currents.

PACIFIC OCEAN

CANADA

Cartier explored Canada with native North Americans as his guides.

Montreal

CENTRAL AMERICA

Explorers brought back pineapples from Central and South America.

ATLANTIC OCEAN

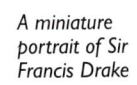
Amazon

SOUTH AMERICA

Important dates

1519-1521	Spanish conquistadors conquer the Aztecs.
1519-1522	Magellan's ship sails around the world.
1532-1534	Spanish conquistadors conquer the Incas.
1534-1536	Cartier explores eastern Canada.
1542	Orellana sails along the Amazon.
1576	Frobisher reaches northern Canada.
1577-1580	Drake sails around the world.
1596	Barents reaches the Arctic Ocean.

THE WORLD

297

The Ottoman Empire

The Ottomans were Muslim Turks who were governed by a powerful ruler called a sultan. By 1500, they had built up a large and well-organized empire with its capital in the magnificent city of Istanbul.

The empire grows

During the 16th century, the Ottomans gained land in the Middle East, North Africa, Russia and Hungary. In 1529, they threatened western Europe by attacking Vienna, but eventually a Christian army drove them out of the city.

Struggle for sea power

By the 1550s, the Ottoman navy had gained control of the Mediterranean Sea. This frightened the rulers of Spain and Italy, and in 1571 they fought the Ottomans in the sea battle of Lepanto, near the Greek coast. The Ottomans lost the battle, but they soon won back control of most of the Mediterranean.

The Ottomans built many beautiful mosques including this, the Blue Mosque in Istanbul.

Strong sultans

The Ottoman sultans lived a life of luxury in the Topkapi Palace in Istanbul. The most powerful sultan was Suleiman, a great ruler and warrior, who became known in Europe as Suleiman the Magnificent.

Sultan Suleiman

Using Christians

The Ottomans captured boys from Christian areas of the empire and brought them up as Muslim slaves. Many of the slaves were trained as soldiers, called janissaries, but the most intelligent ones became officials in the empire. The slaves were very useful to the sultans, because they were completely obedient to their Ottoman masters.

THE MIDDLE EAST

298

Map of the Ottoman Empire

- Ottoman Empire around 1500
- Ottoman Empire around 1700
- Borders of the Persian Empire around 1600

Persian warriors

Persian rivals

From around 1500 to 1750, the Ottomans' greatest rivals were the Persians. Like the Ottomans, the Persians were Muslims, but they belonged to a group known as Shia Muslims. Led by their rulers, the powerful Safavid family, the Persians fought the Ottomans for land. They also encouraged Shia Muslims in the Ottoman Empire to rebel.

The empire weakens

After 1600, the Ottoman Empire continued to grow, but it was ruled by a series of weak sultans who couldn't control their people. At the same time, some of the sultans' enemies, such as Russia and Austria, grew stronger.

The end of the empire

In 1683, the Ottomans attacked Vienna again, but they were driven back. After this defeat, the empire gradually became smaller and weaker. It lasted until the 20th century, but by the end of World War I it had collapsed completely.

Important dates

1520-1566 Sultan Suleiman rules the Ottomans.
1529 The Ottomans attack Vienna.
1571 The Battle of Lepanto
1683 The Ottomans attack Vienna for the last time.
1918 The Ottoman Empire comes to an end.

THE MIDDLE EAST

The Mughal Empire

The Mughals were Muslims from the area now called Afghanistan. Like their ancestors, the Mongols, the Mughals were great warriors, but they also loved poetry and art, and created beautiful gardens.

The first emperor

In 1526, a Mughal prince named Babur led his army into India. He defeated the Sultan (ruler) of Delhi at the Battle of Panipat and took control of northern India, becoming the first Mughal Emperor.

Akbar the Great

Babur's grandson, Akbar, won large areas of land from the Hindu princes who ruled most of India, but he still managed to keep the Hindus loyal to him. He did this by marrying a Hindu princess, and by allowing the Hindus to worship their own gods and goddesses. Akbar ruled for almost 40 years. He ran his empire very efficiently, and invited painters, poets and scholars to his splendid court at Agra.

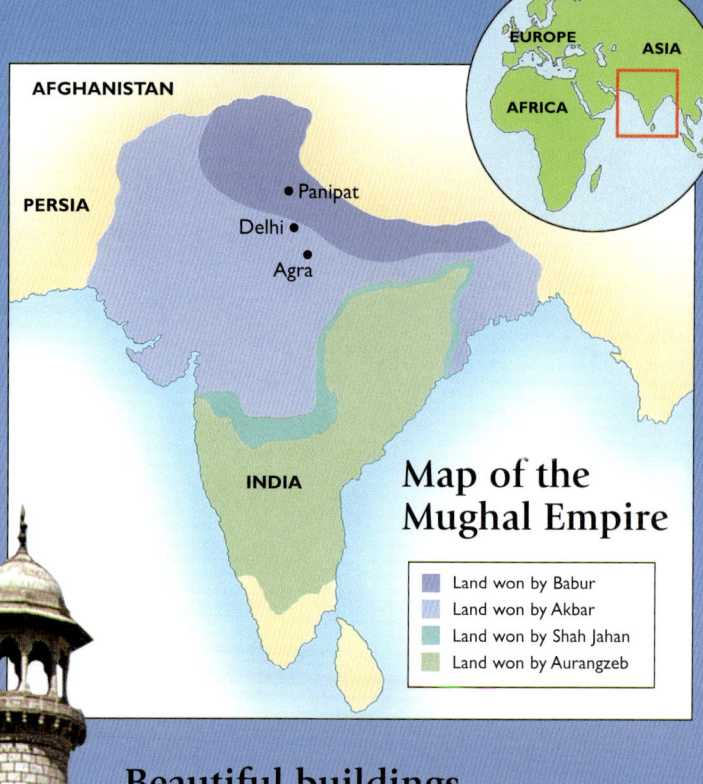

Map of the Mughal Empire

- Land won by Babur
- Land won by Akbar
- Land won by Shah Jahan
- Land won by Aurangzeb

Beautiful buildings

The Mughals built amazing mosques, forts and palaces, but their most famous building is the Taj Mahal, near Agra. It was built by Akbar's grandson, Shah Jahan.

Emperor Shah Jahan built the Taj Mahal as a tomb for his beloved wife, Mumtaz Mahal.

A Mughal painting showing the marriage of Emperor Akbar's brother

SOUTH ASIA

A cruel emperor

The Mughal Empire reached its greatest size under Shah Jahan's son, Aurangzeb. But Aurangzeb was a cruel man and an unpopular ruler. In order to become emperor, he put his father in prison and murdered his two older brothers. Once he had gained power, Aurangzeb forced the Indian peasants to pay very high taxes. He also destroyed many Hindu temples and built mosques on top of their ruins.

The Taj Mahal is built from white marble and took 11 years to complete.

Armies and traders

After Aurangzeb's death in 1707, there were no more strong emperors. A Persian army invaded northwest India, and the Hindu princes slowly won back land from the Mughals. Meanwhile, traders from Europe began to set up trading stations all over India.

A Hindu soldier

The end of the Mughals

By 1750, the Mughal emperors were losing control of their empire. India became divided into small states ruled by princes, and the European traders grew more and more powerful. Gradually, the British East India Company took over the running of India, and the Mughal emperors lost all their power (see pages 328 and 329).

Important dates

1526	Babur wins the Battle of Panipat
1526-1530	Babur is the first Mughal Emperor.
1556-1605	Akbar is emperor.
1628-1658	Shah Jahan is emperor.
1658-1707	Aurangzeb is emperor.
1714	The Hindu princes start to win land.
1737-1739	The Persians invade northwest India.
1857	The last Mughal Emperor gives up his throne.

Catholics and Protestants

By the 1500s, many people were unhappy with the Catholic Church. They thought that its leaders were only interested in wealth and power, and complained that many of its priests were badly educated and lazy.

A few determined people protested about the Church. At first, they tried to reform or improve it, but later they broke away completely. Their followers became known as Protestants, and the movement they started was called the Reformation.

Martin Luther, the leader of a growing protest against the Catholic Church

Luther's protest

In 1517, a German monk named Martin Luther wrote a list of 95 ways that the Catholic Church could be reformed. He nailed the list to the church door in Wittenberg, and his ideas soon spread. This made the Church leaders furious, and in 1520 the Pope issued a document that banished Luther from the Catholic Church for ever.

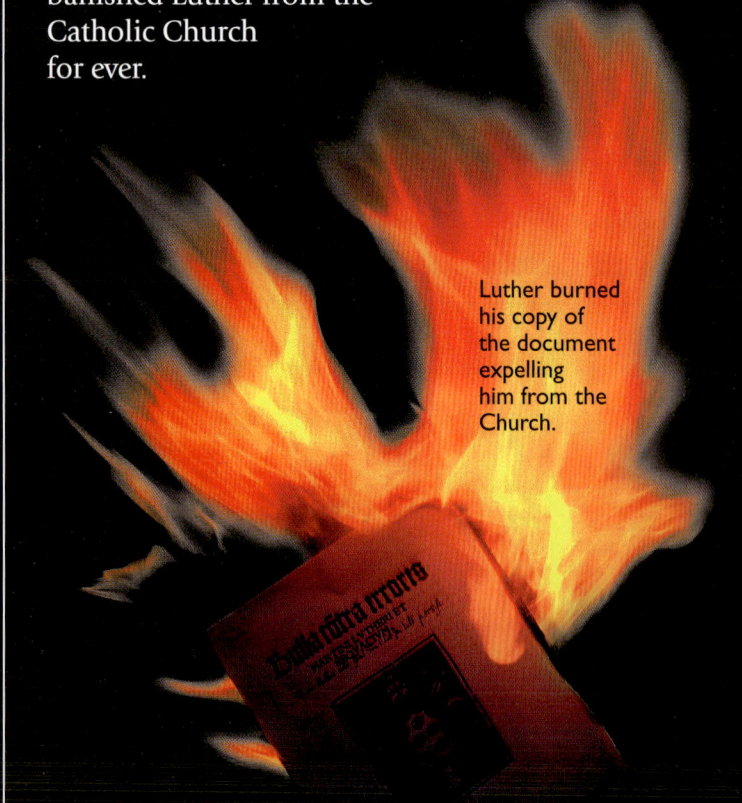

Luther burned his copy of the document expelling him from the Church.

Luther's changes

Luther went into hiding and worked on his ideas for how the Church should be run. He believed that church services should be kept simple, and that people should read the Bible for themselves, instead of learning everything from priests. Luther translated the Bible from Latin into German, and many copies of his Bible were printed.

By 1525, people all over Germany were holding simple services based on Luther's ideas, and the Lutheran Church was born.

John Calvin

In 1541, John Calvin, a French reformer, started the Calvinist Church in Geneva. Calvinism is a strict form of Protestantism, and it was very popular in Switzerland and Scotland. By 1560, large numbers of people in northern Europe had become either Lutherans or Calvinists (see map).

John Calvin, founder of the Calvinist Church

Henry's rebellion

King Henry VIII of England argued with the Pope because he refused to allow Henry to divorce his wife, Catherine of Aragon. In 1531, Henry decided to take the place of the Pope, and made himself head of the Church in England, which later became known as the Anglican Church.

Henry VIII thought many monks and nuns did not lead holy lives, so he closed down the abbeys where they lived. Most of these abbeys are now in ruins, like Rievaulx Abbey shown here.

Catholics fight back

The leaders of the Catholic Church tried hard to win people back to their Church. They made many changes, which together became known as the Counter-Reformation.

During the Counter-Reformation, sculptors carved beautiful statues for Catholic cathedrals and churches. This statue of St. Teresa and an angel is by the Italian sculptor Bernini.

Catholic leaders set up colleges for priests, built elaborate churches, and trained teacher-priests, called Jesuits. They attacked the Protestants in sermons and books, and also used the Inquisition, a system of courts run by monks, to find and punish Protestants.

Map of Europe

SWEDEN
SCOTLAND
IRELAND
DENMARK
ENGLAND
POLAND
• Wittenberg
GERMANY   AUSTRIA
FRANCE
SWITZERLAND   HUNGARY
Geneva
SPAIN

The map shows the different Christian groups in 1560.

- Mainly Catholic
- Mainly Lutheran (Protestant)
- Mainly Calvinist (Protestant)
- Mainly Anglican (Protestant)
- Mixed Catholic and Protestant

Religious wars

During the 16th century, Protestants and Catholics fought each other all over Europe. One of the bloodiest struggles took place in France where French Protestants, known as Huguenots, fought the Catholic king and his supporters. The most horrific event in the French wars was the St. Bartholomew's Day Massacre, when thousands of Huguenots were slaughtered by Catholics. Eventually, after 30 years of war, the Huguenots were given the freedom to worship.

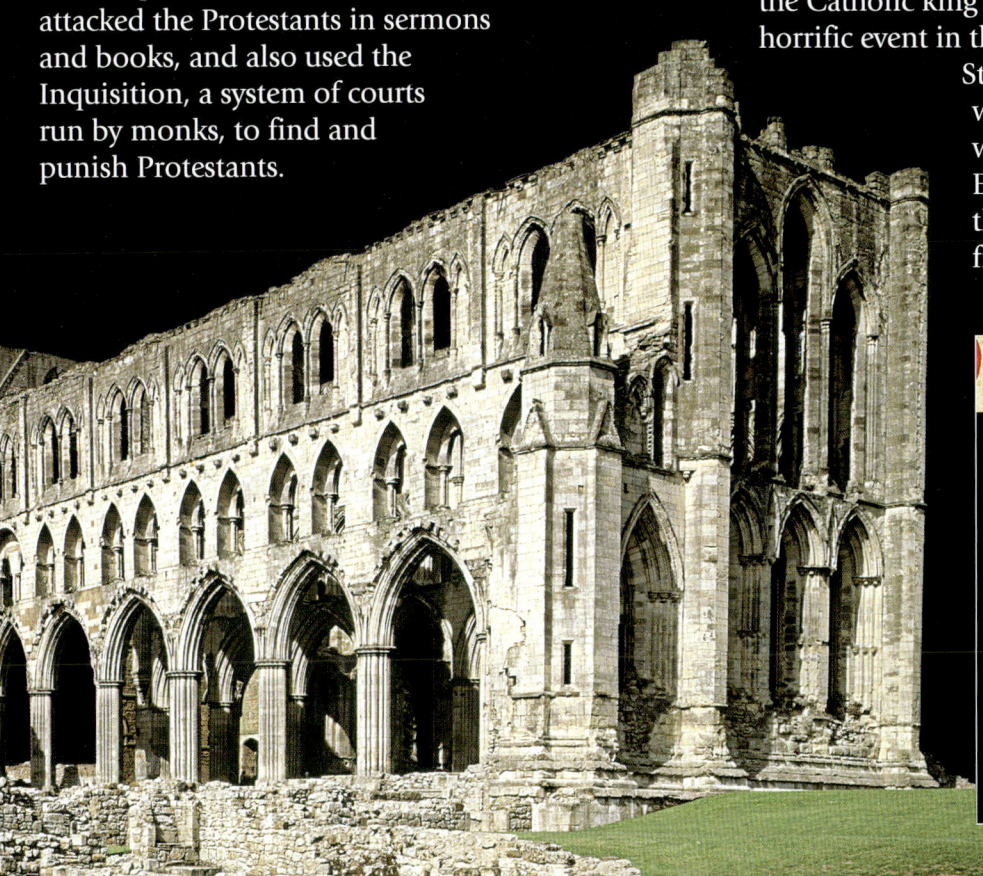

Important dates

1517	Luther writes his list of 95 suggested reforms.
1531	Henry VIII declares himself head of the English Church.
1541	Calvin starts his Church.
1545	The Counter-Reformation begins.
1562-1589	Religious wars in France
1572	St. Bartholomew's Day

EUROPE

303

Elizabethan England

Elizabeth I was the last and greatest of the Tudors, a line of kings and queens who had ruled England since 1485. She reigned for 45 years, making England a rich and powerful country that was respected throughout the world.

Great entertainment

Elizabethan England was famous for its writers and composers. The queen invited poets and musicians to entertain her at court, concerts were held in nobles' houses, and plays were performed in new London playhouses, such as the Globe Theatre.

In this portrait, Elizabeth I wears thick, white face paint and a dress that is covered with jewels.

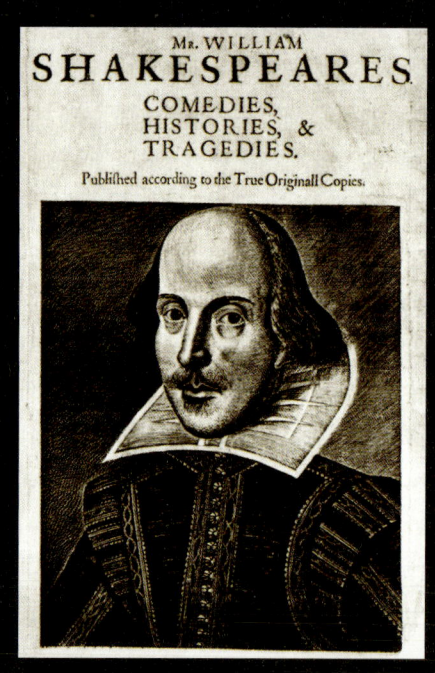

Mr. WILLIAM
SHAKESPEARES
COMEDIES,
HISTORIES, &
TRAGEDIES.
Published according to the True Originall Copies.

This is the title page from a collection of plays by William Shakespeare, the most brilliant of all the Elizabethan writers.

Elizabeth's people

Although lots of merchants became rich in Elizabeth's reign, many of her people were still very poor, and some had to beg in order to survive. In 1563, the first Poor Law was passed. This allowed local officials to raise money to look after the poor.

An Elizabethan picture of a beggar being chased through the streets

Catholic plots

Elizabeth was a Protestant, but some people wanted a Catholic ruler instead. A group of English Catholics tried to replace Elizabeth with her Catholic cousin Mary, Queen of Scots, but all their plots failed.

Explorers and raiders

During Elizabeth's reign, the great explorer Sir Francis Drake sailed around the world (see page 297), and Sir Walter Raleigh started a colony in North America. But English captains like Drake and Raleigh were raiders as well as explorers. They attacked Spanish ports and stole treasure from Spanish ships.

The Spanish Armada

King Philip II of Spain was furious that the English were raiding Spanish ships, and he decided to lead a Catholic attack on England. In 1588, he sent a large fleet of ships, called an armada, to invade England. The Spanish ships sailed to the Netherlands, where an army was waiting to join them, but on their way through the English Channel they were attacked by English warships.

Frightening fire ships

After four fierce sea battles, the Spanish fleet anchored close to Calais, on the northern coast of France. During the night, the English surprised the Spaniards by sending eight fire ships (ships that had been deliberately set on fire) into the middle of the fleet. The Spaniards panicked, and their ships scattered in all directions.

In this scene, English fire ships are approaching the Spanish Armada.

The fire ships are packed with rags, timber and oil.

The end of the Armada

The morning after the fire ships attacked, the English and the Spaniards fought the sea battle of Gravelines. The battle lasted all day, and the Spaniards were defeated.

After the battle, the Armada's ships were blown north. The Spaniards were forced to sail around Scotland and Ireland, and most of their ships were wrecked in terrible storms.

Map of western Europe

- ■ Lands ruled by Spain
- → Route taken by the Armada

The fire ships are carried toward the Armada by the wind and the tide.

As the fire ships approach, the Spanish sailors panic and cut their anchor ropes.

The Spaniards are terrified by fire because their ships are carrying gunpowder which might explode.

Heat from the flames makes the ships' guns fire.

Important dates

1558-1603	Elizabeth I is queen.
1563	The first Poor Law is passed.
1564-1616	Life of William Shakespeare
1577-1580	Sir Francis Drake sails around the world.
1588	The Spanish Armada is defeated.

EUROPE

305

Kings, Cavaliers and Roundheads

In 1603, James I became King of England and started a new line of Stuart rulers. James I and his son, Charles I, believed that God had chosen them to be supreme rulers and so they refused to accept any control from Parliament. This led to violent arguments.

The Civil War

In 1629, after several clashes with Parliament, King Charles I decided to rule without its help. Charles ruled alone for 11 years, but eventually he was forced to ask Parliament for money. Parliament refused to help, and in 1642 fighting broke out between the king's supporters and Parliament. This struggle is known as the English Civil War.

Followers of the king were called Royalists or Cavaliers, and supporters of Parliament were known as Parliamentarians or Roundheads. Some Cavaliers had flowing hair and fancy clothes, while most of the Roundheads were Puritans (very strict Protestants), who disapproved of fine clothes, acting and dancing.

The New Model Army

At first, the Cavaliers won most of the battles in the Civil War, but then a Puritan named Oliver Cromwell decided to reorganize the Roundheads' troops.

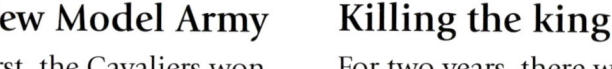

A 17th-century portrait of Oliver Cromwell

Cromwell's new fighting force was called the New Model Army. In 1645, it won the Battle of Naseby, and the following year the king was forced to surrender.

Killing the king

For two years, there was no more fighting, but then war broke out again. Eventually, Parliament gave up any hope of agreeing with the king, and in 1649 Charles I had his head chopped off in front of a stunned crowd in London.

The dramatic death of Charles I, as shown by an artist of the time

Commonwealth and Cromwell

After Charles' death, Parliament ruled England for four years. This period of time was known as the Commonwealth. But Parliament did not govern well, and in 1653 Oliver Cromwell took control of the country, calling himself Lord Protector of England. Cromwell ruled efficiently but strictly. He closed down many ale-houses and declared that Christmas Day was no longer a holiday.

King Charles I, painted by the artist Van Dyck

King Charles II

When Cromwell died, many people wanted to have a king again. The son of Charles I had escaped to France, and he was welcomed back and crowned King Charles II. The return of Charles II is called the Restoration.

Charles II, a popular king who loved music, dancing and beautiful women

Plague and fire

During Charles II's reign, a dreadful disease, known as the plague, killed thousands of people in London. The following year, a terrifying fire swept through the city. The fire destroyed hundreds of buildings, but it also killed the rats that helped spread the plague.

Rebuilding London

After the fire, large areas of London were rebuilt, using stone instead of wood. The architect Sir Christopher Wren designed over 50 churches for the city, and by the 1690s London had many elegant new buildings. People strolled through public gardens, and merchants met in coffee houses to make deals with each other. Theatres were reopened and women appeared on stage for the first time.

This is St. Paul's Cathedral in London, Sir Christopher Wren's most famous building.

A strong wind helps the fire to spread quickly.

The Great Fire of London raged through the city for four days. In this scene, the flames have reached London Bridge.

London Bridge has many wooden houses on it and they burn very easily.

People try to cross the Thames to safety.

Important dates

1603-1625 James I is king.

1625-1649 Charles I is king.

1642-1648 The English Civil War

1649-1653 Parliament rules England (the Commonwealth).

1653-1658 Oliver Cromwell is Lord Protector of England.

1660-1685 Charles II is king.

1665 The Great Plague of London

1666 The Great Fire of London

EUROPE

307

The Power of the Habsburgs

The ambitious Habsburg family began ruling Austria in the late 13th century. By marrying into some of Europe's richest families, they gained vast areas of land, and soon became the most powerful rulers in Europe.

The empire of Charles V

In the first half of the 16th century, the Habsburg emperor Charles V governed large areas of Europe, as well as colonies in the Americas. Charles was a strong ruler who defended his empire well. He won wars against the French and drove an army of Ottoman Turks out of Vienna (see page 298).

The empire divides

In 1556, Charles V retired to a monastery, dividing his lands between his son, Philip II, and his brother, Ferdinand. Philip II became King of Spain, and also controlled Italy, the Netherlands and Spain's American colonies, while Ferdinand ruled from Austria and inherited the title of emperor.

This is King Philip II of Spain, who became fabulously wealthy when Spanish settlers in America started mining gold and silver.

Map of Europe

- Empire of Charles V

SWEDEN
DENMARK
ENGLAND
Magdeburg
BOHEMIA
NETHERLANDS
Vienna
HUNGARY
AUSTRIA
FRANCE
SPAIN
ITALY
AFRICA

The Thirty Years' War

The Thirty Years' War started as a religious struggle between Protestants and Catholics in central Europe. It began in Bohemia (now part of the Czech Republic), when a group of Protestant nobles threw some officials of the Catholic Habsburg emperor out of a window.

This 17th-century drawing shows the event which helped to start the Thirty Years' War.

Spain and the Catholic German states supported the Habsburg emperor, while Bohemia was joined by Denmark and the Protestant German states. Later, Sweden and France also fought against the Habsburgs. By the end of the Thirty Years' War, the Habsburgs had become much less powerful.

The War of the Spanish Succession

The last of the Spanish Habsburgs was Charles II, who died in 1700. Charles had no children, so the French king claimed the throne for his grandson, Philip. The English and the Dutch were afraid that France and Spain would unite, so in 1701 they formed a "Grand Alliance" to fight against France.

The war lasted for 13 years and many European countries joined in. Eventually, the Alliance allowed Philip to become King of Spain, on the understanding that France and Spain would always remain separate. This was the end of the Habsburgs in Spain, but they still ruled in Austria.

Maria Theresa

In 1740, the 23-year-old Maria Theresa became the new ruler of the Habsburg Empire. When she took over, the empire was poor and weak, but she managed to make it strong again. Maria Theresa welcomed many musicians and artists to her court in Vienna. One of these musicians was the brilliant composer Wolfgang Amadeus Mozart.

This portrait shows Maria Theresa, who ruled the Austrian Habsburg Empire for 40 years.

The later Habsburgs

During the 18th and 19th centuries, the Habsburgs lost more and more land. But they managed to stay in power until 1918, when the last Habsburg emperor gave up his throne.

Here you can see the Schönbrunn Palace in Vienna, which was rebuilt by Maria Theresa.

★

Important dates

1519-1556	Charles V rules a vast Habsburg Empire.
1556	The Habsburg Empire is divided in two.
1618-1648	The Thirty Years' War
1701-1714	The War of the Spanish Succession.
1740-1780	Maria Theresa rules the Habsburg Empire.
1918	The last Habsburg emperor gives up his throne.

EUROPE

The Rise of the Dutch

By the 1550s, the low-lying lands that are now Holland, Belgium and Luxembourg were divided into 17 areas, called provinces. The people of the provinces had grown rich by weaving cloth and trading, but they weren't independent. Instead, they were ruled from Spain by the powerful Habsburg family (see page 308).

Catholics and Protestants

In 1556, King Philip II of Spain became the new Habsburg ruler of the provinces. Many people in the provinces were Protestants, but Philip was determined that they should all be Catholics. He sent the Duke of Alba to punish any rebels, and when two Protestant leaders were executed, war broke out between the provinces and Spain.

Map of the Netherlands

— Border of the 17 provinces in 1550

▨ Republic of the United Netherlands

EUROPE
ASIA
AFRICA

NORTH SEA

Amsterdam

Antwerp

The Dutch Revolt

Led by a Dutch prince named William of Orange, the people of the provinces fought fiercely for their independence. This struggle is known as the Dutch Revolt, because the most determined fighters were the Dutch, who lived in the northern provinces.

A miniature painting of Prince William of Orange

Dutch independence

In 1581, the seven northern provinces declared that they were independent from Spain. They called themselves the Republic of the United Netherlands and chose Prince William of Orange as their ruler.

In 1648, Spain finally accepted that the Republic was independent. This was the start of a new country called the Netherlands, which is sometimes also known as Holland.

The city of Amsterdam

During the Dutch Revolt, the wealthy port of Antwerp was destroyed by Spanish troops, and many of the provinces' merchants and bankers moved north to Amsterdam. The city of Amsterdam was rebuilt around a network of canals, and by the 1600s it was the busiest port in Europe.

This picture shows the bustling port of Amsterdam.

Merchant ships from all over Europe visit Amsterdam.

French trading ship

Art and science

This painting is by Jan Vermeer, who was famous for his scenes of everyday life.

During the 17th century, many great artists, thinkers and scientists lived and worked in the Netherlands. Inventors made microscopes, telescopes and clocks, and artists painted portraits and scenes of daily life.

The Dutch Empire

The Dutch built up an efficient navy and set up trading bases in Asia, South Africa, America, and even Japan. But their most valuable bases were in the East Indies (present-day Indonesia and Malaysia). From there, Dutch merchants sent shiploads of precious spices to Europe.

Using the land

The flat fields of Holland were often flooded by sea water, but Dutch engineers discovered new ways of draining the land. Some farmers made a fortune by growing exotic flowers from Turkey, known as tulips.

Dutch tulip-growers developed a wide range of flowers. Here are three kinds of tulips, painted by a 17th-century artist.

One tulip bulb could cost as much as a large country house.

William and Mary

In 1677, Prince William of Orange, great-grandson of the first Dutch leader, married the English princess Mary, and in 1689 they were crowned joint rulers of England. William ruled the Netherlands and England until his death in 1702, but the Dutch lost control of England when Mary's sister Anne became the next English queen.

This Dutch merchant ship is bringing spices from the East Indies to the Netherlands.

Important dates

1568 The Dutch Revolt begins.

1581 The Republic of the United Netherlands is created.

1584 Assassination of William of Orange.

1648 The Republic of the United Netherlands is recognized by Spain.

1689-1702 William of Orange is ruler of the Netherlands and King of England.

EUROPE

311

France and the Sun King

King Louis XIV of France, known as the Sun King, was the most powerful ruler in 17th-century Europe. He controlled all of France for over 50 years, without ever consulting his nobles or the

Louis XIV became known as the Sun King after he played the role of the Sun in a 12-hour ballet. This golden carving shows Louis as the Sun King. ★

Early lessons

Louis was only five when he became king, so his mother ruled for him. But after five years, the people of Paris rebelled, angry at the high taxes that they had to pay. Many nobles joined in the revolt, and Louis was forced to leave Paris.

In 1653, the rebellion collapsed, but Louis was still too young to rule on his own, so a powerful Church leader, Jules Mazarin, governed France on his behalf. Louis finally took control in 1661 when he was 22. He was determined that there would be no more revolts, so he kept all the power for himself, becoming what is known as an "absolute" ruler.

Running France

To help him run the country, Louis chose advisers who were talented and loyal, even if they were not nobles. His chief adviser, Jean Colbert, reorganized laws and taxes, set up new businesses in France and increased trade with other countries. Colbert also built new roads, canals and bridges all over France.

The Palace of Versailles

Louis gave orders for a magnificent palace to be built at Versailles, near Paris. Over 30,000 workers were needed to build the palace, which was filled with priceless statues, tapestries and paintings. In 1682, Louis moved to Versailles with his family and thousands of servants. He also forced many French nobles to live in the palace, so that he could keep an eye on them all the time.

Here you can see Louis XIV's palace at Versailles. Its extravagant Baroque style was copied all over Europe.

Wars in Europe

Louis wanted to conquer more land, and he fought many wars against other countries in Europe. The wars made France feared and respected, but they were very expensive and the French gained only small areas of new land.

Anger in France

In 1685, Louis took away the French Protestants' right to worship, and many of them fled abroad. Meanwhile, the French middle classes and peasants began to resent the taxes that they had to pay to keep the king and the nobles in luxury.

This is the glittering Hall of Mirrors in Louis's palace at Versailles.

A splendid court

Louis XIV's court at Versailles was famous for its drama, music and art. The playwright Molière wrote comedies to amuse the king, the musician Lully composed operas for the court, and artists painted flattering portraits of the king and his family.

This dramatic portrait of Louis XIV shows him as a dashing young horseman.

After the Sun King

The two French kings who ruled after Louis XIV were both very extravagant. Like the Sun King, they fought expensive wars and lived in incredible luxury. Meanwhile, the French people continued to pay heavy taxes, and 70 years after the Sun King's death, the French Revolution began (see pages 332 and 333).

The palace gardens were laid out in a very formal design.

Important dates

1643-1715   Louis XIV is King of France.

1643-1651   Louis's mother rules for him.

1648-1653   Rebellion in Paris

1661   Louis XIV takes control of France.

1667-1713   France fights wars against other countries in Europe.

The Age of Ideas

Between 1600 and 1800, there was an explosion of new ideas in Europe. Scientists made dramatic discoveries, thinkers questioned the power of their rulers, and some daring writers challenged the teachings of the Church. Many people started to see the world in a new light, and the 18th century became known as the Age of Enlightenment.

Discoveries in science

By observing the world around them and doing experiments, scientists made amazing progress. Johannes Kepler studied the way planets move, and Galileo Galilei used the newly invented telescope to help him prove that the Earth circles the Sun. Robert Boyle experimented with chemicals and gases, and Isaac Newton discovered how gravity works.

The photograph on the left shows the surface of the Moon. Galileo studied the mountains of the Moon with the help of a telescope.

★

Kepler's diagram of the Solar System shows how the planets travel around the Sun.

Advances in medicine

During the 17th and 18th centuries, doctors studied the human body, and surgeons performed difficult operations. Many doctors were forced to study secretly because the leaders of the Church wouldn't allow them to cut up dead bodies.

In 1628, William Harvey described the way blood moves around the human body. This is a diagram from Harvey's book.

This painting by the Dutch artist Rembrandt shows a group of 17th-century doctors examining the arm of a dead man.

Collecting knowledge

Many books were produced to record the new discoveries that were being made. Denis Diderot put together a 35-volume encyclopedia. Dr. Samuel Johnson wrote a vast English dictionary, and Carl Linnaeus published detailed studies of plants, dividing them into types, or species.

Linnaeus gave each plant a Latin name. The pansy shown here was named *Viola tricolor.*

Spreading ideas

The new ideas spread fast among educated people. Discoveries were published in books, pamphlets and newspapers, and scientists formed societies where they shared their findings.

Rich people invited guests to their homes to discuss the latest discoveries, and people also met in coffee houses to read newspapers and talk about ideas.

Scientists often used models to help them explain their ideas. This is an 18th-century model of the Sun and the planets.

Dangerous ideas

By the 1750s, thinkers in Europe had become very daring. In France, Jean Jacques Rousseau made the bold new claim that all people are equal, while Voltaire attacked the French king and the Church. Ideas like these got their writers into trouble, and Voltaire was sent to prison three times.

Like Voltaire and Rousseau, the writer Thomas Paine encouraged ordinary people to think about their rights. His most famous book, *The Rights of Man*, supports the ideas behind the French Revolution.

The writing in this 18th-century cartoon suggests that Thomas Paine's ideas were dangerous nonsense.

This golden ball represents the Sun.

These smaller balls represent the planets, which all move around the Sun.

Some planets have moons circling them.

The model works when its handle is turned.

Rulers and ideas

Some European rulers encouraged the search for knowledge. King Louis XIV of France set up a society which paid scientists to carry out experiments, while Charles II of England started the Royal Society for scientists and thinkers. Charles also built an observatory, where astronomers could study the stars.

Important dates

1620s	Kepler studies the movement of the planets.
1630s	Galileo proves that the Earth travels around the Sun.
1660s	Newton discovers the laws of gravity.
1694-1778	Life of Voltaire
1712-1778	Life of Rousseau
1791-1792	Thomas Paine writes *The Rights of Man*.

EUROPE

315

Changes in Russia

Russia in the 1500s was a fast-growing country ruled by a powerful tsar, or emperor. But Russia's position on the eastern edge of Europe made it isolated from the wealthy west. Large areas of Russia were too cold to grow food, and most Russians were peasants who were desperately poor.

This is a portrait of Ivan the Terrible, a powerful ruler who was often violent and cruel.

Ivan the Terrible

In 1547, Prince Ivan IV of Moscow became Tsar of Russia. He was a strong ruler who encouraged trade with western Europe, built up the Russian army, and won land in the valley of the Volga river.

At home in Russia, Ivan was ruthless and cruel, earning himself the title of Ivan the Terrible. He seized land from Russian nobles, called boyars, and gave it to his personal followers. He also made a law that took away all the peasants' rights, turning them into serfs who couldn't leave their master's land.

St. Basil's Cathedral in Moscow was built by Ivan the Terrible to celebrate his victories in the Volga valley.

The time of troubles

The chaotic period that followed the reign of Ivan the Terrible is known as the "time of troubles". During this time, several men claimed that they were the true tsar, and the country was divided by civil war. Meanwhile, Russia was attacked by Sweden and Poland. However, the Russians did manage to win more land, in the vast eastern area known as Siberia.

Map of Russia

Russia at the end of Ivan the Terrible's reign

Russia at the start of Peter the Great's reign

Land invaded by Peter the Great

Peter the Great

In 1613, the Romanov family took control of Russia, starting a dynasty that would last for 300 years. The greatest of the Romanovs was Peter the Great, who became tsar in 1682. By the end of his reign, Russia was one of the strongest countries in Europe.

Learning from the west

Peter decided to modernize Russia by copying the way western countries were run. He spent 18 months in northern Europe, visiting factories, farms and hospitals, and he even worked in a shipyard.

Peter the Great was an energetic and inspiring leader, but he could also be frighteningly brutal.

Changing Russia

Back in Russia, Peter reorganized his country's government, and reduced the power of the boyars. Workers from Europe helped to build canals, ships and factories, and a new iron industry was set up in Russia.

Peter forced the boyars to cut off their beards, to show that they had given up their old powers. This cartoon shows him as a barber.

Peter's wars

Peter strengthened the Russian army, created a navy, and won several victories against the Swedes and the Ottoman Turks. From Sweden, Russia gained a stretch of land beside the Baltic Sea. This meant that the Russians could at last build some ports which were close to western Europe and didn't freeze solid every winter.

A new capital city

Peter gave orders for an elegant new city to be built on the Baltic coast. He named it St. Petersburg and made it into Russia's new capital. The land around St. Petersburg was extremely swampy, and hundreds of serfs drowned while they were building the city.

Important dates

1480-1505	Prince Ivan III of Moscow is the first Tsar of Russia.
1547-1584	Ivan the Terrible is tsar.
1613	The Romanov dynasty begins.
1682-1725	Peter the Great is tsar.
1695-1706	Russia fights the Ottoman Empire.
1700-1721	Russia fights Sweden.
1712	St. Petersburg becomes the new Russian capital.

EUROPE

317

Russians and Prussians

During the 18th century, eastern Europe was dominated by two very powerful rulers. Catherine the Great of Russia and Frederick the Great of Prussia both insisted that they should have complete power, and both of them used their power to make their countries rich and successful.

Catherine the Great

Catherine the Great was an intelligent and determined ruler who demanded total obedience from her people.

Catherine II became Tsarina (empress) of Russia in 1762, and ruled for more than 30 years. She encouraged Russian trade, set up universities, and invited thinkers and writers to her splendid court at St. Petersburg. Later, she became known as Catherine the Great.

New lands

Catherine's army won new land around the Black Sea and the Baltic Sea, and the Russians built ports on both of these coasts. But Russia's most important gains came from the break-up of the weak kingdom of Poland. Poland was split between Russia, Austria and Prussia, and Catherine made sure that Russia had the largest share.

Life in Russia

While Catherine and her courtiers lived in luxury, the Russian peasants paid heavy taxes and had to fight in the army. At first, Catherine planned to make life better for her people, but most of her plans were never put into action. Peasant rebellions were brutally crushed, and when Catherine drove through Russia, her officials paid wealthy farmers to pretend to be peasants so that she wouldn't see how poor her people really were.

In this scene, Tsarina Catherine is driving through the Russian countryside in her sleigh.

Catherine's sleigh passes well-built houses like this, but most Russian peasants live in tumbledown shacks.

Wealthy farmers in warm clothes wave at the tsarina.

An official pushes the real peasants out of sight.

Map of eastern Europe

RUSSIA

BALTIC SEA

St. Petersburg

PRUSSIA

POLAND

AUSTRIA

BLACK SEA

EUROPE ASIA

AFRICA

- Russia before Catherine the Great
- Lands won by Catherine the Great
- Prussia before Frederick the Great
- Lands won by Frederick the Great

Frederick's wars

Frederick the Great was a brilliant soldier who used his well-trained army to conquer large areas of land. He won outstanding victories against France and Austria in the Seven Years' War, and by the end of his reign he had doubled the size of Prussia.

This 18th-century painting shows a violent battle in the Seven Years' War.

The rise of Prussia

In 1618, the weak state of Prussia was inherited by the ruler of the German state of Brandenburg. Prussia's new rulers built up a strong army and united all their lands under an efficient government. In 1701, the ruler of Brandenburg was crowned King of Prussia, and an ambitious new country was born.

Frederick the Great

Frederick II, known as Frederick the Great, became King of Prussia in 1740. He was a talented musician, a brave general and a stern ruler who believed that only a king with total power could make a real difference to the lives of his people.

Frederick improved education for middle-class boys, encouraged the study of science, and helped to build up farming and trade in Prussia. He also made it illegal to torture prisoners, and allowed both Catholics and Protestants to follow their own religion.

Important dates

1701-1713	Frederick I is the first King of Prussia.
1740-1786	Frederick the Great is King of Prussia.
1756-1763	Prussia and Britain fight France, Russia and Austria in the Seven Years' War.
1762-1796	Catherine the Great is Tsarina of Russia.

EUROPE

Early Settlers in the Americas

Soon after Christopher Columbus reached America in 1492, the first settlers from Europe began arriving in the New World. By 1550, there were thousands of Spanish and Portuguese settlers in the West Indies and South America. At the same time, settlers from France had begun to make their homes in the land that is now called Canada.

Soldiers and priests

Spanish soldiers conquered large areas of South America and set up colonies with Spanish rulers, called viceroys. Some soldiers and priests from Spain also settled in North America, building forts and churches in Florida and California.

This 19th-century painting shows a lakeside town in the Spanish colony of New Granada.

Silver and gold

Spanish settlers opened up mines in Mexico and Peru, and sent back shiploads of silver and gold to Spain. The Spanish forced the Native Americans to work in their mines, and many workers died of exhaustion or disease.

★ Spanish cross made from South American gold

French settlers

The early French settlers in Canada built their homes close to rivers, and lived by trapping and hunting animals and catching fish. Slowly, the settlers spread out, and in 1699 they claimed all the land around the Mississippi River, naming the area Louisiana after the French king, Louis XIV.

French losses

The French were not the only Europeans to settle in North America, and by 1700 the British also owned large areas of land. In 1754, the French and the British began fighting each other for land. At first, the French managed to fight off the British, but in 1759 British troops, led by General James Wolfe, captured the French city of Quebec. After this victory, the British won more land from France, and in 1763 the French signed the Peace of Paris, giving most of their land in Canada to Britain.

General James Wolfe

Portuguese plantations

Portuguese settlers in Brazil grew sugar on vast farms called plantations, and brought slaves from Africa to work on their farms. (For more about slavery see pages 324 and 325.)

Map of the Americas

The map shows land owned by European countries in 1750.

- Spanish land
- British land
- Portuguese land
- Dutch land
- French land

CANADA, NORTH AMERICA, Quebec, California, Louisiana, Mississippi, Florida, MEXICO, WEST INDIES, NEW GRANADA, SOUTH AMERICA, PERU, BRAZIL

Important dates

By 1600 The Spanish, Portuguese and French all have colonies in the Americas.

1699 The French create the colony of Louisiana.

1754 War breaks out in North America between the British and the French.

1759 The British capture Quebec.

1763 The Peace of Paris gives Britain control of Canada.

THE AMERICAS

321

Settlers in North America

Near the end of the 16th century, groups of settlers from England tried to set up colonies on the east coast of North America. The first English settlers either died or returned home, but in 1607 a successful settlement was started in Jamestown, Virginia.

Pilgrim settlers

In August 1620, a group of English settlers set sail for Virginia in a ship called the *Mayflower*. The settlers belonged to a strict religious group who wanted to be free to worship God in their own way. Later, they became known as the Pilgrims, or the Pilgrim Fathers.

The *Mayflower* took three months to sail from England to America.

The first Thanksgiving

The *Mayflower* was blown off course and landed in a place that the Pilgrims named Plymouth. The first winter was extremely hard, but, with the help of the local Indigenous Americans, half of the settlers survived.

After their first harvest, the Pilgrims made a simple meal and held a service of thanksgiving. Every November, Americans remember this event with a Thanksgiving meal.

This picture shows the Pilgrims preparing their first Thanksgiving meal.

Land and freedom

By the 1650s, many settlers were sailing from Europe to North America. Groups of Puritans (strict Protestants) and Catholics settled in America so that they could be free to follow their own religion. But many other settlers left Europe in search of land and adventure.

New Amsterdam

In 1624, a group of Dutch settlers built a settlement on an island in the Hudson River and named it New Amsterdam. The Dutch controlled the island until 1664, when it was captured by the English, who renamed it New York.

Fish hung up to dry

These women are plucking wild turkeys.

House built from wooden planks, called clapboards

Some of the settlers are very weak and ill.

The Thirteen Colonies

By 1733, the British ruled 13 colonies on the east coast of America. The colonists grew tobacco, rice, and a blue dye called indigo. They sold these things to people in Europe in exchange for guns, clothes and tools.

Wars for land

At first, the settlers from Europe lived peacefully with the Indigenous North Americans, but as their colonies grew, battles for land began. By the 1720s, most of the indigenous peoples on the east coast of America had been wiped out or had been driven west.

Map of the Thirteen Colonies

MASSACHUSETTS
NEW HAMPSHIRE
RHODE ISLAND
NEW YORK
Plymouth
CONNECTICUT
New York (New Amsterdam)
PENNSYLVANIA
NEW JERSEY
MARYLAND
DELAWARE
VIRGINIA
Jamestown
NORTH CAROLINA
SOUTH CAROLINA
GEORGIA

NORTH AMERICA

Indigenous North Americans have taught the settlers how to fish, hunt and grow crops.

Fence to keep out wild animals

These Indigenous North Americans are bringing deer for the meal.

Chickens are kept for their eggs.

This woman is reading aloud from the Bible.

The settlers wear very plain clothes.

Important dates

1607 The English build a settlement in Jamestown, Virginia.
1620 The Pilgrims arrive in America.
1624 The Dutch settle in New Amsterdam.
By 1733 The British have 13 American colonies.

NORTH AMERICA

323

The Slave Trade

People had bought and sold slaves since ancient times, but in the 1580s this terrible trade increased dramatically. Millions of Africans were captured and sent across the ocean to the Americas. Those who survived the journey were sold as slaves, and most slaves had to work so hard they died within a few years.

Workers wanted

Since the 1500s, settlers from Europe had grown sugar and tobacco in the West Indies and South America. The settlers used indigenous people to work on their vast farms, which were called plantations. However, by the 1550s, so many indigenous people had died that the settlers were desperate for more workers.

Charleston, July 24th, 1769.
TO BE SOLD,
On THURSDAY the third Day
of AUGUST next,
A CARGO
OF
NINETY-FOUR
PRIME, HEALTHY
NEGROES,
CONSISTING OF
Thirty-nine MEN, Fifteen BOYS,
Twenty-four WOMEN, and
Sixteen GIRLS.
JUST ARRIVED,
In the Brigantine DEMBIA, Francis Bare, Master, from SIERRA-LEON, by
DAVID & JOHN DEAS.

African slaves were sold to the buyer who offered the most money. Posters like this advertised the sales.

The slave trade begins

The Portuguese had colonies on the west coast of Africa and they began to buy Africans who had been captured by rival tribes. The captives were chained together and forced to march to the coast. Then they were packed onto ships and sent to the Americas to be sold as slaves.

A triangle of trade

By 1600, many European countries had joined in the slave trade. Their ships made a three-stage journey in the shape of a triangle (see map opposite). First, the slave ships sailed from Europe to Africa, carrying goods such as guns and cloth. In Africa, they exchanged their goods for slaves, and sailed on to the Americas. There, the slaves were sold in exchange for sugar, tobacco and cotton before the ships returned to Europe. This triangle of trade made the slave traders extremely rich.

This 19th-century painting shows slaves from Africa working on a tobacco plantation in the West Indies.

Slave ships

Conditions on board the slave ships were appalling. The slaves were packed tightly together and were kept chained up in the dark for all of their eight-week voyage. Diseases spread rapidly on the ships, and more than a third of the slaves died before they even reached the Americas.

This diagram of a slave ship shows how tightly the slaves were packed together.

Slaves at work

Most slaves worked in the plantations of the West Indies and South America, but some of them were sent to the USA to pick cotton and harvest tobacco. A few masters were kind to their slaves, but many slaves were treated cruelly and forced to work very long hours.

Map of the slave trade

Slave rebellions

Some courageous slaves led rebellions against their masters, but most of these rebels were punished severely. In 1791, however, a successful revolt took place in Haiti in the West Indies, and the slaves' leader, Toussaint L'Ouverture, became ruler of Haiti.

Ending the slave trade

By the 1780s, many people in Europe had become unhappy about the slave trade. In 1792, Denmark became the first country to stop buying and selling slaves, and over the next 40 years the European slave trade slowly died out.

In 1804, slavery was banned in the northern states of the USA, but the people of the southern states continued to keep slaves for another 60 years. Gradually, slavery was made illegal all over the Americas, and the last slaves were set free in 1888.

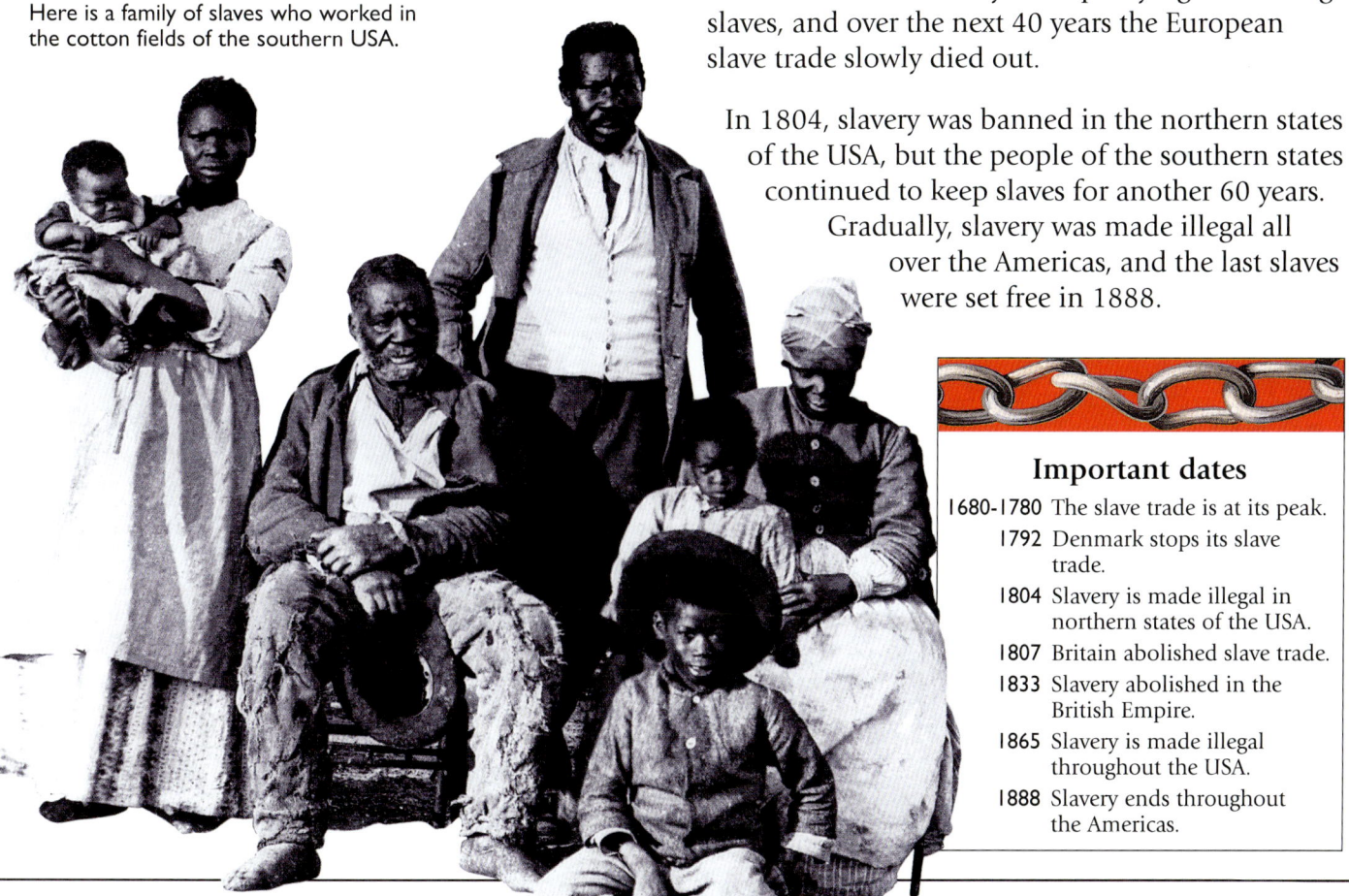

Here is a family of slaves who worked in the cotton fields of the southern USA.

Important dates

1680-1780	The slave trade is at its peak.
1792	Denmark stops its slave trade.
1804	Slavery is made illegal in northern states of the USA.
1807	Britain abolished slave trade.
1833	Slavery abolished in the British Empire.
1865	Slavery is made illegal throughout the USA.
1888	Slavery ends throughout the Americas.

THE WORLD

Exploring the South Seas

By the 1600s, European explorers had reached most parts of the world, but the South Pacific Ocean was still unknown to them. Sailors began to travel there, searching for new lands and riches.

Dutch explorers

In 1606, Dutch explorers reached the north coast of Australia, and in 1642 a Dutchman, Abel Tasman, sailed as far south as New Zealand. Tasman was also the first European to see the island of Tasmania, which was named after him.

Captain Cook

In 1768, Captain James Cook set out from Britain to explore the lands of the South Pacific. In some places, Cook's men were welcomed by the people who lived there. But when Cook's ship reached New Zealand, the people, called the Māori, tried to frighten him away. Cook eventually made peace with the Māori, and later drew detailed maps of New Zealand's coastline.

This picture shows Māori canoes approaching Captain Cook's ship, the *Endeavour*, as it arrives on the coast of New Zealand.

The ship is flying a British flag called the Red Ensign.

Scientists have come on the voyage to study wildlife in new lands.

Captain Cook

Cook's soldiers fire guns into the air, to drive the Māori away.

The Māori canoes are covered with carvings.

AUSTRALASIA

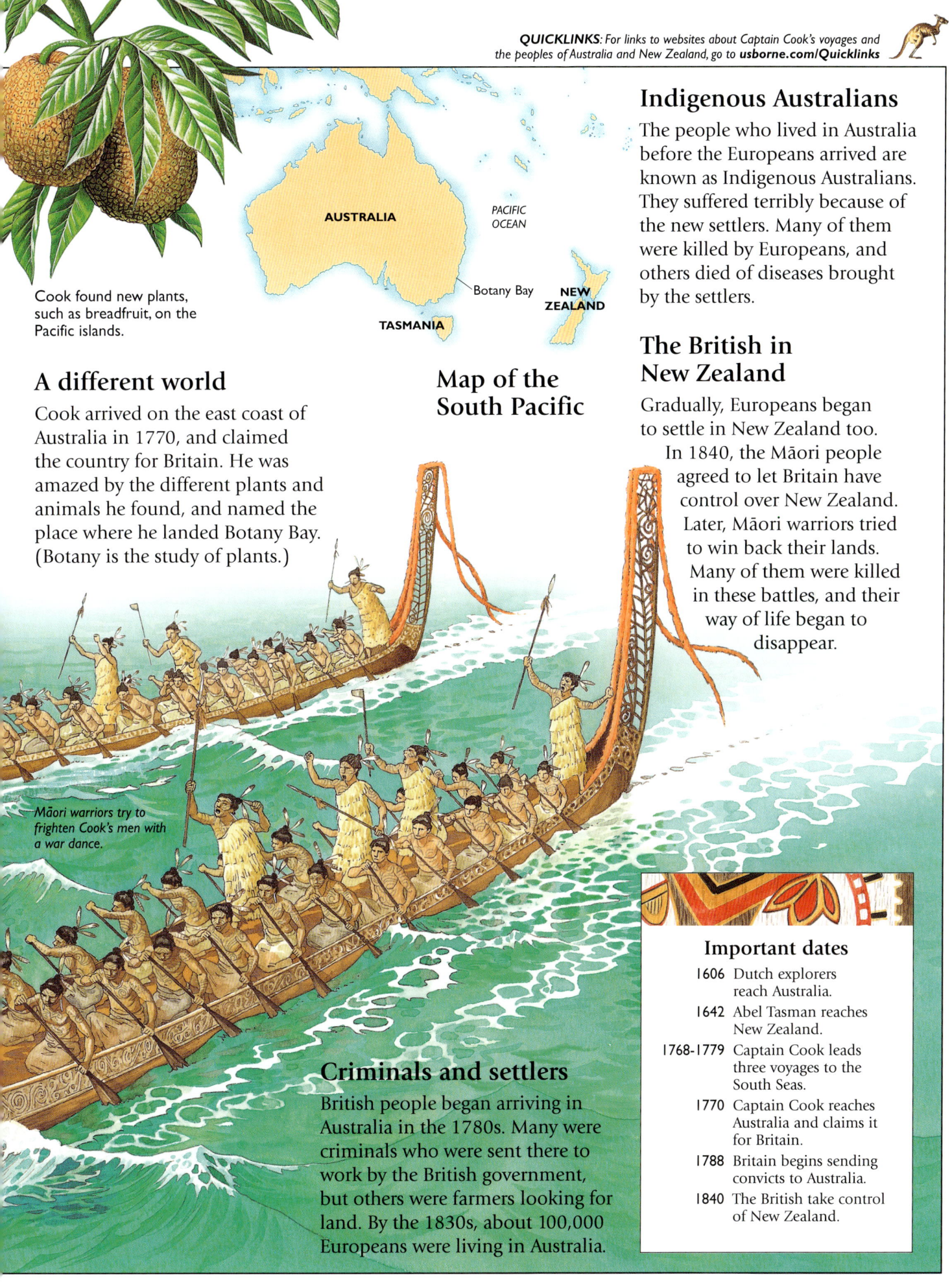

QUICKLINKS: For links to websites about Captain Cook's voyages and the peoples of Australia and New Zealand, go to **usborne.com/Quicklinks**

Cook found new plants, such as breadfruit, on the Pacific islands.

Map of the South Pacific

AUSTRALIA

PACIFIC OCEAN

Botany Bay

NEW ZEALAND

TASMANIA

A different world

Cook arrived on the east coast of Australia in 1770, and claimed the country for Britain. He was amazed by the different plants and animals he found, and named the place where he landed Botany Bay. (Botany is the study of plants.)

Indigenous Australians

The people who lived in Australia before the Europeans arrived are known as Indigenous Australians. They suffered terribly because of the new settlers. Many of them were killed by Europeans, and others died of diseases brought by the settlers.

The British in New Zealand

Gradually, Europeans began to settle in New Zealand too. In 1840, the Māori people agreed to let Britain have control over New Zealand. Later, Māori warriors tried to win back their lands. Many of them were killed in these battles, and their way of life began to disappear.

Māori warriors try to frighten Cook's men with a war dance.

Criminals and settlers

British people began arriving in Australia in the 1780s. Many were criminals who were sent there to work by the British government, but others were farmers looking for land. By the 1830s, about 100,000 Europeans were living in Australia.

Important dates

1606 Dutch explorers reach Australia.

1642 Abel Tasman reaches New Zealand.

1768-1779 Captain Cook leads three voyages to the South Seas.

1770 Captain Cook reaches Australia and claims it for Britain.

1788 Britain begins sending convicts to Australia.

1840 The British take control of New Zealand.

AUSTRALASIA

327

The British in India

During the 16th century, many merchants from Europe arrived in India. They bought silk, cotton, jewels, tea and spices, and built up wealthy trading companies.

Indian crocuses, and a spice called saffron which comes from their flowers

By the 1700s, India was split into areas ruled by local princes. The princes often fought each other, and the Europeans sometimes took sides in their battles.

Clive of India

In 1756, the Prince of Bengal captured a British trading base and killed more than a hundred people. The following year, a British general named Robert Clive led an army that defeated the Prince. Clive forced everyone in Bengal to pay taxes to the British East India Company, which became very powerful.

Robert Clive, who became rich by seizing gold that belonged to the Prince of Bengal

The rise of the British

The East India Company gradually built up a big army. It was led by British soldiers, but many Indians joined as well. The army defeated more and more princes, and took control of large areas of

This mechanical toy belonged to an Indian prince. It shows a tiger eating a British soldier.

The Indian Mutiny

Many Indian soldiers in the British army became angry. They felt that the British didn't respect Indian religions and were changing the country too much. In 1857, some Indian soldiers in Bengal began a mutiny, or rebellion, against the British.

★ *This scene is based on a 19th-century painting of a battle in the Indian Mutiny.*

The fighting spread to many areas of northern India, but in 1858 the rebels were defeated. The British government took charge of the country, and India became an important part of the British Empire.

Princes and servants

After the mutiny, some Indian princes still lived in splendid palaces, but they no longer had any power. Most Indians remained poor, and many of them worked as servants for the British.

Making changes

The British built roads, railways and schools in India, and made the Indians learn English. Many British missionaries went to India and tried to persuade Indians to become Christians.

Life in the Raj

By the 1880s, lots of British families were living in India. They tried to keep to a British way of life, but they were also influenced by Indian culture. The British stayed in India until 1947, when the country became independent. The period of time when the British ruled India is known as the Raj.

Map of India

- ■ Areas controlled by the East India Company by 1805
- — Main area where the Indian Mutiny took place

EUROPE
ASIA
AFRICA
BENGAL
INDIA
ARABIAN SEA
BAY OF BENGAL

★

Europeans were not used to the hot Indian weather and many died from the heat and tropical diseases. Women used parasols to protect themselves from the sun.

This photograph shows King George V of Great Britain hunting tigers during a visit to India in 1911.

Important dates

1600 The British East India Company is created.

1757 Robert Clive defeats the Prince of Bengal at the Battle of Plassey.

1757-1857 Britain conquers large areas of India.

1857-1858 The Indian Mutiny

1858 The British government takes control of India.

The American Revolution

By the 1700s, Britain had 13 colonies on the east coast of North America (see page 323). The British government ruled its colonies with strict laws, and made the colonists pay more taxes than people in Britain. Many colonists thought that this was unfair, and riots broke out.

Map of the Thirteen Colonies

British colonies

NORTH AMERICA

Boston

ATLANTIC OCEAN

Yorktown

Tea in the sea

One very unpopular tax made it extremely expensive to buy tea in America. In 1773, colonists climbed on board ships delivering tea to the port of Boston and threw all the tea into the sea. This famous protest is known as the Boston Tea Party.

Fighting begins

The British government punished the colonists with even stricter laws, and moved a large army into North America. Fighting soon broke out between the colonists and the British.

Breaking free

The colonists thought of themselves as Americans and wanted to break free from Britain. In 1776, the leaders of all 13 colonies signed a statement called the Declaration of Independence.

This painting shows the leaders of the colonies signing the Declaration of Independence.

The Declaration said that the colonies were now an independent country. The colonists called their new country the United States of America (USA).

Early battles

The British didn't want to lose control of their North American land, and they fought hard against the new American army. Although the Americans had a strong leader, named George Washington, the British soldiers were better trained and more experienced. The British won several early battles and captured some important cities.

George Washington, a skilled soldier and an inspiring leader

NORTH AMERICA

French friends

In 1777, France decided to support the USA against Britain. By this time, the American army was stronger and, with the help of the French, the Americans began to win more battles. In 1781, the British surrendered after a long battle at Yorktown, and the war was over.

Here you can see the American army attacking a British fort during the Battle of Yorktown. The Americans have started their attack at night, in order to take the British by surprise. ★

A new nation

Soon after the war, Britain signed a peace treaty and accepted the United States as an independent country. In 1787, a group of American lawyers and politicians wrote a set of laws for the new country. These laws are known as the American Constitution. In 1789, George Washington was elected the first President of the USA.

Americans from all 13 colonies fight alongside each other.

The American flag has 13 stripes, one for each of the 13 colonies.

The American soldiers wear blue jackets.

The British have built a wall of soil and tree trunks to protect themselves.

American cannons have destroyed parts of the British wall.

This gun is called a musket.

Metal cannonballs

The British soldiers are known as "redcoats".

Important dates

1773	The Boston Tea Party
July 4, 1776	The 13 colonies declare independence.
1777	France joins the Americans in their war against Britain.
1781	Britain is defeated by the USA and France.
1787	The American Constitution is written.
1789	George Washington becomes the first President of the USA.

NORTH AMERICA

331

The French Revolution

By the 1780s, many French people were angry with their ruler, King Louis XVI, and the way he ran the country. Although the French government was running out of money, the king's nobles still led a luxurious life and paid no taxes. Meanwhile, the peasants and workers had to pay high taxes, and there wasn't enough work or food for them all.

Facing disaster

By 1789, the government had no money left at all, and France was in a desperate situation. In order to solve the country's problems, the king was forced to call a meeting of the Estates General, the French parliament, which had not met for almost 200 years.

Tax troubles

Some of those who came to the meeting of the Estates General were middle-class people, such as merchants and lawyers. Unlike the nobles, the middle classes had to pay taxes. They demanded that everyone should pay fair taxes, but the king refused. This made many French people furious.

Storming the Bastille

On July 14, 1789, a crowd of poor people, helped by some of the king's soldiers, attacked and captured an important prison in Paris, called the Bastille. This dramatic event is known as the storming of the Bastille.

In this scene, French rebels are attacking the Bastille. This was the start of the French Revolution.

A guard plummets from the battlements.

Cannonballs smash the prison walls.

The king's army has joined the rebels.

People shout and cheer.

QUICKLINKS: For links to websites where you can find out more about the French Revolution, go to **usborne.com/Quicklinks**

The revolution spreads

The news that the Bastille had been captured encouraged many other people to rebel, and a revolution soon broke out all over France. The middle classes took control of the country, and in 1793 the king was executed.

Maximilien Robespierre, leader of the French people during the Reign of Terror

The Reign of Terror

The revolution quickly became very violent. The queen was executed, as well as thousands of nobles, and anyone else who was thought to be against the revolution. This frightening period became known as the Reign of Terror.

★ This is a guillotine, a machine used by the revolutionaries to execute their enemies.

Map of France

• Paris

FRANCE

☐ French land in 1789
☐ French land by 1795

War in Europe

The revolutionaries promised to help people in other nations to rebel against their rulers, and France began to invade nearby countries. Many European rulers were worried and wanted to stop the revolution. In 1793, several countries, such as Britain and Austria, attacked France, and war began. By 1795, the French had defeated most of their enemies and won new land in Europe.

Red, white and blue ribbons, like those worn by the French revolutionaries

★

Some buildings have been set on fire.

Rebels have broken through the prison gate.

Peasants use their farm tools as weapons.

Important dates

May 1789   Louis XVI calls a meeting of the Estates General.

July 14, 1789   The Bastille is captured by revolutionaries.

1793   Louis XVI is executed.

1793-1794   The Reign of Terror

1793-1795   France is at war with most of Europe.

The Empire of Napoleon

During the wars that followed the French Revolution, a brilliant young general named Napoleon Bonaparte won many battles for the French army. Napoleon became popular and powerful, and in 1799 he seized control of France.

Napoleon Bonaparte, painted in 1801 by the French artist Jacques Louis David

New laws

Napoleon made many new laws, giving everyone in France the right to own land and to find a good job. However, he was also an extremely strict ruler who wanted as much power for himself as possible.

Napoleon the Emperor

In 1804, Napoleon made himself Emperor of France. His army won a series of spectacular victories, and by 1812 he had conquered most of western Europe. Napoleon ruled from Paris, and put his relatives in charge of parts of his empire.

Defeat at sea

One country that Napoleon failed to take over was Britain. Britain was hard to invade because it had a powerful navy. In 1805, British ships, under the command of Admiral Lord Nelson, defeated the French navy just off Cape Trafalgar, in southern Spain. The British encouraged other countries to stand up to Napoleon.

This 19th-century painting shows a scene from the Battle of Trafalgar.

The French and British ships have moved close together to fire at each other.

Disaster in Russia

In 1812, Napoleon invaded Russia. He won several battles, then marched his men into Moscow. But Russian soldiers had set fire to the city and taken away all the food.

Napoleon's army was forced to leave Moscow and march all the way back to France through the freezing winter snow. Thousands of men died, and Napoleon's attempt to conquer Russia ended in disaster.

Napoleon Bonaparte

Napoleon's army retreating from Moscow

Enemies in Europe

When Napoleon's invasion of Russia failed, many European countries joined together against him. In Spain and Portugal, British forces, under Sir Arthur Wellesley (later the Duke of Wellington), drove the occupying French back into France. In 1814 Napoleon was captured and imprisoned.

Cape Trafalgar

Map of Napoleon's Empire

Land ruled by France in 1812

Napoleon's downfall

A year after he was captured, Napoleon escaped and took control of France once more. However, after only a hundred days in charge, he was finally defeated by the British and the Prussians at the Battle of Waterloo. Napoleon was sent to live on the tiny island of St. Helena in the middle of the Atlantic Ocean. He died there in 1821.

Important dates

1799	Napoleon takes control of France.
1805	The Battle of Trafalgar
1805-1812	Napoleon conquers most of western Europe.
1812	Napoleon invades Russia, but is forced to turn back.
1814	Napoleon is defeated and captured.
1815	Napoleon returns to power, but is defeated at Waterloo.
1815-1821	Napoleon is imprisoned on the island of St. Helena.

EUROPE

335

Changes in Farming

Until the late 1600s, farming in Europe had hardly changed for hundreds of years. Most families grew their own food on small strips of land in big fields that belonged to wealthy landowners. There were no farm machines, and people had to manage with just a few simple tools.

By 1700, new ideas and machines were being tried out on farms in Britain and the Netherlands. The new ideas soon spread across Europe, and the changes that they brought became known as the Agricultural Revolution.

Rotating crops

Planting the same crop in a field year after year wears out the soil, so farmers regularly left a field unplanted to let the soil recover. But in the 18th century, some farmers discovered that they could stop the soil from wearing out by planting a different crop in each field every year. This new system was called crop rotation. It meant that farmers could use all their fields all the time, and grow more food.

Corn

Turnip

Potatoes

New crops grown by European farmers in the 18th century

This scene shows how a British farming village might have looked by the year 1800.

Wheat has been planted in this field. Next year, turnips will be grown here.

Manure (animal dung) is spread on the land to help crops grow.

Village inn

Village shop

This open space is called the village green.

This man is making deep furrows (grooves) in the field.

A seed drill is used to plant seeds in the furrows.

The landowner rides around the village, inspecting his land.

Planting seeds

One of the most important new machines was the seed drill, which was invented by an English farmer named Jethro Tull. Instead of scattering seeds onto the ground by hand, people could use the seed drill to drop seeds straight into the soil. This meant that far fewer seeds were blown away or eaten by birds.

EUROPE

Better breeding

Some farmers began using only their biggest, healthiest animals for breeding. These animals often had big babies, and over time farm animals became larger, so they could feed more people.

Wealthy farmers had pictures painted that made their animals, such as this sheep, look even bigger than they were.

Fields and fences

Large landowners wanted to use new farming methods and machinery, so they got permission from Parliament to grow crops in large fields, rather than in lots of small strips. They built fences and planted hedges around their fields, and villagers were forbidden from farming them.

Many small farmers could not afford the hedges and fences around their land, so they had to sell. This meant that many people no longer had anywhere to grow their food. They either had to work for a landowner or find a job in a town.

The vicar, or priest, lives in this house.

Church

This house belongs to the wealthy landowner who owns most of the land in the village.

The land has been divided into fields for the landowner.

Hedges have been planted around the fields.

Blacksmith's workshop

The landowner built these cottages for villagers who work for him.

Steam power

By the 1850s, some farmers were using new steam-powered machines (see page 338). The machines helped to harvest crops, dig the fields and pump water out of marshy land.

Here are some farm workers with a steam-powered machine for threshing crops. The machine separates the grain from the stalks.

This family is leaving to find work in a town.

EUROPE

337

The Industrial Revolution

In the 18th century, many changes began to take place in the way that people lived and worked in Britain. These changes later spread across the world, and together they became known as the Industrial Revolution.

New machines

In 1700, most people in Britain lived in villages. Many villagers worked on farms, but others worked at home, spinning wool and cotton thread, then weaving the thread into cloth.

This way of life began to change in the 1700s, when British inventors first designed machines that could spin and weave cloth very quickly. The machines were too big and expensive for people to use at home, so wealthy businessmen built factories that could hold lots of machines.

★ This machine, called a Spinning Jenny, could spin 16 threads at once, instead of just one.

Mining coal

Steam for the new engines came from boiling water, and huge amounts of coal were needed to heat the water. Deep coal mines were dug, and men, women and children worked in the mines. Working underground was very dangerous, and many people were killed or injured.

★ Children working in a coal mine

Steam power

At first, running water was used to turn the wheels that made the machines work, so all the factories had to be built near rivers. Then, in 1782, James Watt invented a powerful engine that was driven by steam. Hundreds of these new steam-engines were built to run machines in factories all over Britain.

Factories and towns

Busy towns soon grew up around the factories, as thousands of people moved out of their villages to work on the new machines. People had to work very long hours, and many workers were injured while using the machines.

During the Industrial Revolution, iron was used to make engines, boats, trains and bridges. This is the world's first iron bridge, built at Coalbrookdale in England in 1779.

EUROPE

Canals and trains

Roads were muddy and bumpy in the 18th century, and carts were often attacked by robbers, so factory owners had to find a different way to transport their goods. For many years, they used canals, but canal boats were slow. Then, early in the 19th century, British inventors discovered how to build steam-powered trains. This made it much easier to travel long distances.

The *Rocket*, a famous early steam train, designed by George Stephenson ★

The Rocket could travel at up to 50km (30 miles) an hour.

ROCKET

Britain booms

Here you can see inside the Crystal Palace, which was built to contain the Great Exhibition of 1851.

Britain had so many factories that it became known as "the workshop of the world" and by the 1800s it was an extremely rich and powerful country. In 1851, many British inventors displayed their machines at a huge event in London, known as the Great Exhibition. Millions of people came from around the world to admire the new inventions.

Important dates

1767	James Hargreaves invents the Spinning Jenny.
1782	James Watt invents a powerful steam engine.
1804	Richard Trevithick builds the first steam train to run along a track.
1811	The Luddites start smashing machines.
1825	Passenger trains start running in Britain.
1829	George Stephenson builds the *Rocket*.
1851	The Great Exhibition

The machine-smashers

The new machines worked so fast that people who made cloth at home couldn't earn a living. This made some people angry, and they tried to destroy the machines. The most famous machine-smashers were the Luddites, named after their leader Ned Ludd.

However, protesters like the Luddites could do nothing to stop the Industrial Revolution, and the number of factories continued to grow.

A Luddite

EUROPE

339

Life in the New Towns

By the 1850s, there were factories in many parts of Britain, and large, busy towns were growing up around them. Although the factory owners became rich and lived in grand houses, the workers were paid very little and were extremely poor. They lived in dirty, crowded parts of the town, known as slums.

This scene shows part of a British town around 1850.

Life in the slums

Factory workers lived in rows of tiny houses on narrow streets. Their houses had no inside toilets or running water, the air was full of smoke from the factories, and the streets were filthy, so diseases spread quickly. There was a lot of crime, because some poor people had to steal food or money to survive.

Thick smoke from the factories pollutes the air.

Cloth factory

Up to 20 people live in each tiny house.

Gas lamp

The factory owner drives past quickly.

Ditch full of smelly waste

This policeman is chasing a thief.

People get water from a pump in the street, called a standpipe.

This boy is a chimney sweep. He earns money by climbing inside chimneys to clean them.

Wealthy people, such as lawyers and businessmen, live in larger houses on the edge of town.

Steam train

Houses are built back-to-back and in rows.

Outhouse for toilet

Workhouses

People who had no money or who couldn't work were sent to live in places called workhouses, which were almost like prisons. Once inside the workhouse, people had to work very long hours, and it was hard to get out again. Families were split up and hardly ever allowed to see each other.

The workers protest

Many workers, like these matchmakers, became ill because of the dangerous chemicals they had to handle.

Lots of factory workers felt they were being treated unfairly, so they started to form groups, called trade unions. The unions demanded better pay, shorter hours and safer places to work.

At first, trade unions were banned by the government, but in 1825 they became legal. When the members of a union wanted to protest about something, they all agreed to stop working and go on strike.

Making changes

Members of the trade unions and some wealthy people put pressure on the government to make life better for the poor. In the second half of the 19th century, factories became safer, and better houses were built. New drains and sewers made the streets cleaner, which helped to prevent diseases from spreading.

Going to school

In 1800, parents usually had to pay to send their children to school, so many children from poor families never learned to read or write. Over the next hundred years, laws were passed which allowed children to have a free education. By 1900, all children had to go to school until the age of 12. Schools were very strict, and pupils were often beaten by their teachers.

A group of children from the slums of London

EUROPE

The Year of Revolutions

By 1848, various groups of people in Europe had become unhappy with their rulers, and wanted more say in how their countries were run. In many places, there weren't enough jobs for everyone, and people were desperately short of food. They remembered the French Revolution of 1789, and thought they could solve their problems with more revolutions.

A year of chaos

In February 1848, a rebellion broke out in Paris and the rebels took control of France. When people in other countries heard about this, a wave of revolutions swept across Europe, and 1848 became known as the Year of Revolutions.

By the end of 1849, the revolutions had been crushed and most of the old rulers were back in power. However, rulers all over Europe realized that they would have to pay more attention to their people in the future.

New ideas

At the same time as the revolutions were spreading through Europe, some powerful new ideas were beginning to change the way people thought.

In 1848, a British group called the Chartists demanded that men of all classes should have the right to vote. In the same year, a German thinker named Karl Marx wrote a book called *The Communist Manifesto*. This said that workers everywhere should unite to gain more power for themselves.

Karl Marx and the title page of *The Communist Manifesto*

The rebels used whatever they could find to build barriers, or barricades, in the streets. This is part of a poster showing French rebels defending a barricade.

New Nations

At the start of the 19th century, the countries now known as Greece, Italy and Germany did not exist. Germany and Italy were made up of lots of small states, and some of these states were ruled by foreign countries. Greece was part of the Turkish Ottoman Empire.

The nation of Greece

In 1827, the Greeks who lived in the Ottoman Empire decided to join together to fight against their Turkish rulers. The rebels defeated the Turks and formed the independent kingdom of Greece.

Greek soldiers fighting for independence

Italy unites

By 1859, the Italian states of Piedmont and Sardinia, led by Count Camillo Cavour, had taken control of most of northern Italy. At the same time, a soldier named Giuseppe Garibaldi led an army of rebels that conquered large areas of southern Italy. In 1860, Count Cavour and Garibaldi agreed to join the north and south of the country together, and a year later the new nation of Italy was created.

Map of Germany

- Prussian land in 1815
- German border in 1871

PRUSSIA
Berlin
WESTPHALIA
FRANCE
AUSTRIA

The prime minister of Prussia, Otto von Bismarck, was a strong leader. This cartoon from the 1800s shows him sweeping away German rebels.

Germany unites

In the 1860s, the most powerful German state was Prussia, governed by King Wilhelm I and his prime minister, Otto von Bismarck. Prussia already ruled Westphalia, and gradually took control of many other German states. Prussia also won impressive victories against Austria and France, and in 1871 the rest of the states decided to join the growing nation. Germany was united and Wilhelm became its first emperor, or kaiser.

Map of Italy

The map shows the Italian states before 1861.

LOMBARDY
VENICE
PIEDMONT
PARMA
MODENA
LUCCA
ROMAGNA
TUSCANY
PAPAL STATES
NAPLES
SARDINIA
SICILY

Giuseppe Garibaldi

Important dates

1827 Greece becomes an independent country.

1848 Revolutions in many parts of Europe

1861 The Italian states join together to form Italy.

1871 Germany is united under Wilhelm I.

EUROPE

343

Revolutions in South America

Since the 16th century, Spain and Portugal had owned vast colonies in South America. The colonies were ruled by a few rich landowners, but most South Americans were poor.

Fighting for freedom

By the 1800s, many South Americans wanted to break free from their foreign rulers and form their own nations. Portugal allowed Brazil to become a separate country in 1822, but the Spanish were determined to keep control of their land. This meant that all the Spanish colonies had to fight for their independence.

Bolivar the rebel

The most famous South American rebel leader was Simon Bolivar, from the northern colony of Venezuela. Bolivar became commander of Venezuela's rebel army in 1811, and fought the Spanish for three years, before being defeated.

This is a portrait of Simon Bolivar. He was determined to free South America from Spanish rule.

Across the mountains

Bolivar realized he couldn't beat the huge Spanish army in Venezuela, so he planned a surprise attack on the nearby colony of New Granada. In 1819, he led his soldiers on a dangerous journey over the Andes mountains and into New Granada. There, he defeated the Spanish army and helped the colony to become an independent nation, known today as Colombia.

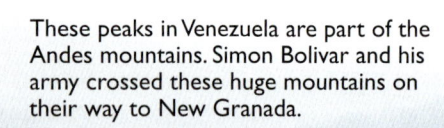

Flag of New Granada

People in New Granada celebrating independence with Bolivar's soldiers

★

These peaks in Venezuela are part of the Andes mountains. Simon Bolivar and his army crossed these huge mountains on their way to New Granada.

Defeating the Spanish

Bolivar spent the next few years moving around South America, fighting the Spanish in different colonies. In 1821, he finally freed his home colony of Venezuela, and the next year he drove the Spanish out of Ecuador.

San Martín strikes

Another great rebel leader was José de San Martín. He led Argentina to independence and helped to free Chile.

A 19th-century painting of José de San Martín

Peru and Bolivia

In 1824, Simon Bolivar drove the Spanish from the rest of Peru. He then made part of Peru into a new nation, which was named Bolivia after him.

Freedom and war

By 1830, all of the South American colonies had become independent. However, in the years that followed, many wars broke out between the new nations, and life remained hard for the people of South America.

Map of South America

- Spanish land in 1800
- Portuguese land in 1800

Map labels: ATLANTIC OCEAN, VENEZUELA, GUIANA, NEW GRANADA (COLOMBIA), ECUADOR, BRAZIL, PERU, BOLIVIA, PARAGUAY, CHILE, URUGUAY, ARGENTINA

Important dates

1808 Some South American colonies start fighting against the Spanish.

1816-1824 Bolivar and San Martín help to win independence for many colonies.

1822 Portugal declares Brazil an independent country.

1825 Bolivar creates the country of Bolivia.

By 1830 All the South American colonies are independent.

SOUTH AMERICA

345

The Scramble for Africa

For hundreds of years, the vast continent of Africa was divided into kingdoms led by powerful African rulers. In 1652, the Dutch conquered an area called Cape Colony in the south, and by the 1800s French, British and Portuguese traders had settled along the coast. However, most of Africa was still unknown to Europeans.

Things began to change in the 19th century, when European countries tried to win land for their empires. The Europeans also hoped to find gold and precious stones in Africa, and they competed fiercely against each other. This struggle became known as the Scramble for Africa.

This picture shows Zulu warriors attacking Dutch settlers, who were called Boers, during the Great Trek.

★

Map of Africa

EGYPT

LIBERIA

ETHIOPIA

The map shows the areas ruled by Europeans in 1910.

- French land
- British land
- German land
- Land belonging to Britain and Egypt
- Belgian land
- Portuguese land
- Italian land
- Spanish land
- → The Great Trek

Victoria Falls

Orange Free State

Transvaal

Cape Colony

The Boers shelter behind their wagons.

Zulu warriors fight with spears.

Thorn bushes protect the wagons.

The Great Trek

In 1806, Britain seized control of Cape Colony. Most of the people who lived there were Dutch farmers, known as Boers, and they soon became very unhappy with their new British rulers.

In 1836, thousands of Boers set off on a long journey in search of a different place to live. This journey became known as the Great Trek. Eventually, the Boers took over some land and set up two colonies, called the Transvaal and the Orange Free State.

The Zulu wars

The Africans whose land the Boers seized were called the Zulu people. For many years, Zulu warriors tried to win back their homeland by fighting bravely against the Boers. But the British helped the Boers, and the Zulu people were defeated in 1879.

Exploring Africa

Although Europeans had settled on the African coast, many of them were scared of the deadly diseases and wild animals that they thought they would find inland. However, a few explorers went on dangerous expeditions. The most famous was the Christian missionary David Livingstone, who explored large parts of Africa and made maps of the land.

The Boer War

Here are some Boer soldiers. Most of the soldiers were not very well trained, but they fought hard to defend their land.

Despite the Europeans' agreement in Berlin, they continued fighting over land. In 1899, Britain tried to take over the Dutch colonies, and war broke out between the British and the Boers. The British imprisoned many Boers and destroyed their farms, and the Boers were forced to surrender. In 1902, the Boers' land became part of the British Empire.

Europe moves in

By the 1880s, many European countries had begun to win land in Africa. The new nations of Italy and Germany were especially eager to build up empires for themselves, and soon the Europeans had conquered huge areas of the continent. Any Africans who tried to fight back were killed.

Europe takes over

In 1884, European leaders met in Berlin and decided to divide up Africa between them. Each country took over a different part of the continent, until eventually only Ethiopia and Liberia were still ruled by Africans (see map). Many Africans were treated very badly by their new rulers, and they often rebelled against the Europeans.

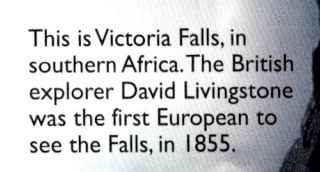

This is Victoria Falls, in southern Africa. The British explorer David Livingstone was the first European to see the Falls, in 1855.

Important dates

1806 Britain takes control of Cape Colony.

1836-1845 The Great Trek

1841 David Livingstone starts to explore Africa.

1879 The Zulus are defeated.

1884 European leaders divide Africa between them.

1902 The British defeat the Boers. Transvaal and the Orange Free State become part of the British Empire.

AFRICA

The American Civil War

In the middle of the 19th century, the north and south of the United States seemed like two different countries. In the north, there were lots of big cities and factories, while most of the south was farmland.

Slavery in the south

In the southern states, the two most important crops were cotton and tobacco, which were grown on vast farms, called plantations. Thousands of people had been brought from Africa to work as slaves on these plantations. But slavery was banned in the north, and this led to bitter arguments with the people of the south.

The USA splits

In 1860, Abraham Lincoln was elected President of the United States. Lincoln was against slavery, and this made many people in the south angry. A group of southern states decided to break away and form their own independent country.

This is Abraham Lincoln. He was a strong leader who was determined to keep the United States together.

Map of the USA in 1861

Gettysburg
Bull Run
Atlanta
ATLANTIC OCEAN

Union states
Confederate states
■ Important civil war battles

Robert E. Lee, an outstanding Confederate general

The war begins

The American government told the southern states that they had no right to become a separate country, and in 1861 civil war broke out. For four years, the south, known as the Confederacy, struggled against the north, called the Union.

The Union had more soldiers and factories to make weapons, but the Confederacy had brilliant generals, and the southern troops fought fiercely for their independence. The south won many battles in the early part of the war.

NORTH AMERICA

The Union advances

In 1863, Union troops won an important battle at Gettysburg, in the state of Pennsylvania. After this victory, Union armies began to advance into the south, burning and destroying all the farms and towns they found. Union ships surrounded the southern ports and prevented the Confederacy from bringing in more food and weapons.

This scene shows Union soldiers destroying a southern town.

The end of the war

Soon, the Confederate troops became weak and hungry. By 1865, large areas of the south had been destroyed, and the Confederacy surrendered. The war was over, but it had cost the lives of hundreds of thousands of soldiers on both sides.

A difficult peace

After the civil war, the United States became a single nation once again. Slavery was made illegal, and thousands of Black slaves were freed. However, there were still problems between the north and south. Five days after the war ended, Abraham Lincoln was assassinated by an angry Confederate supporter, and Black people continued to be treated appallingly in many parts of the south.

Confederate flag

Important buildings, such as factories and banks, have been set on fire.

BILLIARD

This soldier is waving the Union flag.

Union soldiers smash the railway line to stop the Confederacy from transporting supplies.

Important dates

1860	Abraham Lincoln becomes President of the United States.
April 1861	Civil war breaks out.
1863	The Battle of Gettysburg
1863-1865	Union armies destroy many southern towns.
April 1865	The civil war ends. Lincoln is murdered.

NORTH AMERICA

349

The Growth of the USA

By the start of the 1800s, the United States of America was a large and growing nation. Over the next hundred years, the USA won huge areas of land, and millions of people came to settle in this exciting new country.

Buying land

Since 1700, France had owned the enormous colony of Louisiana in the middle of the North American continent, but in 1803 the US government bought it from the French. This dramatic deal is known as the Louisiana Purchase, and it doubled the size of the USA. Americans began to settle on this new land and set up new states there.

War with Mexico

Many people from the USA settled in a southern area called Texas, which was owned by the country of Mexico. In 1835, the Texans declared that they were independent from Mexico. The Mexicans fought to keep Texas, but after two years they were defeated. In 1845, Texas joined the USA.

This is Davy Crockett, who fought for Texas against the Mexicans. He was killed in the Battle of the Alamo at the town of San Antonio, in Texas.

Moving west

Gradually, people moved farther and farther west, and the government encouraged settlers, known as pioneers, to make their homes there. When gold was discovered in California in 1848, many people rushed to live in the area, hoping to make a fortune.

★ Pioneers heading for California during the Gold Rush

Lots of families travel together in groups of wagons, called wagon trains.

This photograph shows a rocky valley in the state of Utah, one of the places the pioneers passed through on their difficult journey to the West.

REWARD
($5,000.00)

Reward for the capture, dead or alive, of one Wm. Wright, better known as

"BILLY THE KID"

Age, 18. Height, 5 feet, 3 inches. Weight, 125 lbs. Light hair, blue eyes and even features. He is the leader of the worst band of desperadoes the Territory has ever had to deal with. The above reward will be paid for his capture or positive proof of his death.

JIM DALTON, Sheriff.

DEAD OR ALIVE!
"BILLY THE KID"

The Wild West

For many years, the American West was a wild and dangerous place, full of crooks and bandits.

This poster from the 1870s offers a huge reward to anyone who captures the famous bandit Billy the Kid.

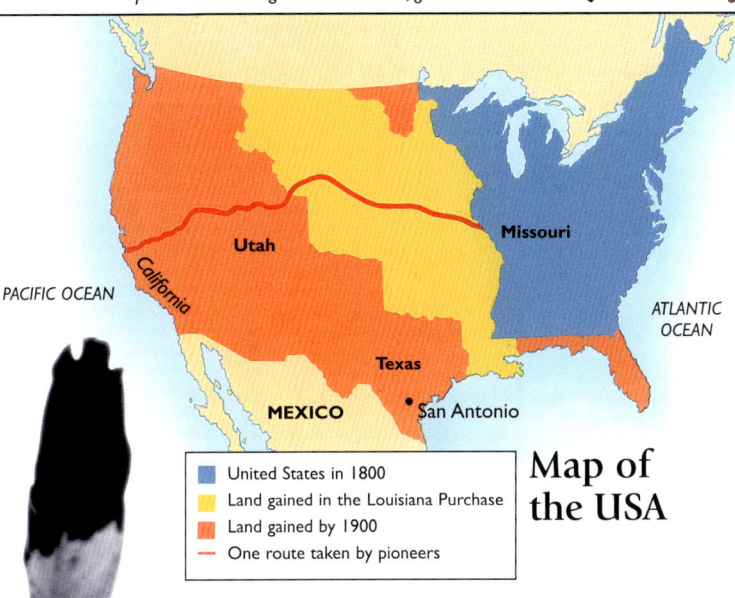

Map of the USA

- United States in 1800
- Land gained in the Louisiana Purchase
- Land gained by 1900
- One route taken by pioneers

Cattle herders, or cowboys, drove cattle over the plains to be loaded onto trains and sold in the east. There were many clashes between the cowboys and the Indigenous Americans who lived on the plains.

Taking land

As the USA grew bigger, settlers moved into many areas where Indigenous Americans lived. At first, the government promised to leave the Indigenous Americans alone, but most of their land was gradually taken away.

Struggling to survive

Some tribes of Indigenous Americans refused to leave their land, and they fought hard against the settlers and the US army. The Indigenous Americans won some battles, but many peoples were completely wiped out. US troops and settlers also killed most of the buffalo that roamed the plains, leaving the remaining peoples with very little to eat. By 1890, many Indigenous Americans had been captured and were forced to live in camps guarded by US soldiers.

Sitting Bull, an Indigenous American chief who fought the US army

A new world power

By the 1890s, the USA stretched all the way from the Atlantic Ocean to the Pacific. Despite the wars against the Indigenous Americans, and the terrible civil war in the 1860s, the country became extremely successful.

The USA was soon growing more crops and building more machines than any other country. By the beginning of the 20th century, it was one of the biggest, richest and most powerful nations in the world.

Important dates

1803 The Louisiana Purchase
1835-1836 War between Texas and Mexico
1836 Battle of the Alamo
1848 Gold is found in California.
1860-1890 Indigenous Americans fight the US army for land.
1876 Indigenous Americans win the Battle of Little Bighorn.
1890 Indigenous Americans are finally defeated at the Battle of Wounded Knee.

NORTH AMERICA

351

The Ming and the Qing

The vast empire of China was ruled by powerful emperors for thousands of years. In the 14th century, a new family, or dynasty, took control of China. They were called the Ming dynasty, and their emperors ruled for the next 280 years.

The Forbidden City

The Ming emperors governed from the northern city of Beijing, where they lived in a fabulous walled palace, called the Forbidden City. Only the emperor's family and advisers were allowed to enter the palace.

Art and medicine

During the Ming period, the Chinese made exquisite vases and elegant wooden furniture. They also designed amazing gardens and made beautifully illustrated books. Doctors treated their patients by sticking lots of needles into their skin. This treatment is called acupuncture and it is still used today.

This photograph shows the Hall of Supreme Harmony in the middle of the Forbidden City.

China and the world

By 1500, China was almost completely cut off from the rest of the world. The Ming emperors thought all foreigners were savages, and wanted to keep them out of China. Foreign merchants were only allowed to trade at a few Chinese ports.

Problems for the Ming

For a long time, China was peaceful, but problems began in the 16th century. The south coast was plagued by Japanese pirates and smugglers, and tribes from Mongolia often attacked northern China. To defend themselves against these attacks, the Ming emperors strengthened the Great Wall of China, which had been built in ancient times, and used thousands of soldiers to guard it.

★

A decorated jar from the Ming period

Chinese rebels

By the 1630s, many Chinese people were angry with the government, because there wasn't enough food for everyone and people were forced to pay heavy taxes. Rebellions broke out in many areas, and the country was thrown into chaos.

Attack of the Manchus

In 1644, rebels seized the city of Beijing, and the last Ming emperor committed suicide. The emperor's advisers asked the Manchus, a group of people from the north, to help them crush the rebellion. But the Manchus took advantage of the Ming's problems and took over Beijing. The Manchus gradually won more land, and by 1681 they had conquered all of China.

Map of China

- Ming Empire
- Land added by the Qing
- The Great Wall

Manchu warriors, painted by a Chinese artist

The Qing dynasty

The Manchus started a new line of rulers, known as the Qing dynasty, which lasted until 1912. The Qing emperors won vast areas of new land to the north and west. They also made sure that China stayed independent from the rest of the world.

THE FAR EAST

Changes in China

In the 18th century, European merchants were eager to buy Chinese goods, such as silk and tea. But China's Qing emperors wanted to keep foreigners out of their country, so Europeans were only allowed to trade at the port of Canton.

Kangxi, a powerful
Qing emperor
★

Silver and opium

The Qing emperors made European traders pay Chinese merchants with silver, which was very costly for the Europeans. But in the 1720s, the British began paying the Chinese with a drug called opium instead.

Many Chinese people smoked opium, but the emperors disapproved of this, and in 1813 smoking opium was banned. However, the British continued selling opium to Chinese merchants, and this made the Manchu government angry.

The Opium War

In 1839, a government official burned thousands of chests of opium, and the emperor banned all trade with Britain. This made the British furious, and they attacked China. The British had much better ships and weapons, and they easily defeated the Chinese navy. After losing the war, China was forced to allow British merchants to trade at lots of Chinese ports.

This 19th-century British painting shows Chinese ships being destroyed by the British during the Opium War.

ASIA

AUSTRALIA

CHINA

Beijing

EAST
CHINA
SEA

Guangzhou

Map of China

— Area where the Boxer
Rebellion took place

The Europeans advance

Soon, other European countries began forcing
the Chinese to trade with them. They moved
soldiers into China and took control of many
ports. The Europeans wanted to persuade the
Chinese to become Christians, so they began
to send missionaries to China.

The Taiping Rebellion

The Manchu emperors also faced other problems
during the 19th century. Their government
had become weak, and in the 1850s a violent
revolution, known as the Taiping Rebellion, broke
out. For more than ten years, peasants all over
China attacked their rulers and destroyed cities. By
the time the Manchu emperor regained control in
1864, up to 20 million people had been killed.

Trying to change

Some Chinese people thought China could only
overcome its problems by becoming more like a
modern European country. They encouraged the
government to build lots of factories and trains, but
change was slow.

The Boxer Rebellion

Many people in China hated the way Europeans
had changed their country. In 1900, a secret society
of warriors, known to Europeans as the Boxers,
started attacking Europeans and Chinese Christians.

The Manchu government supported
the Boxers, hoping that they would
get rid of the foreigners, but the
rebellion was crushed by
European soldiers. The
government became
even weaker, and
in 1912 there was a
revolution in China
(see page 364).

Boxer warriors like
these thought they were
protected by magic powers.

Important dates

1368-1644   The Ming dynasty
1644-1912   The Qing dynasty
1839-1842   The Opium War
1850-1864   The Taiping Rebellion
1900   The Boxer Rebellion

THE FAR EAST

355

Changes in Japan

At the start of the 16th century, Japan was in the middle of a long civil war. Fierce warlords, called samurai, fought each other for land, and the Japanese emperor had very little power.

Strong samurai

The civil war ended in 1568 when the powerful samurai Oda Nobunaga took control of Japan. After him, another samurai, Toyotomi Hideyoshi, became chief minister of Japan. Hideyoshi set up an efficient tax system and worked hard to create a united country.

Map of Japan

The first Tokugawa

After Hideyoshi's death, war broke out again. Tokugawa Ieyasu defeated his rivals at the Battle of Sekigahara, and in 1603 the emperor made him shogun (military commander) of Japan.

This is Osaka Castle, which was seized by Tokugawa Ieyasu from a rival samurai.

The Edo period

While the emperor stayed in his palace in Kyoto, Ieyasu set up his capital in Edo. This was the start of a long line of shoguns from the Tokugawa clan who ruled Japan on behalf of the emperor. Thy controlled Japan for over 250 years, and this period of time became known as the Edo period.

Japan's isolation

In the 1630s, the shogun Tokugawa Iemitsu became frightened that European merchants and priests in Japan had too much influence over his people. He banned Christianity and declared that only the Dutch and Chinese were allowed to trade with Japan. Foreigners could not set foot on Japanese soil, so the Dutch had to trade from an island in Nagasaki Bay.

Peace and wealth

Japan remained cut off from the world for over 200 years. During this time, the Tokugawas ruled very strictly and made sure that there were no more civil wars in their country. Japanese towns grew fast, and Edo became one of the largest cities in the world. As the towns grew, Japanese traders became wealthy, but the peasants and samurai didn't share in this wealth. By the 1800s, there were many rebellions against the Tokugawa family.

Contact with the west

In 1854, a group of American warships waited in Edo Bay while their commander, Commodore Perry, forced the shogun to sign a trading agreement with the USA. Other agreements followed, and by 1860 Japan had started to trade with several western countries.

The end of the Tokugawas

Most of the samurai hated the western traders and blamed the Tokugawas for allowing them in. Civil war broke out, and in 1867 a samurai army defeated the Tokugawas. In 1868, the victorious samurai helped the Japanese emperor to take control of Japan. This is known as the Meiji Restoration. The emperor moved from Kyoto to Edo, which he renamed Tokyo.

Even in the 1800s, the samurai still wore their traditional costumes. In this 19th-century Japanese print, two samurai warriors are fighting each other.

Modernization

The Japanese began building steam trains in the 1880s. Here are two engine drivers in front of their train.

In spite of the samurai's hopes, the emperors continued trading with the West and copied many western ideas. They set up a parliament, improved schools, and built factories, trains and ships. Meanwhile, the samurai lost most of their power, and most of them had to do ordinary jobs.

Japanese wars

In 1894, Japan tried to conquer Korea, and this led to war with China. The Japanese won an easy victory, but in 1904 they had to fight the Russians for control of Korea. Once again, the Japanese were victorious. In 1905, the Treaty of Portsmouth gave Japan control of Korea and some land in China. This made Japan the most powerful country in the Far East.

Important dates

1568-1582	Oda Nobunaga controls Japan.
1591-1598	Toyotomi Hideyoshi controls Japan.
1603-1867	The Tokugawa shoguns rule Japan (the Edo period).
1854	Japan signs a trading agreement with the USA.
1868	The emperor takes control of Japan (the Meiji Restoration).
1894-1895	Japan fights China.
1904-1905	Japan fights Russia.
1905	The Treaty of Portsmouth gives Japan control of Korea.

The First World War

World War I, also known as the Great War, involved more countries and killed more people than any other war that had ever been fought before. But how did it all start?

Friends and enemies

By 1914, the five strongest countries in Europe had split into two rival groups. Britain, France and Russia (called the Allies) were on one side, with Germany and Austria-Hungary (called the Central Powers) on the other. The situation became very tense. If a war were to start between any two rival countries, all the others would probably join in.

Murder in Sarajevo

The event that actually sparked off the war took place on June 28, 1914. Archduke Franz Ferdinand, the heir to the Austrian throne, was visiting the town of Sarajevo in Bosnia, when he was shot dead by a Serbian student.

On July 28, Austria, backed up by Germany, declared war on Serbia. Russia stepped in to help the Serbs, and soon the Allies and the Central Powers were at war.

The Western Front

German soldiers moved quickly into northern France, but they were soon stopped by the Allies. The two sides faced each other along a line known as the Western Front. Both sides dug deep ditches, or trenches, to defend themselves. After this, neither side was able to advance very far, and the war dragged on for four years.

Soldiers lived in the trenches for weeks at a time. During a battle, they climbed out of the trench and charged at the enemy across an area known as No Man's Land. Millions of men died in these terrible battles that sometimes lasted for months.

This scene shows British soldiers in a trench on the Western Front.

A shell explodes in No Man's Land.

A soldier, called a sentry, keeps watch.

Machine gun

Officers live in underground shelters, called dug-outs.

Boxes of machine-gun bullets

Wooden walkways, called duckboards, stop the soldiers from sinking into the mud.

The trenches swarm with rats, flies, fleas and lice.

THE WORLD

Poppies that grew on the battlefields of the Western Front became a symbol ★ for remembering the war.

Map of Europe

NORTH SEA

IRELAND

BRITAIN

GERMANY

RUSSIA

ATLANTIC OCEAN

BELGIUM

FRANCE

AUSTRIA-HUNGRY

ITALY

ROMANIA

BULGARIA

PORTUGAL

Sarajevo

SERBIA

MONTENEGRO

TURKEY

MEDITERRANEAN SEA

GREECE

	Allies
	Central Powers

The map shows the two sides during World War I.

The war spreads

Other countries soon became involved in the war. Turkey and Bulgaria joined the Central Powers, while Italy, Greece and Portugal supported the Allies. The two sides also fought in Africa and the Middle East, where Britain, Germany and other European countries had colonies.

Ships and submarines

Both sides tried to stop their enemies from getting food and raw materials to make weapons. German submarines, called U-boats, sank any ship going to a British port. Some of these ships were American, and this provoked the USA into joining the war, in April 1917, on the side of the Allies.

The war ends

By March 1918, the Russians were exhausted by the war, and they made peace with Germany. German soldiers made a series of final attacks on the Western Front, but they were forced back. Germany surrendered, and on November 11, 1918, the war finally came to an end.

Walls supported by wooden planks

Barbed wire

Sandbags

This man has been sent some extra food by his family.

The men rest in holes dug into the sides of the trench.

The soldiers' feet are always wet and often get infected.

Important dates

June 1914	Archduke Franz Ferdinand is murdered.
July 1914	Austria-Hungary declares war on Serbia.
Sep 1914	The Germans are stopped by the Allies at the Battle of the Marne.
Jul-Nov 1916	Over a million soldiers die at the Battle of the Somme, in France.
April 1917	The USA joins the war.
March 1918	Russia makes peace with Germany.
Nov 11, 1918	The war ends.
1919	League of Nations formed.

THE WORLD

359

The Russian Revolution

At the start of the 20th century, Russia owned a vast empire that covered one sixth of the Earth's surface. Most of its people were peasants who lived in terrible poverty, but in the capital city of St. Petersburg, wealthy nobles lived a life of luxury.

Map of Russia

Russian Empire in 1905

Tsar Nicholas II of Russia with his wife and family, photographed around 1900

Russia was ruled by a powerful emperor, or tsar, who believed he had been chosen by God. The tsar was advised by officials from noble families, but most Russians had no say in how their country was run.

Time for change

Many Russians were unhappy that the tsar had so much power. Some wanted him to rule with the help of a parliament chosen by the people. Others wanted a revolution to get rid of the tsar altogether. One group of revolutionaries were the Bolsheviks, led by Vladimir Ilyich Ulyanov, better known as Lenin.

The Bolshevik leader Lenin

The 1905 Revolution

In January 1905, over 150,000 workers marched to the tsar's Winter Palace in St. Petersburg to protest about their dreadful working conditions. The army fired on the protesters, killing over a hundred people. Workers across Russia went on strike, and Tsar Nicholas was forced to set up a parliament. But he made sure it had very little power.

Russia at war

In 1914, Russia entered the First World War (see pages 358 and 359). The Russian army suffered terrible defeats, losing over a million men in the first six months.

At home, the war caused shortages of food, and people began to starve. Many Russians blamed the tsar for all these problems.

Revolution!

By March 1917, St. Petersburg (which had been renamed Petrograd) was running out of bread. Riots broke out and workers went on strike. When the army joined in the riots, Tsar Nicholas realized he had lost control and gave up the throne.

A temporary government was set up, but it did nothing to solve Russia's problems and soon became unpopular. In November 1917, the Bolsheviks, led by Lenin, seized power and took control of the country.

Civil war

Lenin made peace with Germany and took Russia out of the First World War. He moved the capital to Moscow, gave land to the peasants and put workers in charge of the factories. Many wealthy Russians didn't like these changes, and this led to a bitter civil war between the Bolsheviks (now known as Communists) and their enemies. In 1918, Tsar Nicholas and his family were killed by a group of Communists.

A civil war poster urging people to join the Communist fighting force, known as the Red Army

Communist control

By 1921, the Communists had won the civil war, and Lenin was in complete control of Russia. He began the massive task of rebuilding the country, which was in chaos after years of fighting. In 1922, Russia was renamed the Union of Soviet Socialist Republics (USSR), also known as the Soviet Union.

These Russian soldiers are joining the Revolution in March 1917. One of them is holding a red flag, which was a symbol of the Revolution.

Important dates

1894	Nicholas II becomes Tsar of Russia.
January 1905	Soldiers fire on protesters in St. Petersburg.
1914	The First World War begins.
March 1917	Riots break out in Petrograd. The tsar gives up his throne.
Nov 1917	The Bolsheviks seize power.
1918-1921	Civil war in Russia
May 1918	Tsar Nicholas II and his family are shot.
Dec 1922	Russia is renamed the USSR.

EUROPE

Stalin's Soviet Union

After the Russian Revolution, the Communist leader Lenin was seen as a hero by many Russians. But Lenin did not rule the new Soviet Union for long. From 1922, he was often unwell, and he died in 1924.

After Lenin's death, several leading Communists struggled for power. One of these men was Josef Stalin, the Secretary of the Communist Party. Stalin had many friends in the Party, and he used them to get rid of his rivals. By 1928, Stalin had complete control of the country.

Josef Stalin in military uniform

Factories and workers

Stalin launched a Five Year Plan to turn the Soviet Union into a modern, industrial country. He forced people to leave their villages and work in factories in the city. Factories were expected to produce much more than before, and workers who didn't work fast enough were punished like criminals.

A Soviet poster urging workers to carry out the Five Year Plan

Farms and peasants

To keep the factory workers well fed, Stalin needed to reorganize farming. Peasant farmers were told to give up their tiny strips of land, and these strips were then joined together to create vast farms, called collective farms. The peasants were paid to work on the farms, and the crops they grew were sold to the government at a low price.

This statue of a factory worker and a peasant woman makes the Soviet way of life look heroic.

The worker holds a hammer, while the peasant woman has a farm tool called a sickle.

Kulaks and camps

Some peasants, known as kulaks, owned their own land, and when they refused to give it up Stalin used force. Millions of kulaks were arrested and sent to live in remote parts of the Soviet Union. There, they had to work in harsh prison camps, where many of them died of cold, hunger and exhaustion.

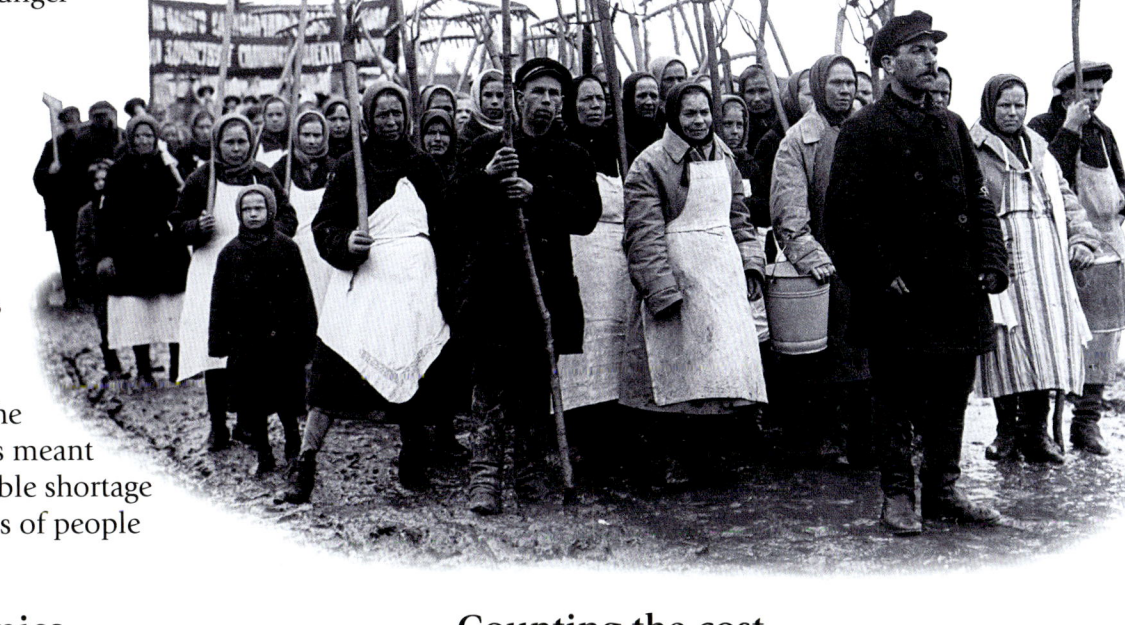

These Soviet farmers are carrying a banner which says that they will destroy the kulaks.

Many peasants destroyed their crops and killed their animals rather than hand them over to the collective farms. This meant that there was a terrible shortage of food, and millions of people died of hunger.

Removing enemies

By 1934, Stalin was worried that his enemies were plotting against him, so he decided to get rid of them. Anyone who criticized him was arrested by the secret police and executed, or sent to a prison camp. As many as 24 million people may have died in these brutal attacks, known as purges.

War and after

At first, Stalin supported Hitler, but then, in 1941, the Soviet Union was invaded by Germany. After many fierce battles and much suffering, the Soviet army drove the Germans back across eastern Europe, and set up a new block of communist countries (see page 378).

Counting the cost

Under Stalin, the Soviet Union became a strong, industrial country with factories, steel works, power stations and railways. Lots of new hospitals were built, and all children were given a free education. But Stalin was a ruthless leader. By the time he died, he had caused the deaths of as many as 40 million Soviet people.

The worker's hammer and the peasant's sickle became part of the symbol of the Soviet Union.

Important dates

1924	Lenin dies.
1928	Stalin begins a Five Year Plan to modernize industry and farming.
1929	Collective farms are set up.
1932-1933	Millions die in a terrible famine.
1934	The purges begin.
1941-45	The Soviet Union is at war with Germany.
1953	Stalin dies.

EUROPE

363

The People's Republic

Since 1644, China had been ruled by a family of powerful emperors called the Qing Dynasty. By 1900, the Qing were very unpopular, but they refused to change the way the country was run.

In 1911, a revolution broke out. A group of nationalists, called the Kuomintang, seized power and set up a republic. The Kuomintang leaders found it hard to bring the country under control, but by 1928 they governed most of China.

Not everyone supported the Kuomintang. The Chinese Communist Party wanted China to be run by the workers and peasants, rather than by the rich. One group of Communists, led by Mao Zedong, set up their own government in Jiangxi (say "jang-shee"), in the south.

The Long March

In 1934, the Communists in Jiangxi were surrounded and attacked by the Kuomintang army. The Communists escaped and set off to find a safe place far away from the Kuomintang. This famous journey, which covered a distance of 8,000km (5,000 miles), is known as the Long March. Out of 100,000 people who set out on the march,

The marchers are trudging down a rocky mountain path.

This picture shows Communists on the Long March. Most of the men have had to leave their wives and children behind.

The men are wearing the uniform of the Communist Red Army.

During the Long March, the Communists had to cross 18 mountain ranges, including these mountains in Sichuan, in western China.

Map of China

➡ Route of the Long March

Mao Zedong, leader of the Chinese Communist Party from 1935 to 1976

Communist China

Between 1937 and 1945, China was at war with Japan. After the war, the struggle between the Communist Party and the Kuomintang continued. In 1949, the Communists, led by Mao Zedong, defeated the Kuomintang. Mao set up the People's Republic of China and took control of the country.

The Great Leap Forward

In 1958, Mao started a campaign, known as the Great Leap Forward, to try to build up industry. Many peasants were taken away from farms to work in factories. This meant that not enough crops were planted, and millions of people died of hunger.

The Cultural Revolution

Mao became worried that China was moving away from true Communism. In 1966, he started a new campaign, called the Cultural Revolution. He encouraged young people to attack traditional ideas and to criticize their teachers, bosses and parents.

Schools and universities were closed, and educated people were forced to work on the land. Groups of teenagers, known as Red Guards, beat and tortured anyone they thought was against the Revolution.

A young Chinese ★ Red Guard

After three years of chaos, the army was sent in to stop the violence. The Cultural Revolution finally came to an end when Mao died in 1976.

Important dates

1911	The Kuomintang starts a revolution in China.
1912	The Kuomintang sets up a republic.
1934-1935	The Long March
1949	Mao Zedong sets up the People's Republic of China.
1958-1960	The Great Leap Forward
1966	Mao Zedong starts the Cultural Revolution.
1976	Mao Zedong dies.

THE FAR EAST

Good Times, Bad Times

During the 1920s, the United States of America was the richest country in the world. Businesses boomed and factories produced lots of new goods, such as washing machines, vacuum cleaners and cars. Not everyone was rich, but most Americans thought life was getting better.

The Jazz Age

The 1920s are often known as the Jazz Age because of the new music and dances that were popular at that time. Some daring young women, known as flappers, cut their hair short and wore their skirts above the knee.

These two people are performing a popular 1920s jazz dance called the Charleston.

Banning alcohol

From 1920 to 1933, it was illegal to make or sell alcohol in the USA. This period of time is known as Prohibition. Many people drank secretly in illegal bars, called speakeasies, and gangsters, such as Al Capone, grew rich by making, smuggling and selling alcohol.

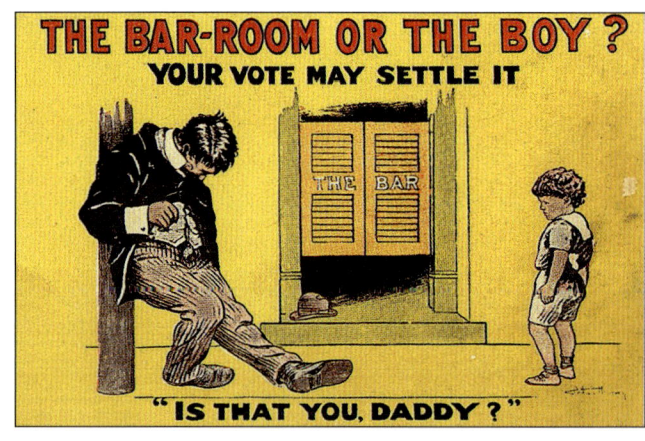

This 1920s postcard encourages Americans to vote for the banning of alcohol.

The Wall Street Crash

The good times came to an end in 1929, when thousands of people were ruined in a financial disaster known as the Wall Street Crash.

During the 1920s, many Americans had bought shares in businesses on credit, hoping to make money by selling them later at a higher price. But in October 1929 share prices began to fall. People panicked and started selling their shares. This made prices drop even lower, until the shares were almost worthless.

This disaster is known as the Wall Street Crash because Wall Street is the home of the New York Stock Exchange, where shares are bought and sold.

The Great Depression

After the Wall Street Crash, banks and businesses failed, and millions of people lost their jobs. Thousands of families lost their homes as well, because they couldn't afford to pay the rent. This period of terrible poverty is known as the Great Depression. It lasted for most of the 1930s and affected countries all over the world.

Some homeless families had to live in shacks like this that they built out of cardboard.

The Dust Bowl

The Great Depression also affected farmers. In the USA, the situation was made worse by the weather. In some central areas, fierce winds blew away the dusty soil, making it impossible to grow crops. These areas became known as the Dust Bowl. Many farming families left their homes to look for work in California, on the west coast.

Here you can see a farm in the Dust Bowl being battered by a violent dust storm.

The New Deal

In 1932, Franklin D. Roosevelt became President of the USA. He started up a series of projects, known as the New Deal, to help industry and farming, and create new jobs. This did not end the Depression, but it made life easier for many Americans.

Important dates

1920-1933	Prohibition
Oct 24, 1929	The Wall Street Crash
1932	Franklin D. Roosevelt becomes President.
1933	Roosevelt launches the New Deal.

NORTH AMERICA

367

The Rise of Fascism

After the First World War, many countries in Europe faced huge problems. Governments had very little money because they had spent so much on weapons for the war. Lots of people were out of work, and there wasn't enough food for everyone. People began to think that these problems needed drastic new solutions.

The first fascist

In Italy, the problems were particularly bad. Many people turned to Benito Mussolini, the leader of the Fascist Party. Mussolini became prime minister of Italy in 1922. Soon, he banned all other political parties and took complete control of the country. This way of ruling is known as fascism.

Mussolini salutes the crowd at a huge public meeting.

Germany defeated

After World War I, the winning countries decided that Germany should pay for the damage caused by the war. The Germans were forced to reduce the size of their army and navy, and were not allowed to have an air force. Germany also had to give up large areas of land. Many Germans felt angry and humiliated by all of this, and they blamed their government for agreeing to it.

The Depression

In 1929, Germany was hit by the Great Depression (see page 367). Millions of Germans lost their jobs, but the government did nothing to help. People became desperate, and some turned to the National Socialist Workers' Party (the Nazi Party), led by Adolf Hitler.

New hope

Hitler persuaded people that their problems were caused by foreigners, especially Jewish people. He believed that the Germans were superior to other races, and said he would make Germany powerful again. He promised strong leadership, jobs for everyone and an end to poverty.

Total power

The Nazis held huge meetings, or rallies, all over Germany to persuade people to vote for them. By 1932, they were the biggest party in the German Reichstag (parliament), and in 1933 Hitler became chancellor (head of the government). He then persuaded the Reichstag to give him complete control of the country.

This is the badge of the Nazi Party. The symbol in the middle is called a swastika.

Nazi Germany

Once Hitler was in power, he banned all political parties except the Nazi Party. He took control of all newspapers and radio, and forced schools and universities to teach Nazi ideas. Children had to join Nazi youth groups, and anyone who disagreed with the Nazis was arrested by the secret police, which was called the Gestapo.

In this photograph, the German leader Adolf Hitler (in the middle of the picture) is inspecting members of a Nazi organization called the SA.

Persecuting Jews

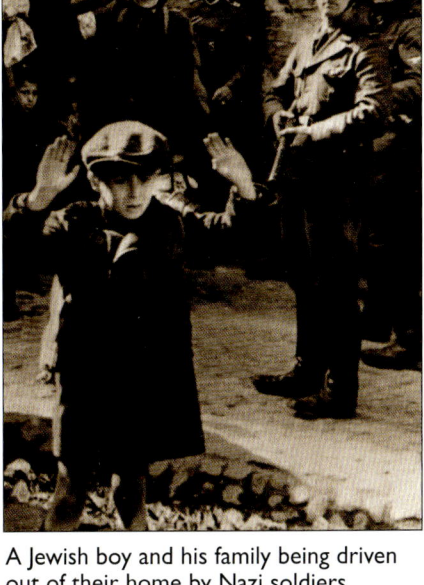

A Jewish boy and his family being driven out of their home by Nazi soldiers

The Nazis made life impossible for Jewish people. They weren't allowed to marry Germans, own land, do certain jobs, or even go out at night. Gangs of Nazi thugs attacked Jewish people, vandalized Jewish shops and burned synagogues.

Important dates

1919	Mussolini sets up the Fascist Party in Italy.
1922	Mussolini comes to power.
1929	The Great Depression begins.
1933	Hitler becomes chancellor of Germany.
1934	Hitler takes complete control as *Führer* (leader) of Germany.
Nov 9, 1938	On *Kristallnacht* (the Night of Broken Glass) Nazis attack thousands of Jewish homes, shops and synagogues.

EUROPE

Europe at War

By 1934, the Nazi leader Adolf Hitler had complete control of Germany (see pages 368 and 369). Hitler planned to create a powerful empire made up of all the German-speaking people in Europe. He began by taking over Austria in March 1938.

Hitler's next target was the German-speaking part of Czechoslovakia, known as the Sudetenland. Britain and France wanted to avoid another war with Germany, like the First World War, so they agreed to let Hitler have the Sudetenland. But he soon took over the rest of Czechoslovakia as well.

On September 1, 1939, Hitler invaded Poland. Britain and France had already agreed to help Poland if it was attacked, so two days later they declared war on Germany. Italy later joined the war on the German side. Together, Germany and Italy were known as the Axis Powers.

German troops with a machine gun

Europe under attack

Nothing much happened for the first six months of the war. Then, in April 1940, Hitler's troops began their attack. They used tanks and planes to advance at incredible speed. By June 1940, Hitler had taken over most of western Europe.

Escape by sea

As the Germans swept into northern France, many French and British soldiers were trapped near Dunkirk, on the north coast. The British organized a huge rescue, using small boats and yachts, as well as ships from their navy. In nine days, over 330,000 men were taken safely to Britain.

The Battle of Britain

Hitler planned to invade Britain, but he knew he needed to destroy the British Royal Air Force first. From August to October 1940, British and German planes fought a fierce battle in the skies over southern England. The British had fewer planes, but still managed to win. After this defeat, Hitler gave up the idea of invading Britain.

Map of Europe

NORWAY

DENMARK

GREAT BRITAIN

Moscow

SOVIET UNION

Berlin

GERMANY

POLAND

Dunkirk

Dresden

Stalingrad

FRANCE

CZECHOSLOVAKIA

SUDETENLAND

AUSTRIA

ITALY

ALBANIA

NORTH AFRICA

LIBYA

El Alamein

Axis Powers

Land occupied by Axis Powers in the 1930s

Land occupied by Axis Powers by June 1940

The British Prime Minister Winston Churchill, who inspired his country during the war

The Blitz

Hitler then tried to make the British surrender by bombing their cities. Night after night, German planes attacked, wrecking buildings and killing thousands of people. These attacks are known as the Blitz. The British fought back by bombing German cities, such as Dresden, where over 35,000 people were killed in one night.

This scene shows a typical London street during the Blitz. The bombing continued for nine months.

★

Powerful searchlights are used to spot German planes.

Anti-aircraft guns fire at the bombers.

Firefighters use water pumped from the river to fight the flames.

The Eastern Front

At the start of the war, the Germans and the Russians had agreed not to fight each other. But in June 1941, Hitler broke this agreement and invaded the Soviet Union. By December, the Germans had almost reached Moscow. But they weren't prepared for the freezing winter weather, and the Russians managed to drive them back.

This building has been hit by a fire bomb.

Hundreds of families have lost their homes.

This bus was thrown into the air by an exploding bomb.

HOVIS

Rescue workers dig survivors out of the rubble.

The bombs have made huge holes, or craters, in the street.

Gas and water pipes have been shattered.

This unexploded bomb could blow up at any minute.

Thousands of British children were sent to live in the countryside, away from the bombing.

EUROPE

371

The World at War

At first, the war against Hitler was fought mainly in Europe. The USA supported Britain and the Soviet Union by sending them weapons and tanks, but the US government didn't want to get involved in the fighting.

All this changed on December 7, 1941, when ships from the US navy were bombed by Japanese planes, at Pearl Harbor in Hawaii. The next day, the USA declared war on Japan. Hitler had signed an agreement with the Japanese, so he then declared war on the USA.

US battleships on fire after the Japanese attack on Pearl Harbor

War in the Pacific

The Japanese already controlled parts of China, which they had invaded in 1937. Determined to build up a new Japanese empire, they now advanced with frightening speed. By June 1942, Japan had taken over most of Southeast Asia and many of the islands in the Pacific Ocean (see map) September 1944.

The Allies advance

The countries that fought against Japan and Germany were known as the Allies. From June 1942, the Allies began to push the Japanese back across the Pacific. They also won important battles in other parts of the world, such as El Alamein in North Africa and Stalingrad in the Soviet Union.

D-Day

On June 6, 1944, known as D-Day, the Allies made a surprise attack on the Germans in northern France. Thousands of Allied soldiers crossed the English Channel and landed on the beaches of Normandy. Slowly, they fought their way across France, reaching Germany in September 1944.

Map of the Pacific

- Japan
- Area controlled by Japan by 1942

This photograph, taken on D-Day, shows US soldiers wading from their landing craft onto one of the Normandy beaches.

THE WORLD

Victory in Europe

Meanwhile, Russian troops were advancing into Germany from the east. In April 1945, they reached the capital, Berlin. Hitler realized he was defeated and killed himself on April 30. The Germans finally surrendered on May 8, known as V-E Day. (V-E stands for "Victory in Europe".)

The war ends

Although the war in Europe was over, fighting continued in the Pacific. On August 6, 1945, the USA dropped the first ever atomic bomb on the Japanese city of Hiroshima. About 80,000 people died in the explosion. Three days later, another bomb destroyed the city of Nagasaki, and the Japanese surrendered.

The Holocaust

As the Allies advanced across Europe, they found prisons, or concentration camps, where the Nazis had sent Jewish people, Romani people and people with mental health conditions. Many of these people had been murdered by the Nazis. As many as 15 million people died in this way. This horrific event is known as the Holocaust.

Atomic bombs, like the ones that destroyed Hiroshima and Nagasaki, form a huge, mushroom-shaped cloud when they explode.

Important dates

Sep 3, 1939	Britain and France declare war on Germany.
April-June 1940	Hitler occupies most of western Europe.
Aug-Oct 1940	The Battle of Britain
June 22, 1941	Hitler invades the Soviet Union.
Dec 7, 1941	Japan attacks US ships at Pearl Harbor.
June 6, 1944	The Allies land in France (D-Day).
April 30, 1945	Hitler kills himself.
May 8, 1945	Germany surrenders.
June 1945	United Nations formed.
Aug 6, 1945	Hiroshima is destroyed by an atomic bomb.
Aug 14, 1945	The war ends.

From Colonies to Countries

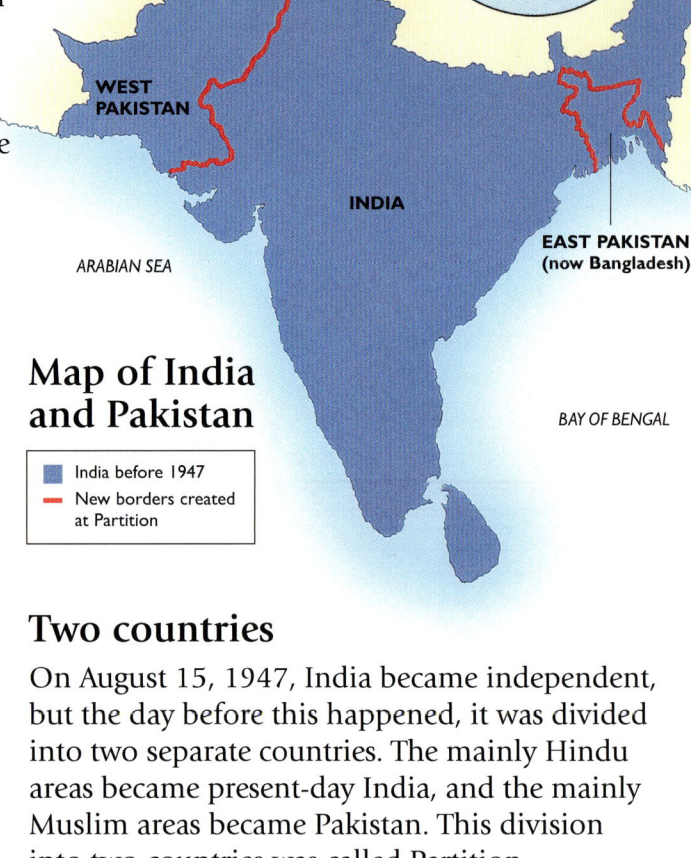

Since the 19th century, all of India and most of Africa had been ruled by Europeans. But by 1945, Europe had been weakened by the Second World War. The people of India and Africa at last saw their chance to break free and govern themselves. At the same time, some Europeans began to think it was time for the countries of Europe to give up their colonies.

Gandhi and India

A group called the Indian National Congress had fought against British rule in India since the 1880s. This group became much stronger in 1920, when a Hindu lawyer named Mohandas Gandhi took over as leader. Gandhi led many protests against the British, and although he protested peacefully he was often thrown into prison.

Gandhi was an inspiring leader and he became known as Mahatma, which means "Great Soul".

The British give in

During the Second World War, thousands of Indians fought on the British side and this helped to change Britain's attitude to India. In 1942, Britain promised that it would grant India its freedom after the war, provided that the Indians continued to help the British.

Two religions

Although most Indians wanted independence, fierce arguments broke out between Hindus and Muslims. They clashed because the Muslims did not want to be ruled by the Hindu majority after India had become independent.

Map of India and Pakistan

KASHMIR

WEST PAKISTAN

INDIA

ARABIAN SEA

EAST PAKISTAN (now Bangladesh)

BAY OF BENGAL

- India before 1947
- New borders created at Partition

Two countries

On August 15, 1947, India became independent, but the day before this happened, it was divided into two separate countries. The mainly Hindu areas became present-day India, and the mainly Muslim areas became Pakistan. This division into two countries was called Partition.

Partition happened very fast, and riots broke out when people found themselves trapped in the "wrong" country. In 1999, arguments were still going on between India and Pakistan over areas of land such as Kashmir.

This photograph, taken in 1999, shows Indian soldiers celebrating a victory over Pakistani troops in Kashmir. The soldiers are holding up the Indian flag.

THE WORLD

African independence

Until the 1950s, most of Africa was divided into colonies ruled by European countries (see page 346). This began to change in 1951 when Libya became the first African country to win its independence.

This is Jomo Kenyatta, a leading fighter for independence in Kenya and first president of his country.

Over the next 30 years, more than 40 African countries became independent. In some countries, such as Kenya and Mozambique, rebel soldiers known as guerrillas fought savage wars against their European rulers. These struggles for independence often lasted many years, but most of them were successful in the end.

White rebels

In parts of southern Africa, power was seized by white Europeans who had settled there. The Prime Minister of Rhodesia, Ian Smith, declared his country's independence from Britain in 1965. Britain did not support Smith, and eventually the African majority took control. In 1980, Rhodesia became an independent African country and was renamed Zimbabwe.

Civil wars

After breaking free from European rule, many African countries still faced huge problems. Civil wars broke out in countries such as Nigeria, Angola, Chad and Somalia when people from different tribes or religions fought each other for power. Today, wars are still being fought in many parts of Africa.

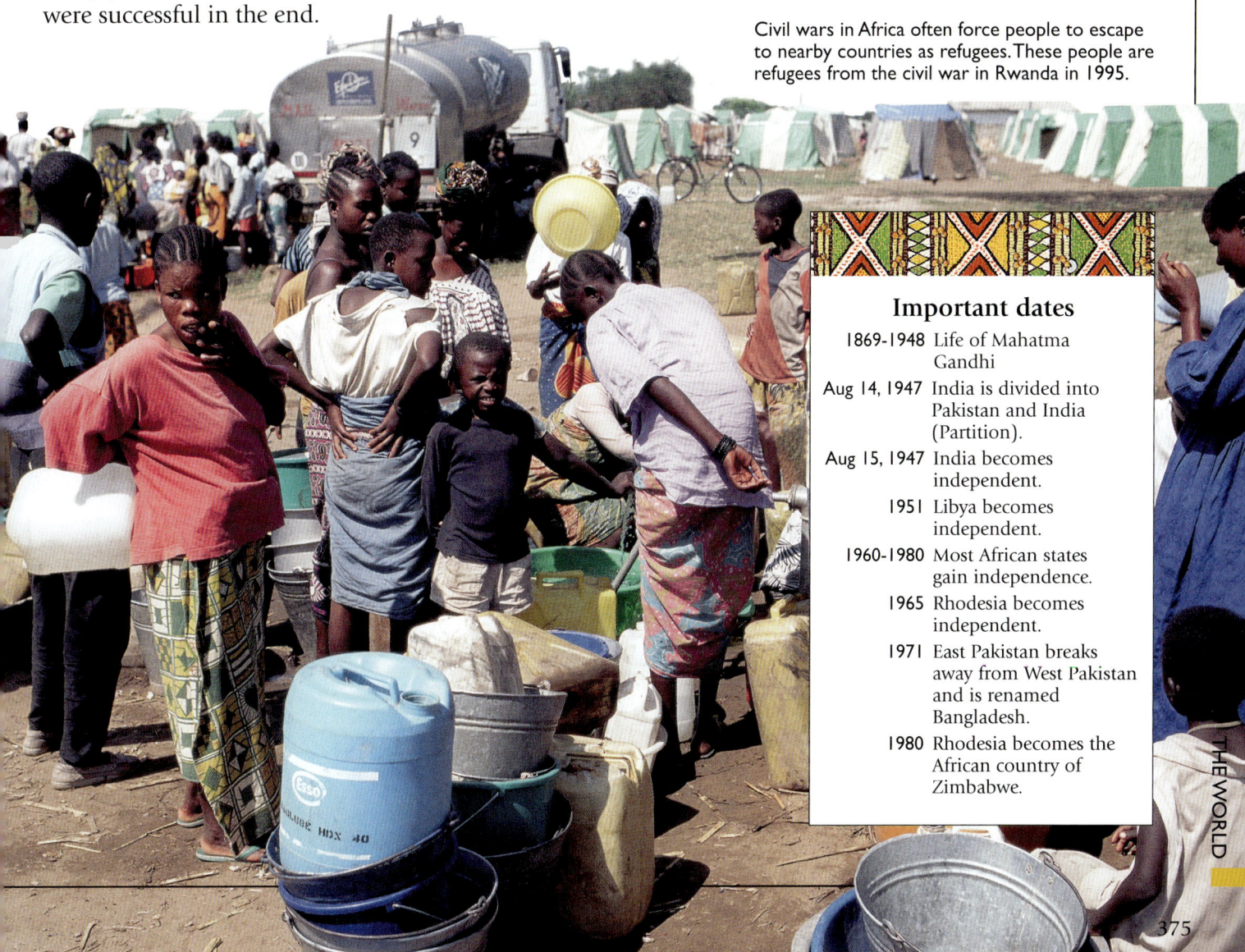

Civil wars in Africa often force people to escape to nearby countries as refugees. These people are refugees from the civil war in Rwanda in 1995.

Important dates

1869-1948	Life of Mahatma Gandhi
Aug 14, 1947	India is divided into Pakistan and India (Partition).
Aug 15, 1947	India becomes independent.
1951	Libya becomes independent.
1960-1980	Most African states gain independence.
1965	Rhodesia becomes independent.
1971	East Pakistan breaks away from West Pakistan and is renamed Bangladesh.
1980	Rhodesia becomes the African country of Zimbabwe.

THE WORLD

War in the Middle East

The Middle East is the area around the Red Sea and the Persian Gulf. Since 1945, there have been many changes, invasions and wars in this troubled part of the world.

Israel is born

In 1945, the country that is now Israel was called Palestine. It was ruled by Britain, though its people were mostly Arabs. However, many Jews had moved there hoping to set up a Jewish state in what had once been biblical Israel. Many of them had escaped from Europe, where they had been brutally persecuted by the Nazis during the Second World War. There was often fighting between the Jews and the Arabs, and the British had been unable to solve the problem.

After the war, an organization called the United Nations voted to split Palestine into a Jewish state, called Israel, and an Arab state. However, the Arabs wouldn't agree to this plan. The British decided to leave Palestine, and on May 14, 1948, the Jewish people set up the new state of Israel.

The Arabs attack

The Arab Palestinians couldn't accept the new Jewish state because they felt that it was part of their country. They were supported by other Arab countries, such as Egypt and Syria. In May 1948, the Arab countries attacked Israel and war broke out. By January 1949, Israel had won the war, and thousands of Arab Palestinians had fled or been driven from their homes.

The fighting continues

Over the next 20 years, fighting continued between the two sides. Palestinian attacks increased after 1964 when the Palestine Liberation Organization (PLO) was formed to fight for the liberation of what they saw as their country.

Palestinian refugees, who have had to leave their homes

In 1967, Israeli troops seized large areas of Arab land in the dramatic Six-Day War. To get this back, in 1973, Egypt and Syria launched a surprise attack on Israel in the Yom Kippur War. Eventually, Egypt and Israel signed a peace agreement in 1978 at Camp David in the USA.

Peace plans

In 1993, Israel and the PLO signed a peace deal recognizing each other for the first time. The Palestinians were given control over some of their cities and towns, and hoped to have their own state next to Israel. However, in 2000, peace talks broke down and fighting began again between the two sides, as well as clashes between rival Arab groups.

Israeli leader Yitzhak Rabin (on the left) and PLO leader Yasser Arafat shake hands during the 1993 Middle East peace talks, while US President Bill Clinton looks on.

Revolution in Iran

For most of the 20th century, Iran was ruled by a series of kings, or shahs. The last shah tried to modernize his country, but he was opposed by strict Muslims who wanted to keep the old traditions. In 1979, the Shah was overthrown and Ayatollah Khomeini, a Muslim leader, took control of Iran. The Ayatollah ruled Iran very strictly and ordered all Iranian women to wear traditional dress.

Here, a young Iranian woman in traditional dress is walking past a gigantic portrait of Ayatollah Khomeini.

Map of the Middle East

■ Areas claimed by Israel but occupied by Palestinians

The Gulf War

In 1990, Iraq invaded nearby Kuwait, hoping to gain control of Kuwait's oil wells. This led to the Gulf War, which started in 1991. A group of countries led by the USA and Saudi Arabia attacked Iraq to force it to free Kuwait. After just two months, Iraq lost the war, but both Iraq and Kuwait had been badly damaged.

Oil wells like this were set on fire by Iraqi troops as they retreated from Kuwait at the end of the Gulf War.

The Iran-Iraq War

War broke out in 1980 between Iran and nearby Iraq. The war was really based on ancient differences between the two countries, but it began when Iraq invaded an area on Iran's border. The Iraqi leader, Saddam Hussein, thought Iran would be easy to beat, as it was in chaos after the revolution in 1979. In fact, the war dragged on for eight years and neither side won. By the time Iran and Iraq made peace in 1988, over a million soldiers had been killed.

Important dates

1948	Israel is created.
1964	Palestinians form the Palestine Liberation Organization (PLO).
1967	Six-Day War
1973	Yom Kippur War
1979	Revolution in Iran
1980-1988	Iran-Iraq War
1990	Iraq invades Kuwait.
1991	Gulf War
1993	Middle East Peace Accord between Israel and the PLO

THE MIDDLE EAST

The Cold War

During the Second World War, the USA and the Communist Soviet Union fought on the same side. But soon after the war, they became suspicious of each other. For the next 40 years, they fought a war of words and threats that became known as the Cold War.

Communism spreads

By the end of World War II, the Soviet Army had advanced across eastern Europe and into Germany. After the war, Soviet soldiers remained in eastern Europe, and the Soviet leader, Stalin, helped to set up Communist rulers there.

Taking sides

Western countries, such as the USA and Britain, grew worried that the Soviets wanted to control all of Europe. So, in 1949, these countries formed an organization called NATO (the North Atlantic Treaty Organization). All the members of NATO agreed to defend each other if the Soviets attacked.

In 1955, the Soviet Union and the Communist countries of eastern Europe made a similar agreement among themselves, called the Warsaw Pact.

Map of eastern Europe

SOVIET UNION
EAST GERMANY
Berlin
POLAND
WEST GERMANY
CZECHOSLOVAKIA
HUNGARY
ROMANIA
YUGOSLAVIA
BULGARIA
ALBANIA

■ Communist countries
🚩 Iron Curtain

Germany divided

At the end of World War II, Germany was divided into four zones. The eastern zone was controlled by the Soviet Union, while the three western zones were run by the USA, Britain and France. In 1949, the Soviet zone became the Communist country of East Germany. The rest became West Germany.

The Berlin Wall

Berlin, the old capital city, now lay inside East Germany, and it too was divided into East and West. Life was much harder for people in East Berlin, and many of them tried to move to West Berlin. To stop this from happening, the Soviets built a huge wall between the two parts of the city. Any East Germans who tried to escape over the wall were shot.

This is part of the Berlin Wall, which became a symbol of the "Iron Curtain" that separated eastern Europe from the West.

East German flag

This is the Brandenburg Gate in East Berlin. It was built between 1788 and 1791 as a gateway into the city of Berlin.

West German police

Crisis in Cuba

During the Cold War, both sides built up huge supplies of weapons. In 1962, the USA discovered that the Soviet government was planning to use the island of Cuba, near the American coast, as a base for its nuclear missiles. The situation became very tense, as neither side wanted a nuclear war. After six days, the Soviet government was persuaded to back down.

Map of Southeast Asia

Communist countries

Wounded American soldiers being rescued by helicopter during the Vietnam War

Korea and Vietnam

The USA and the Soviet Union never actually fought each other during the Cold War. But both sides sent weapons and troops to support Communists and anti-Communists who were fighting each other in different parts of the world. The main places where this happened were Korea and Vietnam.

Changing times

During the 1970s, the USA and the Soviet Union became more friendly. This changed when the Soviets invaded nearby Afghanistan in 1979, and the USA began planning powerful new weapons. In 1991, the Soviet Union split up, and the Cold War finally came to an end (see pages 382 and 383).

This sign near the Berlin Wall warns people that they are about to leave West Berlin.

ACHTUNG!
Sie verlassen jetzt
WEST-BERLIN

East German guards

Important dates

1945 World War II ends.

1949 NATO is formed. Germany becomes two separate countries.

1950-1953 The Korean War

1954-1973 The Vietnam War

1955 The Warsaw Pact is signed.

1961 The Berlin Wall is built.

1962 The Cuban Missile Crisis

1979 The Soviet Union invades Afghanistan.

1991 The Cold War ends.

THE WORLD

379

The Space Race

For hundreds of years, people dreamed of exploring space, but space travel only became possible when the rocket was invented in the 1930s. The first rockets were used during World War II to carry German bombs. After the war, scientists set about building a rocket powerful enough to travel into space.

Once the Cold War began in the 1950s, the USA and the Soviet Union competed fiercely to be the first country to send a rocket into space.

Satellites in space

In October 1957, the Soviets launched *Sputnik 1*. This was the first man-made object to go into space, and circle, or orbit, the Earth. Today, objects like this, called satellites, are used to take detailed photographs of the Earth and to send television pictures all around the world.

The photograph above was taken by a modern satellite orbiting the Earth. It shows the Sacramento River and the city of Sacramento, in California.

People in space

The Soviets scored another first in April 1961, when Yuri Gagarin became the first person to travel into space. During a flight that lasted 108 minutes, Gagarin made one complete orbit of the Earth. When he returned to the Soviet Union, he was treated as a hero.

Yuri Gagarin, photographed on the way to his spacecraft *Vostok 1*

Flying to the Moon

In the early 1960s, the Soviets were winning the space race and the Americans were desperate to change this. The US president, John F. Kennedy, announced a daring plan to put American astronauts on the Moon.

This is one of the giant *Saturn 5* rockets that were used to send American astronauts to the Moon.

In December 1968, an American spacecraft, *Apollo 8*, flew around the Moon for the first time. Six months later, US astronauts Neil Armstrong and Buzz Aldrin became the first people to set foot on the Moon.

Buzz Aldrin on the surface of the Moon on July 20, 1969

The space shuttle

The early manned spacecraft of the 1960s and 1970s could only be used once. Their crews returned to Earth by dropping out of the sky in a tiny capsule that had parachutes attached to it to help break its fall.

All this changed in 1981 when the American space shuttle flew for the first time. The shuttle took off like a rocket, but landed on a runway, like a plane, so it could be used many times.

The space shuttle *Endeavour* blasting off from Cape Canaveral in the USA

Two rocket boosters helped the shuttle reach a speed of 84km (54 miles) per minute.

These wings helped the shuttle glide back down to Earth.

At a height of 43km (27 miles), the boosters fell away. They dropped into the sea and could be used again.

Space stations

During the 1970s, both the USA and the Soviet Union launched space stations, where scientists could live for weeks at a time and carry out experiments.

When the Cold War ended, the two countries began to work together. From 1995 to 1998, American scientists worked on the Russian space station *Mir*.

The space station *Mir*

At the end of the 20th century, engineers around the world started work on an exciting new project, called the International Space Station. The first two parts were built in Russia and in the USA. They were launched separately and were joined together in space, in December 1998.

Important dates

1957	*Sputnik 1*, the first satellite, is launched.
1961	Yuri Gagarin is the first person in space.
July 20, 1969	*Apollo 11* reaches the Moon. Neil Armstrong and Buzz Aldrin make the first Moon landing.
1971	The Soviets launch the world's first space station, *Salyut 1*.
1981	The space shuttle makes its first flight.
1986	The space shuttle *Challenger* explodes after lift-off, killing seven astronauts.
Dec 1998	The first two parts of the International Space Station link up.

THE WORLD

The Fall of Communism

By the 1980s, the Communist countries of Eastern Europe were facing serious problems. People there were much poorer than in the West, and in some of the countries there wasn't enough food for everyone. The Communist rulers were very unpopular, and they relied on the support of the Soviet Union and its army to keep them in power.

A new leader

In 1985, Mikhail Gorbachev became leader of the Soviet Union and began modernizing the country.

Mikhail Gorbachev, Soviet leader from 1985 to 1991

Gorbachev allowed people to set up their own businesses and to vote freely in elections for the first time. He also made it clear that the Soviet Union would no longer help the Communist leaders of Eastern Europe to stay in power.

Map of former Communist countries

■ Countries that were part of the Soviet Union
■ Eastern European countries

EUROPE ASIA
AFRICA

ESTONIA
LATVIA
LITHUANIA
RUSSIA
Berlin
GERMANY POLAND BELARUS
CZECH
REPUBLIC UKRAINE
AUSTRIA SLOVAKIA
HUNGARY MOLDOVA
ROMANIA GEORGIA
KAZAKHSTAN
CASPIAN SEA
BLACK SEA
YUGOSLAVIA BULGARIA
ALBANIA MACEDONIA ARMENIA
AZERBAIJAN

People power

In 1988, thousands of workers in Poland went on strike to protest against the government. The Polish Communist leaders were forced to allow elections, and the workers' trade union, known as Solidarity, won a huge victory. In August 1989, a non-Communist prime minister was elected, and a year later the Solidarity leader, Lech Walesa, became President of Poland.

★ The Solidarity logo, which includes the red and white flag of Poland

Opening borders

East Germany was one of the strictest Communist countries, and people there were forbidden to travel to the West. In September 1989, Hungary opened its border with Austria. Thousands of East Germans began escaping through Hungary into Austria and West Germany. Meanwhile, inside East Germany, there were massive protests against the Communist government.

The Wall falls

On November 9, the East German government agreed to let people travel freely to the West. In Berlin, people climbed onto the wall that divided the two parts of the city. The gates were opened for the first time in over 25 years, and thousands of East Germans crossed into West Berlin.

In March 1990, East Germany voted to join West Germany and, on October 23, the two countries became one again. Berlin later became the capital of the new, united Germany.

Here you can see people from East and West Germany celebrating together at the Berlin Wall, just after the Wall was opened up in November 1989.

A violent end

By the end of 1989, all the old Communist leaders of Eastern Europe had been replaced. In most countries, this happened peacefully, but in Romania the brutal Communist ruler, Nicolae Ceausescu, was taken prisoner and executed.

The break-up of the Soviet Union

Meanwhile, in the Soviet Union, the republics of Latvia, Estonia and Lithuania decided to break away and form countries of their own. Other regions tried to do the same, and fighting broke out in some places.

Boris Yeltsin, President of Russia from 1991 to 1999

President Gorbachev resigned, and on December 31, 1991, the Soviet Union split up into 15 independent countries. The largest of these was the republic of Russia, led by the non-Communist Boris Yeltsin. With the fall of Communism, the Cold War between the West and the Soviet Union was finally over.

Important dates

1980	The Polish trade union Solidarity is set up.
1985	Mikhail Gorbachev becomes leader of the Soviet Union.
August 1989	A non-Communist becomes prime minister of Poland.
Sep 1989	Hungary opens its border with Austria.
Nov 9, 1989	East Germans cross the Berlin Wall.
Oct 23, 1990	East and West Germany become one country.
Dec 31, 1991	The Soviet Union splits up.

Rights for All

Human rights are based on the idea that all people should be treated fairly and equally, whatever their race, religion or sex. They should be able to live in freedom, express their opinions, have a fair trial and vote in elections. Today, these basic rights are often taken for granted, but a hundred years ago things were very different.

Votes for women

In 1900, most countries in the world did not allow women to vote in elections. New Zealand had given women the vote in 1893, but other countries were slow to follow. In Britain and the USA, women known as suffragettes campaigned fiercely for the right to vote. Britain finally gave women the vote in 1918, and the USA did the same two years later.

Many suffragettes, like this woman, were arrested and sent to prison.

Black rights

In the USA, during the 1950s, African Americans began to protest at the way they were being treated. In many southern states, Black people were prevented from voting and weren't allowed to send their children to white schools, or sit in bus seats reserved for white people.

This is Martin Luther King, a Baptist minister who led many Black protests in the USA.

The largest protest took place in August 1963, when 200,000 people marched through the streets of Washington, DC. The next year, the US government passed new laws, making it illegal to treat people differently because of their race. In spite of this, even today, many Black Americans do not have the same advantages as whites.

In some countries, such as China, people are not allowed to protest against the government. Here you can see Chinese students protesting in Beijing, in May 1989. Hundreds of them were killed when the army was sent in to stop the protests.

South Africa

Meanwhile, in South Africa, Black Africans were treated appallingly by the white people who ruled the country. They weren't allowed to vote, and laws were passed to keep them out of white areas. This system of keeping Black and white people apart was known as apartheid, and thousands of Black Africans were jailed, beaten or killed for protesting against it.

In 1989, a new president, F. W. de Klerk, came to power and began changing the system. The following year, he released the Black leader Nelson Mandela from prison. In 1994, Black Africans were allowed to vote for the first time, and Nelson Mandela was chosen as South Africa's first Black president.

Nelson Mandela surrounded by supporters during the election campaign of 1994.

The right to land

Many indigenous people around the world have been treated unfairly by white settlers. In Australia, Indigenous Australians lost their land and their way of life when Europeans arrived in the 18th century. Since the 1930s, indigenous people have been campaigning to win back their land, but so far they have only been given a tiny fraction of what they lost.

Protecting rights

Today, there are still many parts of the world where people's rights are not respected. In many countries, women are still seen as second-class citizens, and people are treated unjustly because of their race.

International organizations, such as the United Nations, try to persuade governments to make fairer laws, while groups such as Amnesty International speak out on behalf of people whose rights are being ignored.

This is the symbol of Amnesty International, which campaigns for people imprisoned for their beliefs.

Important dates

1893	Women in New Zealand are given the right to vote.
1945	The United Nations is set up to encourage peace and to protect human rights.
1949	Apartheid is introduced in South Africa.
1964-1965	Civil rights laws are passed in the USA.
1989	Hundreds of protesters are killed in Tiananmen Square in Beijing, China.
1990	Apartheid ends in South Africa.

Sound and Pictures

In 1900, radios and moving pictures, or movies, had only just been invented, and television did not exist at all. Over the next hundred years, these new inventions created a whole new area of entertainment and completely changed our view of the world.

The birth of cinema

In 1895, two brothers, named Louis and Auguste Lumière, invented a machine called a Cinématographe, which could project moving images onto a screen. The brothers gave their first movie show in Paris in December 1895, and cinema was born.

Moving pictures quickly became very popular, and the craze soon spread to the United States. By the 1920s, Hollywood, on the west coast of the USA, was the movie capital of the world.

This is an advert for the London premiere of the talking picture, *The Jazz Singer*, starring the American singer, Al Jolson.

The comic actor Charlie Chaplin was the most famous movie star of the 1920s.

The first talkie

Early moving pictures had no sound, but were accompanied by music from an orchestra or piano. The first major talking picture, or talkie, was *The Jazz Singer*, which was made in 1927.

Radio days

During the 1920s, radio also became popular. The first radio stations were set up in the United States in 1920, and by 1930 there were 12 million radio sets in the USA. Politicians soon realized that they could use radio to speak directly to people in their homes. During the Second World War, governments on both sides made radio broadcasts to encourage their own side and show the enemy in a bad light.

The start of television

The first public demonstration of a mechanical television was given by the British inventor John Logie Baird in 1926. The TV system we use today was developed in the 1930s, and in 1936 the BBC began regular TV broadcasts from London. At first, very few people had a TV set, as each one cost about the same as a small car. But by the 1950s, television was the most popular form of entertainment.

Satellite service

In 1962, for the first time, live TV pictures were sent across the Atlantic Ocean by a satellite orbiting the Earth. This meant that images filmed in the United States could be shown at the same time in Europe. Today, people can watch the news all over the globe as it happens, and our world seems a much smaller place.

This scene from 1998 movie *Lost in Space* shows a robot inside a space ship. The movie used a vast number of special effects to create a fantasy world in space.

Too much television?

By 1990, in the USA, the average teenager was spending 23 hours a week watching television. Some experts thought that too much television made people too lazy to think for themselves. Others worried that watching a lot of violence on television could make people behave in a violent way.

Movie magic

In order to compete with television, movie-makers had to create more spectacular effects. In the 1950s, new techniques were invented to improve sound and produce bigger, widescreen pictures. By the 1990s, movie companies were spending vast amounts of money on truly amazing special effects.

Important dates

1895 The Lumière brothers project moving images onto a screen.

1920 The first radio stations are set up in the USA.

1926 John Logie Baird demonstrates his television.

1927 *The Jazz Singer* is the first major movie with sound.

1936 The BBC begins regular television broadcasts.

1962 The satellite Telstar sends a TV image across the Atlantic.

THE WORLD

387

Our Polluted Planet

During the 20th century, daily life changed dramatically. People now had cars to take them from place to place, gas and electricity for cooking and heating, and a vast number of gadgets and machines to make life easier. But as early as the 1960s, scientists began to realize that the modern way of life was gradually destroying the world around us.

Global warming

Much of the world's electricity is produced in power stations that burn coal, oil or gas. When these fuels burn, they release a gas called carbon dioxide into the air. Exhaust fumes from cars and buses also contain carbon dioxide. Scientists now believe that this gas may be making the Earth warmer. This is known as global warming.

Trees use up some of the carbon dioxide in the air, helping to reduce global warming. But all over the world, forests like this are being burned to make room for farmland.

The greenhouse effect

As carbon dioxide rises high into the air, it forms a blanket around the Earth, trapping heat underneath. This is known as the greenhouse effect and it is what causes global warming. As the Earth warms up, the weather all over the world could change dramatically. Sea levels might also rise, flooding large areas of low-lying land.

Poisoning the air

Cars, factories and power stations continuously pump out fumes which dirty, or pollute, the air. In cities, these fumes sometimes form a smoky fog, called smog, which makes it hard for people to breathe. The fumes also mix with clouds to form acid rain that kills plants.

The ozone hole

The Earth is surrounded by a layer of gas called ozone, which blocks out harmful ultraviolet light from the Sun. In 1973, scientists discovered a hole in the ozone layer above Antarctica. The ozone was being destroyed by man-made gases called chlorofluorocarbons, or CFCs, found in some aerosols and refrigerators. The thinner ozone layer let through more ultraviolet light, damaging people's eyes and skin.

In 1987, countries around the world agreed to stop making harmful CFCs. By the year 2000, the ozone layer had started to recover. It's still continuing to recover now.

Plastic pollution

Plastic is one of the most common materials around today. Because it is cheap, it is often used to make bags, bottles and wrappers which people throw away. Plastic doesn't rot, so it's very hard to get rid of. Lots of it ends up in the sea, where it kills millions of fish, birds and animals every year.

Turtles can die from eating plastic bags, which look like jellyfish in the water.

Here you can see the hole in the ozone layer above Antarctica. It is shown by the deep purple and bright pink areas in the middle of the picture.

Saving the planet

Protest groups, such as Greenpeace, try to persuade governments to do something about pollution and climate change, and most world leaders now accept that there is a real problem.

In 1992, politicians from around the world met at the Earth Summit in Brazil to talk about the future of the planet. A total of 154 countries signed an agreement to cut the amount of carbon dioxide they produce, use alternative fuels that don't cause global warming, and protect the Earth's water and oceans. But more still needs to be done.

Polluting the water

The world's seas and rivers are being polluted by sewage (waste from drains and toilets) and poisonous chemicals dumped from factories. Our seas and rivers are also being poisoned by fertilizers that are washed off farmland. All around the world, beaches are ruined and seabirds are killed when oil leaks out of tankers that have run aground.

One way to reduce global warming is to find cleaner ways of making electricity. These are wind turbines, which can produce electricity without releasing carbon dioxide into the air.

Important dates

1967 Scientists first become aware of the greenhouse effect.

1971 Greenpeace is set up.

1987 International agreement to protect the ozone layer.

1992 The Earth Summit is held in Rio de Janeiro, in Brazil.

THE WORLD

The Computer Revolution

Computers allow us to do things that people used to think were impossible. We can test cars and planes before they are even built, explore imaginary worlds using virtual reality, and send information around the world in seconds on the internet. Today, computer technology is changing incredibly fast, but progress was slow at first.

The first computers

The very first computers were invented in the 19th century. They made calculations mechanically, using lots of connected cogs and wheels. The first electronic computers did not appear until the 1940s, over a hundred years later. These early computers were immense. ENIAC, completed in 1946, filled a whole room and weighed as much as 500 people.

From valves to chips

Computers use electrical signals to process, or work on, information. Early computers, such as ENIAC, had thousands of large valves which switched on and off to produce these signals. Then, in 1947, a much smaller switch, called a transistor, was invented. Computers no longer needed to be quite so huge.

In 1958, an American scientist named Jack Kilby invented the microchip, which contained more than one transistor. By using microchips, it was possible to build computers that were much smaller and more powerful than before.

Today, microchips, like the one shown above, can contain millions of tiny transistors.

Personal computers

The first small home computer, the Altair, was sold in 1975. It was named after a planet in the TV series *Star Trek*. The Altair had to be bought as a kit and then built at home. Most modern computers are based on a type of computer called a PC that was first made in 1981.

The internet

The internet is a huge network that links together millions of computers all around the world. It grew out of a network called ARPANET, which was set up in 1969 by the US armed forces. At first, computers had to be connected to the internet by special cables. It wasn't until the 1990s that people could link up by using their own phone line.

Here are some web pages from the internet.

This is the website for the British Museum, where you can find pictures of amazing treasures from the ancient world.

This is the website for the Natural History Museum, where you can find out about the natural world.

The World Wide Web

Using the internet, we can send electronic messages, or email, around the world in seconds and find information on any topic we want, by searching web pages. Lots of people now shop on the internet, buying anything from groceries to plane tickets.

Living with computers

Computers have had a huge effect on the way we live. Today, many people work from home, using a computer to connect to their workplace. Other jobs, such as assembling cars, can be done by computers instead of people. Many of the gadgets in our homes, such as washing machines and CD players, rely on tiny computers to make them work.

This is the website for the musician and artist Jeb Loy Nichols.

This is the website for the Royal Horticultural Society, where you can find out about plants and gardenning.

This is the Usborne website, where you can find out about the latest books.

Just for fun

The first popular electronic game, a simple tennis game called Pong, appeared in 1972. Today's computer games are much more complicated, with realistic images and dramatic sound effects. Computers are also used to create the amazing special effects you see at the movies. These techniques are now so good that it's impossible to tell what's real and what isn't.

Important dates

1834-1871	Charles Babbage designs the first mechanical computer.
1946	The ENIAC computer is completed.
1947	The transistor is invented.
1958	Jack Kilby makes the first microchip.
1969	The computer network ARPANET is set up.
1975	The first small home computer is sold.
1981	The first PC is made by the American firm IBM.
1989	British scientist Tim Berners-Lee invents the World Wide Web.

THE WORLD

391

The End of the Century

The end of the 20th century was an exciting time, as new discoveries and inventions changed people's lives faster than ever before. At the same time, several parts of the world were devastated by terrible wars.

Yugoslavia breaks up

At the start of the 1990s, the country of Yugoslavia, in eastern Europe, split into separate republics. The largest of these republics, Serbia, wanted Yugoslavia to remain a single country, and war soon broke out between Serbia and the other republics. Fighting was especially violent in the republic of Bosnia-Herzegovina and in Kosovo, in southern Serbia.

Kosovo Albanian refugees crossing the Albanian border

East Timor breaks free

In August 1999, violence broke out in East Timor, in Southeast Asia. For more than 20 years, East Timor had been ruled by Indonesia, and when the East Timorese voted to become independent, Indonesian soldiers began attacking them. The United Nations (UN) sent troops to protect the people of East Timor, and Indonesia soon agreed to let East Timor govern itself. UN soldiers stayed there to make sure the area remained peaceful.

The symbol of the UN

New technology

By the 1990s, advances in technology were changing the way many people lived and worked. New satellite phones allowed people to talk to each other from very remote places. More and more people used mobile phones and computers to connect to the internet. A whole new industry grew up, as companies began using the internet to sell things directly to people in their homes.

Understanding genes

By the end of the century, scientists had built up a vast amount of knowledge about human genes, made up of DNA, the coded chemical messages that are passed on from parents to children. In 1990, a project was set up to discover how each gene in the body works. This is known as the Human Genome Project, and scientists hope that it will help them find cures for many diseases.

This is a computer image showing the structure of DNA, the chemical from which genes are made.

GM food

In the 1990s, scientists discovered how to transfer genes from one type of plant or animal to another. They used this knowledge to create crops that were protected against insects and diseases. Food from these crops is known as genetically modified, or GM, food. Although GM crops could help to provide enough food for everyone in the world, many people are afraid that they could also damage the environment.

The year 2000

The century ended with a bang as many countries held spectacular firework displays to celebrate the start of the year 2000. For the first time ever, television made it possible to watch people celebrating the dawn of a new century in different places all over the world.

Fireworks exploding in Paris at midnight on December 31, 1999

THE WORLD

393

Ancient World Time Chart

This chart shows what was happening at the same time in different parts of the ancient world.

DATE	THE AMERICAS	EUROPE	
BEFORE 10,000BC	By c.13,000BC People arrive in North America.		
10,000BC	c.6000BC Farming begins in Central America.	c.6000BC Farming begins in Greece and spreads across Europe.	c.6000BC People in the Sahara tame cattle.
			Saharan rock painting
5000BC	c.1200BC The Olmecs build temples. The Chavín way of life begins. Olmec ball-players	c.3500-2200BC Stonehenge is built in Britain. c.1900-1450BC The Minoans build palaces on Crete. c.1600BC The Mycenaeans become powerful in Greece. c.1450BC The Mycenaeans invade Crete. c.1100BC The Greek Dark Ages begin. Mycenaean woman	c.5000BC Farming begins in the Nile Valley. c.3100BC King Menes unites Upper and Lower Egypt. c.2686BC The Old Kingdom begins in Egypt. c.2530BC The Egyptians start building the Great Pyramid at Giza. c.2040BC The Middle Kingdom begins. c.1650BC The Hyksos invade Egypt. The Middle Kingdom ends. c.1570BC The New Kingdom begins. c.1450BC The Egyptian Empire is at its largest under Thutmose III.
1000BC	c.100BC The Hopewell culture builds earth mounds. The Great Serpent Mound	c.800BC The Celtic way of life spreads across western Europe. c.776BC The first Olympic Games. 753BC The city of Rome is set up, according to legend. c.509BC Rome becomes a republic.	c.814BC The city of Carthage is built by the Phoenicians.
500BC	c.500BC The Adena culture begins. c.100BC The Nazca start to draw lines in the desert.	c.500-350BC The Greeks are at their most successful. 431-404BC The Peloponnesian War. 356BC Alexander the Great is born. 44BC Julius Caesar is murdered. 27BC Augustus becomes the first Emperor of Rome.	c.500BC The Nok way of life begins. 332BC Alexander the Great conquers Egypt. 146BC The Romans destroy Carthage. Nok sculpture 30BC The Romans conquer Egypt.
AD1	c.AD100-800 The Moche are ruled by warrior-priests. c.AD250-900 The Maya are at their most successful. c.AD500 Teotihuacán is the sixth largest city in the world.	AD117 The Roman Empire is at its largest under the Emperor Trajan. AD395 The Roman Empire splits permanently in two. AD476 The Western Roman Empire collapses.	c.AD100 The kingdom of Axum becomes powerful. c.AD500 The Bantu people reach southern Africa.

ASIA

THE MIDDLE EAST

c.10,000BC Farming begins in the Fertile Crescent.

c.3500BC The wheel is invented in Sumer.

Sumerian wheel

c.3300BC Writing is invented in Sumer.

c.2350BC Sargon of Akkad creates the world's first empire.

c.2000BC The Hittites settle in Anatolia.

c.1792-1750BC King Hammurabi rules Babylon.

c.1400BC An alphabet is invented in Canaan.

c.1250BC The Hebrews arrive in Canaan.

c.1200BC The Phoenicians become successful sailors and traders.

c.1000-663BC The Assyrians build up a strong empire.

c.965-928BC King Solomon rules Israel.

605-562BC King Nebuchadnezzar II rules the Babylonian Empire.

559-530BC King Cyrus II rules Persia and builds up an empire.

490-479BC Wars between the Persians and the Greeks.

331BC Alexander the Great defeats the Persians.

64BC The Romans conquer parts of the Middle East.

Alexander the Great

c.AD29 Jesus Christ is crucified.

Jesus on the cross

SOUTH ASIA

c.3500BC Farmers settle in the Indus Valley.

c.2500-1800BC The Indus Valley people are at their most successful.

c.1500BC Settlers arrive in the Indus Valley.

c.560BC Siddhartha Gautama (the Buddha) is born.

272-231BC Ashoka rules the Maurya Empire.

AD320-535 The Gupta Empire in India.

THE FAR EAST

c.10,000BC The Jōmon people of Japan hunt and fish for food.

c.7000BC Farming begins in China.

c.2700BC Silk is first made.

1600-1046BC The Shang kings rule China.

c.1400BC People in China write on oracle bones.

1046BC The Zhou kings take control of China.

c.1000BC Farming begins in Japan.

Confucius

551BC Confucius is born.

481-221BC The Warring States Period in China.

221BC Qin Shi Huang becomes China's first emperor.

202BC The Han Dynasty begins.

c.AD100 Paper is invented in China.

c.AD250 The first emperors rule in the Yamato area of Japan.

Yamato warrior

AUSTRALASIA

c.65,000BC People known as Indigenous Australians arrive in Australia.

Indigenous Australian

c.1500BC People have begun settling on islands in the Pacific

Medieval World Time Chart

This chart shows what was happening at the same time in different parts of the medieval world.

DATE	THE AMERICAS	EUROPE	AFRICA
Before 500		c.450 The Angles, Saxons and Jutes begin to rule Britain.	429 The Vandals invade North Africa.
500	c.600 The Maya are at their most successful. Maya mask	456-711 Visigoth kingdom in Spain 481-511 Clovis creates the kingdom of the Franks. 527-565 Justinian rules the Byzantine Empire Coin showing Justinian	533 The Byzantines conquer North Africa. 697 The Arabs conquer North Africa.
700	c.750 The Puebloans start to build villages. c.850 Many Maya towns are abandoned.	711 African Muslims invade Spain. c.790 The Vikings begin raiding Europe. 800-814 Charlemagne rules his Empire. c.862 Rurik creates a kingdom in Russia.	c.700 The empire of Ghana is at its most successful. c.850 The kingdom of Benin begins.
900	c.900 The Mississippians start to build towns. c.900-1000 The Toltecs are powerful. c.1000 Leif Ericson reaches North America.	962-973 Otto I is the first Holy Roman Emperor. 1037-1492 Christians win back Spain from Muslim settlers. Emperor Otto's crown 1054 The Church in eastern Europe splits from the Church in western Europe. 1066 The Normans conquer England.	969-1171 The Fatimids rule Egypt. c.1000 The state of Ife is created.
1100	c.1100 The Chimú start to build their Empire.	c.1100 The Viking raids end. 1215 King John of England signs Magna Carta. c.1250-1480 The Mongols rule southern Russia. King John	c.1200 The empire of Mali is created. 1250-1517 The Mamluks rule Egypt.
1300	c.1300 The Pueblo people abandon their towns. c.1345 The Aztecs start to build their Empire. Aztec warrior 1438 The Incas start to build their Empire.	c.1300 The city of Moscow starts to become powerful. 1337-1453 The French and the English fight the Hundred Years' War. 1347-1353 The Black Death spreads through Europe. c.1350 The Renaissance begins in Italy. 1378-1417 Rival popes rule in Avignon and Rome. Florence Cathedral	c.1350 The city of Great Zimbabwe is at its largest.
1450	1492 Columbus reaches the West Indies.	1453 The Ottoman Turks capture Constantinople and the Byzantine Empire collapses.	c.1450 The Portuguese start trading in West Africa.

THE MIDDLE EAST	SOUTH ASIA	THE FAR EAST	

Sui Emperor's boat

c.570-632 The life of Mohammed.

632 Arab caliphs (rulers) start to build the Islamic Empire.

581 The Sui dynasty begins in China.

618 The Tang dynasty begins in China.

750 The Abbasid Caliphs start to rule the Islamic Empire from Baghdad.

711 Arabs forces invade northern India.

886 The Chola empire is created in southern India.

802 The Khmer empire is created in Cambodia.

858 The Fujiwara family take control in Japan.

868 The earliest printed book is produced in China.

Māori good luck charm

1055 The Seljuk Turks capture Baghdad and control the Islamic Empire.

1071 The Seljuk Turks beat the Byzantines at the Battle of Manzikert.

1096 The Crusades begin.

1099 The Crusaders capture parts of the Holy Land.

960 The Song dynasty begins in China.

Painting by a Song artist

c.900 Settlers reach Easter Island.

1206 The Sultans of Delhi start to rule northern India.

1258 The Mongols capture Baghdad.

1290 Osman I starts to build the Ottoman Empire.

Osman I

1291 The Crusades end.

1192 Shoguns start to take control in Japan.

c.1230 The Sukhothai kingdom is created in Thailand.

Statue from the Sukhothai kingdom

1206-1226 Genghis Khan builds the Mongol Empire.

1279-1368 The Mongols rule China.

c.1250 The Easter Islanders start to build stone heads.

1360-1405 Timur builds a new Mongol Empire.

Timur

1336 The empire of Vijayanagar is created in southern India.

1398 Timur invades northern India.

1368 The Ming dynasty begins in China.

c.1350 Māori settlers reach New Zealand.

World Time Chart for the Last 500 Years

This chart shows what was happening at the same time in different parts of the world.

DATE	THE AMERICAS	EUROPE	AFRICA
1500	1500s Portuguese settlers arrive in Brazil. 1519-1521 Spanish conquistadors conquer the Aztecs. 1532-1534 Spanish conquistadors conquer the Incas. Inca priest 1580s The Slave Trade begins.	1520s The Reformation begins. 1545 The Counter-Reformation begins. 1547-1584 Ivan the Terrible is Tsar of Russia. 1556 Charles V divides the Habsburg Empire in two. Flag of the Habsburg Empire 1558-1603 Elizabeth I is Queen of England. 1581 The Republic of the United Netherlands is created.	1505 The Portuguese establish ports on the coast of East Africa. 1516-1560 The Ottoman Turks conquer large areas of North Africa.
1600	1603 French settlers start to set up colonies in Canada. 1620 The *Mayflower* arrives in North America carrying English pilgrims. 1699 The French create the colony of Louisiana.	1618-1648 The Thirty Years' War. 1630s Galileo proves that the Earth travels around the Sun. 1642-1646 The English Civil War. 1643-1715 Louis XIV is King of France. 1660s Isaac Newton discovers the laws of gravity. 1689-1725 Peter the Great is Tsar of Russia.	1616 Dutch and French traders set up trading posts in West Africa. 1652 Dutch settlers conquer Cape Colony.
1700	1759 British troops capture Quebec from the French. 1776 American colonists sign the Declaration of Independence. 1789 George Washington becomes the first President of the USA.	1740-1780 Maria Theresa rules the Habsburg Empire. 1740-1786 Frederick the Great is King of Prussia. 1750s The Industrial Revolution begins in Britain. 1762-1796 Catherine the Great is Tsarina of Russia. 1789 The French Revolution begins. Ribbons worn by French Revolutionaries 1799-1815 Napoleon Bonaparte rules France.	1700-1800 The African states of Benin, Oyo and Ashanti are flourishing. Ashanti gold ornament
1800	1816-1824 Simon Bolivar and José de San Martín win independence for colonies in South America. 1860 Abraham Lincoln becomes President of the USA. 1861-1865 The American Civil War. 1888 Slavery ends throughout the Americas. US President Abraham Lincoln	1848 Revolutions in many parts of Europe. 1861 Italy is unified. 1871 Germany is unified. 1895 Karl Benz, a German engineer, builds the first motor car. Benz's first motor car 1895 The Lumière brothers give the first ever movie show, in Paris.	1806 Britain takes control of Cape Colony. 1836 The Boers set out on the Great Trek. 1841 David Livingstone starts to explore Africa. 1879 The Zulu people are defeated by the British and the Boers. 1899 The Boer War begins.

A S I A

THE MIDDLE EAST

1502 The start of the Safavid dynasty in Persia.

1520-1566 Sultan Suleiman rules the Ottomans.

Sultan Suleiman

1680s The Ottoman Empire begins to weaken.

Persian Safavid warriors

1730 The Safavid dynasty in Persia ends.

1854-1869 The Suez Canal is built in Egypt.

Symbol of the Indian National Congress

SOUTH ASIA

1526-1605 Babur is the first Mughal Emperor of India.

1556-1605 Akbar is the Mughal Emperor of India.

1600 The British East India Company is created.

1632 The Mughal Emperor Shah Jahan starts to build the Taj Mahal in India.

1690s The Mughal Empire is at its largest.

1714 Hindu princes start to win land in northern India.

1757 Robert Clive defeats the Prince of Bengal at the Battle of Plassey in India.

1857-1858 The Indian Mutiny.

1858 The British government takes control of India.

1885 The Indian National Congress is set up to campaign for independence.

THE FAR EAST

1568-1582 Oda Nobunaga controls Japan.

1591-1598 Toyotomi Hideyoshi controls Japan.

1595 Dutch traders start to set up colonies in the East Indies.

1603 The Tokugawa shoguns start to rule Japan.

1644 The Ming dynasty ends and the Qing dynasty takes over China.

Ming jar

1839-1842 The Opium War in China.

1850-1864 The Taiping Rebellion in China.

1868 The Emperor takes control of Japan.

1894-1895 War between Japan and China.

1898-1900 The Boxer Rebellion in China.

Boxer warrior

AUSTRALASIA

Indigenous Australian musical instruments, called clapsticks

1606 Dutch explorers reach Australia.

1642 Abel Tasman reaches New Zealand.

Australian kangaroo

1770 Captain Cook reaches Australia.

1788 Britain begins sending convicts to Australia.

1840 The British take control of New Zealand.

1860-1861 Explorers cross Australia.

1893 Women in New Zealand are given the right to vote.

DATE	THE AMERICAS	EUROPE	AFRICA

1900

THE AMERICAS

1914 Opening of the Panama Canal.

1917 The USA joins World War I.

1920 Prohibition begins in the USA.

1927 The Jazz Singer is the first major movie with sound.

1929 The Wall Street Crash.

1933 US President Roosevelt launches the New Deal.

1941 The USA joins World War II after Pearl Harbor is bombed.

EUROPE

1914-1918 World War I.

Poppies from the battlefields of World War I

1917 The Russian Revolution.

1922 Benito Mussolini takes control of Italy.

1928-1953 Josef Stalin controls the Soviet Union.

Symbol of the Soviet Union

1933 Adolf Hitler becomes Chancellor of Germany.

1939-1945 World War II.

1948 Communists come to power in Czechoslovakia, Hungary, Romania, Bulgaria and Poland.

1949 Germany is divided into East and West.

AFRICA

1902 The Boer War ends.

1942 The Allies defeat the Germans at El Alamein in North Africa.

1949 Apartheid is introduced in South Africa.

1950

THE AMERICAS

1958 Jack Kilby invents the microchip.

1962 The Cuban Missile Crisis.

1963 US President Kennedy is assassinated.

1968 Martin Luther King is assassinated.

1969 US astronaut Neil Armstrong is the first man on the Moon.

US astronaut Buzz Aldrin on the Moon, photographed by Neil Armstrong

1981 The US space shuttle makes its first flight.

1992 The Earth Summit is held in Rio de Janeiro, Brazil.

EUROPE

1953 The structure of DNA is discovered in Britain by Rosalind Franklin, Francis Crick and James Watson.

1957 The Soviet Union launches Sputnik I into space.

1961 Yuri Gagarin of the Soviet Union is the first person in space.

1980 Solidarity is set up in Poland.

1985 Mikhail Gorbachev becomes leader of the Soviet Union.

1989 The Berlin Wall falls.

1989 Tim Berners-Lee invents the World Wide Web.

1991 The Soviet Union splits up.

1991-1995 War in Yugoslavia.

1998-1999 War in Kosovo.

AFRICA

1951 Libya becomes independent.

1952-1955 Rebellion in Kenya against British rule.

1957 Ghana becomes independent.

1960-1980 Most African states become independent.

1967-1970 Civil war in Nigeria.

Flag of South Africa

1990 Apartheid ends in South Africa.

1994-1999 Nelson Mandela is President of South Africa.

2000

A S I A

THE MIDDLE EAST

1918 The Turkish Ottoman Empire ends.

1922 The Republic of Turkey is formed.

1948 Israel is created.

1948-1949 Arab-Israeli War.

1956 Second Arab-Israeli War.

1967 Six-Day War between Israel and the Arab states.

Israeli fighter plane ★

1973 Yom Kippur War between Israel and the Arab states.

1979 Ayatollah Khomeini takes control of Iran.

1980-1988 Iran-Iraq War.

1990 Iraq invades Kuwait.

1991 The Gulf War.

1993 Peace agreement between Israel and the Palestinians.

SOUTH ASIA

Mahatma Gandhi

1920 Mahatma Gandhi starts a non-violent campaign for Indian independence.

1947 India and Pakistan become independent.

1960 Mrs Bandaranaike of Ceylon (now Sri Lanka) is the first woman prime minister in the world.

1971 Bangladesh is formed.

THE FAR EAST

1904-1905 War between Japan and Russia.

1910 Japan gains control of Korea.

1911 The Kuomintang start a revolution in China.

1912 The last Qing Emperor of China gives up his throne.

1934 Communists in China set out on the Long March.

1941-1945 Japan fights the Allies in World War II.

1945 The first ever atomic bomb is dropped, on Hiroshima in Japan.

1949 Mao Zedong sets up the People's Republic of China.

1950-1953 The Korean War.

1954 The Vietnam War starts.

1966 The Cultural Revolution in China.

A Chinese Red Guard from the time of the Cultural Revolution

1973 The Vietnam War ends.

1976 Death of Mao Zedong.

1989 Hundreds of Chinese protesters are killed in Tiananmen Square.

Symbol of the UN

1999 UN soldiers are sent to East Timor to help it become an independent nation.

AUSTRALASIA

1914-1918 Troops from Australia and New Zealand fight in World War I.

1939-1945 Troops from Australia and New Zealand fight in World War II.

1993 The Native Titles Bill gives some land rights to Indigenous Australians.

401

Word List

This list explains some of the words that are used in the book.

allies People who fight on the same side in a war. During the two world wars, the countries that fought on the same side as Britain were known as "the Allies".

amphibian An animal that can live on land, but lays its eggs in water. Frogs are amphibians.

apartheid The South African system of keeping different races of people apart. Apartheid lasted from 1949 to 1990, and meant that non-whites were treated as second-class citizens.

archbishop An important Christian priest, in charge of the Church over a large area.

arthropod A creature with jointed legs and a hard, outer skeleton. Spiders and insects are arthropods.

assassinate To murder a leader or a politician.

Axis Powers The countries that fought on the same side as Germany in the Second World War.

barbarian A member of one of the warlike tribes that came from the lands outside the Roman Empire.

bishop An important Christian priest, who has the rank below an archbishop.

Bolshevik A Russian Communist who supported Lenin. The Bolsheviks led the revolution against the Tsar of Russia in 1917.

caliph An Arab ruler.

carnivore An animal that only eats meat.

Catholic A person beonging to a branch of the Christian Church led by the Pope in Rome.

cells The tiny "building blocks" from which all living things are made.

Central Powers The countries that were on the same side as Germany in the First World War.

city-state A city and surrounding land, which has its own rulers.

civilization An advanced way of life, where people live in towns and have a system of laws and a way of writing.

civil war Fighting between different groups of people within the same country.

Cold War The struggle for power between the United States and the Soviet Union, which was at its height during the 1950s and 1960s.

colonists People who set up a colony, or their descendants who live there.

colony
1. A settlement created in a foreign land, by people who have moved away from their homeland.
2. A group made up of large numbers of one kind of plant or animal. All the members of a colony live or grow together.

Communism A form of government where the state owns all land and factories, and provides for people's needs. Today, China is the world's largest Communist country.

constitution A set of laws used to rule a country.

continent A large area of land on the surface of the Earth. Africa and North America are two of the Earth's continents.

convict A person who has been found guilty of a crime.

crusade A war fought for a religious reason.

culture The shared ideas, beliefs and values of a group of people.

cuneiform writing An ancient form of writing made up of wedge-shaped symbols.

democracy A system of government where the people have a say in how their country is run.

DNA The chemical containing the instructions that make living things what they are.

dynasty A series of rulers from the same family.

ectothermic A word used to describe cold-blooded creatures that cannot produce their own body heat. Snakes and lizards are ectothermic.

empire A large group of lands that is ruled by one powerful person or government.

endothermic A word used to describe warm-blooded animals that can produce their own body heat. Mammals are endothermic.

evolve To change or develop gradually.

extinct A word used to describe a creature or plant that has died out. Dinosaurs are extinct.

famine A serious shortage of food which causes many people to die.

Fascism The military form of government in Italy from 1922 to 1943, led by Benito Mussolini, which banned all opposition. Fascism is also used to describe similar forms of government in other countries, such as Hitler's Germany.

fortress A group of buildings surrounded by a wall so that they can be easily defended.

fossil The remains of a prehistoric creature or plant. Fossils are often made of stone.

fossilize To turn into a fossil.

fresco A picture painted on a wall while the plaster is still damp.

general A person who leads an army.

gills The parts of an underwater creature that take in oxygen from the water. Fish have gills.

global warming The slow warming of the Earth's climate, caused by gases from power stations, factories and car exhausts.

government The group of people who run a country.

Great Depression The period of worldwide unemployment and poverty, which began after the Wall Street Crash of 1929 and lasted until the late 1930s.

guild An organization for craftworkers or traders, with strict rules for all its members.

hadrosaur A plant-eating dinosaur with bird-like feet and a beak shaped like a duck's bill.

herald A person in medieval times who made announcements and carried messages.

herbivore An animal that only eats plants.

heretic A Christian whose ideas were different from the teachings of the Church.

hieroglyphs Picture writing that was used in Ancient Egypt.

Hindu A person who follows the Hindu faith, the main religion of India. Hindus pray to many gods and goddesses.

Fossilized skull of a dinosaur called *Triceratops*

Holocaust The murder of six million Jews by German Nazis between 1940 and 1945.

hominin An ape that has a large brain and walks upright. Humans are hominins.

ice age A period of time when large parts of the Earth were covered with ice.

ichthyosaur A sea reptile that was shaped like a dolphin.

icon A religious picture, usually painted on a wooden panel.

incense A sweet-smelling substance that was burned in ancient temples or in the presence of kings.

Indigenous Australians The people who lived in Australia before the Europeans arrived.

Internet The vast computer network that links millions of computers around the world.

Iron Curtain A phrase used to describe the boundary that existed until 1989 between Western Europe and the Communist countries of Eastern Europe.

Islam The religion based on the teachings of the Prophet Mohammed and on the holy book, the Koran.

Jew A person who belongs to the race of people who are descended from the ancient tribes of Israel. The Jewish religion is based on the teachings of the Old Testament of the Bible.

khan A Mongol ruler.

knight A man in the Middle Ages who was trained to fight on horseback for his lord.

lacquer A substance that can be painted onto wood, to make it shiny and waterproof.

lance A long pole with a pointed end, used as a weapon.

mammal An animal with hair on its body that feeds its babies with milk. Dogs and humans are mammals.

mammoth A large prehistoric elephant with long, curved tusks. Some mammoths had thick, woolly coats.

manuscript A handwritten book or document.

Māori people The people who lived in New Zealand before Europeans arrived.

marsupial A mammal whose babies stay in a pouch on their mother's stomach until they are large enough to survive on their own. Kangaroos are marsupials.

Middle Kingdom The second main period in Ancient Egyptian history (c.2040BC-c.1720BC).

missionary A person who travels to a foreign country and tries to persuade the people living there to follow a different religion.

mosaic A picture made from lots of small pieces of stone or glass.

mosque A building where Muslim people pray.

Muslim A person whose religion is based on the teachings of the Prophet Mohammed and on the holy book, the Koran.

nationalism The shared feeling among people who live in the same region and who have the same culture, language or religion. Nationalism often leads people to form their own independent nation.

NATO The North Atlantic Treaty Organization, an international organization which was set up in 1949 to defend Western countries against the Soviet Union. The USA, Canada and Britain are members of NATO.

Nazi Party The German National Socialist Workers' Party, led by Adolf Hitler who ruled Germany between 1933 and 1945. The Nazis were extremely anti-Jewish, and used force against anyone who opposed them.

New Kingdom The third main period in Ancient Egyptian history (c.1570BC-c.1070BC).

noble A member of a family that belongs to the ruling class of a country.

nomads People who have no permanent home, but who move around from place to place.

observatory A building from which people study the stars.

Old Kingdom The first main period in Ancient Egyptian history (c.2686BC-c.2180BC).

ornithopod A plant-eating dinosaur with bird-like feet and a beak.

oxygen A gas that all living creatures need to breathe.

pagan A person who believes in many gods.

parliament A group of people who meet to make decisions and create laws for their country.

particle A tiny speck.

patron A rich person who pays artists, architects or writers to produce works of art.

peasant A person who works on the land.

pharaoh An Ancient Egyptian king.

photosynthesis The process that plants use to make food from water and sunlight.

pilgrimage A journey to a holy place.

pioneer A person who explores a new country or a new area of a country. Pioneers usually settle in the place they have explored.

placental A mammal whose babies grow inside their mother's belly until they are large enough to survive in the outside world. Rabbits and humans are placentals.

plague A disease that spreads fast and kills many people.

planet A huge ball of rock, gas or metal that spins around a star.

plantation A large farm where crops such as cotton, coffee and tobacco are grown.

plesiosaur A sea reptile that had a long neck and big, paddle-shaped flippers.

predator An animal that hunts and eats other animals.

prey An animal that is hunted by another animal for food.

primate A mammal with hands and feet and a large brain. Apes and humans are primates.

prime minister The leader of a government that has been chosen by the people.

proteins Chemicals that form part of all living cells.

Protestant A person who belongs to a branch of the Christian Church that started in western Europe in the 1500s. The Protestant Church does not have the Pope as its leader.

province An area within an empire, such as the province of Britain in the Roman Empire.

pterosaur A prehistoric reptile that could fly.

pueblo A village or town built by the Puebloans in the southwest of North America between 700 and 1300.

Puritan A person who belongs to a very strict Protestant branch of the Christian Church.

refugee A person who is forced to leave their homeland and live somewhere else. Refugees have usually escaped from wars or famines.

reptile An animal with scaly skin that lays its eggs on land. Lizards and snakes are reptiles.

republic A country without a king or queen, whose leaders rule on behalf of the people.

revolution A successful rebellion by the people against a leader or a government.

rodent A mammal with very strong teeth that gnaws on roots, bushes and tree trunks.

satellite An object that circles the Earth in space. Man-made satellites can take photographs of the Earth, and are also used to send phone calls and television pictures from one part of the world to another.

sauropod A large, plant-eating dinosaur that had a long neck and tail and walked mainly on four legs.

scavenger A creature that eats meat from dead animals that it finds.

scholar A person who studies, teaches, and writes books.

scribe A person in the ancient world whose job was to read and write for everyone else.

shrine A sacred building or place, where people worship or where something holy is kept.

Soviet Union The Communist country that was formed in 1922 after the Russian Revolution. It was also known as the USSR.

species A group of similar plants or animals that can breed together. Lions are one species and tigers are another.

standard-bearer A soldier who carries his leader's flag into battle.

state An area with its own laws. A state can be independent, or part of a larger country.

stegosaur A large, plant-eating dinosaur with a row of upright bony plates along its back.

stocks A heavy wooden frame with holes in it, used in the Middle Ages for locking up criminals.

strike A protest in which workers demand better pay or

fairer working conditions by refusing to work.

suffragette A woman who campaigned for the right to vote at the end of the 19th and the beginning of the 20th century.

sultan A ruler of the Turkish Ottoman Empire or of other Muslim lands.

synagogue A building where Jews worship.

taxes Money collected from the people by a government or a ruler.

theropod A meat-eating dinosaur.

trade union An organization of workers who campaign together for better pay or fairer working conditions.

treaty An agreement between two or more countries.

tsar A Russian emperor.

tsarina A Russian empress.

UN The United Nations, an international organization which was set up in 1945 to encourage world peace.

vertebrate An animal with a backbone.

the West The western part of the world which includes Europe and America. During the Cold War, the non-Communist countries of Europe and America were known as "the West".

World Wide Web A vast network of linked pages which are stored on computers around the world, providing information on a huge variety of subjects.

yurt A circular tent made from felt or animal skins, used in central Asia.

Index

Pages where you can find out most about a subject are shown in **bold** type.
The Latin names of prehistoric plants and creatures are shown in *italic* type.

taxes, 135, 146, 152, 163, 168, 188, 208, 232, 246, 260, 301, 312, 313, 318, 328, 330, 332, 353, 356

technology, 112, 169, 172, 189, 209, 292, 336, 337, 338-339, 380-381, 386, 390-391, 392

teeth, 16, 17, 18, 30, 36, 39, 40, 41, 42, 44, 45, 47, 48, 55, 57, 60, 66, 67, 68, 70, 71, 74, 79, 85

telescopes, 286, 292, 311, 314

television, 292, 380, **386-387**, 393

temples, 110, 111, 117, 121, 136-137, 143, 158, 159, 178, 179, 180, 181, 188, 264, 265, 266, 267, 276, 278, 280, 281

Ten Commandments, 143

Tenochtitlán, Aztec city, 278-279

tentacles, 26, 28, 29

tents, 93, 101, 142, 162, 171, 176, 187, 211, 250, 251, 252, 259

Teotihuacán, city, 180

Terra Amata, France, 87

terracotta warriors, 167

Tertiary Period, 13

Teutonic Knights, 241, 255

Texas, USA, 350

Thanksgiving, 322

Theodora, Byzantine empress, 202

Theodosius, Roman emperor, 193

Theosodon, 72

Thera, island, 127

therapsids, 41, 42

theropods, 44-45

Theseus, Greek prince, 125

thieves, 235, 242, 243

Thirty Years' War, 308

Thomashuxleya, 72

Thoth, Egyptian god, 136

Thrinaxodon, 42, 60

Thuthmose III, King of Egypt, 134

Thylacoleo, 63

Thylacosmilus, 72

Tiber, river, 184

Tigris, river, 110, 146

Timbuktu, African city, 262-263

Timur, Mongol ruler, 251, 264

togas, 184

toilets, 118, 188, 210, 340, 341

Tokugawa Iemitsu, 356

Tokugawa Ieyasu, 356

Tokugawa shoguns, 356-357

Tokyo, Japan, 357

Toltecs, 281

tombs, 105, 113, 116, 117, 121, 123, 129, 163, 165, 167, 169, 170, 171, 172, 173, 280, 300

tools, 80, 82-83, 85, 86, 87, 89, 90, 92, 93, 96, 100, 123, 172, 173, 180, 182, 214, 336

Tower of London, 221, 244, 249

towns, 109, 126, 188-189, 207, 208, 221, 228-231, 242, 256, 261, 262-263, 268, 276, 277, 278-279, 280, 282, 284, 338, 340-341, 349

Toxodon, 72

Toyotomi Hideyoshi, 356

toys, 119, 139, 191

trade & traders, 93, 112, 119, 123, 126, 131, 134, 135, 140, 144, 163, 169, 171, 173, 177, 180, 207, 208, 209, 213, 227, 228-231, 250, 256, 258, 261, 262, 263, 265, 266, 268, 269, 274, 277, 279, 283, 288, 296, 301, 310, 311, 323, 324, 328, 346, 354, 355, 356, 357

trade unions, 341, 382

Trafalgar, Battle of, 334

trains, 339, 349, 351, 355, 357, 363

Trajan, Roman emperor, 186

transistors, 390

Transvaal, Africa, 346

Transylvania, 255

travel & transport, 112, 118, 126, 130, 133, 134, 135, 141, 144, 146, 152, 168, 169, 187, 209, 212, 213, 231, 235, 250, 251, 264, 266, 269, 272-273, 274, 283, 286, 288-289, 292, 296-297, 326, 339, 357, 380-381

treasure, 113, 116, 123, 129, 163, 165, 169, 214, 296, 297, 304

trees, 36, 37

trenches, 358, 359

Trevithick, Richard, 339

Triassic Period, 13, **42-43**, 52, 54, 60

Tribrachidium, 25

tribute, 135, 257

Triceratops, 51

trilobites, 26, 28, 29

triremes, 155

Troy, siege of, 131

tsars of Russia, 257, 316, 317, 360, 361

Tudor rulers, 249, 302, 304-305

Tull, Jethro, 336

tundra, 76

Turkey, **133**, 141, 182, 192, 203, 209, **240**, **252-253**, 260, **298-299**, 308, 343, 359

tusks, 42, 48, 68, 74, 75, 96

Tutankhamun, King of Egypt, 116, 117

Tyler, Wat, 221

Tyrannosaurus rex, 45

Tyre, Phoenician city, 144, 160

U

U-boats, 359

Ugarit, Canaanite city, 140

Uintatherium, 64

Union (northern US states), 348, 349

United Nations, 373, 376, 385, 392

United States of America, 75, 325, **330-331**, **348-351**, 357, 359, **366-367**, 372, 373, 376, 377, **378-379**, 380-381, **384**, 386, 387

universe, beginning of, 20

universities, 208, 262, 265, 318, 365, 369

Upper Egypt, 114

Ur, Sumerian city, **110-111**, 113

Urban II, Pope, 240

USSR, 361, **362-363**, 371, 372, 373,

378-379, 380-381, **382**, **383**

V

Valhalla, 211

Valley of the Kings, Egypt, 117

van Eyck, Jan, 246

Vandals, 195, 204, 260

V-E Day, 373

Vedas, 174

Venezuela, 344, 345

Venice, Italy, 230, 241, 269, 273

Versailles, Palace of, 312-313

vertebrates, 19, 30, 31, 38

Vespucci, Amerigo, 289

Victoria Falls, Africa, 347

Vienna, Austria, 298, 299, 308, 309

Vietnam, 379

Vijayanagar empire, 265

Vikings, **210-213**, 215, 217, 218, 256

villages, 101, 108, 120-121, 164, 170, 184, 204, 212-213, 214-215, 226-227, 243, 255, 274-275, 277, 336-337, 338

Vinland, 213

Visigoths, 195, 204, 258

Vladimir, Prince of Kyiv, 256

volcanoes, 12, 21, 22, 23, 24, 59, 127, 189

Voltaire, 315

voting, 159, 292, 342, 382, 384, 385

W

Wales, 183, 244

Walesa, Lech, Polish president, 382

wall paintings, 105, 125, 135, 137, 175, 189

Wall Street Crash, 366

Wallace, William, 245

Wars of the Roses, 248-249

Warsaw Pact, 378

Warwick, Earl of, 248

Washington, DC, USA, 384

Washington, George, US president, 330, 331

Waterloo, Battle of, 335

Watt, James, 338

weapons, 84, 85, 87, 93, 96, 101, 123, 130, 133, 141, 146, 147, 154, 162, 182, 183, 186, 187, 194, 219, 222-223, 225, 244, 245, 250, 251, 259, 264, 271, 279, 282, 358, 359, 370, 371, 373, 379

weather, changes in, 34, 59, 68, 73, 75, 76, 77, 81, 100, 108, 120, 172

weaving, 108, 119, 137, 156, 178, 182, 210, 214, 274, 277, 279, 282, 338

Wessex, kingdom, 215

West Germany, 378, 383

West Indies, 289, 320, 324, 325

Western Front, 358, 359

Western Roman Empire, 194, 195, 202

Westphalia, German state, 343

whales, 65

wheel, invention of, 112

Wilhelm I, Kaiser of Germany, 343

William of Orange, King of England, 311

William of Orange, Ruler of the Dutch Republic, 310

William the Conqueror, King of England, 218

wine, 115

wings, 18, 36, 37, 54-55, 56-57, 65

witches, 219, 233

Wittenberg, Germany, 302

Wiwaxia, 26

Wolfe, General James, 321

wolves, 67, 69, 75, 100

women's rights, 384, 385

wood henges, 122

wooden horse of Troy, 131

workers, 166, 332, 338, 340, 341, 342, 360, 361, 362, 364, 382

workhouses, 341

World War I, **358-359**, 360, 361, 368, 369

World War II, 363, **370-373**, 374, 376, 378, 380, 386

World Wide Web, 390, 391

worms, 25, 26

Wren, Sir Christopher, 307

writers, 199, 246, 247, 258, 270, 286, 287, 304, 313, 315

writing, 105, 111, 119, 126, 129, 137, 140, 145, 165, 167, 170, 181

X

Xerxes I, King of Persia, 153

Xianyang, China, 166

Xuanzang, 273

Y

Yangtze River, 164

Yaroslav, Prince of Kyiv, 256

Year of Revolutions (1848), 342

Yellow River, 164

Yeltsin, Boris, Russian president, 383

Yom Kippur War, 376

York family, 248-249

Yorktown, Battle of, 331

Yugoslavia, 392

yurts, 250, 251, 252

Z

Zarathustra (Zoroaster), 153

Zeus, Greek god, 124, 157, 161

Zheng He, 273

Zhou dynasty, 165

Zhoukoudian, China, 86

ziggurats, 110, 150

Zimbabwe, 375

Zulu people, 346

Photo Credits

Every effort has been made to trace and acknowledge ownership of copyright. If any rights have been omitted, the publishers offer to rectify this in any subsequent editions, following notification. (t = top, m = middle, b = bottom, l = left, r = right):

front cover ©Erik von Weber/The Image Bank/Getty Images; **cover** ©Bob Elsdale/Eureka/Alamy; **p1** ©Dagli Orti/CORBIS; **p2** ©Kevin R. Morris/CORBIS; **p4** ©Adam Woolfitt/CORBIS; **p7** ©Digital Vision; **p8** ©Hubert Sadler/CORBIS; **p10** ©Roger Ressmeyer/CORBIS; **p12** *(bl)* ©Digital Vision, *(br)* ©Digital Vision; **p18** ©JT Vintage/Glasshouse Images/Alamy Stock Photo; **p19** *(bl)* ©Digital Vision, *(m)* ©Digital Vision; **p23** ©Bill O'Connor/Still Pictures; **p24** *(tl)* ©Dr. Kari Lounatmaa/SPL, *(bl)* ©Digital Vision, *(r)* ©Sinclair Stammers/SPL; **p25** ©Sinclair Stammers/SPL; **p31** ©Peter Scoones/Planet Earth Pictures; **p38** ©Digital Vision; **p59** ©Digital Vision; **p67** ©Peter Weimann; **p73** ©Bill Ivy/Tony Stone Images; **p75** ©Digital Vision; **p76** ©akg-images/Universal Images Group/Movoto; **p102** ©Egyptian Museum, Cairo/Dagli Orti/The Art Archive; **p105** (main) ©Roger Ressmeyer/CORBIS, *(tl)* ©The British Museum, London/Werner Forman Archive; **p106-7** ©Jim Zuckerman/Alamy Stock Photo; **p122** ©Martin Bennett/Alamy Stock Photo; **p125** ©The Art Archive/Shutterstock; **p136** ©Epix Travel/Alamy Stock Photo; **p159** ©James Green/Robert Harding Picture Library; **p167** ©Tony Stone Images/Julian Calder; **p171** ©vladphotos/Alamy Stock Photo; **p179** ©Werner Forman Archive/Bridgeman Images; **p181** ©Robert Frerck/Robert Harding Picture Library; **p189** ©J. E. Stevenson/Robert Harding Picture Library; **p196** ©The Art Archive; **p198** ©Archivo Iconografico, S.A./CORBIS; **p199** *(tl)* ©John Heseltine/CORBIS, *(br)* ©Michael T. Seddam/CORBIS; **p200-1** ©Carol Carpenter/Alamy Stock Photo; **p203** ©Ronald Sheridan/Ancient Art and Architecture; **p205** *(br)* ©The Art Archive/Shutterstock; **p207** ©Ronald Sheridan/Ancient Art and Architecture; **p220** ©Ronald Sheridan/Ancient Art and Architecture; **p239** ©The National Gallery, London/Scala, Florence; **p246** ©National Gallery, London/Scala, Florence; **p249** ©Royal Holloway, University of London/The Bridgeman Art Library; **p259** ©Michael Holford; **p275** ©Clive Gifford; **p281** ©Sybil Sassoon/Robert Harding Picture Library; **p285** ©Photodisc; **p290** ©Musée d'Orsay, Paris/Dagli Orti/The Art Archive; **p292** *(bl)* ©Shawshot/Alamy Stock Photo; **p292-3** *(b)* NASA; **p293** *(tr)* ©dpa picture alliance/Alamy Stock Photo, *(br)* ©Niday Picture Library/Alamy Stock Photo; **p294** ©Gail Mooney/CORBIS; **p297** *(tr)* ©Kunsthistorisches Museum, Vienna, Austria/Bridgeman Images; **p298** ©Wolfgang Kaehler; **p300** *(bl)* ©The Art Archive, (main) ©Estate of Sheldan Collins c/o Valerie Shepherd; **p302** *(bl)* ©Image Bank/Getty Images, *(t)* ©Art Collection/Alamy Stock Photo, *(mr)* ©PRISMA ARCHIVO/Alamy Stock Photo; **p302-3** ©Heritage Images/English Heritage/Diomedia; **p303** *(tl)* ©NPL - DeA Picture Library/Bridgeman Images; **p304** **(t)** ©PBL Collection/Alamy Stock Photo; **p306** *(tl)* ©The Print Collector/Alamy Stock Photo, (tr) ©The British Library Board, Shelf E.561.(14), *(b)* ©Fine Art Images/Diomedia; **p307** ©Fraser Hall/robertharding.com; **p308** *(bl)* ©Alfredo Dagli Orti/Shutterstock,*(r)* ©Pictorial Press/Alamy Stock Photo; **p309** *(tr)* ©The Art Archive/Superstock; **p311** *(tl)* ©Heritage Images/Heritage Art/Diomedia, *(tr)* ©Wageningen UR Library; **p312** ©Dave G. Houser/The Image Bank Unreleased/Getty Images; **p313** *(t)* ©photo RMN/J. Derenne, *(m)* ©Alfredo Dagli Orti/Shutterstock; **p314** *(ml)* ©Digital Vision, *(bl)* ©Heritage Images/Fine Art Images; **p315** ©Science Museum Group; **p316** ©Galen Rowell/Getty Images; **p317** *(b)* ©Fine Art Images/Diomedia, *(tr)* ©De Luan/Alamy Stock Photo; **p318** ©Corbis Historical/Getty Images; **p319** ©The Art Archive; **p320** ©Art Heritage/Alamy Stock Photo; **p324** (main) ©Corbis Historical/Getty Images, *(t)* ©CBW/Alamy Stock Photo; **p325** US Library of Congress; **p328** ©NTPL/Erik Pelham; **p329** ©Hulton Deutsch/Corbis Historical/Getty Images; **p330** *(bl)* ©Philadelphia Museum of Art/Gift of Mr & Mrs John Wagner, 1986/Bridgeman Images, *(tr)* ©Peter Newark's American Pictures; **p333** ©Josse Fine Art/Diomedia; **p334** *(t)* ©Diomedia/De Agostini Picture Library, *(b)* ©Whpics/Dreamstime.com; **p337** *(t)* ©The Art Archive, *(br)* ©National Museums & Galleries of Wales (Museum of Welsh Life); **p338** ©Robert Estall; **p339** ©Corbis Historical Picture Archive/Getty Images; **p341** *(m)* ©Well/BOT/Alamy Stock Photo, *(br)* © Topical Press Agency/Hulton Archive; **p342** *(mr)* ©The Granger Collection/Alamy Stock Photo, *(b)* ©Universal Images Group/Christophel Fine Art/Diomedia; **p343** ©INTERFOTO/Alamy Stock Photo; **p344** (bl) ©The Art Archive; **p344-5** *(b)* ©Pablo Corral Vega; **p345** *(tl)* ©The Art Archive; **p347** *(mt)* ©Hulton Deutsch/Corbis Historical/Getty Images, *(r)* ©Eric and David Hosking/FLPA/Minden Pictures; **p348** *(bl)* Illustrated London News, *(m)* Illustrated London News; **p351** *(tl)* ©Everett Collection/Alamy Stock Photo, *(m)* ©Classic Image/Alamy Stock Photo; **p350-1** ©Dave G. Houser; **p352-3** ©Ric Ergenbright; **p354-5** ©The Art Archive; **p356** ©Jackyenjoyphotography/Moment/Getty Images; **p357** *(t)* ©George Rinhart/Corbis Historical/Getty Images, *(b)* ©Michael Holford; **p360** *(tl)* Illustrated London News, *(mb)* ©Brian A. Vikander/Getty Images; **p361** *(b)* ©akg-images/Alamy Stock Photo, *(t)* ©GRANGER - Historical Picture Archive/Alamy Stock Photo; **p362** *(tl)* ©Pictorial Press Ltd/Alamy Stock Photo, *(bl)* ©akg-images/Elizaveta Becker, *(r)* ©Robert Harding Productions/ robertharding.com; **p363** (t) ©Bettmann/Getty Images; **p364-5** ©OSCAR DAVID TOLEDO MARIN/Alamy Stock Photo; **p365** ©akg-images; **p366** *(bl)* ©Hulton Archive/Getty Images, *(tr)* ©Pictorial Press Ltd/Alamy Stock Photo; **p367** *(tr)* US Library of Congress, *(br)* ©Digital Vision; **p368** (main) ©Hulton Archive/Getty Images, *(tr)* ©PictureLux / The Hollywood Archive/Alamy Stock Photo; **p369** ©US National Archives; **p370** *(mt)* ©Everett Collection/Shutterstock, *(br)* Illustrated London News; **p371** ©Hulton-Deutsch/Corbis Historical; **p372** *(t)* ©Science History Images/Alamy Stock Photo, *(br)* ©Shawshots/Alamy Stock Photo; **p373** ©Everett Collection Historical/Alamy Stock Photo; **p374** *(tl)* Illustrated London News, *(b)* ©Ravi Batra/AFP/Getty Images; **p375** *(t)* ©Bettmann/Getty Images, *(b)* ©Howard Davies/The Image Bank/Getty Images; **p376** *(tr)* ©Suhaib Salem/Reuters, *(b)* ©David Ake/AFP-Popperfoto; **p377** *(tl)* ©Damir Sagolj Reuters/Alamy Stock Photo, *(b)* ©Roberto Borea/AP/Shutterstock; **p379** ©Tim Page/Corbis Historical/Getty Images; **p380** *(l)* ©Digital Vision, *(t)* ©stock imagery/Alamy Stock Photo, *(bm)* ©Digital Vision, *(br)* ©Digital Vision; **p381** (main) ©Digital Vision, *(tr)* ©Corbis Historical/Getty Images, *(br)* ©Digital Vision; **p382** ©Bettmann/Getty Images; **p382-3** ©Rex Features; **p383** *(tr)* ©REUTERS/Stringer (RUSSIA); **p384** *(l)* ©The Print Collector/Alamy Stock Photo, *(tr)* ©Bettman/Getty; **p384-5** ©Peter Turnley/Archive Photos/Getty Images; **p385** *(mt)* ©Peter Turnley/Corbis Historical/Getty Images; **p386** *(bl)* ©GRANGER - Historical Picture Archive/Alamy Stock Photo, *(mt)* ©Lordprice Collection/Alamy Stock Photo; **p387** Copyright ©1998, New Line Productions, Inc./The Moviestore Collection; **p388-9** (main) ©Digital Vision, *(bl)* ©Digital Vision; **p389** *(tl)* ©NASA/ SPL, *(tr)* ©Digital Vision, *(br)* ©Digital Vision; **p390** *(bl)* Photo courtesy of STMicroelectronics, *(br)* ©The Natural History Museum, www.nhm.ac.uk, *(mr)* ©The Trustees of the British Museum, www.britishmuseum.org/explore; **p391** *(ml)* ©Jeb Loy Nichols, with kind permission, www.jebloynichols.co.uk, *(m)* Credit ©Royal Horticultural Society, www.rhs.org.uk, *(tr)* ©Digital Vision, *(br)* ©Digital Vision; **p392** ©David Brauchli/Sygma/Getty Images; **p393** *(tl)* ©Alfred Pasieka/SPL, (main) ©Reuters/Corbis; **p398** Illustrated London News; **p400** ©Digital Vision; **p401** Illustrated London News.

Illustrated by:	Inklink Firenze, Giacinto Gaudenzi, Ian Jackson, Jeremy Gower, Nicholas Hewetson, Lorenzo Cecchi, Justine Torode, David Cuzik, Gary Bines and David Wright
Managing editor:	Jane Chisholm
Managing designer:	Mary Cartwright
Cover design:	Michael Hill & Karen Tomlins
Digital imaging:	John Russell
Additional designs:	Robin Farrow, Matthew Hart & Susannah Owen
Additional consultants:	Stuart Atkinson, Chris Chandler, Dr. John Rostron & Dr. Margaret Rostron
Additional illustrations:	Susanna Addario, Stephen Conlin, Peter Dennis, Richard Draper, John Fox, Bob Hersey, Jason Lewis, Chris Lyon, Susie McCaffrey, Joseph McEwan, Malcolm McGregor, Cecco Mariniello, Peter Massey, Sean Milne, Louise Nixon, Andrew Robinson, Simon Roulstone, Claudia Saraceni, Chris Shields, Sue Stitt, Ross Watton & Gerald Wood
Picture researchers:	Ruth King, Sophy Tahta & Ehimare Ogona
Website research:	Jacqui Clark
Artwork co-ordinator:	Cathy Lowe
Additional contributions:	Anna Claybourne

First published in 2025 by Usborne Publishing Limited, 83-85 Saffron Hill, London EC1N 8RT, United Kingdom. usborne.com